Eyes Like Mine

Lauren Cecile

ISBN: 1508457727
ISBN 13: 9781508457725
Library of Congress Control Number: 2015902458
CreateSpace Independent Publishing Platform
North Charleston, South Carolina

Design Consultant, Brooke A. Siggers
Cover design by Brian D. Siggers
Author photo by Brian E. Siggers
Cover photo courtesy of the Ragland family
Other images from the public domain: No Known Restrictions

"Swing Low, Sweet Chariot" lyrics by Wallis Willis circa 1862
"Jesus Loves Me" lyrics by Anna Bartlett Warner circa 1860
"Oh, Let My People Go" lyrics by Horace Waters circa 1862
"After My Death" by Hayyim Bialik 1904

Disclaimer:

Dedicated To "Daddy"
and
My Loving and Supportive Family

First they came for the Communists,
and I didn't speak out because I wasn't a Communist.
Then they came for the Socialists,
and I didn't speak out because I wasn't a Socialist.
Then they came for the trade unionists,
and I didn't speak out because I wasn't a trade unionist.
Then they came for me,
and there was no one left to speak for me.
-- Martin Niemoller

We all should know that diversity makes for a rich
tapestry,
and we must understand that all the threads of the
tapestry
are equal in value no matter what their color.
-Maya Angelou

CHAPTER 1

June 1936
Justinia

AT FIRST MOTHER was content just knowing the name and profession of the man I met at the NAACP convention in Baltimore. She liked the fact that his name, Julius Sommerfeldt, had an aristocratic ring to it and that he was a lawyer. In subsequent telephone conversations, however, my mother, Magdalena Treadwell, a grande dame of black Washington D. C., kept pressing me about who his people were and what organizations besides the NAACP he belonged to. She wanted to make certain he was not too "militant" or lacking in "proper connections."

I assured her I was not intending to elope and continued being evasive. Julius was not exactly what she had in mind for me, but she was satisfied as long as she thought he was part of the "talented tenth," that venerable group that my father's friend, W.E.B. Dubois, said would be the intellectual and political saviors of the Negro race. That was important, because now that I had my college degree, my social circle dictated that it was time to make a decision about whom to marry and cautioned that he be a "tenther" – well-educated, well-bred and preferably well-off.

The NAACP convention was to be the highlight of my summer. For months I'd been looking forward to exploring the city, meeting new people and being out "on my own" with no real obligations for an entire week. The convention was sure to be more interesting than our family's annual trek to the exclusive, all-Negro resort town of Highland Beach, a couple hours from Baltimore, where

I'd grown bored with the croquet tournaments, bonfires, tea parties and clam-bakes and traipsing over the same stretch of Chesapeake I've splashed around in all my life.

One of Frederick Douglass' sons founded the picturesque retreat because Negroes weren't allowed at nearby beaches or hotels. Our Highland Beach home had been in my mother's family since the century's turn and every-one who visits says they prefer our tiny beach to the "Inkwell" on Martha's Vineyard because it was quainter, more intimate, attracted the most prominent people and was "all ours." We had our own mayor, and the resort was not governed by, or shared with, white people. As a new Howard graduate and yet unmarried, I was still expected to accompany my parents and participate in the activities.

Every June for the past several years, my friends and I left our homes, as nearby as Washington and as far away as New York, and arrived at our cottages with freshly coiffed hair and a chic, new skirt and blouse ensemble because wad-ing into the warm, gently lapping waves in our bathing suits was not as alluring as when we were younger. Now all we wanted was a pillowy chaise lounge and idle chatter over icy glasses of sweet tea. So we posed and preened far enough away from the shoreline to avoid the evening mist, the gulls and the trample of Howard and Harvard pretty-boys pretending to be serious rugby players.

Still I was tired of the same conversations regarding who was graduating, debuting, betrothing, marrying or traveling and I knew that my best friend Georgine Kirkwood, who'd somehow survived the all-female Wellesley College and was now on a frantic hunt for a proper husband, would be grabbing me and squealing news of someone's engagement before I could even alight from my taxi. Of course I'd squeal and hug her back, but I knew I couldn't spend another summer doing the same mindless things.

I was a college graduate now. It had taken me five years, but that was because, though I loved Spelman, it was too strict for me – early curfews, compulsory chapel and a dress code that often required white gloves. And by Thanksgiving the following year, I realized I couldn't tolerate the snow and cold blowing through the campus of Oberlin College. So I ended up close to home after all, at Howard, my third-choice school, the Negro intellectual, educational and cultural capital of the country – or the black Harvard, as it was known in our circles.

Howard, too, had unbendable rules and meddlesome, eagle-eyed dorm mothers, but I made the most of it because my parents refused to indulge another transfer. Instead of pining for Radcliffe, I pledged Alpha Kappa Alpha Sorority, dabbled with the Glee Club, the debate team, swim team, German Club, NAACP and other miscellaneous activities and graduated *summa cum laude*. I still wasn't sure what I wanted to do next but was ready for the bright, new horizons that our commencement speakers had promised us.

Meanwhile I still appreciated the *idea* of our annual summer retreats. They provided much-needed sanctuary from big-city indignities and Jim Crow policies, from all the mean looks, intimidating police officers and nasty clerks who seemed to relish kicking us out of the parks and keeping us out of their restaurants. At Highland Beach we were never the interlopers. We could skip and run around with barefoot abandon and picnic 'til dawn without being hassled. We laughed out loud, swam under the stars, danced in moonlight and our neighbors smiled and said "Aw, look at that." We toted buckets and spades for clam-digging, nets for butterfly-chasing and no one demanded to know what we were up to. We took long hikes through the trees and brush and never expected to be startled by anything more threatening than a rabbit or a quail – no *person* ever leaped out to challenge our right to be wherever we happened to be. And we could enjoy watermelon without ever worrying about perpetuating a stereotype. I loved the residents, the freedom and tranquility, but two decades of Highland Beach summers have rendered me restless.

Every year, Mr. Andrews, who'd been born a slave, summoned all the young people to his apple orchard for a history lesson and to lecture us about the value of education, hard work and perseverance so that, Lord willing, maybe we too could find outrageous fortune in the Depression-proof funeral home business; the "Countess," another centenarian, sitting in her wicker peacock chair while her great-great-granddaughters took turns fanning her, would tell anyone willing to hear for the hundredth time how Paul Laurence Dunbar had recited his poetry to her while they roasted marshmallows on the beach; inevitably, a visitor's hard-headed child climbed up too high in a towering oak and Daddy had my brother Emery go fetch the groundskeeper for a ladder; and every year, Inez Harper would drape herself over someone's spanking-new Roadster, flaunting the evidence of her Cherokee heritage and flirt with old and new arrivals; and of course there were the elders who tried to arrange courtships and marriages by steering someone's doctor-son towards another's ballerina-daughter, or someone's hazel-eyed lawyer-nephew to another's fair-haired author-granddaughter in an unrelenting quest to strengthen bloodlines, communities and the race as a whole.

The only thing different this year was that my older sister, Charlotte, always good for spicing things up by getting into a squabble with a snotty girl from another clique, had gotten married the previous summer – it had been the social event of the year – and was now living in Liberia doing missionary work with her new husband, an African Methodist Episcopal priest. My brother Emery was planning on spending the better part of the summer at the sprawling plantation home of his Morehouse classmate in Atlanta. So my parents could spend all their time and energy focusing on me.

I was ready to try something new, exciting and unconventional. After the NAACP convention and my obligatory sojourn at Highland Beach, I had a teaching assignment in D. C. waiting for me. Regrettably, many of my college girlfriends, brilliant and ambitious as they were, had no career opportunities yet, and were considering working as a domestic or a factory drone until the Depression ended, the racial climate improved or a good, marriageable man came along.

They considered me lucky. I had a job I didn't need and was obtained through family connections. So I was sensitive enough not to complain about being unfulfilled when so many had already reached a professional dead end. But I was worried I was falling into a rut. I wanted to explore whether my future portended more than graduation from college, a part-time assignment teaching underprivileged kindergarteners, marriage to a doctor, dentist, lawyer or businessman, a couple of children, then a lifetime of hosting dinner parties and charity balls. Nine months in D. C., then summers in Highland Beach, year in and year out. I loved Magdalena, but I didn't want to become her. That was *her* life.

I thought about what other women had done or were doing. Bessie Coleman, bless her soul, was about my age when she became an international sensation as a stunt pilot. She'd probably be more famous than Amelia Earhart had she been wearing a seatbelt and not fallen out of her plane when it malfunctioned and catapulted. I adored Katharine Hepburn, loved her movies, independence and the fact that she wore trousers without regard to what others thought.

I was obsessed with the beautiful and fabulous Josephine Baker who could sing, dance, act and speak out authoritatively against injustice. She was loved all over the world, especially in Paris which was known to be more tolerant and appreciative of different races. I didn't want to be an entertainer – Magdalena would be mortified – but I coveted her panache and audacity. I'd had pictures from magazines of Bessie, Katharine and Josephine taped all over my dormitory walls at Howard.

One of my sorority sisters and fellow Howard graduates was going to Harvard Law School and said in her valedictory address that "our generation will change the world," and that one of us could quite possibly become President one day when discrimination against Negroes and women was a thing of the past. Smart and dynamic, I knew if anyone could accomplish that goal, she could. Inspired by Madame C. J. Walker, some of my friends were manufacturing and marketing their own cosmetics line. Even my sister Charlotte was in Africa. Like all these ladies, I wanted to pursue extraordinary goals and do something different. I was searching for my special niche and didn't think it was in D. C. And after meeting Julius Sommerfeldt, I was sure.

CHAPTER 2

AT THE SHARP Street Memorial Methodist Episcopal Church, home of the oldest Negro congregation in Baltimore, Juanita Jackson, secretary of the newly formed Youth and Young Adult division, addressed the crowd, the largest ever at an NAACP convention. It was a diverse group – white, black, young, old, men and women, working stiffs and professionals – and all eyes were on Juanita. Despite her pixie-hair, impish smile and cute, polka dotted dress, she gave a fiery speech about how it's the young people who need to begin organizing demonstrations all over the country to protest discrimination, segregation and lynching. She said we also needed to address police brutality, especially in D. C., where deadly police encounters were rampant and considered new-style lynching.

"Slavery has been over for more than seventy years and they still think they can torture and kill us with impunity!"

"We have to make them stop!" shouted a young boy in a too-big suit who looked to be no older than twelve.

"We need everyone, from the youngest to the oldest, to work together. We got complacent during the twelve short years of Reconstruction and now many of our political, social and economic gains are gone – stripped by goons in white sheets *and* three-piece suits." The crowd roared. Juanita exhaled and wiped perspiration from her brow.

"We once had senators and congressmen; Louisiana had a Negro governor! We had several Black Wall Streets where Negroes owned entire towns until jealousy and resentment burned them down."

"Truth!"

"But we will have empires again because we as a people always persevere despite everything they do to keep us down! We must be forever vigilant!" She was on a roll.

"Forever!"

"That's right!"

"It will take all of us!" Juanita continued. "Just like former Secretary James Weldon Johnson says in his song – we must lift *every* voice and sing. But we must also lift every foot and *march*!" Some people excitedly waved handkerchiefs in the air. "Lift every hand and *vote*!"

"Vote! Vote! Vote!"

One man was so moved, he took it upon himself to go sit at the organ and punctuate the end of Juanita's every phrase, just like I'd noticed organists do when I visited a Baptist church.

"It's the NAACP that's helping to save the lives of those Scottsboro Boys," she said, referring to the nine innocent teenagers sentenced to the electric chair for allegedly raping two white prostitutes on a train. The people roared and the impromptu musician struck strong chords.

"And it's the NAACP that will help save the lives of countless other innocent young men and women who might get trapped in a situation where a blood-thirsty mob or a corrupt criminal justice system wants to destroy them!"

Everyone was on their feet. The organist's hands were flying over the keyboard. "It could happen to any one of us. We could walk out these church doors right now and be falsely accused and condemned by nightfall." There was deafening applause.

"Let's not forget George Armwood right here in Baltimore."

The lynching of feeble-minded George Armwood was huge news a few years ago. The Armwood atrocity dominated barbershop discussions and Sunday sermons for weeks later. Accused of the usual crime of attacking a white woman, he was taken from jail by an angry mob, beaten, had his ears sliced off, gold fillings yanked out, dragged behind a car, doused with gasoline, set on fire, and hanged from a tree next to the judge's house. The next day, everyone went about their business as if nothing had happened; it was barely mentioned in mainstream newspapers. Despite a public outcry from citizens, the *Baltimore Afro-American*, the *Washington Bee* and the *Chicago Defender*, no one was ever arrested, let alone prosecuted. Nationwide, there'd been at least twenty known lynchings the previous year – thousands overall – and little, if anything, was ever done to prevent them or bring the perpetrators to justice.

"There has to be a federal anti-lynching law."

"Amen!"

CHAPTER 3

THE SUNDAY FOLLOWING the Armwood murder, at St. Luke's Episcopal Church, Reverend Crawford called it one of the worst cases of overkill ever. He called the perpetrators savages and said they had the audacity to call Negroes un-civilized! Reverend Crawford's sermons were usually rather dull and cryptic with liberal doses of obscure scripture, but this time I interrupted my romantic daydreaming and actually paid attention. He said that the people who watched these lynchings were as much to blame as the ones who actually snatched up the victims, coiled the rope and smacked the horse's rump so that it bolted away, leaving its would-be rider – someone's brother, son, husband or father – to hang and twist.

He went on to say that any decent person who didn't use their power to stop lynchings was as guilty as Pontius Pilate who believed Jesus to be inno-cent but, to placate the Jews and maintain his popularity and position, handed him over to the Roman mob anyway. Reverend Crawford said it was too convenient for people to ignore their conscience and pretend to have no in-dividual culpability. Those who enjoyed a family picnic while a lynched body still twitched just a few feet away were no different from Pilate. Their very presence at the scene communicated assent and encouragement. They may as well have strung the body up themselves just as Pilate essentially nailed Jesus to the cross.

Even Emery stopped squirming to pay closer attention. "Think about it," Reverend Crawford said, "who are these bystanders? They are customers, busi-ness leaders, teachers, friends and relatives of the lynch mob and have influence;

they can shun, rebuke, boycott and vilify. That's power. And when a few people stand up, others follow. Just ask the first abolitionists.

"Instead they just eat their sandwiches and go home whistling a tune to keep from screaming. Because they know it's wrong. All of them, including the preachers who justify the lynchings with perverted interpretations of biblical verse, encouraged by the hallelujah chorus and the nodding parishioners, are to blame. And they cannot, as Pilate did, simply go scrub their hands to absolve themselves of guilt.

"Brothers and sisters," Reverend Crawford thundered in an unusual display of pulpit passion, "silence is acquiescence. Lynch men, like bullies, are empowered by the silence and weakness of others. We cannot stand idly by and watch evil have its way. Or we *will* be held accountable on Judgment Day when we lie prostrate before the Lord Almighty!"

This homily earned him a few "amens" from the ultra-conservative congregation that did not believe in random interjections during the service, no matter how moved the listener may become. Glancing at my mother, her subtle nod and pursed lips indicated that she agreed with Reverend Crawford in substance, but disapproved of the congregants' liturgical faux pas and the minister's uncharacteristic fire-and-brimstone flourish at the end. My father looked thoughtful as he pulled out his checkbook for the offering.

My sister Charlotte, who was a perennial teachers' pet and once rescued a puppy from a creek while wearing her First Communion dress, was considered a Goody-Two-Shoes; and she sat there looking quite pleased with herself. "I'm no Pilate," her expression said. Granted, she was the first person to defend an underdog and didn't hesitate to rebuke Georgine and other girls from snickering behind their hands at someone they considered too fat, too dark, or too unfashionably attired. On the drive home, Charlotte said that she'd have stood up for Jesus and tried to convince the crowd to free Jesus and crucify Barabbas instead. "And if I were white, I'd never be silent about all the terrible things going on today."

Not to be outdone I said, "Neither would I."

Reverend Crawford's sermon really did resonate with me. It was the first *practical* message I'd received at church in a long time.

CHAPTER 4

IN THE SHARP Street Memorial pulpit, Juanita Jackson spoke on. "George Armwood and his family got no justice! But we honor him by committing to the anti-lynching cause and *all* our righteous causes!"

I noticed a young lady in front of me suddenly break down in sobs and the people on both sides of her comforted her and rubbed her back. I figured some-one very close to her must have had a fateful encounter with a ragtag bunch of vicious marauders wearing white hoods or star-shaped pieces of tin.

Many people probably knew of someone who'd been lynched or had some-how miraculously escaped being lynched. Years ago in Lexington, Kentucky, my father's uncle outsmarted a lynch mob that was after him for killing a white man, a dry goods store owner, who attacked my aunt. She'd gone to buy fabric for curtains and found herself being forced into a back storage room just as Uncle Jett came in from gassing up his car at the filling station next door. In defense of his wife, he beat the man to death. The yokels discovered the body, jumped to conclusions and came to abduct Jett from his house which, along with his coveted Packard, horse stable and tobacco fields, was duly torched. By that time, Aunt Esther and the kids were ensconced in the colored section on a train to Baltimore and Uncle Jett, to hear him tell it in his usual irreverent manner, was in a freight car lying in a casket underneath "some peckerwood's dead momma." Uncle Jett and his family eventually settled in Prince George, Virginia, started a thriving textiles and interior decorating business which catered to upper class Negroes and whites, and have been there ever since.

CHAPTER 5

JUANITA SAID, "IMAGINE politicians who are against anti-lynching laws. How low do you have to be to support random torture and killing?"

I joined in the applause. It was hard to believe that, in the age of airplanes and helicopters, people were still doing the kinds of things they did when there were stage coaches and mules.

"It's sick!" she said.

I was amazed at the intensity of Juanita's indignation as she echoed the sentiments of previous speakers, reminding us of the nationwide barbarity of Red Summer in 1919 and the Ku Klux Klan, looking remarkably like the mythical ghosts of confederate soldiers in their white, hooded robes, marching down Pennsylvania Avenue in '25. This was less than a generation ago and these events were still vivid in our minds.

"They can't continue to ignore this problem when they have the power to curtail it!" The organ chords were frenzied, angry.

"Dr. DuBois says, 'Whenever the government allows the mob to rule, the fault is not with the mob.'"

"Amen!" said someone in the very back of the room.

"We'll vote the right ones in and the wrong ones out! There's power in the ballot!"

Someone started a chant. "FDR! FDR!" It caught on for a few seconds, and then petered out.

Most Negroes had gone from being staunch Lincoln Republicans to milquetoast Roosevelt Democrats but felt FDR owed them something besides vague

New Deal promises, impotent Negro cabinet appointments, and meager relief benefits for the Depression's worst victims. Even Eleanor Roosevelt was imploring her debonair and seemingly compassionate husband to do something to end lynching.

"We have a lot to do between now and November. We have to register people to vote, educate them about the issues and what's at stake. Then we have to get them to the polls!"

"Jim Crow be damned!"

"But politicians are just part of the solution," Juanita said. "We still have to fight our own battles and make our own way!" People responded, excited about the challenge.

"That's right!"

"But we also can't just let these elected officials off the hook. They must do the right thing and end lynching now! Today, Mr. President, today!" She looked pointedly at Harold Ickes, a committed NAACP member and FDR's Secretary of the Interior. He nodded.

"End it now!"

"Together we'll make a difference! We have to make a difference! Or we will perish! So let us march on, 'til victory is won!" People applauded wildly.

"Juanita Jackson is the next Ida B. Wells," someone shouted, referring to the late anti-lynching crusader.

After Juanita's powerful speech, people began shouting out spontaneous commitments to the anti-lynching cause.

"So what are we gonna do?"

"Let's march. I'll carry the banner. Who's with me?"

"Count me in."

The Baltimore delegation suggested staging a protest downtown. The Washington delegates were more specific, suggesting that protestors line the streets with "nooses" loosely hanging down from their necks for shock value, to confront good, bad and indifferent people with the barbarity of hanging human beings from a tree until their necks break or they are strangled to death. Everyone agreed that it was just the kind of dramatic staging needed to bring more attention to the problem.

After various delegations reported on incidents and action plans for their individual cities, there was a prayer and a rousing rendition of the NAACP's official song, "Lift Every Voice and Sing," sung by a group of school children, and a rush to shake hands with Juanita and NAACP bigwigs. We hugged and greeted each other, sharing thoughts about the convention so far.

The Youth and Young Adult division was emerging as a real action coalition and taking immediate steps to help solve problems. They wanted an immediate protest. As secretary of the Howard University NAACP, I went to many meetings where there was a lot of grumbling and over-intellectualizing of the issues, though we did manage to *do* some things. I was excited to be at the national convention but it was not exactly what I'd expected. I thought it would be a week of inspiring speeches, rallies and meeting new people. It was. But I didn't know there'd be real work and immediate commitments.

I was caught off guard. I didn't think I wanted to join the noose demonstrations because it seemed like a morbid exercise in futility and I was also in Baltimore to have some fun, to exercise some freedom after five years of demanding professors, college exams, student teaching, and a lifetime of Magdalena's scrutinizing eyes. So I intended to enjoy myself before I had to re-join the family for the monotony, predictability and seclusion of Highland Beach. I was told that, after convention business, there'd be lots of fun mixers, concerts and some good shopping. There was supposedly a nearby boutique that didn't require Negro customers to trace the outline of their foot on a piece of paper but actually allowed us to try on the shoes before buying them.

"What a great session," my friend Millie said, linking elbows with me. "Such powerful stuff."

"Yes it was," I said. "Now let's go shoe shopping. My treat. I heard there's a real nice place that will let us try them on first. No getting home and discovering they're too tight."

It was a common letdown. Those wooden shoe stretchers didn't work and if the shoes were too loose, we put balled-up newspaper in the toe and hoped we wouldn't falter. The opportunity to get perfectly fitted shoes was exciting. Custom ordering is better, but shopping in brick-and-mortar stores, especially in a new city, is so much more fun.

"Fat chance," Millie said as we navigated the crowd to meet and greet. She'd heard that the President of a Negro college hadn't been permitted to purchase a suit from Kaufman's Department Store just that day. Johns Hopkins University was reneging on an invitation to allow the convention to use its McCoy Hall for a banquet. "The word is that a lot of whites are riled up about the convention being hosted here and acting pretty nasty."

"Some things never change."

CHAPTER 6

JIM CROW WAS alive and well even though the D.C./Baltimore area wasn't nearly as bad as the Deep South. In Georgia there were "No Negroes Allowed" signs which were ubiquitous and supported by law. While at Spelman, every time we took a walk to the drug store, a luncheonette, or just because, we passed a Laundromat that displayed a sign saying "No niggers, Jews, chinks or dogs" and it was always crowded despite the limited clientele. The patrons inside peered out at us, practically daring us to cross the threshold. As instructed, we passed by with nonchalance and represented our school with utmost dignity.

"*Up* south," in D. C. and Baltimore, however, there was a "No Negroes Allowed" *mentality* which was supported by custom but not law. Signs, but not the attitude they represented, were considered outmoded and sleazy, something you'd find in lesser, backwoods places like Mississippi and Alabama, and there had to be some tangible, modern-day distinction from those old confederate liens. But Negroes didn't need a sign to know we weren't welcome at many establishments. If we *were* allowed in, we might get skipped over until all the whites were served or be made to enter through a rear door, and my mother said there was nothing anyone could need so badly that they would go through an alternate door to get it. It could wait, and there was always another store.

There was always U Street, a mecca of Negro businesses. As my integrationist father says, we still need to have our "own stuff" – our own stores, restaurants, facilities, schools, banks, communities, newspapers, even sports teams like the Washington Elite Giants who played in the Negro League and who my father loved almost as much as family and making money. Many of our establishments failed during the Depression, but we had to support the ones still standing.

During a time when so many had lost so much, this unwritten custom of racial separation was all some whites had to hold onto to make them still feel good about themselves. Instead of banding together in populist solidarity – black and white together – many continued to maintain their sense of racial superiority. Broke, tattered, at least they could request a glass of water or a piece of stale bread at the corner diner without having a meat cleaver shaken at them. That was an advantage they'd always have and even Magdalena held her tongue when a disheveled man said, "Step aside, aunty," and walked into the bank before she did.

If they aren't lynching us, they're making us sit in the back of the trolley because *Plessy versus Ferguson's* "separate but equal" doctrine was the law of the land and being enforced all over. Amid the razzle-dazzle of New York City even Josephine Baker, the toast of the town, was prevented from eating in certain restaurants.

President Woodrow Wilson reneged on his promise to have "fair dealing" with Negroes. One of the first things he did after winning office with Negro support was to re-segregate federal government offices which resurrected the specter of Negro inferiority among the employees. A family friend, Mr. Beverly, a war veteran and one of the first and only Negroes with a desk job at the Department of Labor, suddenly found himself eating lunch in a broom closet instead of the sunny lunchroom with his chummy, white colleagues and a community urn that dispensed the strong, pungent coffee he'd grown to appreciate. The Negro janitor emptying wastebaskets and scrubbing toilets could be ignored, but the sight of Mr. Beverly typing and shuffling papers was so offensive that a partition was built around his desk to separate him from the whites. The policy was a major blow to Negroes who'd "made it" by snagging a government *office* job; but despite the demeaning treatment, they were still considered big shots in the community. Mr. Beverly was even on the vestry at our church. I remember Emery and me, sitting at the "kiddie table" at one of Magdalena's dinner parties, giggling uncontrollably when Mr. Beverly said, "They could've banned me from the toilets and made me shit in a bucket and I wouldn't have quit that job."

My father says we would've been better off if Negroes had re-elected Teddy Roosevelt who'd done the unthinkable by having Booker T. Washington over for dinner with the First Family. Wilson would've never invited a former slave, or any Negro, to the White House, let alone to his private quarters. Daddy was no fan of Booker T. Washington, but was impressed by Roosevelt's gesture.

CHAPTER 7

MY FATHER IS an attorney, and while there were many down-and-out attorneys, Negro and white, my father, in addition to his *pro bono* clients, had some wealthy clients, clients who were mum about it because the world needn't know they had a Negro lawyer making big things happen for them behind the scenes. He also made some sound investments over the years, so fortunately the Depression had minimal impact on our lifestyle.

Growing up, on the hottest days, my city friends like Millie were routinely turned away at public swimming pools and amusement park rides and had to be content peering through the chain link fence at the white kids who stuck their tongues out at them until some meaner person came and shooed them away. But I was able to walk out of my Highland Beach cottage, run down a path and jump into our own private waters. We sipped from bottles of imported San Pellegrino sparkling mineral water while gathered on a neighbor's sail boat catching the lusty Chesapeake breezes to cool off. We also carried Pellegrino in our handbags to avoid the unpleasantness of segregated water fountains when out and about.

We belonged to an exclusive organization for privileged Negro children and teens called "Dukes and Duchesses," a necessary complement to day school and Sunday school since the National Honor Society, Scouts, Junior Achievement, the Kiwanis Key Club, intramural sports and most recreational facilities were "white-only" and the D & D founders thought there needed to be a way for the upper crust to learn and play together. It would've been nice to go to the Aquarium, but since we couldn't, we enjoyed the exotic fish collection at the posh home of one of the "Dukes." A "Duchess" had a lanai and heated pool at

Lauren Cecile

her house, and several others had tennis courts. The Sinclairs' house was a virtual museum of Negro art with paintings by artists like Joshua Johnson, Henry O. Tanner, Archibald Motley and Howard professor Lois Mailou Jones. We took turns hosting meetings and parties. Cotillions and golf were at the swank Lincoln Colonnade and the Martinique sporting club.

To get around, we ordered a cab or Chauncey, our driver/security guy/handyman, took us where we needed to go; so unlike many, I've never been forced to sit in the back of a cold or stifling bus. I didn't think it was fair, but Daddy says life's not fair, but that it's incumbent on us all to work to make things fairer.

⸺

"I'm not doing the noose demonstration," I told Millie.

"You just haven't suffered enough," she said, pulling me into a huddle of impassioned protest collaborators.

"Maybe not, but really, what would another protest accomplish?"

"Every little effort sharpens the focus and gets folks talking. Think about it first."

She was right, I hadn't suffered enough, but I could commiserate with those who had. Millie's family had suffered greatly during this Depression. She had to leave Howard and her mother, an apron-wearing, pie-baking homemaker, had to take a job at the telephone company. Her father, who'd been a longshoreman for over twenty years but was "let go" ostensibly because of the Depression, but really for union activity, still wore a starched white shirt and tie everyday as he scouted around for day labor. As a former, solidly middle-class family, they were still remarkably upbeat despite their smaller house in a rougher neighborhood, a cancelled YMCA membership and no car.

I realized I took a lot for granted but hesitated to spend the week trying to dismantle the entire institution of Negro oppression. I saw no glory in participating in symbolic demonstrations that yielded no immediate results. But voicing that opinion would be blasphemous. From what I've seen, unless there's something strangely fascinating like a Klan march, no one pays much attention to demonstrations. Some people might stop and show support, but preaching to the choir seemed like a waste of time.

Fighting discrimination and working to eradicate lynching was inherently gratifying, but it was hard work with mostly disappointing results. I would happily wear a noose and carry picket signs all day long if I knew that the next day we could use the ladies' room at Barrington's Department Store or matriculate at the University of Maryland without getting lawyers and the courts involved. Even when elite Washingtonians like Mary McLeod Bethune and Mary Church Terrell, whose late husband had been the first Negro D. C. judge, joined picket lines, it wasn't enough to make People's Drugs integrate their lunch counters or work staff.

It takes a special person to be dedicated to a centuries-long struggle. It takes a patient person to be satisfied with only slow and barely perceptible change and return to the trenches time after time. They say Juanita Jackson helped desegregate dormitories while a student at the University of Pennsylvania and that made my feeble attempts to get later curfews and better food on campus seem totally frivolous. Juanita was amazing and I could never match her level of passion and commitment.

Magdalena would say that, once again, I liked the *idea* of something, but not necessarily what it took to achieve it, that I would start off gung-ho, then become half-hearted shortly thereafter. When I was twelve, I wanted a harp because I thought it was the most beautiful instrument in the world. I begged my parents to buy one for my birthday. As far as I knew, there were no famous American Negro harpists. I could be the first. Magdalena loved Negro firsts. But when the harp arrived – special delivery from Italy – I realized that though it was magnificently handsome, a work of art actually, it was difficult to learn, and I lost interest after the third lesson.

I wanted to be part of the NAACP's successes, but I was impatient and didn't want to risk failure, ridicule, arrest, injury, the loss of valuable social time, or the cold realization of futility. My sister Charlotte would readily participate in the demonstration and say that I was wishy-washy and never knew what to do with myself. We're both right. At least I'm aware of my shortcomings.

I was also not like Millie who walked picket lines and marched for jobs and against police brutality. She inherited the activist gene from her father, described as a rabble-rousing Negro union organizer by certain shipyard owners. Millie was already battle-tested-and-scarred; she had a small scar by her eyebrow from a sharp, little stone that got thrown in her direction during a march to support unions. She was still pretty and her courage and clear sense of purpose were some of the things I admired about her. She was also a lot of fun.

I met Millicent Thomas when we were both students at Dunbar Public High School. She was one of the few friends I had who wasn't involved with D & D and sometimes it was difficult to balance my friendship with her and my friendship with Georgine and some of the other "Duchesses." Magdalena approved of the association even though Millie's family was not of our station and was a bit too militant with their "angry looks and all that hollering and fist pumping." But she was also "smart, well-spoken and refined" and Chauncey spied that her mother kept a "tidy" home.

I appreciated the idea of protest, but at the same time, I was weary from having the obligation to do battle being constantly ingrained into my psyche at home, at church, at school, D & D, sorority meetings, even the neighborhood LeDroit Park knitting club. Often I've just wanted to be unburdened from the perpetual obligation to uplift the race, the other ninety percent. Even so, I've done a lot in the pursuit of equal rights, but I'd still love to have a normal, uncomplicated life while hoping that the country would just phenomenally right itself.

I envied the few white acquaintances I had who could hear about a church being burned, the plain-spoken pastor being lynched, the family rendered homeless, and just sigh, shake their heads and go right back to polishing their nails. How wonderful it must be to harbor only fleeting outrage, to be self-righteously appalled for only a moment, and be unbothered by a prickly conscience. How liberating it would be to not expend so much energy figuring out how to just *be*, to not have to strategize the simple task of going to the store to get talcum powder and sanitary supplies. How nice it must be to have no duty beyond doing for self, family, or the occasional charity case and not having it extend to an entire race of people.

In principle, I was totally committed to "the cause," but the part of me that was fickle and self-centered fretted about the noose demonstrations and brooded about mundane things, like whether I'd ever enjoy a Katharine Hepburn movie in the "nice" seats instead of being relegated to the rickety balcony, or "nigger heaven," as it was called by the smug locals and the contemptuous ushers who claimed they were just doing their job as they pointed to the staircase.

After listening to the preliminary plans for the noose demonstration and seeing everyone's eyes light up with enthusiasm, I told Millie, "I'll think about it."

"Good, that's all anyone can ask."

CHAPTER 8

As THE DAUGHTER of Attorney and Mrs. Jasper Treadwell, noted philanthropists and volunteers for numerous social causes, I was well aware of the civil rights struggle. Our entire family has always had some degree of involvement. Charlotte, Emery and I, often as part of a Dukes & Duchesses initiative, have taken up collections to benefit everything from Negro orphanages to the Howard Theater. My father writes numerous checks to the NAACP and other various charities. Many prominent people and civil rights leaders were frequent guests at our home. Magdalena has hosted dinners for many of Washington's Negro elite, from bank presidents and shipping magnates to the influential owners and editors of Negro newspapers. Everyone sits around discussing Jim Crow politics and trying to solve all society's ills over a single meal or a cocktail or two. Even Dr. DuBois has sampled my homemade lemon squares while visiting us at Highland Beach. He and my father would play chess and discuss fine arts and literature, the racial divide and their shared disdain for the Amos and Andy radio show and all that buffoonery.

And my parents, unlike many of my friends' parents, were rather progressive in that they didn't believe in banishing children while adults were talking so I always knew everything that was going on. Nor did they discourage our questions and comments as long as they were serious and well thought out so guests could be impressed by how bright we were. So we were present for some provocative discussions, including the constant debates about whether or not the late Booker T. Washington was an Uncle Tom.

Washington believed that Negroes should abandon the goal of equality and integration and be content with second-class status. He thought we should be apolitical and unconcerned about voting and just concentrate on becoming skilled and industrious. He spent a lot of time promoting the school he founded, Tuskegee Institute in Alabama, which emphasized "useful trades" like bricklaying, carpentry or dressmaking. Washington was anointed as *the* Negro leader and spokesman, a necessary counterpoint to the "radical" Dr. DuBois and was financially rewarded by the many white benefactors who agreed with him that Negroes should be patient and have low expectations and simple goals. Yet he sent his own children to expensive boarding schools and colleges for classical academics and encouraged them to become fully engaged citizens. Washington's "accommodationist" philosophy and perceived hypocrisy didn't sit well with Dr. DuBois or my father. However, many a Booker T. Washington admirer has broken bread at our table and the discussions were always good-natured but high-spirited.

"I met Booker T when I was down in Tuskegee for a meeting," said an older gentleman, a retired Howard professor. "I'll tell you, he was one arrogant son of a bitch. But, deep down, I believe he meant well."

The other guests, already feeling privileged to sit at Jasper Treadwell's dinner table, were also impressed that they sat in the company of someone who actually spoke with the legendary Booker T. Washington. They smiled at the professor's memory of him.

"Yeah," my father said, "he meant to do well for himself and sell out everybody else."

"Well you must admit the practicality of his 'go-slow' approach," some other guest would say. "Most of our people have barely transitioned out of slavery. Putting the focus on agricultural and industrial jobs just makes sense. I have a cousin who's not very bright but has done very well for himself as a brick mason. Voting is the last thing he's thinking about. People like him need to worry about making a living so they can take care of themselves. What good are voting and integration if you're begging in the streets because you have no skills?"

"Bull!" my father said, pounding the table and making the silverware bounce. "First, we can have *both*. And, second, every Negro can be educated. They just need exposure and the opportunity to fail or succeed on their own merits. It's fine to be a bricklayer, but not if you really want to be a lawyer."

"But with all due respect, Mr. Treadwell, not everyone can be a lawyer."

"Why not?" he'd ask, peering over the tops of his glasses.

"Well, because…"

"Ain't no because," my father would say, unafraid to slip into comfortable vernacular in erudite company. "Of course everyone won't actually *become* a lawyer, but everyone should have the *opportunity* to become one. I could pluck any pickaninnie from the tobacco field and, in ten to fifteen years, I could have him going toe to toe with any white lawyer.

"You really think so?"

"I know so. I was one of those pickaninnies."

"But…"

"Education is the key to success. You can be the best bricklayer this side of the Mason-Dixon, but without education and the ballot, you can only get so far! Waiting and begging get us nowhere. I don't care what Booker T said."

Sitting at the head of his Chippendale 18-place mahogany dining table, he would conclude the conversation in order to move on to the next friendly debate. "He was the worst kind of Uncle Tom, did everything but buck dance." The guests would chuckle and some would clink their water goblets with each other. "It's great we have Tuskegee; it's a valuable institution, but that Negro set us back fifty years."

"Hear, hear!" they said, in deference to the illustrious Jasper Treadwell. And this scenario played out over and over again with various arrays of guests and my father always getting the last word with a light-hearted sneer and a table slap.

CHAPTER 9

CHARLOTTE, EMERY AND I were present at dinner conversations where people gossiped about who'd been publicly humiliated by some Jim Crow antics or had lost all their money and possessions after the stock market crash.

"The Logans tried to integrate St. Bonaventure last Sunday and some of the parishioners literally pushed them back out the door," one guest shared. "And bolted it shut."

"Goodness!" said my mother. "They should just stay at St. Luke's."

"You can't tell them anything. They're going to try again in a few months."

"Godspeed."

There were guests like Georgine's mother who couldn't wait to share that she'd spotted one of their old friends in line at a soup kitchen.

"Rowena put a newspaper up to her face and pretended not to see me," Ann Kirkwood said. "It was pitiful."

"How tragic," said my mother. Rowena Maxwell was, at one time, the Queen Bee. Her husband, a mogul in the barrel manufacturing industry, had a reversal of fortune and absconded somewhere west.

Daddy said, "I told them all that wild, phony stock speculation would lead to ruin."

"Had that been me," Georgine's mother said, "I'd have moved to Cleveland or some place where no one knew me."

"Relocating costs money," my father said. "And Rowena is broker than the windows in an abandoned factory in Foggy Bottom."

Mrs. Kirkwood laughed. "She could always borrow some."

"She'd rather die," my mother said.

During another conversation between my father and the president of the Washington bureau of the NAACP, I learned about their desire to integrate one of Washington's most exclusive private schools. I saw an opportunity to do something other than write letters to the President or collect money for causes. I could be a race pioneer and, at seven years old with wide-eyed optimism, I immediately volunteered my services because people needed to realize that Negro children were just as good and capable as white children.

Georgine always said that the "dirty, raggedy, black kids" scrounging around D.C. were an embarrassment to her and she could only imagine what "others" thought. And the dark and brooding photographs of accused Negro thieves and assailants were often plastered in the newspapers and were perceived as typical Negro denizens. My mother was so disturbed by the images that she slammed the papers shut as if that erased the disgrace. Unlike whites, Negroes are defined by the least, not the best, elements of our community. The "tenthers" were obliged to dispel the stereotypes.

We'd been taught in our Dukes and Duchesses' etiquette and elocution classes that when we stepped out in public, we represented our families, the greater D. C. Negro gentry and the sum and substance of all Negro people. We had to strive for perfection and teach image consciousness to the Negroes who unfortunately lacked the education, deportment and thoughtful breeding that we had. We did this with the children we tutored while upholding the principle of *noblesse oblige* and fulfilling D & D's once-a-month community service requirement to help the underprivileged. According to the D & D leadership, we needed to look and act like equals to be treated as equals. Otherwise white people were justified in their refusal to mix socially with us and for treating us all as inferior. So, as Mary Church Terrell puts it, "we lift as we climb," and this benefits everyone.

But Georgine's father, tipsy from too much spiked eggnog, once thanked God during a midnight champagne toast at a New Year's Eve party, for keeping him "at the top of the heap" for another year, for separating the descendants of "house niggers" and "field niggers" and for granting white America the ability to discern the difference between the two. Half the room politely chuckled and the other half looked stricken.

"That fool is delusional," I overheard someone say. "We're all the same to them. They disdain all of us."

"The *nerve* – black as he is," someone said, though Dr. Kirkwood was, at most, brick-colored.

"Who does he think he is – a Roosevelt?"

Magdalena, after tucking us into bed and explaining that "field *Ne*-groes" were dark-skinned, full-blooded African slaves who tended the crops and got whipped if they worked too slowly or tried to escape, and that "house *Ne*-groes" were light-skinned Mulatto slaves who wore nice clothes and helped cook and set the table in the owner's mansion, said that she found Dr. Kirkwood's toast to be a crass assessment but that she understood his point. She dodged our follow-up questions, blew us kisses and went back downstairs to the party.

There were kernels of truth in Dr. Kirkwood's slurred assertions. We *were* different. I was always aware of being watched and judged whenever we ventured out and we were taught to handle the scrutiny with aplomb. There was always some thinly veiled scorn that we were just a bunch of worthless Negroes. But people would often do a double take when they saw us with Magdalena, a mother duck leading her three ducklings, single file, never abreast, to avoid any sidewalk hassles with approaching whites who still felt we should be the ones to stand aside or step off the curb to let them pass. Depending on the mindset of the pedestrians, a chance, two-second rendezvous on a narrow sidewalk could turn into a full-blown racial incident. We walked briskly, with a purpose. "Always walk like you have somewhere to be," Magdalena would warn. "No meandering or dawdling. Never give those people a reason to question your intentions."

Whites and Negroes alike would gawk at Magdalena's perfectly aligned seamed stockings with the taut, movie-star fit that didn't sag at the ankles and knees like they did on a lot of women, the elaborate but tasteful hat and the patrician chin jutting forward unabashedly. Charlotte, Emery and I followed behind, trying to keep her pace. Emery had blade-sharp pants creases and a tie he knotted perfectly himself, and Charlotte and I were colorfully dressed, hands burrowed in a mink fur muff if it was chilly or clasping a matching parasol if it was warm and the sun threatened to scorch our sensitive complexions. We met our friends and D&D associates at the Howard Theater for a concert or maybe Chez Olivet for a birthday party.

But whether it was a trip to the library, the zoo or a store, heads turned and tongues wagged as people wondered who we were disembarking from sparkling sedans and promenading up and down streets without a care in the world, especially in later years during the Depression. We walked past people who wore their poverty like a shroud, limbless military veterans and those who'd been movers and shakers until Black Tuesday rendered them bankrupt and despondent.

Occasionally, Magdalena would recognize an old acquaintance who'd fallen on hard times. They would often be holding a sign saying "Bank lost all my money, please help!" or "Will work for food" and my mother would press a dollar into their hand and tell them "You take care of yourself now." Bringing up the rear of Magdalena's processional, I would sometimes contribute a dime if I could dig one out of my coin purse fast enough, before Magdalena, who apparently had eyes in the back of her head, said, "Come along, Justinia, what do I say about dawdling?"

Even as youngsters we were aware of the looks of awe, resentment or admiration we received. And we were taught that the proper racial etiquette was to acknowledge anyone who acknowledged us – no matter how rude or crude the acknowledgment. With whites, it was "Good day to you" in their general direction without meeting their eyes but without looking down or away either. One white lady stopped my mother to say "Your children are quite fetching. They prance like prime specimens at the Westminster Dog Show." Magdalena gave her a tight smile then railed to my father about the left-handed compliment later at home. We looked Negroes in the eye and nodded – even the ones who eyed us with caution or contempt, even the wine-soaked vagrant who asked, "Hey, where y'all from – England?" By acknowledging *all* persons, everyone's sense of pride and propriety was preserved and the "uppity" indictment was less likely to be leveled against us. Negroes didn't feel belittled and whites didn't feel the racial hierarchy was being breached.

Magdalena didn't mind being called uppity. She said it was a term invented by whites to express their displeasure at observing the dignified and cultured bearing of well-bred Negroes. If you didn't have a bent back and downcast eyes, you were considered uppity. Magdalena's spine was always ramrod straight, her chin raised and eyes forward, but she didn't have the accompanying head-tilt, the nose-to-the-sky posture caricatured by some of her friends. "So yes," she'd concede, "I guess I am uppity. Though I prefer up*lifted.* Would that we all could be up*lifted.*"

When a Negro called another Negro uppity, it was usually out of resentment for someone perceived as thinking themselves superior to others. If that happened, my mother, who was reserved but kind, quiet but cordial would feel sorry for them. She said, "People may assume what they wish, but only insecure people and frustrated social climbers call other Negroes uppity."

So in addition to participating in the fight for equality and working to uplift the masses, I had to be conscientious about my image each time I walked out the door. I could really only relax when sprawled across my canopied bed reading or daydreaming. Once when Magdalena took us all out to Woodward and Lothrop to buy Easter clothes, I accidentally brushed up against a little white girl who'd reached for the same yellow, beaded collar dress that I did. Her mother pulled her back like I was a hot iron, muttered something and left the store without the dress.

I immediately wondered if I had inadvertently portrayed a poor image. Looking in the store mirror, I saw that my shoe laces were not untied, my slip was not showing, my knees and elbows were still free of ashiness, and my braids were still tight and unraveled. And although my parents constantly assured me that I was pretty, smart and talented, that simple gesture stung for a while. My young mind still couldn't grasp the concept that society thought Negroes were inferior beings and that we had to do everything separately from whites. It made no sense. Were white dogs better than brown or black dogs? I'd seen them romping together and nobody cared. I thought if that little girl and her mother actually knew me, they'd invite me over to play.

That incident was worse than the typical name-calling tomfoolery. When I was a teen, a group of young guys yelled out "jungle bunny" or "tar baby," I forget which, from a moving truck, but it didn't have nearly the same effect on me; it was an impersonal affront, more mischievous than vicious. It was like they were playing a stereotypical role in some satirical race play, and their contempt didn't come from a deep, visceral level like it did with the department store lady. So I just lifted my chin up and stepped lively into Clarabelle's beauty salon for my weekly shampoo and hair straightening and thought nothing else of it.

CHAPTER 10

AFTER THE CONVERSATION between my father and the NAACP president, and after some wrangling with my parents, particularly the overprotective Magdalena who always said I was impetuous, I was to be one of two Negroes to participate in a voluntary integration experiment that upcoming autumn at Citizens Academy, a private school that served upper-middle-class whites. I was eager to see what all the fuss was about, find out what they had that was so precious they couldn't bear to share it with Negro children. I never found anything.

Though I excelled, I stayed for only one semester because the segregated Negro school was better. It had an accelerated curriculum, and no one stared, fingered my hair or threw spitballs at me. The parents of the other boy allowed him to stay even though we had proven our point, even though Citizens' third graders weren't yet learning long-division or cursive writing, even though they were taught that Columbus discovered America and we learned in kindergarten that one couldn't "discover" a place that was already inhabited. The exalted Citizens Academy with its state-of-the-art pool and Jungle Gym, master chef and equestrian training was nothing more than a facade.

My classmate who stayed wouldn't be adequately prepared for Paul Lawrence Dunbar, the Negro high school on M Street, named after the famous poet, which was the best, most rigorous public school in the entire city and the first of its kind in the nation. The entire D. C. Negro school district was excellent and was the only one in the country run exclusively by Negro administrators. But Dunbar was the standout. Dunbar students could compete with any students in any arena where there was a level playing field and Negroes weren't held to stricter, subjective standards. Many of the Dunbar faculty had Ph.Ds and ivy-league or European educations and expected and elicited the best from all the students and produced an impressive number of future doctors, lawyers and educators. Between Dunbar High School and Howard University, the "talented tenth" was kept well-stocked.

Whether one's father was a professor, a laborer or unemployed, everyone was expected to be neat and clean, to stand up straight, use proper grammar, keep their hands to themselves, say "Yes ma'am" and "No sir," obey the Golden Rule and be dignified at all times. The teachers always said, "Poverty is no excuse to not be respectable." I still recall how Principal Austin twisted the ear of a boy whose pants would not stay up, exposing his dingy undershorts. The boy explained that the pants were hand-me-downs from his older brother and that he didn't have a belt. "You are a *Dunbar* student," Mr. Austin said. "You're supposed to be sharp and resourceful." The boy found some twine to thread through his belt loops until he could acquire a proper belt.

When the Washington NAACP president came to dinner after our little experiment was over, I learned that the Citizens' administrators had hoped we'd fail but were pleasantly surprised by our performance and the way we fit in. I also learned about something he called Negro Low-Self-Esteem Syndrome – a condition that had some Negroes thinking anything Caucasian is always inherently superior. It is precisely this malady that had the other boy remaining at the inferior Citizens Academy for another year.

"What do you mean?" I asked, taking a sip of milk.

"People," my father said, "have been conditioned to think that everything black is ugly, gross and immoral and everything white is right, beautiful and virtuous."

"A crying shame," said the NAACP president.

"How do the Indians fit into that analysis?" Charlotte asked, cutting her roast beef into tiny pieces.

"It's complicated..." My father answered.

"What about the Chinese?" Emery asked, grinning as he stretched the outer corners of his eyes towards his pointy little ears. "Or the Jews, what about them?"

"You're being silly, Emery," my mother chastised. "Eat your peas."

"Jews are white," Charlotte said.

"Not exactly," said my father.

"Did Jews really kill Jesus?" I asked. "Georgine's dad says that's why Christians hate Jews."

"Jesus *was* Jewish," Charlotte said. "Why would Christians be mad about Jews killing another Jew?"

"Well if he was Jewish, why do we call him Christ – like in Christian?" I asked.

"Yeah," said Emery, genuinely confused. "And like Christmas."

"And was Jesus really white? Doesn't the Bible say he was swarthy with woolly hair?" I was a bit confused myself. "Doesn't swarthy mean dark?"

"Maybe he was Mulatto," Emery offered. "Like Nana." My mother nodded. "That would mean that either God or the Virgin Mary is a Negro."

"If God or Mary were Negro," Charlotte said, "Negroes would be in charge of everything."

"Excellent point," my father said.

I decided to change the subject, ignoring the fact that she may have had a valid point. "Georgine's dad may go to St. Luke's every Sunday, but he says he's an atheist."

"Georgine's father talks too much," my mother said.

"What's an atheist?" Emery asked.

My mother sighed and asked Lily to refill her wine glass. "An atheist does not believe in God."

"No God?" Emery was astonished. "Will the devil get him?"

"Well," my father said, "these are all excellent questions. We'll have to have Reverend Crawford over for dinner one day and maybe he can explain everything to you. But as far as the different races go, Charlotte, suffice it to say that Indians, Chinese and Jews are all despised. But Negroes are the most despised. We have it worse than anyone else."

"I think the Indians do," Charlotte said. "We took their land and gave them smallpox."

"The white man did." He leaned back in his chair. "But I'll bet if you asked one of those Cherokee who work down at the tobacco plant if they'd rather be Indian or Negro, they'd say Indian."

"Maybe."

"No maybe, little girl. That's a fact. But back to my original point," my father said, pointing his fork at the adults at the table. "Zack and Meredith need to take their son out of that over-rated Citizens Academy and put him back in Douglass Prep. He has to be ready for Dunbar or he may not even get accepted there. And he'll need Dunbar if they still want him to go to Yale."

The NAACP president said, "That's right. Integration is not always in our best interest."

"We have to get Negroes to stop thinking that the white man's ice is always colder."

"Amen, Brother Jasper" laughed the NAACP president, helping himself to another serving of mashed potatoes.

"And maybe if some of those bourgeois Negroes had trusted some of those whip-smart Negro lawyers and accountants out there to handle their business affairs, they wouldn't have gone broke when the bottom fell out." He took a sip of water. "Then maybe Webster Norris wouldn't have put that pistol to his temple."

"Really, Jasper, we're eating!" My mother pushed her plate away.

"Well it's true. Negro Low Self-Esteem Syndrome – it can be fatal."

"Beg your pardon, Magdalena, but Amen again," said the NAACP president, barely suppressing his grin. "Justinia, will you please pass the gravy?"

CHAPTER 11

BACK AT SHARP Street Memorial, Millie and I were on our way to the reception in the church basement. Two guys intercepted us and interrupted my reverie about cute, designer shoes that I could actually try on in the store. They thrust some political fliers into our hands.

"What's this?" I asked.

"It's a brochure of Roosevelt's accomplishments," said the young man wearing a "Re-elect FDR" campaign badge. "We need your support. Vote democrat."

"I plan to," Millie said.

"Not so fast," said the young man wearing a "Landon & Knox" badge. "The Republicans need to take control of this country again. Deeds not deficits. Vote for Landon."

"I probably will," I said.

"Whichever way you go," said the Democrat, "just make sure you go. Exercise your God-given right to vote."

"Tell that to everyone you know," said the Republican.

"You're preaching to the choir," said Millie.

"Absolutely," I said and the two guys walked off shaking hands.

When our housekeeper Lily and members of her church had problems registering to vote, I was the one who asked my father to help them although she didn't want to get him involved. "He does so much for me and my family already," Lily said. "Seems I'm always running to him for something or other." But I insisted.

Although I wasn't old enough to vote yet, I understood that voting was too important to take nonchalantly. I was six years old when women won the right to vote in 1920 and remember accompanying my mother to the voting booth for her first time. She ordered a dress from the Spiegel catalog and the "hat lady" on U Street made her a natty cloche special for election day. She wore her nicest strand of pearls and went as part of one of her women's groups who'd planned for suffragettes to show up en masse at the polls. Out of hundreds of white women, she was one of only a few Negroes at her polling place.

This was truly a momentous occasion, a dream come true for her. It had always bothered her that she was denied the ballot when she was as intelligent and propertied as any man, if not more so; and she was third-generation college-educated, practically unheard of for anyone in the early 1900s, particularly Negroes. Years earlier, while pregnant with me, she was prepared to march in the National Woman Suffrage Parade with Mary Church Terrell, Ida B. Wells and members of Delta Sigma Theta Sorority until the event coordinators announced that all Negroes had to walk with the "black delegation" at the back of the line. The irony was obviously lost on the people who made that decision. Thoroughly disgusted, my mother declined to participate, went home and soaked her swollen feet in warm water and Epsom salts.

At the poll, we sipped Pellegrino while waiting in the long line. There were men, even a few women, shaking their fists, heckling, and calling everyone lesbians, bull dykes and whores – labels my mother had to explain later. They carried signs demanding that women return to the kitchen where they belonged and stop trying to be men. One sign said "Next they'll want to be President." Most of the women voters ignored them, held their heads higher, pulled their children nearer, clutched their pocketbooks tighter. A few tried to engage in unwinnable debates with men whose veins pulsated dangerously from their foreheads as they gesticulated wildly all because women were voting. Adding to their aggravation, an Amazon of a woman pulled out her driver's license, thrusted it at one wild-eyed man. "Read it and weep," she said. "I voted and drove my own car down here to do it. A car I paid for all by my lonesome. How ya like them apples?" The women in the queue cheered her on.

A poll worker checked for Magdalena's name against a ledger and looked her up and down. It was obvious that he'd never seen a Negro woman quite like my mother, one so finely dressed and coiffed, one who radiated with self-confidence and entitlement. Some women were giddy, some seemed cautious, some cried tears of joy. Magdalena looked as if she'd done this before, as if the act of voting was commonplace for her. The poll worker pointed toward an available booth, observed her every step as she entered like it was her personal boudoir. I watched her proudly retract the privacy curtain and pull the lever for the Republican Warren Harding. When she reopened the curtain, a photographer from the Baltimore *Afro-American* newspaper was waiting to take her picture, blinding me and Charlotte with the bright, popping flash. Magdalena made the front page of the *Afro-American* and the *Washington Bee*.

The best thing about the day, in addition to our candidate winning, was seeing one of my mother's rare smiles; she radiated from within. This was not the smile she shared with the camera though – the photograph revealed only smug vindication, the cool countenance of a woman who knows that her club members and lunch companions would be critiquing the picture for weeks to come. The real smile occurred at the moment she recorded her votes; it was involuntary, involving all the parts of her face – crinkling eyes, wrinkling nose and beautiful, straight, white teeth all showing. I knew then that voting was a monumental privilege, an obligation even, if it evoked such an emotional response from my normally stoic mother. Anything that interfered with that hard-fought suffrage was serious business and my father lived for those kinds of challenges.

So after Lily shared her misadventure with me, I pulled her into Daddy's office and told her to tell him the same sordid story she'd tearfully told to me – how it took so much courage for them to go...how many of them used the last of their pin money for the carfare needed to get to the Anne Arundel County registrar's office...how the staff made them wait over two hours even though they weren't doing anything or registering anyone else...how this man with big, bulging eyes finally came out and accused them of being Communists because they were probably going to vote for that Communist Roosevelt because they were "plum-lazy" and just wanted a handout...how the man gave them written "voter-qualifying tests" with questions that asked them to explain the Tenth Amendment to the Constitution, to describe the Maryland state flag in detail, to state how many seeds were in a watermelon, to state how many bricks it took to build the White House, and to list the occupation of their grandparents...how her friend Linc had brought a knotted-up handkerchief with exactly 233 seeds because he'd been told to anticipate the watermelon question and wanted to have verification of his answer... how they were gleefully told some 90 minutes later that all nine of them had failed, were not smart enough to vote and were not eligible anyway because they each had some family history of slavery...how the bulgy-eyed man threatened to fetch the sheriff to arrest them if they didn't leave immediately and slammed the door so hard after them that one of the panes of glass shattered...how Lily and her church family vowed never to return again...how they should have known that was going to happen.

"Thank you for hearing me out, Mr. Treadwell," Lily said breathlessly, having thoroughly purged herself of the egregious grievances perpetrated on her and her church members. "I know you're a very busy man, but Miss Justinia thought you might be able to help us out."

When she excused herself to go finish preparing dinner, I thought my father would rant and rave about the injustice, call the NAACP president, yell about how this was 1932, not 1832, and that what they did was illegal and they could not just make up rules and apply them arbitrarily. Whites were not required to take this test unless, perhaps, they were dirt-caked, barefoot and toothless, and probably not even then. Yet a Negro mechanic in his Sunday best and painstakingly de-greased fingernails and palm creases, who had a hanky full of watermelon seeds, was subjected to a test designed for him to fail. It violates the Equal Protection Clause, Daddy would normally fume. I'd heard this argument before at the dinner table, on the beach, wherever the subject came up, but not this time. Instead he got on the phone and asked the operator to connect him to the Anne Arundel County sheriff.

"Sheriff Casey, Jasper Treadwell here. How are you, sir?...Excellent!..Look, two things...I wanted to know if you were planning to run for re-election again, because I've been approached by Horton Cook for a contribution to his campaign, so I'm checking with you because you know I've always supported you... You are? Good. I'll get a check out to you. One other thing. My housekeeper and some of her church members had a problem registering to vote today... Yes, they did take the test...no, they were told they failed, but you know as well as I do that that test is ridiculous and it's unconstitutional...And you're a fair minded public servant, that's why I like you...And these are good, hard-working Christian people; they'd make good, loyal constituents, you can build your base....That's right, every vote does count...Excellent!...So you tell Orville to stand down at the registrar's office and I'll be sure to get Lily and her friends in there Monday morning sharp!...Excellent!...And I'll tell Horton Cook I'm already committed...Yes, and I'll see you at the Governor's Ball...Good day, sheriff." My father winked and gave me a thumb's up. I gave my father a tight squeeze and ran to tell Lily.

The relationship between Sheriff Casey and my father could only be described as one of both mutual admiration and mutual contempt; but they made it work. Daddy says Casey sees him as a "rich, uppity nigger," and he sees Casey as a "savvy, undercover redneck" who will do whatever is expedient as long as he gets to strut around in his sheriff's badge and snap his suspenders. For years, Sheriff Casey grudgingly greased the wheels of justice and my father delivered Negro votes for him and other elected officials. Casey beat his last opponent by only six votes. With Sheriff Casey's cooperation, our family was able to register and vote in Maryland, using our Highland Beach address, instead of Washington which was our principal residence. But in Washington D. C., citizens ironically could not vote for President or Congress, nor even a mayor or council, and my father refused to pay all those taxes just to help elect a dogcatcher. Since he didn't believe in taxation without representation, he had the rules bent. Casey bent them.

So our franchise was in Maryland. Lily lived-in with us but maintained a tiny house in Baltimore where extended family stayed. Her home church was also in Baltimore. That Monday after the phone call, Daddy sent carloads of people from First Pilgrim Baptist Church to the registrar's office with instructions to tell the bulgy-eyed voter registrar, Orville, that Attorney Jasper Treadwell had sent them. One of the registrants was a 99-year old man who had migrated from Alabama and last voted for President Rutherford B. Hayes in 1876, a year before the watchdog federal troops were withdrawn from the secessionist states, when Reconstruction effectively ended, Jim Crow policies set in, and Negroes who tried to keep voting or running for office got lynched. The Klan only had to make an example of one person, usually on the eve of election day, to keep people at home and far away from the polls. So the old man was ecstatic about being able to vote again come November.

Orville's staff registered over fifty people that day, did not administer a single, so-called voter-qualifying test, and Orville paced the floor, mashing his lips into a thin, pink line and made his eyes even bulgier. Lily said she thought he was going to pop like a balloon. And when Lily left the county building, registration papers in hand, she felt like Magdalena had felt all those years ago, and she hadn't even cast a ballot yet.

CHAPTER 12

I JOKINGLY SAY that, as an ice cream connoisseur, my greatest sacrifice to the cause of desegregation was giving up those luscious strawberry ice cream cones from High's Ice Cream parlor in support of the New Negro Alliance's boycott because High's refused to hire Negro clerks. The NNA's slogan was "Don't buy where you can't work!" I told everyone I knew, and everyone I saw, to stay out of High's. Many children and Howard University students and families participated in the boycott and High's lost a lot of customers.

They especially missed their Sunday afternoon customers who came by for their after-church treat. Instead of going inside, people milled around outside their door keeping cool and slaked by ice water provided by the Howard University chapter of the NAACP and Coca-colas purchased from street vendors. The NNA members wore sandwich boards saying "Don't Buy Where You Can't Work (Out Front)." One young man sat on the curb and played bongos while some co-eds shook their hips in time with the rhythm. The younger children who whined about not getting ice cream were sufficiently bribed with Mary Janes and chocolate drops that my fellow NAACP members and I fished out of brown paper bags.

It was an opportune time to catch up with friends and neighbors, teach the children about the fight for equality and be mocking of High's at the same time. There was a festival-like atmosphere which made protesting seem fun. The second week, the police made everyone leave because we were "interfering with commerce." The next few times, however, the police looked the other way and left us alone. Eventually High's discovered they liked profit more than they liked not having Negroes behind the counter in white paper hats making root beer floats. So they promoted one of their Negro employees from dishwasher to soda jerk. The decision was made out of self-interest, but we regarded it as a victory anyway. The NNA, the NAACP and the Urban League have always said that we had to hit these segregationists in the pocketbook to make any progress.

The NNA had a huge victory party on Howard's campus. We celebrated the fact that we'd brought about change, and also saluted the Washington community whose cooperation by staying out of the store made it possible. As High's reward for its capitulation, the following Sunday, the after-church crowd formed a line that streamed outside the door and down the block.

The victory party was even better because there were so many prominent guests who attended. A. Philip Randolph, a labor leader and civil rights icon, was in town and he came to the party, made some profound comments, then joined our conga line and proceeded to cut quite a rug. I made sure to get a dance with him. Who knew that the man who unionized Negro train attendants into the Brotherhood of Sleeping Car Porters could jitterbug with the best of them?

Public protests, though not always successful, were still great ways to show businesses that they couldn't take our patronage for granted. The fight over High's hiring practices had been gratifying. Fighting discrimination was sober, serious business but we made it a little fun. If only every battle were that easy.

That tingly feeling of contentment that one got from a well-earned triumph was wonderful and contagious but lasted only as long as the next indignity, the next challenge. Millie's father says that the fight for rights shouldn't be approached like climbing hills – one selected mound at a time. He wouldn't pound his chest until Everest was conquered, until there was absolute equality in all aspects of our lives. Mr. Thomas has remarked on my efforts, "That's nice, but the fight has to be in your marrow, not just something to do from time to time."

He was right, but I still didn't feel I was totally naïve to the world, blind to the struggle or absent from the crusade. I may not be a Juanita Jackson or a Millie Thomas, but in my own way, I feel I've made small but valuable contributions to the pursuit of desegregation and civil rights. I had to remind myself of these little things so I wouldn't feel guilty about not wearing a noose while walking solemnly down Baltimore's Federal Hill with the others.

CHAPTER 13

WE WERE HAVING the requisite after-church refreshment of red punch and butter cookies in the church basement when he approached. I'd noticed him earlier sitting several rows back. He knew all three verses of "Lift Every Voice." With his wavy hair, dimpled chin and slightly olive complexion, I couldn't tell at first if he was white, very light-skinned or trying to "pass" like several of my friends and family members were doing. But on second thought, someone trying to pass for white would probably not be caught dead at an NAACP convention.

Magdalena, a quadroon, taught me how to instinctively spot a "passer," someone trying to elude the "one drop rule" which declared that anyone with an ounce of black blood was a Negro. But she also taught me that it would be in poor taste to expose someone who was passing because it was understandable why a person, or an entire family, would want to disappear, live out a fantasy existence and assimilate into the dominant culture during times of such racial strife. Just nod and let them be, Magdalena would advise.

They didn't always try to pass for white. Sometimes they'd claim to be Dominican, Filipino, Brazilian, Palestinian – anything to explain away the more exotic features of their appearance. It was often considered complimentary to be asked, "What *are* you?" They would profess to being *anything* but black unless it gave them some kind of leverage. My father would say they were suffering from extreme cases of Negro Low Self-Esteem Syndrome. Or maybe it should be ABB – Anything But Black. I hoped to never have those issues. When a young man approached me at a party and asked if I was Puerto Rican, I said "No, I'm Negro just like you." He bristled and asked Georgine to dance instead.

Regardless, ambiguous ethnicity never ceased to intrigue me. Washington was full of racial ambiguities.

I was standing with Millie and some other people when he walked up and introduced himself, much to the irritation of Xavier Brathwaite III who, much to my irritation, considered himself to be courting me and resented the intrusion by this decidedly handsome man. I gave him the once-over. He reminded me a little of Rudolph Valentino, a matinee idol who died too soon.

I deduced that he was not Negro. There were none of the tell-tale signs of a too-broad or flattened nose, flaring nostrils, or lips that were a tad too ample or protruding. There was no orangey-yellow undertone, no hint of kink in his inky hair. The irises of his eyes were dark but not the typical tea-colored dark. I guessed his voice would lack the huskiness and full-bodied timbre common in Negro intonation. I think he was Jewish. My father was not particularly fond of Jews because of some sour business experiences he's had with them. But at the moment, none of that mattered.

"Hello, I'm Julius. Julius Sommerfeldt."

That smile. I was taken by him immediately. This was a man who could change my life.

CHAPTER 14

Julius

SHE WAS PRETTY. Not the prettiest one there, but certainly very pretty. She stood out in looks as well as demeanor. She had a caramel complexion and all these long, corkscrew tresses that were barely contained by the antique-looking barrette that complemented her bright yellow dress. She could've been one of my cousins after being bronzed by a Riviera sun. She seemed young yet worldly, wide-eyed yet knowing, rapt then restless. Depending on what was being said, she vacillated between looking resolute and looking dreamy and ambivalent. One moment she was hugging herself and sitting with knees knocking and legs splayed, the next her slender legs were double-crossed at knees and ankles with her hands steepled under her chin. I thought she was unintentionally coquettish, tossing her head to scan the room with heather eyes and daintily moistening her lips. Our eyes met and held for a few seconds. She blinked first.

The Youth Secretary was saying something about how constituents needed to vote in politicians with the courage to outlaw lynching. I applauded wildly along with everyone else. The American Congress, particularly the southern faction, needed a major overhaul as did the Nazi government in Germany, where I'm from. The girl with the yellow dress glanced back at me and smiled. Something about her intrigued me. I needed to meet her.

I felt right at home at this convention even though some of the attendees regarded me with curiosity, like I was a pork chop in a kosher deli. I was aware that many of the people listening to the lovely Miss Jackson were young people, perhaps relatively unfamiliar with the history of the NAACP and might be surprised to learn that it was actually started by blacks *and* whites.

My great-aunt, a German immigrant, was one of the sixty original members called to action by the great Dr. W.E.B. DuBois and Mary White Ovington, a little Caucasian lady with deep abolitionist roots. They were both determined to create an inter-racial organization to address race relations and the needs and concerns of all oppressed people. The mobilizing incident which brought their idea to fruition was the 1908 riots in Springfield, Illinois. The story was covered in the press from coast to coast because the racial conflagration occurred in a *northern* city and was the hometown of President Abraham Lincoln.

In Springfield, some white citizens went on a rampage because they were denied the thrill of vigilante justice when the sheriff moved two Negro prisoners to a safer jail in another city. Thousands rioted for two days, vandalizing, burning, looting and assaulting people in Negro neighborhoods. They hanged two prominent Negroes – a barber shop owner with a large, diverse clientele and William Donnegan, a cobbler who had made custom size 14 shoes for Abe Lincoln – and neither had anything to do with the alleged original sins that the people were enraged about. Curiosity seekers from all over came to contemplate the colossal property damage as well as the gruesome sight of lynched bodies hanging from trees. Rioters reveled around Donnegan's swaying corpse, taking photos and hacking off souvenir scraps of his clothing and chunks of his hair. The National Guard had to be called in to restore order and protect the besieged Negro citizens. In the end, only one person, a Russian Jew, was convicted on an unrelated charge. Of the two prisoners who'd been ferried off to safety from the avenging posse, one was convicted and executed for murder and the other one was acquitted on an admittedly fabricated rape charge. I remember being aghast when my aunt told me this story years later. It had been the perfect catalyst for civil rights activists to organize.

While Dr. DuBois provided the philosophical agenda and served as editor of *Crisis* magazine which chronicled Negro current affairs, other people like my Uncle Sy, who was on the local Washington D. C. board of directors, did most of the bankrolling and fundraising. Even the best laid plans will die on the vine without money to back them up, and fighting discrimination is expensive. Joel Spingarn, a wealthy Jew and a hell of a guy, was the national president.

I'm certainly aware of the controversy about the NAACP having disproportionate Caucasian leadership, especially at the national level, but am confident that most members are less interested in the internal politics and more concerned about being able to rely on the quality partnership that has sustained for more than twenty-five years and achieved many civil rights milestones along the way.

I knew the black-white issue was going to be discussed at a special session at some point during the convention; but that's a session I planned to skip, just as I'd skip a sausage-making demonstration. I can appreciate a well-funded, well-run organization as well as a tasty knockwurst without taking a peek behind the scenes. In both cases, the less seen and heard, the better.

When I arrived here from Berlin almost three years ago, my Uncle Sy, who I lived with, made sure I became a life member of the NAACP as well as the Anti-Defamation League as soon as I enrolled in law school. The ADL, sort of the Jewish equivalent of the NAACP, was formed in response to the prison kidnapping and lynching of a Jewish man, Leo Frank, who'd been convicted, wrongfully some would say, of murdering a 13-year old girl. I find it interesting that both civil rights organizations essentially came into existence because of lynching.

CHAPTER 15

UNTIL THREE YEARS ago, most of my awareness of racial and religious persecution and violence was limited to isolated incidents and anecdotal history lessons from teachers and rabbis. Since then, however, I've witnessed instances of extreme heartlessness and indifference. Wanting to soak up as much Americana as possible, some colleagues and I, all history buffs, drove to Richmond, Virginia one weekend to see some Civil War battlefields, the house where Confederate President Jefferson Davis lived and the courthouse where Lee surrendered to Grant after so many citizens died defending or opposing the enslavement and brutalization of human beings.

I noticed, strangely enough, that the same rebel flags housed in the courthouse museum were proudly hoisted up on flagpoles outside government buildings. I thought there should be a law establishing "Old Glory" as the official flag and that the "Stars and Bars" relics should be relegated to the basements, attics, and fireplace mantels of those inclined to be nostalgic about the war "of northern aggression." Back home in Germany, the Nazi Party's Swastika flag was more prevalent than the national flag and has become representative of the entire country. There was something unpatriotic, even treasonous, about flaunting flags that promoted hate, separation and exclusion instead of love for a unified country.

While touring Richmond, I saw a burly trolley operator literally push an old Negro woman off the car because she refused to relinquish her seat when there were white people standing. My companions and I jumped out of the car and ran over to see about her. She was conscious but unmoving on the sidewalk. Her fist was half-clenched, clutching some coins, her wages for the day. The bandana tied around her head had blood on it and it looked like her arm was broken, but the nearest hospital didn't treat or admit Negro patients.

A group of several Negroes surrounded us. They all knew her, saw her every day and enjoyed her once-upon-a-time stories. They called her Mama Tess. She used to be a child slave on a tobacco plantation and loved to recount how she was too petrified to throw down her hoe when the Yankees rode in and told them they were free. As we hovered over her, they explained how Mama Tess had washed and ironed laundry all day, was physically tired and mentally sick of the Jim Crow bullshit.

One by one the crowd shuffled away because the paddy wagon, lights strobing and siren blaring, was headed our way. Four cops hopped out with billy clubs drawn, listened to the trolley operator's complaint, grabbed the old woman's arms and legs and tossed her into the back of the truck. I grabbed the elbow of one of the retreating officers. "That woman needs a doctor, you jackasses!" They ignored me and drove Mama Tess away.

I shouted out to the dispersing crowd. "You should do something!" One of the men, almost indistinguishable from the other men with their grimy overalls and lunch pails, turned back and said, "What you thank we oughta do? Write a letter to the trolley comp'ny? Fight the *police*? This stuff happen e'rday, one form or 'nother." He wiped his face with shirt sleeve. "She be aw-right. Mama Tess be tough." I don't know what became of her.

In Berlin, right before I came to America, I saw some Hitler Youth pummel and stomp some satchel-schlepping Jewish kids from the *yeshiva* because they "disrespected" them by failing to cross to the opposite side of the street as they approached. Their books and drawings were snatched from their bags, ripped up and thrown in a mud puddle. The parents of one of the kids ran down six flights of stairs after seeing the assault taking place outside the window of their apartment. The father shook his fist at them, tried to help his boy up, helpless as one of the Hitler Youth, the smallest one, got a few more kicks in. The mother dropped to her knees and wailed at the sight of the kids with their skinned knees, blackening eyes and broken teeth. She stood, grabbed at the shabby lapels of a passerby, demanding "Why...why do they do this to us, to children?" But the old man hurried past with his cart of bruised, mushy apples, head lowered, calling unenthusiastically, "Apples, get your just-picked apples. Best price in town." I could only shake my head and think about how I couldn't wait to get away from there.

I hated seeing Germany, where I'd led a relatively charmed life, morph into something scary and unpredictable. I came to America to go to law school since Jews were no longer allowed at the universities. America, with all its similar problems, still provided the perfect setting to refortify myself mentally, physically and spiritually for future battles which might await me when I returned home. It was obvious that the fates of Negroes and Jews were linked. Jim Crow and the Nazis hated us both. That's why I enjoy the civil rights conventions, the exchange of ideas and action plans; it was why I rejoice in the victories, big and small, and love meeting new and interesting people like the young lady with the yellow dress who had me entranced.

CHAPTER 16

IN GERMANY, SEGREGATION and discrimination against Jews was the law, enforced with an iron fist, and there was nothing anyone could do about it. The American courts might twist the Constitution to uphold discrimination like in the *Plessy* case which said 'separate but equal' was perfectly fine, but at least the plaintiffs were given a hearing and not just rounded up and taken to detention camps for allegations of seditious activity when they complained. In Germany there were no forums for redress. Nothing had to be equal, just separate, and the courts which Adolph Hitler owned, were useless.

I saw the police jump out of a van and grab a nattily dressed man who was walking with his family. They threw him into the back and spirited him away to some God-forsaken place. He was discovered dumped like Friday's garbage on a rain-soaked street – naked, unconscious and severely beaten – three days later. People said he was suing the government for triple-taxing his import-export business. After his ordeal, the lawsuit was dropped. This was a fairly common occurrence. The entire government was corrupt, with zero checks and no balances. Justice is an alien concept. Public officials exist merely to please Hitler – and to hell with the citizens, especially the Jews.

My cousin Gabriel was part of some vague Zionist movement and he and I quarreled about my leaving Berlin. He said I should wait it out for as long as possible, then migrate to Palestine if things became absolutely intolerable. Times would get better, he said; they always have, and our people have endured much worse tribulations.

"Remember the Russian pogroms?" he asked as if I could forget stories about the thousands of Jews, including some of our own ancestors, wounded and slaughtered in the past half-century. "And Germany is nothing like Russia," he added. "Those Russians are diabolical."

"You're right about that."

"We can't just give up," he said. "Germany is our *home*."

"I agree."

"But Palestine, not America, should be our refuge."

"Perhaps."

Gabriel was a gifted artist. He painted wonderful impressionistic landscapes, seascapes, sunrises and sunsets. He enjoyed the solitariness of his work, rarely ventured outdoors and was able to avoid too much contact with Nazis. Gabriel's canvasses used to sell for handsome sums, but then it became unseemly to hang Jewish art in Aryan homes. His livelihood practically decimated, nowadays he painted just to maintain his sanity.

I didn't want to defer law school until Hitler relented or got defeated by someone bold but benevolent. That would be like standing still and I'm much too hyper to stand still, so I vowed to go to school somewhere else and come back. Hitler didn't want Jews to be lawyers and judges, and I planned to use the law as a bludgeon for when the regime ended and Germany returned to its original greatness. I had to be prepared. I told Gabriel this; he understood my concerns, but still accused me of abandonment. That bothered me but I had to do what I thought best.

Our first patriarchs arrived from Russia penniless and ambitious two centuries ago, and we consider Germany to be our native home. My father was a judge, forced into early "retirement" by the Nazi regime, and my mother is a bookkeeper for our family business, Kempner Fine Furniture and Antiques, started by my maternal great-grandparents back when most of Germany was still considered Prussia and was ruled by Kaiser Frederick William III. During the Great War, my grandfather and uncles died for Germany and were given commendations. They're probably rolling in their graves because their patriotism and valor were paying no dividends to their living relatives.

Still I love Germany. I've slalomed the Swiss Alps, but the peaks and lodges in Bavaria offer a more serene romp. I've viewed 360 degrees of Paris from atop the Eiffel Tower, but the breathtaking vista from Neuschwanstein Castle on a rugged hilltop, as well as the castle itself, must be ogled to be believed. On a bet, I jumped from a gondola, tuxedo and all, into the Grand Canal after attending a wedding in Venice. I swam alongside the boat until my cousin told me to get back in before she died from hilarity. But nothing beats walks alongside the Spree River which snakes right through the middle of downtown Berlin or skinny-dipping in the Rhine then sunning on its banks while imagining depth to the fuzzy outlines of Strasbourg in France across the way. Times Square and 42nd Street are dizzyingly exciting, but I still prefer the hustle and bustle of Alexanderplatz and its theaters, cafes, beer gardens and promenades.

I once ate two huge steamed blue crabs and what they called a po' boy sandwich in one sitting at a bayside restaurant in Baltimore. It was all so good, and I enjoyed hammering those meaty claws, savoring the shrimp and slaw slathered in hot sauce, and the act of living dangerously by eating taboo shellfish – though it certainly wasn't the first or last time I've gone rogue from a kosher diet. Still nothing can compare to the rowdiness, the frosty ales and all-you-can-eat brats and cabbage at my favorite Berlin café. I've danced the polka with coy lasses in Czechoslovakia and was taught to jitterbug to the great amusement of my Negro hosts and their friends while traversing the Washington D. C. club circuit. But pipe in some phonographic Mozart, and I could waltz a pretty *fraulein* wall to wall across the grandest, most crowded ballroom at Berlin's Adlon Hotel. I want to see movie sets in Hollywood, look the Egyptian Sphinx in the eye and run with the bulls in Pamplona, Spain. I hope to visit every country in Europe and all seven continents, even Antarctica. But wherever I went, I'd always prefer home.

Rabbi Danziger taught us that Jews should have roots because we were tired of wandering through the proverbial desert. Until Israel was reclaimed and rebuilt, we deserved to claim some country, identify with it and embrace it. I claim and embrace Germany. Berlin, the New York City of Europe, was home. If I never returned, I'd miss my favorite room – the library – with its wall-to-wall books, my own familiar feather bed, my mother plucking out a Beethoven tune on the baby grand. I'd miss Helga, our house servant, serving mimosas and strudel on the balcony which overlooked the explosion of summer rose bushes, the profusion of springtime peonies, the cacophony of fall chrysanthemums, and the occasional voluminous snowdrifts which you could interpret and reinterpret like the clouds in the sky. The rear red brick wall, a veritable bulletin board for the first sixteen years of my life, had been the perfect spot for scratching messages with the sharp end of a stick. Our favorite bakery was right down the street and the aroma of marble rye baking made my mouth water all day long. We had friendly but nosy neighbors. I could always count on at least one of them, Mrs. Eva Dreschler or someone like that, to lean out of a window and ask me how school was going, congratulate me for scoring the game-winning goal at the football game or to call out, "Welcome back, Julius. How was Switzerland?"

"Fantastic," I'd respond. "But it's great to be home."

In school we were taught that Germany was the greatest nation on the planet, and that Great Britain was a close second. I believed it. Germany's supremacy was reinforced by photographs and statues of former rulers of imperial Germany sitting on thrones, on horseback or in swashbuckling poses, images that exuded strength, honor, courage and dignity. I also remember visiting England, sitting astride my father's shoulders as I glimpsed, through thousands of flower-tossing spectators, King George V and his wife Queen Mary in their carriage being driven across Windsor Park on the way to the races. Thinking back, the half-smile and blasé royal wave may have been a little condescending but I was impressed nevertheless. It was the way a head of state should look – aloof, but tolerant and benign.

It was such a contrast to Adolph Hitler, with his stiffened stance and trademark, Jew-hating glower, tooling around in his bullet-proof Mercedes Benz amongst swarms of saluting, jack-booted minions. His image was dark and foreboding, not bright, glorious or honorable. I yearned for Germany's old leaders, ones who didn't thrive on hating people.

Of course, there's always been anti-Semitism, ever since Pharaoh enslaved the Hebrews in Egypt, since Christians blamed Jews for Jesus Christ's crucifixion, since the Europeans blamed Jews for the Black Plague. The Nazi propaganda machine has now convinced people that Jews orchestrated Germany's defeat during the Great War and are responsible for all the country's current economic woes. People hate us even though none of it is true.

Anti-Jew sentiment used to be subtler, a pervasive undercurrent manifested by a sideways glance, a cocked brow, an unreturned greeting, an eye roll and harrumph or, like what happened to me when I was about thirteen – the hasty and unexpected disentanglement of fingers as Gertie, my first real crush, and I walked across the footbridge arching over the Spree River.

"So you're Jewish?" Gertie asked cautiously.

I was taken aback by the accusation and racked my brain to remember what I said or did that gave me away. I was not embarrassed to be Jewish, quite the contrary, but I didn't go around advertising it unnecessarily either. I didn't see the point. I didn't really know whether my friends, colleagues and associates were Lutheran, Catholic, atheist or agnostic; nor did I care. I only required my friends to be good people who liked to have fun.

"Why do you ask?"

"You live in Wilmersdorf."

"Not just Jews live in Wilmersdorf."

"My brother says if you live in Wilmersdorf that you're probably Jewish."

I said nothing.

"And who was that lady you were with in the market the other day? She was talking in some strange language and was wearing one of those funny-looking stars on a chain around her neck."

She was referring to my Grandmother Zipporah, *Oma* Zip. I'd been helping her grocery shop that day. *Oma* Zip insisted on speaking Hebrew out in public and wearing Star of David jewelry everywhere. When she was around it was impossible to pass yourself off as an Aryan which I'd do from time to time out of sheer convenience. Many family members implored *Oma* Zip, proficient in four languages, to stick to speaking German and wearing her diamonds and rubies when she ventured out, and to save the Hebrew talk and Star of David accessories for temple. "This is our heritage and I shall not be shamed!" *Oma* Zip would declare.

"*Mutti*, that's not the point and you know it," my father, her son, would tell her. "You're an educated woman of means. You don't need to flaunt Judaism like these provincial Poles with their side locks and beards and peasant-like head scarves and antiquated customs. Papa never did. You're not one of the *Ostjuden*. What are you trying to prove?"

Oma Zip was the epitome of German assimilation until my grandfather died as a soldier in the Great War. Several years of widowhood did something to snuff out her desire to out-German all her German wine-sipping, soap opera-listening, Skat card-playing Aryan friends. Now it's mostly seltzer, mah-jongg twice a week and "Rabbi Danziger said this, and Rabbi Danziger said that." She used to not really care about what rabbis said. As years passed, she became exceedingly "more Jewish."

The more we complained, the more stubborn *Oma* Zip seemed to become. When her brother died, and I was playing handball with some of my non-Jewish friends, she hollered out the window, "Julius, come in the house and get ready, we have to go *sit shiva* for Uncle Otto." "Sit *what?*" my friends asked, pausing all action. Our neighborhood had Jews and Gentiles and it was hard enough explaining why I went to "church" on Saturdays wearing those "funny skull caps" and ate so much matzo ball soup without her bringing more attention to the fact we weren't part of the dominant culture. I much preferred to be seen as "generic." Another day someone else would want to know why it was okay for *us* to use electricity, cook and do work on the Sabbath, but not the "weird" Jews down the street who wore the long beards and big, black coats and hats. And I'd say, "Come on, fellas, let's just play ball." After all, I didn't ask *them* why they didn't observe *Sunday* Sabbath and were expected to run to the confession booth after every little escapade.

"She was a relative," I told Gertie, my chestnut-haired *fraulein*. I almost said "family friend", but I could never disavow *Oma* Zip.

"Well are you or are you not Jewish?" she demanded.

"Does it matter?"

She said nothing for several moments.

"Well, thanks for the soda. I need to go now." She turned around and walked quickly away.

"I'm every bit as German as you are!" I yelled after her. She didn't bother to look back.

In that split second I felt so isolated as sets of true elbow-locked sweethearts navigated around me. The week Gertie and I spent laughing, see-sawing and enjoying each other's company in the park was already ancient history and didn't even matter to her. The girl who'd shown such delight when I taught her how to skip rocks over the river's surface just a few days earlier simply melted away into the landscape of people.

Chapter 17

THAT WAS YEARS ago. Now it was fashionable to say and do the most vulgar things to the "descendants of Israel" as *Oma* Zip now called us. Now there were the SA – storm troopers – to intimidate, Gestapo secret police to spy, and Hitler youth to parade around and beat up little kids and anyone else. Another layer, the SS, protected Hitler like a jockstrap. Now there were regular German citizens who regarded Jews like we were roaches scaling a wedding cake. I found it amazing that average everyday people could go from treating their fellow countrymen with relative kindness, or at least disinterest, to being downright hostile in the span of a few years. These people were not imports from some other Jew-hating part of Europe, but the same friends, neighbors, acquaintances and strangers that we've intersected with all our lives. They hurled insults without the slightest inhibition. "*Wir hassen Juden!*" a man yelled into a crowd of us as we were leaving temple and he ushered his family "to safety" on the other side of the street.

The lady at the post office from whose window I purchased all my stationery and stamps, evidently sniffed out my Jewishness and pretended not to know me anymore. I was a prolific letter writer and would see her often, but now she acted as if we never *kvetched* about cold, rainy weather, as if she never marveled about how many people I knew and that they were all over the world. We used to joke about my loopy penmanship and her aching feet, but one day she was just cold and all-business, licking and slapping the stamps haphazardly onto my postcards. She dropped my change onto the counter instead of into my cupped hand and yelled "Next!" to the customer behind me when I tried engaging her in our usual small talk.

And then things got really bad. Hitler, in office less than three months, declared April 1, 1933 a national day of boycott against Jewish businesses in retaliation for the anti-Nazi boycotts of German goods taking place in the United States. "Good German Aryans" were discouraged from patronizing our businesses to show solidarity against the "dirty, thieving Jew."

That day, our Aryan neighbors decided to forgo their tailoring needs and loaves of fresh-baked rye. They traveled across town to purchase their shaving cream and toothpaste from other fellow Aryans because there were at least a dozen storm troopers stationed in front of the conveniently located Woolworth's. They suffered through their migraines since going into Grunsfeld's Apothecary for a few grams of Abe's special headache powder might have resulted in a needless showdown with some teenage Nazi. The clock-maker across the street from our store stood outside in his military regalia holding a sign that told potential customers how he fought valiantly in the war. "I have an Iron Cross," he said, but the storm troopers shooed the shoppers away nevertheless.

I was working in Kempner's that day and assumed there'd be little or no business. We were happy to see our Aryan friends and neighbors, Wolfgang and Eva Dreschler, who made a point of coming into the store in spite of the boycott and "Jude" on the display window. Mrs. Dreschler said, "We're not going to let some two-bit dictator tell us where to spend our money."

"Hitler will be gone soon," Mr. Dreschler said. "The Nazis are sure to self-destruct by the time Hanukkah rolls around." He winked.

"We certainly hope so," said my Uncle Erik.

"And it's the Sabbath," Aunt Sarah added. "All the observant Jews' shops are closed anyway. That's quite a few. Their boycott is *damlich*."

Mrs. Dreschler said, "Well we don't need a thing. But show me your, how do you say, *tchotchke*."

My Aunt Sarah smiled at Mrs. Dreschler's attempt at Yiddish vernacular. "Yes. *Tchotchke*. We don't exactly carry *tchotchke*. But we do have some lovely, reasonably priced items throughout the showroom." She escorted them around and they left half an hour later with some marble beverage coasters and an antique

Russian candlestick holder, not exactly the cheap, insignificant clutter they'd come in to buy just on principle.

"*Danke schon!*" We all hugged the Dreschlers as they left carrying their fancy cloth shopping bag with "Kempner's" emblazoned in red cursive across both sides. We peered through the blinds as they walked boldly past some police officers who were patrolling the neighborhood and advising Aryans to "defend themselves" by staying out of the Jewish shops.

A few others came by looking to take advantage of the boycott, thinking we'd be desperate to sell them nice things at fire sale prices. They ducked into the store surreptitiously, ready to haggle over every price. In essence, they tried to "Jew us down," a phrase I heard quite often in America in reference to the stereotype that we were ruthless bargainers. It didn't work.

Aunt Sarah and Uncle Erik would explain that the prices were fair. The chandelier was the finest, clearest Austrian crystal, the settee was covered in handmade, embroidered silk from China, the painting was an original done by a local artist who studied under Kandinsky at Bauhaus and was framed in gold leaf. When their offers were refused, they stormed out, grumbling about "dirty Jews."

Toward the end of the day, traffic was non-existent. Uncle Erik and Aunt Sarah went home and my mother and I were minding the store. I was having coffee and reading, for my own edification, the filth and lies in the Nazi newspaper, *Volkischer Beobachter*, when a married couple came into the store. The man wore a Nazi stickpin in his lapel. A week ago, they'd seen an antique tapestried bench and now wanted us to sell it for a fraction of its value.

I didn't know enough about Kempner's merchandise, so my mother had to come out of her office where she was balancing the ledger. She explained that the bench was nineteenth century from the Ottoman Empire and she wouldn't take less than 1500 reichsmarks for it.

"It is handloomed, 100% merino wool, the best kind. We think it may be from an Ottoman palace. You can see it's very old indeed, yet very well preserved. It's museum quality, one of a kind."

"I could buy a brand new BMW for that price." The man said

I folded the newspaper and stood up from the desk where I was sitting. "Why not do that then. Hitler would love it. You'd be giving him reason to exploit more cheap labor to meet the phony demand and inflate costs."

The husband looked at me like I'd accused his mother of wearing combat boots. "People have been known to disappear for that kind of insolence and disrespect," he said.

My mother looked at me. I shrugged. I sometimes forgot that it wasn't a good idea to criticize Hitler in public. But it was hard.

"I'm prepared to pay you 650 reichsmarks, and not a pfennig more" the husband said, opening a checkbook and taking the pen that his wife was already holding aloft.

"No," my mother answered. "Even 1500 reichsmarks is a bargain for a quality historical showpiece."

The wife sat down on the bench, folding her arms across her chest, planting her feet on the parquet floor, looking petulant and unmovable.

The man became indignant, sticking out his chest. "My wife wants this bench. It will look exquisite in our foyer. But I will not be robbed. Your Ottoman palace story might fool some low-country Jews, but not me. "

We ignored the insults.

My mother stood less than five feet tall but wasn't easily intimidated. She stood on her tiptoes, hands on hips, and looked him dead in his eyes. "Well, sir, I'm sorry we cannot be of help. Perhaps the department store in the next block will be more useful to you. I'm sure you can find something for less than 30 reichsmarks and have the same piece all your neighbors have, nothing special."

"Even if I believed your little fairytale, tell me, how does one acquire something as grand as an Ottoman Empire piece in the first place? How do you people always seem to have stuff like this? Is there a corner of the earth you Jews haven't pillaged?"

Mutti's face reddened. "You don't know anything about me or my background. And not that it's any of your concern," she said, "but my father and brothers have connections in Istanbul and all over the world and come across some real treasures during their travels. We make an honest living. This is, after all, a specialty shop and all our acquisitions have been quite scrupulous."

"You should be investigated. Something seems shysty," he said as he walked around the store fingering fabrics and rubbing his hammy hand across a replica of a rare Faberge egg.

"Well, the bench is no longer for sale." She turned to me. "Julius, please take this to the back room."

"Yes, *Mutti.*"

She turned to the man. "I'm asking you kindly to leave my store." She snatched an ivory rook that he had lifted from an ebony and ivory chess set and was fondling carelessly. "Leave before I fetch one of those SA officers outside and tell them you're disregarding the boycott. Then those rascals can harass you all the way back to your home." She yanked open the door and the overhead bell tinkled.

"We'll see about that!" he answered.

"But I want the bench," the wife whined at purred at the same time. "I've wanted it since the moment I laid eyes on it. No other will do."

"I wouldn't purchase a paper clip from these greedy people."

He turned to my mother and me. "This is not the end."

"As you wish," she said.

"Thieving Jew bitch," he said, grabbing his wife's hand and walking briskly out the door. "I'm done being nice to you people."

I wanted to cold-cock him with a nearby Tiffany lamp, but quickly regained my composure.

"*Guten Nacht!*" we said.

The next day we discovered someone had broken into the store. The beautiful, storied bench was gone. The intricately carved chess set was gone. The replica of a jewel-encrusted Faberge' egg worth 1000 reichsmarks was gone. We knew who the thief was. We called the police. They never came. We could no longer depend on the government to protect us. Our family felt violated and vulnerable.

It took most of the morning, soap, water and razor blades to remove the "Jude" graffiti from the window without damaging it. The Austrian jeweler next door came out of his store shaking his head, saying "That's too bad." He didn't offer to help and said he hadn't seen or heard anything suspicious. Little did we know this was only a mild incident.

CHAPTER 18

SIX DAYS LATER, the Nazi government passed the Civil Service Restoration Act that purged all Jews from the legal profession. I was meeting my father for lunch the day this law was enforced. We were still discussing plans for my immediate future. We'd been researching law schools in both Britain and America and were planning to weigh all my options over liverwurst sandwiches and a couple bottles of cold Krombacher ale in my father's chambers. My list had narrowed to the University of Cambridge in England and Harvard in America where we had relatives.

My father's caseload had decreased since the police were now routinely rounding up vagrants, drunks and petty thieves and taking them directly to labor camps, where they were incarcerated indefinitely without arraignment or trial. But *Vati* was on the bench when I arrived so I took a seat in the back of the courtroom and listened to a rather amusing eviction case.

Thankfully it wasn't one of those criminal cases where the alleged perpetrator, usually some Nazi sympathizer, was accused of breaking out someone's windows or knocking out someone's teeth. All sitting judges were instructed to give the defendant every benefit of the doubt and to acquit them of any charges if it's proven that the alleged crime was in furtherance of high German principles like pride and solidarity.

One such case featured a victim who sustained a broken nose when his boss at the munitions factory where they worked punched him for refusing to leave the building after he was fired.

"Why did you fire him?" the prosecutor asked halfheartedly.

"Because he refused to allow his child to join the Hitler Youth."

"What's wrong with that?"

"All decent people are strongly encouraged to enroll their children in the Hitler Youth program. They teach discipline and moral values and how to maintain optimal physical fitness."

"Go on."

"The boys are taught to become first-rate German warriors and the girls learn how to be outstanding mothers and wives. What kind of person wouldn't want that for their child? Most of the parents in Berlin have already put their children in this outstanding program. You should see them beam with pride when they go marching down the boulevard in their uniforms."

"Bah!" The victim, *Herr* Krauss, jumped up and yelled. "Those kids are turning into sadistic robots! It's frightening!"

"You're about to be held in contempt *Herr* Krauss!" my father said. "Sit down!" *Herr* Krauss sat.

The defendant continued. "*Herr* Krauss will never know that pride. His boy will be as undisciplined as *he* so obviously is. So I fired him, he refused to leave and I socked him. I regret he only got a broken nose. He is foolish and unpatriotic and I wouldn't hesitate to pound him again."

The defense attorney argued that the defendant was within his rights to fire someone who was so deficient in character that he didn't have the best interests of his own child at heart. When he refused to leave the factory, the complainant was an insubordinate trespasser who deserved to be punched.

"Your honor, my client was defending Third Reich principles and should therefore be acquitted." The prosecutor waived a rebuttal.

My father found the defendant not guilty which it pained him to do. Had he not ruled in the defendant's favor, he would've been removed for unfitness and replaced by someone who'd toe the party line. The integrity of the judiciary would not have improved by his removal; *nein*, it would've only been diminished with the addition of a genuine Nazi judge, so it seemed prudent to go along with the national directives and still be a bit of a buffer between "benign" injustice and the most virulent kind. He never got the chance.

I sat back and watched this eviction case which seemed much less contro-versial. No Nazis were involved. It was just two guys with a disagreement. My father sat high up on his polished mahogany perch. The tenant was on the wit-ness stand testifying about how the landlord didn't deserve to be paid.

"I asked this schmuck ten times to fix my sink. My kitchen flooded. Water dripped through to the downstairs neighbor. He sent someone over who didn't know what he was doing – a carpenter trying to do a plumber's job. Always trying to save a buck, that one. Soon as the guy leaves, the water starts spurting again and won't stop. And he claims it's my fault. Your honor, my things are ruined. Neighbor's things are ruined. The place was always a dump, now it's a damp dump. And he sues *me*?! Damn right I paid him no rent. He should be paying me! He's nothing but a crook, I tell you, a crook!" He stood and pointed a long, crooked finger at the landlord seated at the plain-tiff's table.

"Objection!" The landlord's attorney bellowed and stood up so fast that his chair fell over.

"Sustained," my father said, rapping his gavel gently so the parties would settle down. "*Herr* Schumacher, please be mindful of proper courtroom deco-rum. No name-calling. You've been warned once before."

"But he's lying!"

There was a commotion in the corridors. The back doors burst open and the *Sturmabteilung*, better known as the SA, the brownshirts, or storm troopers, came bursting in. "*Stoppen*! Halt! You will halt! By order of the fuehrer, these matters are to be discontinued immediately."

My father peered over his eyeglasses. "What is this?! Order! We're in the middle…"

The Nazi thug continued his announcement. "Pursuant to the Civil Service Restoration Act, all Jewish judges are hereby immediately forbidden from pre-siding over any and all court business. Cases involving Aryan litigants will be rescheduled before an Aryan judge at the earliest convenience."

The courtroom was in stunned silence. My father looked sucker-punched. He stood. I stood, mouths agape. "What do you mean by this? I'm a duly elected judge here. I was elected just as Adolph Hitler was elected. What right……?"

"You shut up! Shut up!" A storm trooper advanced on my father, a distinguished jurist for over twenty years. The court officers stepped aside. The parties and lawyers from the disrupted eviction case looked entertained, like they were watching grand opera at the *Staatsoper Berlin*.

"Come down from there or we will come and bring you down! You're a judge no longer. You're nothing more than a...bug I will squash if you don't come down right now!"

The Chief Judge, also a Jew, walked in wearing his shirt sleeves and looking a little roughed up. He pleaded with my father. "Come down, Alexander. It's over. At least for now. Please don't give them reason to harm you."

My father, the Honorable Judge Alexander Sommerfeldt, would not "shut up." But he did step down. "Is nothing sacred? They come in here and violate the sanctity and solemnity of a court of law? How is this allowed to happen?" His steps were tentative.

I tensed up. I wanted to lash out, do something, but my father was willing me with his eyes to stay where I was; both of us knew that anything I did would be useless and impractical and would probably only earn me a baton jab in the gut. The smell of perspiration suddenly enveloped me and became almost suffocating. The whole thing was surreal.

When my father reached the storm troopers, they grabbed him like he was a common criminal they were about to put handcuffs on. Instead they stripped him of his custom-stitched, velvet-trimmed satin robe with the wide bell sleeves. They scratched his neck trying to undo the waterfall lace jabot and knocked him about the head as they tore off his elegant, matching judicial cap. The storm troopers were also summarily dismissing the Jewish staff – officers, stenographers and prosecutors throughout the courthouse.

They were ushering all the Jews down the staircase and out onto the street. "You're making a big mistake," one of my father's colleagues protested as he was being prodded through the hallways. "I'm a practicing Catholic. You'll pay dearly for this."

They pushed my father into the unfrocked herd. I fell in behind him and held onto his shoulders. He wasn't permitted to collect his overcoat, the handsome, ostrich-leather briefcase, the gavel his father had handed down to him, or the photos, private letters and papers he'd accumulated over the past twenty years.

Signs were being posted everywhere informing the public that the courthouse was now officially free of Jews – except for defendants. No judges, no prosecutors, even the juries would be Jew-free. *Kein juden zugelassen!*, the ugly signs screamed. What a coup this had been. It was bedlam inside, pandemonium outside.

Outside the huge pile of judicial regalia was being spit on and stomped on by the SA. Some of them even spat at the judges. The expressions of the onlookers ran the gamut from confusion to astonishment to abject fear and no one was brave enough to grab a bullhorn, hop up on a milk crate and yell "What the hell?!" Judges were revered and their expulsion represented a breakdown of a stable and orderly society. But Hitler's representatives were deriving great pleasure from reducing them to rabble. If this could be done to judges, despite their prestige, the potential degradation of everyone else was boundless. The expulsion took less than fifteen minutes; the Nazis were surgical in their undertakings, in and out with precision. But the events seemed to unfold in excruciating slow motion.

We soon learned that the new law also applied to Jewish clerks and civil service support staff in all the courts and all other government buildings. Eventually they got around to purging the army, the press corps, schools and universities. Surprisingly, at the Kaiser Wilhelm Society, they dismissed Nobel Prize winning chemist Fritz Haber who was particularly useful to the Reich as he knew how to use ammonia to make explosives, create poison gas and other deadly chemical military weaponry. The Civil Service Restoration Act also targeted the state doctors and dentists and denied them access to practice in state hospitals and institutions.

All Jews who worked in the public sector were being summarily dismissed, stripped of their sense of security, livelihood and dignity. The Nazis said the "exclusion" had been necessary to make room for "true" Germans to make a living in law and government jobs. At that time, Jews were about one per cent of the German population and we made up over half of the lawyers in Berlin. We had a disproportionate desire to enter the legal field and were being unjustly punished for it.

I don't know how they knew who was Jewish and who was Aryan. The Hitler regime considered Judaism to be a race, not a religion. A person was determined to be full-blooded Jewish if they had at least three Jewish grandparents or if they *practiced* Judaism regardless of heritage. The definition was expanded to include converts, quarter-blooded or eighth-blooded Jews, the spouses of Jews, or anyone with a large, hooked nose when it was expedient to do so.

The Nazis must have compiled a master list and we wondered how they garnered the information. My father never distinguished himself as Jewish in his professional life. He always presented himself as a lifelong, loyal *German* citizen. The Nazis were resourceful and obviously combed government records and got help from friends, family and associates to help them identify all these people. I wanted to be angry with people we knew, but realized later the information could've been elicited stealthily, demanded threateningly or offered innocently. My father said later that he'd challenge the dismissal rather than just accept the abrupt termination of a great, unblemished career. They obviously didn't consider his deeply rooted German heritage, his reputation, the two years spent in the army or his father's sacrifices during the war. He would appeal, otherwise his career was *kaput*.

A glob of spit landed on my father's shoe; it roused us from our stupor. They started throwing things. We needed to scram because things were getting more volatile. *Vati* said no, thrust his arm across my body. "We will walk away with dignity. Look them in the eyes and shame them," he said, and I did but they weren't.

Chapter 19

IN RECORD TIME, Hitler also dissolved parliament. He set fire to the Reichstag, the building that housed the German parliament, and blamed it on the communists. That's like Roosevelt burning the Capitol building and blaming the republicans to win favor with the American citizenry. The fire and destruction was an excuse to suspend all civil and constitutional rights. There was no more free speech, press or assembly, no more freedom from unreasonable search and seizure, no breathing room from the dictatorship Germany had quickly become.

Hitler hated Jews but he hated communists, socialists and unions more because they were the only entities standing in his way of absolute rule. However, many of the communists, socialists and union affiliates were Jews, so they had several targets on their backs. Hitler's Nazi henchmen actually fought members of these opposition parties in meeting halls or drinking establishments. After hitting each other over the heads with beer steins and breaking up a lot of the furniture, the violence spilled into the street where they beat and shot at each other, sometimes wounding and killing innocent bystanders, until one day, only the National Socialists – Nazis – were left standing. Americans probably couldn't fathom such a thing – democrats and republicans fighting to the death on Pennsylvania Avenue. A few, short years ago, I never would've believed that a modernized Germany could descend to such depths either.

The unions were the last political "enemies of the state" and Hitler tricked the leaders into attending parades in their honor so they could easily be identified, arrested and thrown into a reform camp located in an old gunpowder factory in Dachau near Munich. Most of the remaining rivals fled the country to avoid being hunted, captured, imprisoned or killed. With all political opposition eliminated, Hitler had complete control of the country.

That May, they burned books – mainly books by Jewish authors. They burned books by Freud, Kafka and Marx, and books by American authors like Upton Sinclair and Jack London. Some of them were my favorites, including H. G. Wells' *War of the Worlds*, Hemingway's *Farewell to Arms* and Theodore Dreiser's *An American Tragedy* which had sustained me on many a train ride or sea voyage. They burned Bibles and Talmuds.

Books were burned if the subject or the author was considered socialist or pacifist because Germany was proud to be fascist and belligerent. Margaret Sanger's writings about birth control were odious because the Germans revered Aryan procreation. The genius of physicist Albert Einstein and the keen insight of a blind, deaf-mute like Helen Keller were considered as reprehensible as an obscenity scrawled across a classroom chalkboard. They were considered too diplomatic, subversive and un-German.

More than 25,000 books were pilfered from libraries, bookstores, churches, synagogues, schools and private homes and destroyed. Librarians, booksellers and sextons stood helplessly flattened against a wall while Nazi thugs raided and trashed their shelves in search of titles on their list. Many of the looters were unread dunces, indiscriminate in their confiscation, taking anything and everything, but programmed enough to spot the works of deranged philosopher Friedrich Nietzsche, Nazi jurist Carl Schmitt, the Jew-hating, Christian-reforming monk Martin Luther, or anything jingoistic and anti-democratic, and leave them unscathed on the shelves.

I'd been at a nearby café having strudel with my cousin Gabriel when we got word that the Nazis were at it again. Storm troopers and right-wing, Nazified college students and professors were burning books at the Opernplatz university plaza. "Come quick!" they said, and we followed the singing and the trail of torch lights to Opernplatz, where tens of thousands of people had gathered. They were saluting, singing Nazi songs, waving swastikas and just acting like this spectacle was more fun than a football game. In the center of the crowd was a fire pit and people were gleefully tossing books into the flames.

Every time a book went in, its title and author were called out, and the crowd cheered like their team scored a goal against an archrival. It was dumbfounding. This must've been what it was like to watch a witch-burning in Salem, Massachusetts, or a "good, old-fashioned necktie party" in Springfield, Illinois or anywhere in the American south. When whole towns gathered to witness witch-burnings, guillotine beheadings or lynchings, it was not about enforcing morality; it was just madness, or often government-sponsored depravity.

Twenty-year olds who just the day before had been fornicating drunks, injecting morphine into a buttock or vein, were now talking about "delivering to the flames" the most "decadent" books in the name of "discipline and morality." These impressionable lads, with a perverted sense of duty, actually thought that burning books – books they'd never read, couldn't read, or had never even heard of before that day – was cleansing the homeland of evil and that the ideas would perish along with the text.

The pungency, sizzle, crackle and pop of fine leather bindings, gilt-edged vellum and moldy, decades-old parchment being consumed by sky-thrashing flames was immensely disturbing to me. I absolutely cherished books, always had my nose stuck in one, and thought destroying them was sinful. Someone had once hugged those books to their bosom, had smoothed their hands over the fresh-off-the-press jacket covers and inhaled that new-book smell. Someone had creased the pages and underlined passages they wanted to return to. Someone had loved those books. It disturbed me even more to think that burning books is only steps away from burning other kinds of personal property – homes, places of worship, or even, God help us, people. It's happened before. I shuddered at the thought.

Again I wondered where the objectors were, who else thought this was dangerous theater but was afraid to speak up.. Most of the mob was caught up in mass hysteria, especially when Joseph Goebbels, the fanatical Nazi Minister of Enlightenment and Public Propaganda – a paradox if ever there was one – spoke at midnight.

"The era of extreme Jewish intellectualism is now at an end," bellowed Goebbels into a microphone invented by a Jew. He could've been Salem's own Cotton Mather 300 years earlier convincing the pitchfork-wielding zealots that they were ridding Massachusetts of satanic influences by burning innocent women alive. "The Fatherland can be great again!"

The crowd went wild as if *extreme* intellectualism was a bad thing. Ironically these sentiments were cheered in the middle of a college campus. The university, which boasted several Nobel Prize recipients, attracted intellectuals from all over the world. Dr. W.E.B. DuBois went there. Dr. Alain Locke, the first black Rhodes Scholar, studied philosophy there. Some of my most stimulating discussions were with Americans, Italians, Parisians and Nigerians who, like me, spoke English like a primary language, were gluttons for knowledge and information, questioned established "truths" (communism is bad, Germany is supreme) and liked to sit around the university cafeteria solving hypothetical and real-world problems. There was nothing more boring than having a conversation with an anti-intellectual. I preferred "extreme."

"Intellectual activity is a danger to the building of German character," Goebbels said, chain-smoking cigarettes manufactured by a Jew-invented machine. He went on talking garbage about Germany rising like a phoenix from the ashes because they were burning books and ridding the country of 'nefarious Jewish influences." All around me were people in the throes of euphoria. I wanted to punch the guy next to me for being so willingly gullible.

CHAPTER 20

"WHAT THE HELL has happened to our fair country?" I said, thinking out loud. "Our beloved Berlin."

"I know," Gabriel said. "I keep thinking this is all a dream, that I'll wake up soon and everything will be back to normal."

"Only it's not a dream, it's a nightmare. And it doesn't even seem close to ending."

"Not if we don't do anything about it."

"What can we do?"

"Fight."

"Easy to say."

We turned to leave, then spotted a familiar face.

"Isn't that Gunther Hertzog?" Gabriel asked me about the young man wheeling a cartful of more books to throw onto the pyre.

"That awkward kid from *Schiller Gymnasium*?" I asked, referring to the German high school we'd attended. "Yes, I think it is."

I wanted to ask him why he was part of this foolishness, why he was wearing SA gear complete with brown shirt, breeches, boots, kepi cap and swastika armbands. I remembered him being a nice kid who appreciated good literature and provocative ideas. He got teased a lot because he stuttered and I found myself defending him several times. He was a favorite target in dodge ball and competitors invariably aimed the ball at his head as hard as they could. I gave one of those bullies a taste of his own medicine one rainy, muddy afternoon and asked him how he liked being hit full force in the noggin. He didn't. Gunther always gave me that look that said "thanks." He didn't have to say it.

I know he did well on his abitur exams and had assumed he went on to university because he wanted to be a teacher. It pained me to see him fall prey to Nazi propaganda. He was too smart, but obviously lacked the mettle to resist the tide. The crowd was full of eager stooges, but there were probably many who'd been subliminally corrupted – other Gunthers – as well. It was dismaying. The Weimer Republic, the Germany I loved, was officially dead.

Instead we had a homeland controlled by some "mad professor" who wanted to – pardon the cliché – "rule the world" and, to that end, was probably cooking up schemes in a "laboratory" at his secluded villa in the Bavarian Alps. It was like a bad movie and we were all bit players trapped in the production. I wanted no part of it.

CHAPTER 21

I ENDED UP at Georgetown Law School. I'd chosen Harvard over Cambridge because I'd been to England several times but had never been to America and wanted an altogether new experience. Harvard was also the alma mater of my legal muse, Louis Brandeis, the first Jewish justice on the United States Supreme Court.

I was already in Boston before learning that some admissions counselor realized at the last minute that I was a Jewish applicant and that their Jewish quota had already been met for the year. How ironic it was that the same discrimination I was running from in Berlin smacked me square in the face in America. My Uncle Sy, who taught Constitutional Law at Howard University Law School, arranged for me to go to Georgetown. He was widowed, had plenty of room and said I could live with him, that he'd appreciate the company.

There I was, a Jew at a Jesuit school, one of a handful, and it was an interesting experience to say the least. I got used to the statues of saints, the crosses and crucifixes that were ubiquitous throughout the campus. I had my share of Friday fried fish dinners and even went to church, including a sunrise Easter service, with some friends. A well-meaning classmate gave me a beautiful rosary for a Hanukkah gift. I'll keep it always.

There was no shortage of friendly ambassadors who derived pleasure just from seeing me marvel at everything from peanut butter and football to the majesty of that great marble obelisk that was the George Washington Monument. I'd never tasted peanut butter before but soon learned that, paired with jam or a palm full of raisins – my personal, German iteration – on ingeniously pre-sliced bread and a glass of cold milk, it made a great and easy midnight study snack. In Germany, football was played by trying to kick a round ball downfield into the opposing team's net, and in America it was completely different and, ironically, barely even involved the foot or kicking. But the Georgetown Hoyas game against Syracuse at Griffith Stadium is especially exciting, and playing catch with the brown, elliptical-shaped ball on the campus lawns was a lot of fun but would have caused my *Oma* Zip to worry about my committing a sacrilege because I was touching pigskin. She would've quoted from Leviticus about avoiding contact with the carcasses of unclean, single-hoof, non-cud chewing animals the way she did after her dramatic transformation from progressive socialite to conservative Jewess and she burned her designer pigskin gloves and shoes in the backyard. And aside from the Eiffel Tower in Paris, there were no skyscrapers in Europe. So I couldn't wait to go inside and climb to the top of the Washington Monument and get a bird's-eye view of D. C.'s landmarks and its fascinating, geometrical layout which supposedly contains a hidden Star of David and some occult symbols.

When I left Germany, I brought expectations of American idealism, naive as it may have been. I assumed that most people would be friendly because it just had to be better than Berlin where people were tired, tense and terrified of being identified as a Jew or the friend of a Jew and consequently draw attention from Nazi troublemakers. In Washington D. C., I mostly blended in with the Catholics and the WASPs. But after telling someone my name, they paused, wrinkled their nose and asked, "Sommerfeldt – is that Jewish? It's not obvious like Goldberg, but it sure sounds Jewish." Depending on the situation, I might just say that it's a *German* name and leave it at that; or sometimes in a casual setting I just introduced myself as Julius *Sommers*.

I didn't know exactly how to interpret the heavy sighs that followed when they heard the word "German." It may have been my imagination or paranoia, but the person became much less affable. They probably still considered Germans to be the pariahs of the world, and the rumblings about Germany instigating yet another imperialistic war didn't help matters. So it seemed being German was as distasteful as being Jewish. Sometimes it seemed I had a double burden.

Some people would hear me speak and instinctively recoil, remarking that I sounded like "one of those damn Nazis." This was because Nazi sympathizers and party representatives were the only Germans they heard speaking on the radio, it was the sole basis of comparison and the indignation and vitriol were never lost in translation. So I suppose German was a rather sinister accent to sensitive American ears. Even after assuring them in my mirror-practiced, Yankee twang that I was no Nazi or German war hawk, they still regarded me with that hooded-eye suspicion.

I understood the cynicism. All the newsstands featured newspapers and magazines that screamed headlines about what was happening in Germany, about what those "crazy Nazis" were doing next, and I got the impression that Americans thought all Germans were Nazis and perceived them to be somehow worse than America's white supremacists.

The notion that I bore some culpability for Germany's misdeeds was often exasperating. I asked a gentleman on the street if he could point me in the direction of Ford's Theater, the site of President Lincoln's assassination. It was fascinating history. Well, this man looked me up and down before asking, "What are you, some kind of Nazi?" I told him to never mind, that I would find it on my own. He watched me trudge down 10th Street as if I bore watching, as if I was Hitler's best friend or John Wilkes Booth reincarnated. Sometimes I just couldn't stand the scrutiny and the pre-judgment and would have to go jogging to let off steam. I left Germany to get away from that sort of thing.

It was easier to assimilate into the mainstream culture, though because of my accent and name, it was not always easy to do so, so I had to get used to the insidious undercurrent of American anti-Semitism and residual anti-German sentiment. Some people, in an effort to appear super-patriotic, still called sauerkraut "liberty cabbage;" hamburgers were "liberty sandwiches" and German shepherds were "liberty pups." It was silly.

I also had professors who notoriously scheduled exams and assigned papers during Jewish holidays and refused to defer them. Practically speaking, I may not have cared; Uncle Sy and I weren't devout, but it was the principle of the matter. Whenever I had an appointment to see the dean of students, he had this lunatic named Father Coughlin, a popular but notorious radio personality, blaring from his radio. I'd tell the dean how I wanted to drop one class and add another, he'd be chain smoking Camels, and Father Coughlin would be railing against Jewish conspiracies, Jewish immigrants, Jew-assisted communism, anything Jewish.

It seemed I was back in Germany except for the fact that the radio screed was in English. But it sounded just as nasty and foreboding. Behind the dean was a portrait of FDR and one of Father Charles Coughlin in his priest collar and phony pious smile and the dean glanced back at this so-called man of God before telling me, through the veil of smoke, that it was too late to make any schedule changes even though the decidedly Nordic-looking fellow who left right before me had accomplished just that. So I postponed taking Advanced Legal Writing and suffered the Wills and Trust class.

My Wills and Trusts professor, who was also a priest, offered extra credit points for attending mass. One of his former students told me he only did that when there were Jews in the class. It was his subtle way of trying to save our souls from eternal damnation. I put a few bills in the collection plate, managed to abide the cloying incense without coughing and look utterly fascinated when Father/Professor Callahan cast his steely look my way. Wills and Trusts could be complicated and I relished the extra points. But when it was time for the communion wine and wafers, said to be the blood and flesh of Jesus, I slipped out the side door.

Then there was the small group of tormentors, alleged members of the pro-Hitler German American Bund who, during my entire first term, took delight in calling me every slur they could think of. "Oh, look, here comes that nickel-nose Kraut...How are you doing, Pinocchio?...Where's your little beanie, Jew-boy?... How's it hanging, you clipped-dick kike?...Get out of my way, herring-breath... Go back to your hymie country, Abraham..." I ignored this verbal abuse and secretly gave them credit for the creativity of their epithets. It even took me a few seconds to figure some of them out. But I drew the line at physical aggression.

The leader of this Bund faction had occasion to grab a fistful of my shirt collar and propel me into a hallway bookshelf after what I thought was just a spirited disagreement between him and me about a point of law which arose in Torts class, but was perceived by him as a personal attack on his intellect. He lost a debate to a "penny-chasing, cotton-picking Jew" and was embarrassed. I told him he should take care not to mix his racist metaphors and shoved him back. Either the force of the push, the smooth soles of his loafers on the waxy floors, or a combination of both, caused him to lose balance and fall, in a most ungainly fashion, on his racist rump and split the crotch of his slacks.

Our fellow law students stepped away rather than erupt into tearful laughter right in front of him. Adding insult to injury, I said to him, "Because you're so obsessed with Jews, it makes me wonder if you're one yourself – perhaps your mother is – and you're overcompensating."

His face reddened even more and he wanted to lunge at me but couldn't muster the wherewithal to do so. I found out later that he also fractured his wrist when he thrust back his arm to break his fall. Karma's a Buddhist concept, but on that day at least, I was a convert because karma was real to me. The universe didn't like what it saw and gave this guy a thump. He never put his WASP-y hands on me or called me a yid, a hebe, or a kosher grocer again.

Other than these instances, my life as a German Jew at Georgetown was pretty much uneventful. Going to Georgetown turned out to be a good decision and by loading up with extra classes I finished well ahead of schedule. The Jesuit traditions of philanthropy and service dovetailed completely with my Jewish teachings and notions of charity and social justice. The academics were top-notch and I quickly got over not getting into Harvard.

Actually I was glad, since I'd become increasingly disillusioned by Harvard's hallowed halls and the administration which catered to the Nazi regime abroad. Harvard's president was part of the welcome wagon that greeted Nazi visitors to Boston with fanfare and a police security detail. The visitors were part of the crew of the Karlsruhe, a Nazi warship, and it was festooned with swastikas as it steamed boldly into Boston Harbor, the same harbor American patriots dumped tea in to protest a foreign power's stranglehold.

The Harvard dignitaries were ridiculously hospitable, allowing them to present a Swastika-adorned wreath in the university chapel and wining and dining them as they proudly wore Nazi regalia to Boston's fanciest, high-profile social events, including a tea at Harvard University President Bryant Conant's home. In contrast, the administration turned a deaf ear to the Jewish community's outcry and reprimanded the students and faculty who protested the Nazi presence and the university's shameless pandering.

I was nauseated that the university president went out of his way to accommodate a 25th reunion alumnus, Ernst "Putzi" Hanfstaengl, Nazi Germany's foreign press secretary who, while benefiting from a Harvard education and the appurtenant prestige, was known to have popularized the straight-armed salute, and the "Seig Heil" chant at American college football games and then co-opted them both for the Nazi party back home. Putzi was better known as the one responsible for grooming Adolph Hitler, garnering him credibility with the upper classes, financing that bullshit rag called "Mein Kampf," and being the celebrated piano player at all the major Nazi events where he pounded out Wagner tunes all evening long. Hitler was even the godfather of his son. I had no idea why Harvard would be so accepting of such a man, alumnus or not.

The picture of Hanfstaengl queued up on the Harvard lawn with his fellow alums, dressed up in white pants, navy Harvard blazer and hat, smiling like everything was fine and dandy despite the expulsion of Jews from academia and civil service in Germany, despite the stripping of their German citizenship and the random kidnappings and violence, was too much for me to bear. In a perfect world, the other classmates would've refused to stand with him, would've turned their backs on this Hitler creator and Nazi sympathizer and shown the country and the world that government-sponsored bigotry and terrorism, wherever it may be, wasn't to be tolerated.

Instead the New York Times depicted students and reunion participants, either mockingly or admiringly, goose-stepping and "Heil-Seig"-ing for the infamous Putzi, Harvard's prodigal son. I'd stare at that picture of him standing there grinning with a fat cigar protruding from his pudgy face and get angry all over again. The only thing more offensive to me would be a photograph of the Roosevelts picnicking with Hitler and his not-so-secret concubine, Eva Braun.

I was destined to be at Georgetown where I discovered my true calling was helping Washington's large indigent population, people with problems, no money and nowhere to turn for help. In Boston I might've been tempted to go work for some giant corporation where my most important work would be finding clever ways to minimize tax liabilities. I wanted to put my education to better use. And if I'd gone to Harvard, in addition to being sick to my stomach watching my tuition money subsidize five-star hospitality for Nazis, I might never have met so many good, ordinary people or such legal luminaries as Joel Spingarn, Charles Hamilton Houston and Thurgood Marshall. And I might not have met Justinia.

CHAPTER 22

SHORTLY AFTER JUANITA Jackson finished her anti-lynching speech, people scattered, cleaved to their familiar factions or came together to plan this noose demonstration. Some of the organization's leaders made a point to come over to shake the hands of the Caucasian members, thanking us again for coming and for our continued support.

"Of course," one of the white conventioneers told one of the Negro convention organizers, "We're all in this together."

Dr. Ralph Bunche, a notable Howard Political Science professor and fond acquaintance of my Uncle Sy, also came over and invited us to a speech he'd be giving the next day about how *class* disparity would soon supersede race as the world's greatest social problem.

"That's an intriguing notion," I said and told him that I looked forward to his presentation.

When Dr. Bunche moved on to the next throng of people, I was immediately conscientious about standing in a group of all white men, including Harold Ickes, a Roosevelt cabinet secretary and past president of the Chicago NAACP, in a room full of Negroes. At least I think they were all white. Sometimes it was hard to tell for sure.

Earlier I was speaking with a blond, blue-eyed man named Walter White before realizing, in the midst of the discussion, that he was Negro. He said he was one of those "voluntary Negroes" because he could easily pass for Caucasian but refused to do so, wanting to be true to himself and his ancestry. He definitely looked "whiter" than I did. At a Cuban restaurant in downtown Washington, I was mistaken for Cuban which amused me to no end. Happy to be given a short respite from being Jewish or German, I just smiled and said "*Gracias*" when they brought me my empanadas.

This white-looking gentleman, Mr. White, also happened to be the executive director of the NAACP and an anti-lynching activist who almost infiltrated the Ku Klux Klan to gather intelligence about riots and 200 murdered sharecroppers in Arkansas, but had to flee when his cover was blown. I was reminded never to assume anything.

Growing up in such a homogenous society as Germany, I was constantly aware of minorities in an all-white setting and felt a need to make a friendly acknowledgment whether they were "the help," a guest, a colleague, client or anyone else. I was also cognizant of being the only white in a majority black setting and felt the need to demonstrate my comfort and ease in their presence.

We were getting a few odd looks. I needed to mix and mingle. When the NAACP was founded almost a quarter-century ago, most of the youth delegates weren't even born. White people at an NAACP convention could understandably be as unsettling as the trench-coated Gestapo forces stationed on neighborhood street corners, or the shifty eyed children – angelic cherubs transformed into Satan's spawn after only a few weeks at Hitler Youth training camps – who were taught to spy and report on the activities and conversations of their friends, family and neighbors. I asked Mr. Ickes to excuse me while I walked around.

As I approached the young lady in yellow, I was encouraged by her smile although I could tell she was sizing me up. I introduced myself and she said her name was Justinia. Justinia Treadwell.

"A lovely name for a lovely lady," I said. Her blushing cheeks were like ripe peaches.

"Thank you."

"I was admiring your barrette," I lied, to explain why I was staring earlier. "It's so unusual."

"It belonged to my grandmother."

"She had exquisite taste."

I resisted the urge to reach out and touch it, a butterfly in gold filigree and colored crystals – something we might have sold in Kempner's – clasping tantalizing, tawny tresses.

"I'm Millie," said her friend, extending her hand and breaking up a rather awkward moment. She was cute but unremarkable, and also very friendly.

The gentleman they were with, an admittedly dashing fellow, was a different story. He challenged my every word, like I was somehow a threat to him.

"That Miss Jackson is quite a speaker," I said.

"Yes she is," Justinia responded.

"The NAACP always has great speakers," said the man Justinia introduced as Xavier.

"I'm aware. That's one of the reasons why I love this organization. The leadership is so inspiring. They make me want to work harder."

"I know exactly how you feel," Justinia said.

"Miss Treadwell, would you like some punch?"

"I'd love some," she said.

CHAPTER 23

Justinia

JULIUS LADLED ME some punch though I really didn't want any and had just told Xavier no thank you. He gave a cup to Millie also.

"Thank you," she said. "So, Mr. Sommerfeldt, are you from Baltimore?"

"Call me Julius."

"Julius. Are you from here?"

"I'm actually from Berlin. But I've been living in Washington for three years."

"Berlin, *Maryland*?" I asked facetiously, referring to the "charming, little Victorian hamlet" where an innkeeper had refused my father a room on his way to a fishing trip at nearby Ocean City with a business partner. Daddy had bitter memories of Berlin, Maryland.

Julius laughed. "Oh, no. Berlin, Germany actually. In Europe." His accent was crisp and staccato. "Approximately four thousand miles away from these shores."

"We know where Germany is," Xavier interjected. "We're all extremely well educated."

"Xavier," Millie scolded. "I'm sure the gentleman meant no offense. He was just trying to be exact. Isn't that right, Julius?"

"Oh, absolutely. No offense intended." He tasted the watery punch and set the Dixie cup down on the table. "But I've been told by friends that I can be a tad pedantic. I'm working on that."

"*Angenehm!*" I said, offering my hand.

He was pleasantly surprised. "Pleased to meet you too. *Sprechen sie Deutsch?!*" He shook my hand. His palm was soft and inviting.

I threw my head back and smiled. "*Ein bisschen,*" I said, explaining that I knew *a little bit* of German, though my teachers would say I was being overly modest. I studied German for many years. I loved languages, loved how unfamiliar words and concepts could be deciphered by recognizing common roots and their origin.

"I learned it first in high school. Then at Oberlin College. That's in Ohio. About 350 miles from here." We both laughed. "I took advanced classes at Howard University. I had excellent instructors."

"Obviously."

Since my days at Dunbar, German had always been touted as the supremely practical foreign language and there were many opportunities to use it in conversation with people like Dr. Du Bois and Mary Church Terrell who'd spent time in Germany and were fluent. At my high school graduation party, Mrs. Terrell told me "*Sie warden eine Macht, mit der zu rechnen!,*" that I'd be a force to be reckoned with – quite the compliment coming from her. To my eyes and ears, German always looked strange and clumsy on the page and sounded halting, strident and agitated in conversation, but coming from the mouth or pen of Mrs. Terrell, it was as gentle and mellifluous as I found the French language to be.

Julius said, "I'm impressed."

"Why are you surprised that a Negro woman can be multi-lingual?" As usual, Xavier's insecurity was showing. "She knows Latin and French too!" He spoke as if I were a trained puppy that could roll over and play dead too.

To Xavier, Julius said, "I'm not surprised at all. Please allow me the privilege of being intrigued. Outside of Germany and Austria, it's not every day that I see people of any color who know the German language."

To me, he said, "*Je parle le francais aussi? C'est magnifique!*"

"*Oui, c'est tres bien,*" Millie said, not wanting to be left out. She may have had to leave college before she got her degree, but she was still one of the smartest, most knowledgeable people I knew. Fortunately she'd almost saved up enough money working double shifts at a mattress factory to pay for another semester at Howard. She had about two years left and was determined to graduate and go on to law school.

"Yes, well this League of Nations moment has been *beaucoup* fun." Xavier said sarcastically as he ladled himself some punch. He looked at Julius suspiciously. "But I'm curious. What brings you here?"

"It's a long story."

"No, I get that you probably left because your Chancellor Hitler is a fiend. But why are you *here*, at the NAACP convention? You don't look like a *colored* person – unless you're trying to pass."

Xavier also tasted the punch, made a face and set his cup down. Both Millie and I looked at Xavier to express that he was being rude. Despite years of superior schooling and a sterling upbringing, he could still be very impolite.

"Well are you?" he asked, leaning in closer. "Passing? You can tell me."

"Sorry to disappoint, but I'm afraid I'm just your garden variety Jew from Germany. Nobody special."

"Xavier," I said, elbowing him. "That wasn't nice."

"I was curious."

"I'm here as an NAACP member," Julius said, seemingly unperturbed. "I have tremendous respect for this organization and support it wholeheartedly." As if he needed to prove his claim, he pulled out his billfold and took out the card that verified his membership and also classified him as a Life Member.

Xavier was a "student" member. He'd be starting his second year at Howard Law School and apparently had yet to learn not to cross-examine witnesses with questions you didn't already know the answer to. I'd tease him later, ask if he thought Julius was there to recruit tobacco farm workers or something. Xavier knew better, was well aware that white people played integral roles in the NAACP. And there were several other whites there.

"My uncle, Symon Sommerfeldt, is on the D. C. Executive Board."

"That figures," Xavier said but thankfully didn't go on one of his rants about Negro organizations being run predominantly by behind-the-scenes white people. It irritated him to see white boards overseeing black institutions – schools, hospitals, cultural centers. And he felt compelled to infiltrate anything all-white like the student government or the Sphinx Head Honor Society at Cornell University where he went as an undergraduate. Xavier was always determined to prove he was as good as – or better than – any white man.

"Funny how they don't allow us to sit on any of *their* boards," he said.

"And," Julius said, "I'm very proud of the fact that my great-aunt was one of the original NAACP founding visionaries who collaborated with Dr. DuBois after the collapse of his first civil rights organization, the Niagara Movement."

"It did not just collapse," Xavier said. "It was sabotaged by Booker T. Washington. Negro progress was a threat to him. He wanted everyone to mope around and grovel while he used them to get ahead and drink champagne with tycoons and Presidents. As for your aunt, Dr. DuBois collaborated with many people."

I was surprised that Xavier was breaking a cardinal rule, one that was taught to us in Dukes and Duchesses-sponsored etiquette classes. A well-bred Negro did not casually reveal Negro discord to white people, even if the disputes were well-known and decades old. Evidence of disharmony could be used as a wedge to divide and conquer. Only Uncle Toms did that – enable whites, for whatever reason, to exploit fissures between rich and poor, light and dark, citified and countrified, Baptists and Episcopalians. Xavier was a lot of things – snobby, yes, arrogant, absolutely – but he was no Uncle Tom.

But there was always someone willing to "Tom" if they thought it would earn them a pat on the head, an economic advantage or some limited entry into the white world and their good graces. It seemed no radio show or movie was complete without someone playing that role. Millie enjoyed mocking people like that. She was funny: "Yes, massa, dem darkies is sho'nuff lazy. . .Yes, sir, I agree he's got no cause to be uppity. . . I don't know why they don't lift themselves up by their bootstraps like I did." Speaking disparagingly about Negroes to other Negroes was another matter, but we were always cautioned about airing "dirty laundry." Xavier knew better.

"Whatever you say," Julian said. "Now, Mr. Brathwaite, have I properly established my bona fides?"

Xavier's face flushed. "Mr. Sommerfeldt, you don't have to prove anything to me."

He took out his pocket watch and looked at the time. He was the only 24-year old I knew who carried a pocket watch. I thought you should be at least forty before you began sporting a pocket watch and vest. "This was my grandfather's watch," he told a group of us one day, as if that explained why he could only cherish it by wearing it every day. "See his initials engraved on the back? XDB, Sr. He was a famous architect." But that was Xavier. My mother even said he was an old soul, but he's really just old-fashioned. He looked around the room.

"Excuse me," he said, going over to where he'd spotted Juanita Jackson with some other NAACP bigwigs.

"I don't think your friend cares for me very much." Julius said.

"Don't mind him. Xavier can be a pill sometimes."

He laughed. "I'm sure people say the same about me sometimes."

"I doubt that." I smiled. "Well, again, it was a pleasure meeting you."

"The pleasure was mine."

"Enjoy the rest of the convention."

"I intend to."

I saw him walk over to shake hands with a prominent attorney named Thurgood Marshall who'd just won a monumental desegregation case in the Maryland Court of Appeals and was becoming quite the star. Marshall had successfully argued that his client, Donald Gaines Murray, an Amherst College graduate, should be allowed to attend the University of Maryland School of Law because he met the qualifications, was rejected only because he was black, and the state of Maryland failed to provide him a "separate but equal" facility. There were no other law schools in Maryland. Marshall brilliantly used the *Plessy* doctrine against the segregationists and, much to our delight and surprise, the court unanimously ordered the university to immediately begin accepting Negro students.

The "revenge" was even sweeter since Marshall himself, a Maryland resident, had been denied admittance to the University of Maryland and had to go to Howard instead. He said commuting back and forth to Washington was brutal, but he still managed to become class valedictorian. Marshall and his mentor, Professor Charles Hamilton Houston, the dean who transformed Howard from an adequate law school to one that was first-class, were going to talk about the case in a symposium entitled "Negro Lawyers as Social Engineers." The room was sure to be packed. Meanwhile several people were requesting that Marshall autograph their Bibles, law books, convention brochures and random scraps of paper. He was Mr. Popularity. Duke Ellington, the King of Swing, may have gone unnoticed had he walked in the door right then.

"I have to meet Thurgood before we leave," Millie said. "The man is gorgeous! But there're too many people around him right now."

"He's married, you know."

"I know, I just want to see him up close," she said. "Besides, you know he's really not my type. I like men like my coffee – strong and black, no cream at all."

"Millie, you are something else."

"I want him to autograph my *Crisis* magazine. There's an article Professor Houston wrote about the Murray case and Thurgood Marshall. I have a feeling Mr. Marshall's going to be famous one day."

"I wouldn't be surprised."

As Millie and I walked around, she gave me a knowing grin. "I think you like him."

"Who?"

"Julius. You know exactly who I mean."

"I just met him not ten minutes ago."

"Well you couldn't tell. You guys seemed like old friends. There was a familiar ease."

"Millie, you're a scream."

"Well I'm pretty perceptive and the attraction was mutual."

"Silly!" I said, playfully slapping her shoulder.

"Is it?"

Had I been flirting? I don't flirt, not with Xavier or anyone. People spoke badly about flirtatious women behind their backs. I'd been taught to be the pursued, not the pursuer. But I was tiring of Xavier's pursuits. His new favorite pastime was taking me on Sunday drives through the country in his new convertible. He liked to make unannounced visits and monopolize large swaths of my day. I'd be deep into reading or re-reading a good book – Wallace Thurman's *The Blacker the Berry* or Fitzgerald's *The Great Gatsby*, the doorbell would chime and Lily would come tell me I had a gentleman caller.

Usually it was Xavier, one of the only ones intrepid enough to sit in the parlor and carry on a conversation with Magdalena until I appeared. Others tried, but allowed throat-clearing, tea-stirring and the loud ticking of the grandfather clock to fill up the silence, causing Magdalena to question their intelligence and upbringing after they'd gone. She thought any well-raised, well-educated person should have the mental and verbal dexterity necessary to carry on a conversation with the king of England if the situation arose.

Xavier would sit in a Chippendale wingback with his legs crossed, an argyled ankle resting on a gabardine, herringbone-patterned knee, unlike the others who sat stiff-armed and reticent like Lincoln in his memorial. He'd shake his foot, check his watch, help himself to the sour balls in the crystal candy bowl and say things like, "What a beautiful dress you have on, Mrs. Treadwell. Is that chartreuse? I understand the Howard Players are performing *Hamlet* at the Theater next weekend. Last year's *Twelfth Night* was sensational. Are you and Mr. Treadwell planning to attend? Perhaps I'll ask Justinia to be my guest. Such world-class thespians have definitely earned my patronage. It looks like rain – perfect for your begonias. Yes, I'm delighted to stay for dinner. But I hope you're not serving spinach."

And because we've known each other so long, he didn't bother to stand when I entered the room. "Good evening, Justinia. You look...pleasant."

Chapter 24

I'VE KNOWN XAVIER Dillon Brathwaite III most of my life. Our mothers have been trying to get us together since we were teenagers. We lived in the same LeDroit Park neighborhood. We both grew up in the Dukes and Duchesses organization. Until high school, we never missed each other's birthday parties. He'd been my prom date and escort at both of my cotillions. We were in school together until ninth grade when his parents thought he needed a boarding school experience and sent him to Phillips Exeter in New Hampshire.

His mother, Abigail, managed to work this fact into any conversation: "Speaking of billiards, Xavier expects to make the golf team at *Exeter.* Xavier has adjusted very well to *Exeter.* . . Speaking of that new haberdashery, you should see Xavier; he looks so handsome in his *Exeter* blazer. . . At *Exeter,* he's the only Negro in his class and teachers and students love him. . . Maybe the NAACP *is* effective because at *Exeter,* they don't see color and don't care that he is Negro." And so on and so on. In his letters to me, however, Xavier said that he hated Exeter, that everyone was rude, obnoxious and not nearly as smart as they thought they were, but that he stayed because it pleased his mother so.

My mother and Abigail Brathwaite thought it would be a great societal contribution to unite the Treadwells and the Brathwaites in holy matrimony, as if the continuation of the black bourgeoisie depended on it. Xavier bought into this notion of blending and enriching bloodlines for perpetuity, but I wasn't interested in mothering a Treadwell-Brathwaite dynasty, especially not any time soon.

My mother thought that Xavier was a good choice for me because, despite his flaws, he was good-looking, came from premium stock and would be an excellent provider. She encouraged me to look around but reminded me that there were a limited number of good fish in the sea – "plenty of bass, but very few sturgeon."

"And stay away from musicians," she cautioned. "Musicians, with the exception of perhaps a classical violinist or a flautist, too often make a mess of their lives, becoming philandering drug addicts. They bring nothing but grief." She said she'd rather see me with a street sweeper than a musician though either scenario would send her reeling.

My reluctance to settle on Xavier had her making a list of other men she thought I should be considering. "That Charles Drew is certainly dashing. He comes from humble beginnings, but is a brilliant surgeon now and doing all kinds of ground-breaking research – something having to do with blood. I know one of the physicians at the Freedmen's Hospital where Charles is the Chief of Staff. I can arrange for the two of you to meet for coffee."

When I told my mother that I wasn't interested in obvious set-ups, she said, "You watch, one of those *common* girls hanging out on the Howard Medical School steps is going to snatch him up real soon." I was even less interested in competing for a man. She was always making suggestions, but ultimately, she wanted me to follow my own heart and make my own choice as she'd done at my age.

If Abigail was a bit ambivalent about me and her only son marrying, it was because, even though Magdalena was light-skinned with a genealogical and mon-eyed pedigree traceable to the mid-1700s, my father was coppery and self-made, and his ancestors had not all been free-born. As far as Abigail was concerned, my genetic makeup is half-tainted because there was a chance our children could turn out too dark and have naps in their hair unresponsive to Madame C J Walker products and vigorous brushing. There was no guarantee her grandchildren would look like porcelain dolls.

But Daddy had money, more than Dr. Brathwaite, and that's what made a possible Treadwell-Brathwaite union so appealing to Mrs. Brathwaite. Georgine's mother even suggested that my mother would not have married my father had he been just a "regular guy" – a carpenter, country preacher or some such thing. When Georgine repeated this, she got into a fight with my sister Charlotte. There was actual shoving and hair-pulling until Georgine finally apologized and promised never to bring it up again. Georgine's mother didn't know my parents at all. Otherwise she'd have realized that Daddy was special and that my mother would want him unconditionally no matter what his job was or how much money he had.

CHAPTER 25

A CELEBRATED NEGRO lightweight boxer, Joe Gans, owned the Goldfield Hotel in Maryland which featured one of the first black-and-tan (integrated) night clubs in the country as well as the superbly talented pianist, Eubie Blake. It was there, amid the blanket of tobacco smoke, the jazzy, ragtime notes, and the swarms of writhing revelers that my mother, sitting with her girlfriends on one side, and my father, sitting with his buddies on the other, glimpsed each other and then experienced love at first touch after dancing one cheek-to-cheek dance. My father said that the universe drew them together, that they were both helpless to avert it, and my mother agreed. Magdalena didn't need a man's money to coax her into a marriage she didn't want; she had her own money, having taken control over her generous trust fund after graduating from Oberlin. She didn't know at the time that my father had amassed a small fortune by making shrewd investments.

Before she met my father, she already lived very comfortably in a cozy, ivy-covered house while working as a librarian at the all-Negro Morgan State College mainly because she thought too much leisure was sinful and she enjoyed helping the students. Unlike her parents, my mother ignored the fact that Daddy was darker hued and that his ancestors had been kidnapped from Africa and shipped like the rum, spices and other Middle Passage goods listed on the traders' invoices. She didn't have anxieties about having brown children or grandchildren. My sister Charlotte was brown, but Magdalena loved all her children equally.

CHAPTER 26

DADDY HAD HIS paternal grandfather's manumission papers and the bills of sale Granddaddy Treadwell received after returning to the tobacco plantation to buy his wife and kids after saving up enough money blacksmithing and doing odd jobs. He purchased his gimpy, club-footed wife "Ginny" from "Master Treadwell" for the "bargain price" of $840 in 1855; then in 1856, he was able to buy his sons, "Slow Willie," age six, and "Johnny," my father's father, age seven, for the "*grand* bargain price" of $650 total. Both these receipts were marked "Paid in Full."

The manumission papers had been carried in my great-grandfather's pants pocket for many years, had been folded, unfolded and re-folded a hundred times to show to paddy rollers, the slave catchers who stalked the southern landscape and earned commission by returning runaways to their owners. Although he'd filed emancipation documents in the Virginia courts, he wanted immediate proof to show that he was a free man. Some of the paddy rollers may not even have been able to read, but they understood what the papers meant when my great-grandfather handed them over. But they sometimes gave him a hard time regardless, pouring out the fresh water from his canteen, ransacking the meager possessions in his burlap bags, frightening his horse or knocking him around, just because they could.

The papers, having been lovingly or roughly handled, depending on whose hands they were in, were in extremely delicate condition. There were tiny rips in the powdery creases and the words, having faded from exposure to sweat, dirt, tears and sunlight, could barely be made out. But looking closely, one could see that they spelled out, "Sonny, a Negro slave of about nineteen years, is hereby set free and relieved from servitude from Cooper Treadwell and other Treadwell heirs forever." One could still decipher Cooper Treadwell's signature, the date, Christmas day 1852, and see traces of the bluish wax with which the document had been sealed.

Daddy kept these documents in a lockbox in his office. The lockbox contained other miscellaneous keepsakes like marriage, birth and death certificates, old newspaper articles, letters, and haunting, sepia-tinted photos of staring, unsmiling Treadwell ancestors in baggy coveralls and faded pinafores. There was also the posthumously bestowed Medal of Honor that his maternal grandfather earned for "rescuing the regimental colors" during a Civil War battle. Ironically, he was awarded for saving the flag of a country that refused to acknowledge him as a full United States citizen; yet he grabbed the tattered "Old Glory" from its fallen bearer and hoisted it up against the unrelenting gunfire and cannon blasts, inspired by the piper and drummer, or they by him.

My father had a fifty dollar bill from 1881 that he was keeping forever because it bore the signature of a black man, Blanche Bruce, a legendary Washingtonian, who'd been the first Negro senator, a vice-presidential running mate, and the Register of the Treasury. Most of the currency with Blanche's stamped signature was removed from circulation and shredded, much like the other vestiges of Reconstruction-era advancements.

Daddy brought out the "freedom papers" from time to time to illustrate our rich heritage of hard work, grit, sacrifice and unerring dedication to family. When he rummaged through his desk drawer to retrieve the skeleton key that opened the cedar lockbox, he waved away my mother's objections. Magdalena felt slavery should be largely ignored, spoken about only in rare instances, and then only in hushed and private tones, much like news that a friend or family member had committed suicide, contracted tuberculosis, was divorcing, or had an unmarried daughter who'd gotten "in the family way." Daddy felt we should acknowledge every family member regardless of their circumstance. When he opened that lockbox, we prepared ourselves for the lesson to follow.

When Charlotte stated matter-of-factly that life would be easier if she had lighter skin, out came the lockbox. "Life is hard regardless. Treadwells have heart; we transcend racial prejudice and color complexes from brainwashed Negroes," he'd say. "Look at this picture of your great-granny Ginny. She was beautiful and you inherited her long neck, her high cheekbones, those big, doe eyes. That's our Yoruba roots speaking. You've got Yoruba tribe blood coursing through your veins. Our people were in the prestigious *Ogboni*, the governing council in Benin that advised the king in the most important of matters. How many people can say that? Be proud of that."

When Emery complained that algebra was too hard or asked why we had to do chores when some like Georgine and her siblings didn't have to do chores, out came the lockbox. "Boy, you don't know what hard is. Algebra's not hard. Digging ditches and laying railroad tracks is hard. Hoeing tobacco is hard. Picking cotton all day in hundred-degree heat – now that's insanely hard," he'd say. "Would you rather do that? And I don't want spoiled, bratty kids. Drying the supper dishes and cleaning your rooms builds character."

When I complained about needing more spending money, out came the lockbox. "I'm sure your great-granddaddy wanted more spending money too. Then he could've bought his whole family in one fell swoop. Instead he shoed hundreds of horses and picked and baled cotton on the side and had to make two trips to get everybody back under the same roof again. You want to go outside and help Roy weed those flower beds to help pay for that new dress you want?"

When Daddy overheard Xavier boasting that no one in his family had ever been a slave, indentured servant or sharecropper, and that some of his people actually *owned* some slaves, out came the lockbox. "There's nothing virtuous about that, young buck" he'd say. "Slaves were the backbone of this nation. Look at the faces in this picture. Honor them. They are worthy. They built the White House and the Capitol. Exploited labor probably built the big, fancy house you live in. You like your big, fancy house, young buck? How many nails did you hammer in? How many of those marble tiles did you lay? You benefited from *their* sweat."

When Georgine's dad, irritated about something or somebody and having enjoyed a little too much cognac, said "Negroes ain't shit," out came the lockbox. "Tell that to either of my grandfathers. Tell that to the legacies of Harriet Tubman or Blanche Bruce or George Washington Carver," he said. "You weren't shit either once upon a time, Clarence. You could still be a messenger boy in Omaha, but by God's grace, look at you now." They both took another gulp from their oversized brandy snifters. "Yeah, look at me now," Dr. Kirkwood said, "but God had nothing to do with it. Gorgeous wife, thriving practice, second home on Highland Beach, sleek, thirty-foot sloop. Life is good." My father looked at him. "And now you're just a big *piece* of shit," my father said. "Yup, I am!" And they both laughed.

CHAPTER 27

THE CREAMY COMPLECTED, strawberry-haired Abigail Brathwaite, who claimed Thomas Jefferson as an ancestor, but whose membership application was roundly rejected by the Daughters of the American Revolution, was willing to disregard my "blemished" background and set aside her preference for pale skin and pristine lineage, qualities she's extolled for as long as I've known her.

She was regarded by some, either reverently or sarcastically, as being the honorary curator of the Brown Paper Bag Guild or the Blue Vein Society. According to my mother's friend, a sworn enemy of Abigail Brathwaite, during her college days, Abby Kane (as she was known back then) was a hellion when it came to keeping her sorority and some other campus organizations as light-skinned as possible. There was a little ditty that went, "If you're light, you're alright, brown – stick around, but black – stay back" and Abby made it her mission to make that a true sentiment.

There were "paper-bag parties" on campus or at private homes where anyone darker than a brown paper bag was denied entrance, charged an arbitrary admission price or made to pay for the punch and snacks that were complimentary for light-skinned guests. Abigail, using all sorts of pretenses, was one of the door lieutenants who decided which persons were worthy enough to gain entry to a party or club and which persons were sent home to sulk, sob or fume.

She would ask to see their invitation although none had been printed. Or she would consult a clip board bearing a blank sheet of paper and tell them "I'm sorry, sweetie-pie, but you're not on our guest list." Or she'd simply walk them away with her arm around them, telling them sweetly that she didn't think they'd

fit in, that it was the wrong crowd for them and she'd hate for them to feel uncomfortable. Sometimes she could be really nasty, dispensing with all pretenses
and telling really dark people "Oh, no, you can't come in here. The spook party
is down the street." After each ugly insult, every pointless rejection, she'd turn
to the huddled "redbone" coeds for a good giggle. At the sorority rush parties,
she told the girls who were darker than paper bags to find three sponsors before
their membership could be considered; "redbone" candidates needed only one.

On a few occasions, instead of comparing the person to a paper bag, Abigail
would turn them away if, after a limp handshake and a sly wrist twist, she couldn't
see the blue veins on the undersides of their wrists. They had to be a credible
candidate for the "Blue Vein Society," a club some say was actually created by
post-slavery mulattoes and others say just alluded to a clique in a fictional short
story by Charles Chesnutt which satirized "uppity" Negroes imitating British
blue bloods during a time when he thought all blacks needed to bond. Instead
they bonded over light skin and privilege and, decades later, Abby Kane still
wouldn't allow "regular" people to mingle with literal "blue veins" lest they ruin
the occasion's ambiance with their excessive melanin.

To complicate matters more, a person could pass the paper bag test but fail
the "ruler test" which mandated at least twelve inches of ruler-straight hair compliments of Mother Nature or Madame C. J. Walker's straightening comb and
pomades. At the College Honor Society's officer installation ceremony, Abigail
allegedly announced that the incoming president needed to "get a hot comb and
tame that porcupine hair" before they proceeded. My mother's friend said Abigail
was just full of venom and tricks and that most people gave up the effort to be-
friend her or infiltrate any group or function where Abigail was the gatekeeper.

Abigail also divided her high-toned acquaintances into even smaller groups.
One may have been light with "good hair," but still not be part of the "in" crowd
until Abigail had scrutinized their outfit, ascertained their father's occupation
and the neighborhood and size of house they lived in, whether their tuition
money came from some sort of strings-attached scholarship, was scraped-up
from a broad network of family and friends, or straight from their daddy's wallet.
She'd become less chummy depending on the information she extracted from
the prospects themselves or various other sources.

It was said that Abigail could observe from any campus vantage point the quality of someone's wardrobe and the social status of their companions. She saw whether they were waiting on a bus, hailing a taxi or ducking into a private car, and noted the color, age and model of the car and who the driver was. These kinds of details were important to her – so important that people wondered how she studied Art History and received dean's list honors while busily concerning herself with the minutiae of people's everyday lives.

Most Negroes, guided by the wisdom of newspapers, clergy and community leaders, divided the race between those who were respectable and those who were not, between those who worked hard, went to church and raised wholesome families and those who did not, between those known for drinking, fighting and swearing and those who were not. But Abigail felt compelled to splice the categories into narrower segments. She was truly the blue-veined, paper bag queen, and the breadth and depth of her biases was multifaceted.

Many surmised that Abigail Kane Brathwaite was single-handedly responsible for the bouts of depression and lowered self-esteem that some students experienced as a result of being regarded as second-rate by their peers. Those who couldn't handle it ended up dropping out or transferring to a school where black-on-black bigotry, considered more hurtful than white-on-black bigotry, was not as shamelessly practiced.

Today, Mrs. Brathwaite denies ever having played such a divisive role. Abigail was a common name, she said; my mother's friend was mistaken, blaming other people for her own unpopularity. But everyone knew it was true. Abigail was embarrassed by her college antics because discrimination against dark-skinned people, while still a very troublesome issue, was to be expressed discreetly, behind closed doors in the company of like minds. It was a dirty, little secret that Negroes had color issues, and those who revealed them were considered gauche and unsophisticated. Being obnoxiously color-struck wasn't fun anymore since Abigail's college accomplices weren't around to make a game of it.

Nevertheless, my mother's maple-colored friend told everyone that Abigail was an insecure, self-hating bitch and that she'd never forgive her for intercepting her bid to pledge a sorority. When the two of them showed up at the same social events, they turned their noses up at each other, flung their sable stoles over their respective shoulders and refused to speak. But my mother's friend got the last laugh when she and her husband, an ebony-skinned real estate developer whom she met at Fisk after transferring there, snatched up some prime real estate that the illustrious Syphax family used to own. The Syphaxes were descendants of both African royalty and George Washington's wife, Martha, and were prominent Washingtonians, so the property was a hot commodity made more valuable by the fact that the Brathwaites wanted it so badly. Abigail told all her socialite friends that she'd never forgive their "treachery" but I doubt if she received anything more than phony commiseration.

So Abigail was willing to overlook the "slave" branches on our family tree only because my father had more money than her Dr. Brathwaite. Pedigree was important, but that alone couldn't buy land, stocks and bonds or European honeymoons. As long as I could pass the paper bag test and was a Treadwell heir, I was acceptable, good enough for Xavier and the Brathwaite clan. Money was obviously important in our tight-knit community, sometimes more important than reputation, education or relationships. Money bought lots of *things*, but it also bought intangibles – peace of mind, status, envy, the ability to shield oneself, to a large degree, from Jim Crowism.

Daddy had money, but that alone wasn't enough to get him invited to join the most exclusive men's clubs, particularly Sigma Pi Phi, better known as the Boule, the first Negro fraternity and quintessentially elite organization for Negro men. Dr. Brathwaite was a member and his wife Abigail never missed an opportunity to remind people of this: "They begged Xavier for years to join the Boule before he finally relented; he's terribly busy – twelve hours a day in the operating room. . . . Roger Whitfield asked for Xavier's endorsement – a no-no right there – but even though he has a trust fund, he's just a sales clerk at Woodie's, so you know that won't fly...The Boule parties for two straight days during Christmas and it is a most exclusive affair – sorry, only members and their families are allowed."

According to Ann Kirkwood, Georgine's mother, my father had never been extended an invitation because the Boule purported to be more about character and culture and less about money and alleged that my father earned the bulk of his fortune by being a "hustler." She was glad about that because they didn't invite her husband either apparently because he was suspiciously "rolling in entirely too much dough" to just be a family physician treating sore throats and broken bones. Daddy says Negroes loved to criticize and speculate about how other Negroes got their money – but no one cared how J. P. Morgan got so rich, or how he got richer while others were wiped out by the crash – and it was ridiculous how nominating committees dissected and probed the backgrounds of prospective candidates.

My father said that he didn't want to belong to any club that did so much talking behind folks' backs. "They're worse than the FBI and gossip more than Ann Kirkwood," he'd say. My mother, who'd normally be embarrassed by malicious prattle, rejected applications, or invitations that never came, was very supportive of my father. She stood behind him, her slender arms around his neck as he sat at his desk, and said that most rumormongers were "just jealous." She picked invisible lint from his suit jacket, saying, "What matters is who you are *now.* Sometimes we're crabs in a barrel. When one of us claws our way to the top, there are others just waiting to claw us back down to where they are. And, yes, this applies to rich, accomplished people too."

She said all this as if he needed soothing when in fact he did not. My father couldn't care less about joining the gold insignia pin-wearing, secret handshake-having Boule – which had some wonderful men and, like the new and exclusive Girl Friends, did many worthwhile things in the community – because of the perception that it was mainly self-congratulatory, a mutual admiration society.

If he seemed a bit disappointed about the slim possibility of ever getting a current member to sponsor him into the Boule, it was only because he knew my mother really wanted him to belong. As a charter member of the Washington Girl Friends, it was only fitting that her husband was in the comparable men's group. While most of the women in exclusive social clubs were known for their husband's reputations, Magdalena was accepted on her own merits. Still she wanted her husband to be seen as her social equal and not just some lowborn guy who got lucky in money and love but could be counted on to occasionally write a generous check for a frivolous cause – like new curtains for the Black Diamond Club House where one of the high-society groups met.

It sometimes seemed Magdalena needed further proof for her family, at least those who were still around and hadn't vanished to assume a Caucasian identity elsewhere, that she'd indeed married well, and not "down." My mother kissed the top of my father's balding head. She was very protective of him and this was one of those rare instances when she revealed her tender side, when her stern countenance was obscured by adoration for him. And, if he could, my father would rearrange the heavens for her.

Most assuredly, Jasper Treadwell didn't need the Boule to validate his existence. It was unfortunate that Alpha Phi Alpha and the other Negro college fraternities were established *after* my father had graduated from Pennsylvania's Lincoln University, the first Negro university in the country. He'd have been a terrific fraternity brother, but he supported all their causes because he admired their commitment to education, the good they did throughout the community, and the strength of their brotherhood.

It was the Alphas who initiated litigation on behalf of their fraternity brother, Donald Murray, and it was the Alphas who held a fundraiser to collect money for Donald's University of Maryland law school tuition right after the landmark decision was handed down, and it was my father who wrote one of the first checks. No one wanted Donald to have to worry about money. He needed to concentrate on studying so the university provost wouldn't be able to go to the press and say, "See, this is why we don't want Negroes at our school. They simply aren't up to the task." His success was crucial to the desegregation cause. So the Alphas helped pay his way and Thurgood Marshall, also an Alpha, arranged for him to have the best tutoring. Howard deans, professors and alumni – the legal elders – volunteered their services so that Donald would excel. My father was one of those elders. He was too busy helping Alpha Phi Alpha to go yachting and skeet shooting with Sigma Pi Phi.

My father was perfectly content with his poker buddies, golfing buddies, baseball park buddies, fellow alums and NAACP buddies. He *tolerated* the Kirkwoods and the Brathwaites because we've known each other forever, but both my parents found them to be shallow and lacking in empathy and Negro consciousness. But for all other intents and purposes, they were "our kind of people." Daddy also had his professional and business associations and was held in high esteem by both Negroes and whites. He's very involved in the National Bar Association which was created for Negro lawyers since they were unwelcome in the *American* Bar Association. He didn't need the Boule at all.

CHAPTER 28

JASPER TREADWELL WAS regarded as smart, knowledgeable and charismatic and received many invitations to speak on legal issues, race issues and current events, although many times they were all one in the same. When asked to be a speaker at the Dukes & Duchesses Annual Career Breakfast to talk about his career as an attorney, he was candid about Negro lawyers and the challenges they face. He dispensed with the usual platitudes about studying hard, having excellent verbal and written communications skills, being a good listener, reading widely and avidly, cultivating an intellectual curiosity, besting the competition, getting a mentor, networking, advertising, staying abreast of developments in the law, balancing the need to do good with the desire to make a decent living, staying close to God and tithing. As usual, he took things to another level.

Daddy stood up and told the gathered D & D teens, "The first day I ever went to court, the judge called me a nigger."

Abigail Brathwaite was the coordinator of the event, and she gasped as if she'd never heard that epithet uttered before, as if she herself had never been called such, as if everyone in town hadn't heard the story about how one Monday she, in the company of some white doctors' wives, was challenged by the head-waiter when she tried to have lunch at a restaurant that only allowed Negro patronage on Tuesdays and Thursdays. The manager reportedly told the hostess to "tell that nigger to come back tomorrow" and called Abigail a "half-black heifer" when she complained. "I can spot one of you people a mile away."

Between the doctors' wives and the Negro busboys, at least one of whom had recognized Abigail from catering some of her social events, word of what happened was all over D. C. by sunrise the next day. In classic Abigail Brathwaite fashion, she denied that the spurned Negro woman had been her, suggesting that someone had their facts wrong and had confused her with some other light-skinned, pinkish-haired woman with a severe chignon and the audacity to try to blend in with the all-white lunch crowd. "Washington is full of light-skinned women trying to pass," she said. "It must've been Doris Taylor they saw. People are always saying we resemble." But I was there when she came by crying to my mother, her confidante, wailing that it was the most humiliating episode of her entire life. My mother had too much class to point out the irony of the situation considering the reputation Abigail had in college and the fact that karma had a way of catching up with folks.

They were having tea on the sun porch and my mother asked Lily to come add a splash of sherry to their Tetley. My mother said, "That's why I would never patronize that place. I mean if they were more discreet about enforcing their segregation policy – name-calling is uncalled for – he was obviously showing off for somebody – I might've been tempted to go there on a Tuesday or Thursday. I understand their prime rib is delectable."

"That's the only reason *to* go," Abigail said, motioning to Lily to add a splash more sherry and to leave the bottle. "*That*, and their fabulous sour apple martinis."

⤖ ⤛

"A nigger," my father repeated. "There I was, straight out of Howard Law, in my brand-new seersucker suit, still smelling of Ivory soap, my derby in one hand and brief case in the other, and I was still just a nigger to him."

Abigail was so shocked that my father said "nigger" a second time that she knocked over her teacup, spilling Earl Grey all over the lace tablecloth. An attendant, about the same age as the D & D attendees and wearing a black house servant's dress and white half-apron, sprang into action and blotted it up with a towel. I looked at her. She resembled my keen-featured sister Charlotte except she was much darker, almost purple-black, but she was striking and had a cute ponytail that swung around as she wiped up. Mrs. Brathwaite looked at my mother sitting across from her at the same table, hoping she was just as appalled. My mother kept her adoring eyes on my father and kept sipping her tea. My father noticed Abigail's horrified reaction but ignored it. Abigail was just being Abigail.

"I had this client, a white fellow, come to me because he couldn't afford any of the white lawyers who wanted their expenses paid up front. I was new, needed some experience, and told him I'd handle his case for next to nothing, pay the pre-trial expenses and agree to take only twenty percent as opposed to the customary one-third. The man lost his arm in a logging accident and was suing the sawmill company because their equipment was old, dull and not properly maintained.

"We walk into the City Courthouse, this is about 1905. The judge looks at me, looks at my client, leans back and says 'Now I've seen it all. A white man with a nigger for a lawyer.'" He imitated the judge's slight southern drawl. Some of the twenty-odd kids in attendance laughed uncomfortably, unsure about what the etiquette rules said about responding to bawdy humor in public.

Abigail began fake-coughing and fanning herself with her pearl-handled fan. She enjoyed feigning shock because it made her feel superior to the person doing the shocking; but "crazy" anecdotes made for juicy conversation at the whist parties and she was not above contributing her own tidbits about who-did-what-who-said-what-who-wore-what or who-did-what-to-whom, and the retellings and embellishments often were livelier than the game.

Abigail knew my father well enough to know that he didn't censor himself unlike some of his more urbane colleagues who could be counted on to deliver a predictable, uncontroversial speech. Daddy thought nothing of describing Booker T. Washington, the patron saint for many Negroes, as an Uncle Tom. He said Ethel Waters had way more "natural" beauty and talent than the "over-rated" Josephine Baker though he liked her politics, and that Ralph Bunche, an admired Political Science professor at Howard, was too unseasoned and too confused about race to be considered an expert on the "Negro problem." He said that the idolized star pitcher of the Negro League, Satchel Paige, did too much hotdogging to be taken seriously, that he needed to "settle down" in order to become a first-class athlete. Abigail knew this but invited Daddy anyway. While Abigail frantically fanned herself, some older, brown-skinned servers entered the room with silver-domed platters of pancakes, fried potatoes and sausage patties, and my father continued to aggravate her.

"The judge said, 'That reminds me of a joke. A nigger with a big, colorful, talking parrot on his shoulder walks into a bar. The bartender said wow, where'd you get that thing? The parrot said: Africa, there're tons of them over there.'

"The judge laughed and laughed. The court officers laughed, the spectators laughed, opposing counsel and his client laughed. The whole courtroom was in stitches. After awhile, my client laughed because, well, it seemed unseemly not to. Everyone felt the need to curry favor with the judge. The jury hadn't been called out yet. The judge was emboldened by the laughter."

"So what did you do, Mr. Treadwell?" Xavier asked from a back table.

"What could I do? I laughed too. I was brand new to the game and needed to show them I was a good sport, that I wasn't one of those ultra-sensitive Negroes, or one of those high-strung, belligerent coloreds. They like that. You'll learn and you'll see."

"I don't think I could do that, Mr. Treadwell." Xavier called out.

"Me either," another boy said.

"Like I said, you'll learn – to roll with the punches and to smile even though you want to scream. Do what you have to do to get where you need to be." Xavier shook his head vigorously.

"You don't have to be Stepin Fetchit," my father said.

Everyone laughed at the mention of the movie actor who made a fortune by "cooning" – acting dumb and trifling for the entertainment of white people. "But you've got to show these people deference and good humor, show them you're smart without making an obvious effort to prove it. There's an art to doing it and still keeping your dignity. Otherwise they'll think you're uppity and that's another problem altogether."

The teenage girl attendant came out with some club soda to prevent the spilt tea from permanently staining the cloth in front of Mrs. Brathwaite. Abigail was busily twisting her pearls, on guard because now she heard the word "uppity," and she barely noticed the girl. My mother, unfazed, spread strawberry jam on a toast point.

"Anyway, after the laughter died down, I said, now, your honor, about my case." The judge called the jury in.

"Did you win it, Mr. Treadwell?" Xavier asked.

"Hold on. This story takes time. The judge did everything he could think of to ruffle my feathers. I was in the middle of my opening statement and his bailiff brought in a plate of cut up watermelon and served it to him right there on his bench. He started eating it, slurping up the juice, telling me it sure was good and didn't I want some of it."

"He didn't!"

"You have to be kidding!"

The whole room was leaning forward, clearly engaged. I'd heard the story before and was enjoying the reactions of my peers, most of whom had been sheltered from racist taunting, and the idea that these antics were coming from a judge, someone who was supposed to be solemn and dignified, made it doubly disturbing. My father's first case took place in the same building as several high-profile cases. It was where the murderer of the son of anthem writer Francis Scott Key was acquitted, a Lincoln assassination conspirator walked free after a hung jury, and where President Garfield's assassin was convicted after his insanity defense was rejected. Regardless of what one thought about the outcomes, justice was presumably well-served and not corrupted by conduct unbecoming a judge who, to me, should be the least conspicuous character.

"It happened just as sure as I'm standing here. He asked me 'what kind of self-respecting nigger would turn away some juicy, ice cold melon on this hellishly hot day. It feels like what I expect Ethiopia feels like – hot as the dickens. You ever been to Ethiopia, boy?'" He was putting on a real minstrel show. All he needed was some blackface.

"I told him no, I had not, but that perhaps I'd take his honor up on his offer for a melon slice at the noon recess. Then I continued telling the jury, who clearly didn't know what to make of any of this, about how my client lost his arm when it got caught in some machinery at the sawmill and how the boss had promised him hospital care after he had another employee get a First Aid kit and put a tourniquet on it. But they waited too late, several days, and gangrene set in. Initially he'd have only lost his arm up to the elbow which was bad enough.

The doctors had to amputate up to the shoulder because the boss didn't provide timely medical care. The doctors did a sloppy job too. So without two functional arms my poor client couldn't work and provide for his wife and seven kids."

"But did you win?"

"I'm getting to that. Keep your pants on, young buck." People tittered; Xavier blushed.

"Later, the judge took a recess and told me to return at 1:00. But he had the court officers tell the jury and everyone else to come back at 12:30. I came back about 12:50 only to see everyone seated at their places and looking at me like I was holding up progress. The judge asked me if I knew how to tell time. 'You were supposed to be here when the little hand is on the twelve and the big hand is on the six. Now the little hand is half-way between the twelve and the one and the big hand is on ten.' He threatened to dismiss my case right then. He asked me if I was really a lawyer, that if I was, I must've gone to that colored school and that he has yet to see a competent attorney emerge from that sorry excuse for a law school. He went on and on."

"I would never stand for that."

"Xavier, you have no idea what you will tolerate until you experience it."

"Why must you be so rude all the time?" Charlotte asked Xavier.

Georgine flipped her hair and turned to Xavier saying, "Yes, Xavier, keep quiet. We want to hear the rest of the story and you keep interrupting."

"I'm sorry, Mr. Treadwell, please continue." He bit into a pastry. "This is all very interesting, but it makes my blood boil."

"Anyway, when he was finished, I apologized for being late and asked him if I could call my next witness. He kept saying he should hold me in contempt, keep me in jail overnight so I would learn to respect the court and not waste the jurors' time and the taxpayers' money.

"Everyone in the courtroom was eerily quiet and I could tell that even *they* thought this judge had gone too far. I kept my hand on my client's bad shoulder the whole time as I stood there and took all this unwarranted abuse. This helped remind the jurors that my fate and my white client's fate were inextricable; it was easier for them to empathize with him, and therefore with me. Any one of them could've been sitting at the plaintiff's table wearing a shirt where the right sleeve flapped around in the breeze from the electric fan because there was no limb in it. Industrial jobs are dangerous.

"The uncomfortable silence let me know then that I'd be able to sway this jury of six white, male working stiffs. Now these jurors might've been the kind of good ol' boys who thought nothing of stringing up a black man from the nearest tree at the slightest provocation, but this was still a courtroom – filled with flags, Bibles, the scales of justice and oil portraits of past judges. The presiding judge, despite his buffoonery, still wore the venerable black robe. These symbols were supposed to *mean* something, not just be hollow tokens of some fanciful, constitutional ideal that has no chance of coming to fruition.

"So when the jurors began looking at the judge like he was crazy, it gave me hope that they believed in the sanctity of the court system, that litigants were in fact entitled to their fair day in court, that minstrel entertainment did not belong in the halls of justice, that I should get a fair shake while trying to represent this injured white man. Many of the jurors had had no prior dealings with the court system, had surely never seen a Negro lawyer before, probably didn't even know we existed; but they had sense enough to know that, despite volatile race relations and their perceptions of *us*, justice should still be transcendent, that it ought not look *common*, or resemble the "justice" they meted out on the street and in dark alleys."

"What if your client was a Negro?" asked one of the Dukes.

"Good question." Daddy took a sip of water. "Things might've gone a lot differently."

"Anyway, when the trial first started, the jurors all sat there with their arms folded across their chests looking skeptical. Now they were looser, more relaxed, watching my and my client's every move and latching on to every word."

Everyone was enjoying their breakfast and the presentation. It wasn't the monotonous speech they had expected. Even Xavier had decided to keep quiet and let my father talk without prompting him to jump ahead of himself. Abigail, having revived herself from pseudo-shock, kept the pretty, young attendant busy with endless requests for more butter, more cream, hotter water, lighter toast, some clover honey – not the dark, buckwheat honey that was served, – another tumbler of orange juice because hers was too pulpy.

It was a shame too because the girl obviously would have preferred to just stand at her post outside the kitchen's swinging doors because she seemed interested in what my father was saying; he could've been inspiring her to reach high and become a lawyer herself. Daddy says that most Negroes had never even met a lawyer, let alone a black one. I couldn't help wondering if she'd be able to rise above her station in life, or if circumstances were such that she'd be doing menial tasks forever. Of course she may have liked her job because it paid the bills and, as my father says, there's dignity in all work.

I wondered what the young girl thought of us, what the kitchen conversation would be like after we'd gone, leaving our crumbs, spills, greasy linens and wasted food for her and her co-workers to tend to. How I'd like to be a fly on the wall to hear that discussion. It wasn't every day that the banquet hall had Negro patrons, mostly teenagers, dressed to the nines, flawlessly speaking the King's English and eating bacon with a knife and fork. What would she tell her friends and family about her workday when she got home? The girl responded graciously to Mrs. Brathwaite, but her smile was wistful. My mother commented later that that young banquet server had been very well trained.

Imagine my surprise when, a few years later, she showed up in my French class at Howard. At first I couldn't place her, but somehow I remembered when I saw her serving lunch in the university cafeteria. She still looked like Charlotte and had the same swingy ponytail and beautiful eggplant-black skin. Of course she had no clue who I was. I just smiled back at her and said thank you when she scooped some mashed potatoes onto my plate. She eventually became good friends with Millie.

My father continued with his address. "Since the judge was not getting the kind of conspiratorial support he was hoping for, since he wasn't getting the thrill that bullies get when they're egged on from the sidelines, he stopped – in the middle of his tirade. He said 'okay, call your next goddamned witness, boy' and was banging his gavel like I was the unruly one.

"Umph, umph, umph," Xavier said, still incredulous.

"By the time I was finished talking about the sawmill's negligence and their depraved indifference to their employee's injuries, and by the time I finished showing off my client's ugly, mangled stump, the jury was eating out the palm of my hand."

"How much did you get, Mr. Treadwell?"

Charlotte twisted around in her seat to fume at Xavier. "Be quiet!"

"Okay, Xavier. Here it is. The jury gave us a judgment of $1750 in actual damages, $3000 in punitives. That was a lot of money back then."

"Wow!"

"I like to think some of those punitives were not just for the callous treatment of my client, but also for the mockery the judge made of the court process. That sawmill essentially paid for the judge's sins too."

"They should've paid more than that!"

"Then I turned around and sued the hospital for another $4000 for the lousy amputation. Those hospitals didn't, still don't, give a... whit about providing good care to poor people. My poor client was plagued by infections and pain for years afterward. Of course the money made it a little easier for him and his family to cope.

"But here's the kicker." He paused and the Dukes, Duchesses and their parents leaned forward. After that trial….." It seemed everyone in the room was leaning forward in their seats. The young, pretty server was rapt.

"That judge became one of my best friends."

"What?!"

"Impossible."

"No way!"

"Mr. Treadwell, that's hard to believe. That racist nut?"

"Well it wasn't right away of course. But after a few years, he grew to respect me and the other Negro lawyers. He eventually saw that the earth didn't open up and swallow everything; the apocalypse didn't come just because he started being civil to Negroes. We played golf together. That man nominated me for "Lawyer of the Year" one year. I got one vote – his. His transformation was remarkable. I don't know if he got struck by lightning, if the Lord caused him to have an epiphany, or if he discovered he was part Negro himself, but he changed. Like water erodes rock, after time, the character of something can change after the right amount of pressure is applied. So yes, as strange as it sounds, that man became a really good friend. I even spoke at his funeral."

Out of deference to the fond, private memories of his unlikely friend, my father left out the parts about how he and the judge had gone fishing one morning and how the judge had sobbed on his shoulder about how sorry he was for the way he'd treated Negroes for most of his life and about how ashamed he was for treating him so horribly when he appeared in his courtroom. The judge told my father about how he'd witnessed several lynchings while growing up in Virginia and how he'd become desensitized to the suffering of the victims and their survivors. It was only that first time that he had to remove his little Klan hood so he could vomit. The nightmares of the swinging corpses coming back to life, stepping down out of their nooses and chasing him through the trees, disappeared after a few weeks. At subsequent hangings though, he just yelled and pumped his fist along with everyone else. His sleep was restless but nightmare-free. He admitted knowing in his head and his heart that what they were doing was wrong, but he went along because he was expected to. His attitude, due to indoctrination from the cradle, was imitative and reflexive but realized that was no excuse and that he was responsible for his own actions.

The judge told my father, "I was practically raised by a Negro woman. I loved Rosie. I knew it was wrong when my father ran her husband off the land they were sharecropping, claiming he was cheating him out of some profit. But it was my father who was cheating *him*. It was a real bad scene and I won't go into detail about it. Pappy wouldn't let her leave as long as they owed us money. Instead of being understanding and compassionate, I made her darn a shirt for me before her husband was even a mile down the road and she was still hysterical. Rosie's heart broke and she was never the same. Oh Rosie, poor Rosie! She died soon afterwards. Her husband came sneaking back to get her a few months later and we all got our rifles and took potshots at him, rather than invite him up on the porch and tell him that his wife was dead and buried in the woods somewhere without a marker. I don't know what was wrong with me. My mother was gentle and kindhearted. But the influence of my father and uncles and the men in the town was greater. So from the bottom of my heart, Jasper, I apologize for everything."

My father said he understood how prejudice and hatred were so often contagious and irrational and told him he could think of no other person he respected more than him at that moment. They hugged. Three hours later, they caught one small trout. They gutted it, sprinkled some salt and pepper on it, cooked it on an open fire, ate it with some Saltine crackers, and washed it down with some moonshine. It was one of the most satisfying meals he ever had. My father came home and still had moisture in his eyes.

Xavier could not believe my father and the judge had become friends. "Unbelievable," he sputtered. "I'd have never forgiven that crazy cracker."

"And that, Xavier, is exactly how one misses out on things. You let emotion trump reason and good sense. That crazy cracker, as you so eloquently put it, endowed a scholarship for needy students at Howard Law School. You need to know that – not that you'll ever benefit from it." He looked around the room. "Now...any questions?"

Mrs. Brathwaite suddenly remembered she was supposed to be moderating the event and rose to her feet to stop the further chastisement of her son. "Oh, my, look at the time. Let's all give Charlotte and Justinia's father a hand for that...interesting...talk." The room applauded politely. A couple of the kids stood up to show their full appreciation of Jasper Treadwell's words of wisdom.

"Very provocative," someone said.

"And now we'd like to invite Robert's father to come up and speak to us about his exciting career as a pharmacist."

"Put your studies first," Robert's father said, reading from a piece of paper. Xavier groaned.

CHAPTER 29

I'D HOPED XAVIER would have found a girlfriend at Cornell, but apparently there was a scarcity of "esteemed" Negro women in the entirety of Ithaca, New York and the surrounding area. After coming back home to D. C., he claimed he was much too busy with his first year of law school classes to date anyone seriously. There were two attractive women in his class and he didn't invite either to his study groups – probably because the idea of women lawyers was repugnant to him, though he'd never come right out and admit it. So here he was still unbetrothed and with no other prospects but me. At 25, and a second year law student, he was beginning to feel the pressure to wed.

A soon-to-be lawyer whose family was in the D. C. Negro social register would need a wife to care for him and support him while he endured years of rigorous legal training and testing and made forays into the right lodges, social organizations and golf foursomes. He would need the right woman to squire around as he jockeyed his way around the circuits of Negro high society. Xavier was a member of Alpha Phi Alpha and there were fraternity balls, Howard Law School dinners, alumni events, NAACP and Urban League functions to attend. The National Medical Association – for Negro doctors – was always having something and Xavier's father would be doling out invitations to those functions, Boule galas and Bachelor-Benedict-sponsored cotillions. Xavier was expected to attend, arm-in-arm with proper accompaniment, preferably a wife.

When he wasn't being obnoxious, Xavier could actually be quite fun and charming and occasionally came by with vaudeville tickets when he wanted to "go slumming." And I did love how he made an effort, especially after a tiff, to gift me with my favorite treats – macadamia nuts or mangoes – which were often impossible to find. He was competitive, but his cut-throat wheeling and dealing during Monopoly tournaments with our friends and his melodramatic outbursts when someone landed on his Boardwalk property always made me laugh til my stomach ached. "I like when you laugh," he'd say and I appreciated that. Of course he opened doors, pulled out chairs, uncapped my Coca-Cola before handing it to me, and threw his suit jacket over my shoulders at the first hint of a chill. But he also felt no compunction telling me that a new hairstyle was unattractive, that my brows were tweezed and drawn too thin (never mind that it was in vogue) or that an outfit was too immodest (never mind that a little daring décolletage was chic and tasteful on the right woman done the right way.) Likewise I had no compunction telling him that his pocket watch, side-parted hair, Clark Gable moustache, and spectator oxfords looked costume-y. We were fond of each other, but were definitely not in love and had never progressed beyond cheek-and-forehead kissing.

Xavier didn't think love was necessary for a good marriage. He thought it was more important to be equally yoked, financially and educationally, to complement each other and have a mutual desire to build a strong, successful family together. It was a pragmatic commitment; love was a bonus, and a well-matched couple could always *grow* to love each other. But I think love, being *in* love, is essential in a relationship. I've told Xavier that just because we waltzed well together didn't mean we were meant to *be* together.

I knew I could easily disappear in his shadow and had no desire to be known as Mrs. Xavier D. Brathwaite III for the rest of my life. I wanted my own identity, independent of a spouse. Once the vows were said and the cake was cut, Xavier would be the kind of man who wanted his wife to recede into a supporting role. I wanted to be able to walk shoulder to shoulder, rib to rib, with my husband.

I've seen what can happen in some "coaxed" marriages. Some couples made it work, but others suffered miserably. First there was a big, beautiful ceremony, a lavish reception and a fabulous honeymoon. But then came the rapid deterioration of the relationship. Dr. DuBois convinced his daughter Yolande to marry poet Countee Cullen even though she was in love with another man – a jazz musician unfortunately – and the "wedding of the decade" ended in divorce two years later. My friend Doyle, a talented but frustrated Yale-trained actor, feels abused and emasculated every day because he doesn't fit in with wife Nadine's family's medical supplies company and is considering absconding to New York.

Adrian Bishop went from being my friend Liza's perfect paramour to a patronizing patriarch as soon as they got back from Bermuda. After eleven months, the affection was gone and Georgine says Adrian was already bored and "sniffing around" Druscilla Chapman who'd dropped out of Howard and, besides having a physique like a Coca-Cola bottle, had nothing else going for her. But Liza's mother was cautioning her not to make any rash decisions until she gave birth to a Bishop Trucking Company heir.

Once they were married, the debonair Caleb Tucker refused to allow my sorority sister Patsy to have any involvement in his family's wine and orchard business even though Patsy had a degree in Horticulture and knew how to improve and develop new varieties of grapes. Patsy was depressed and wouldn't leave the house. Georgine said Patsy just sits on the sofa, all dressed up with nowhere to go, and that the maid has to lift her legs to vacuum the rug beneath her feet. I didn't want to be like Yolande, Doyle, Liza or Patsy. Life was too short.

There was no benefit to marrying into one of Washington's top four hundred "premiere Negro families," only to be unhappy and unfulfilled. My sister Charlotte was still in wedded bliss, having chosen a husband without any outside influence or meddling. Calvin, a Morehouse graduate, was a good man from a good and proper family with a legacy of AME ministry, but his family was not among the Washington 400. Hardly – Calvin was from Memphis and was neither wealthy nor aristocratic. But Charlotte had chosen him and was head over heels. My mother had hoped Charlotte would marry one of the Hamilton brothers who were all third-generation Virginia doctors, but she wasn't the least bit interested in any of them. Like Charlotte, and like Magdalena who chose Daddy with his dark-brown skin and slave roots, I wanted to choose for myself too.

Xavier would think sitting at a desk all day and making a few trips to the book shelves was exhausting and that an evening foot rub should await him at home everyday. Well I wanted a man who would rub my feet just because, and I cannot imagine Xavier rubbing a woman's feet. My mother enjoyed a good foot rub and my father, she said, gave magnificent ones. Xavier would come home and expect to have an aperitif handed to him. Just like his father did. I could see him taking out his pocket watch and gazing at it if dinner wasn't on the table, sending the subtle message that he was annoyed. Just like his father did. Xavier would want children to be seen but not heard, shown off, but not welcomed into the circle of conversation.

Xavier, an only child, wanted lots of children – at least six. He said as much during a game of "Truth or Dare" at a friend's house in high school, hasn't wavered since, and can't wait to have his first son, Xavier IV. I wasn't even sure I wanted children. The world had too many problems – the perpetual brink of war, relentless poverty, virulent racism and segregation that serves no practical purpose.

I cannot imagine having to put up with Abigail who I knew would be constantly examining the tips of my baby's ears, or my boy baby's scrotum which, according to old wives' tales, determined future skin color. She'd deny it, of course, saying she was just making sure everything looked "healthy." I wasn't sure how she'd react if the children didn't have Xavier's curly brown hair, green eyes and girly lashes. My mind's eye sees her chasing the children along the beach, monitoring the depth of their tan lines, the degree of hair frizz and shrinkage and insisting they wear longer sleeves, bonnets and hideous rubber swim caps while near and in the water. She would wring her hands if she didn't think they'd grow tall like Xavier or were too slow developing into the golf and violin prodigy she thought he was.

As long as I lived with her son and grandchildren, Abigail Brathwaite would be hovering nearby, demanding access, questioning my moves and decisions and commenting on every little thing. It'd be worse than living at home with Magdalena. I told Xavier several times that his mother was way too overbearing and he would agree.

At my house in Washington, a few weeks before we left for the convention in Baltimore, Xavier came over and the subject of his mother came up again. "I still remember how your mother secretly campaigned against me to be Miss Ebony Rose at the Dukes and Duchesses Negro History pageant while telling me and my mother that she hoped I'd win."

"I know, I know," he said. "She really wanted the lighter skinned girl to win."

"Yes – Bianca Sloane – who couldn't even walk with a book on her head. Her essay was terrible and she didn't do half the community service I did."

"That's ancient history, Justinia. And anyway you won. Don't you still have the tiara?"

"That's not the point, Xavier. Your mother is duplicitous. What does that portend for the future?"

"She's gotten much better. She's crazy about you."

I told him that he too could be bothersome at times.

"*Moi?*" He acted shock because he thought he was perfect. "Why are you suddenly being so difficult?"

"I'm the same as always, Xavier. You just haven't been paying attention. I don't want to be picking out china patterns, hiring household staff and planning dinner menus before I'm even twenty-four years old. And I'm certainly not ready to be anyone's mother. The world is changing, women have more options and I want to broaden my horizons."

"I thought you wanted to teach. Like your mother. You will make a wonderful teacher."

"Mother was technically a librarian and she hasn't done that in thirty years. And it was just something to do until she got married. I like the idea of teaching, I'm just not completely sure."

"Five years and three colleges later, and you still don't know what you want to do with your life. How is that possible?"

"Xavier, you do realize that college isn't the end of self-discovery."

"You can be married and still do all those things, whatever those things might be," he said, flipping through phonograph album covers.

I'd been listening to Ella Fitzgerald, then mindlessly singing snatches of "Stormy Weather" by Ethel Waters. Xavier stopped it all to put on some Count Basie. I didn't feel like arguing on two fronts, so I let it go.

"Well I don't want to take a chance. Marriage should be forever and I don't want to be stuck in one where I'll feel resentful or regretful. Not every girl is trying to earn an MRS degree."

He just stared at me. "Sure they are. That's the point of most women going to college."

"Oh my God." I just stared at him, then tried to change the subject. "Maybe I want to open a floral shop and sell exotic orchids and bird of paradise. Or…I write in my journal every day and it's enjoyable and cathartic." I spun over to the bay window, "So maybe I'll write for the *world* and become a writer like Jessie Fauset or Zora Neale Hurston."

"If you become a writer, I hope you're more like Jessie Fauset. Most people I know cannot relate to Zora with all that slave dialect and talking mules, but Miss Fauset is sophisticated and at the top of her craft." He loved starting petty arguments.

"You're partial to Fauset because your family knows her personally and her characters are light-skinned and well-off."

"That has nothing to do with it. She's just a superior writer." He paused. "But do you really think writing in a diary is the same thing as being a real author?"

"Oh my goodness, Xavier. Must you be so negative?" I acted nonchalant, tapping my foot to the music. "Or maybe I'll become a lawyer."

"A lawyer? The law is a beast, Justinia. Law school would be a waste of time."

"Rubbish! I could be another Charlotte Ray, the first Negro woman lawyer, educated right here at Howard Law. And I happen to think the law is very interesting."

"I know who Charlotte Ray was. She concealed her gender when she applied for admission, only used her initials. Such dishonesty, yet they reward her with a portrait in the university foyer."

"She was a trailblazer!"

"That doesn't make *your* wanting to be a lawyer any less ridiculous. But I may need a law clerk one day if I ever decide to start my own firm. And as I recall, Charlotte Ray spent most of her life teaching school."

"Well that was a long time ago. There've been many women lawyers since then and some make a decent living."

"They're probably all spinsters."

"Well I need time and space to figure everything out." I raked my hair back with my fingers. "And by the way, you are *such* a male chauvinist."

"How so? Have you been reading Virginia Woolf again? All that feminist, man-hating 'room of one's own' mumbo-jumbo?"

"Have you been studying Freud again? All that macho, anti-woman, penis-envy nonsense?"

"Justinia, I cannot believe you just said that."

"I can't believe all the things *you* say."

I wanted to tell him if he was so eager to "jump the broom" that he should consider giving Georgine a second look. I know that he called on her at home a few times until deciding that she, her sisters, her mother and her father gossip and cackle entirely too much. Their household was chaotic with too much whining and arguing and too many pets – cats, dogs, birds and rabbits – and it all made his eyes water and his head throb. But Georgine would jump at the opportunity to become Mrs. Xavier Brathwaite III. Her mother would be booking St. Luke's Episcopal Church, some fancy hotel that accepted Negro trade, and a dazzling, all-Negro string quartet at the mere thought of such a possibility.

Xavier was clearly aware of my ambivalence about him and marriage in general, so I was bewildered by his persistence.

"Okay, you're being a drag," he said. "Let me beat you in backgammon again."

CHAPTER 30

Julius

THE EMCEE, IN a bow tie and exquisitely tailored suit, was appropriately attired for the occasion. "As you know," he said, "every year since 1914, the NAACP awards the Spingarn Medal, our highest honor, to American Negroes who perform acts of distinguished merit and achievement. Last year's recipient was Mrs. Mary McCleod Bethune." Mrs. Bethune stood at her seat and, leaning on a cane, acknowledging the standing ovation and waved to the admiring crowd. She cut an imposing figure with her salt and pepper hair and the white orchid corsage pinned to her long, black dress. The emcee said she started her own school in Florida with five girls and $1.50 and was part of Roosevelt's "black cabinet."

I made a note to shake her hand before the evening concluded. There were so many pioneering education and civil-rights celebrities in attendance that I hoped there'd be a photographer around at just the right moment to snap my picture with at least some of them. I was eager to show the photographs to people back home.

If people in Berlin could see this awards ceremony or the pictures memorializing it, they'd be confounded and amazed. Since most Berliners had never met a black person, many of their opinions were predicated on the news that was reported by the foreign press. They'd look askance at Thurgood Marshall since they'd never heard of a black lawyer, let alone one who argued and won cases in appellate courts. They believed the stereotypes that the American Negro was illiterate, that the men were prone to spontaneous acts of violence and uncontrollable urges to rape and defile white women. And Negro women, with the exception of glamorous entertainers, were presumably unattractive and undesirable, only good for cooking, cleaning and rearing children.

In Berlin, there were some native Afro-Germans, some African students and professors, ex-patriots, or the occasional American Negro tourist or entertainer. There were also the "Rhineland Bastards," the bi-racial offspring of the African soldiers who patrolled the post-war, de-militarized zone near the Rhine River and the German women from that region. Pervasive stereotypes of black males fueled the misbelief that the "Rhineland Bastards," who I think are quite comely, were the result of rape and not marital or other romantic relationships. Nazis believe France's deployment of African soldiers was a grand conspiracy with Jews to mongrelize and weaken German bloodlines and a way to simply piss off the Germans.

These "bastards" could be hauled before the Nazi-created Genetic Health Court, found to have a "hereditary disease" just like the blind, deaf, schizophrenic, or chronically alcoholic and ordered to be forcibly sterilized. We'd learned the Gestapo kept lists and files on everyone; they made it their mission to find out who the bi-racial youth were and where they could be located.

An Aryan attorney friend was privy to one of these Genetic Health hearings in Dusseldorf. He'd been aghast. Another lawyer in the courtroom sensed his consternation and explained that the idea of eugenics and compulsory sterilization came from America who'd been sterilizing criminals, the mentally ill, immigrants and other "undesirables" for years. "As if that justified it," he said. "But I didn't dare say a word, just watched and listened in disbelief.":

"Dr. Engel submits application for sterilization of this sixteen-year old female of obvious African heritage."

"Doctor?" the judge prompted.

"Yes, *Herr Vorsitzender.* As you can see the subject is mud-colored with wiry hair and fat lips. Agents of Commission #3 have determined she is the product of rape, though her mother is a whore."

"Very well, involuntary sterilization is so ordered. Take her in the back with the others." He banged the gavel.

"Pending appeal." They all laughed.

The petrified girl was taken away to where others "unfit for procreation" awaited the van ride to the hospital where they'd undergo a painful sterilization procedure. Afterwards, they'd be deposited back at the place of their abduction.

"Next case!"

"That's it for today, judge. An albino, a midget, six cripples, two retards, a deaf-mute and three black bastards. It's been a productive afternoon."

"Yes, but the Commission should be expanded so as to expedite the thorough cleansing of Germany."

"I concur. At this rate, it could take years."

"Well," said the judge. "Happy hunting!"

"Heil Hitler!"

"Heil!"

Regardless of the fact that there were black people in Germany, spotting one on the streets of Berlin was as rare as finding a four-leaf clover in a lush Tiergarten field. When blacks were spotted, some people stared as if they were from outer space, and it took a few moments to realize these "strangers" weren't dark-skinned Tarzans with bestial impulses. They seemed surprised to see them walk and talk like regular people. Except for being gawked at, these blacks went about their business unmolested.

CHAPTER 31

"I saw some *black* people last week," my cousin Gretchen announced at *Oma* Zip's apartment where we'd gone to celebrate Rosh Hashanah, the holiday also known as the Jewish New Year, the literal *head* of the year, the anniversary of the creation of Adam and Eve, or the birthday of all mankind. Rosh Hashanah was my favorite holiday, the only one except for Yom Kipper – the Day of Atonement, Hanukkah – the Festival of Lights, and Passover – the observance of the exodus from Egypt, that my family actually celebrates. *Oma* Zip has taken to celebrating some of the more obscure holidays with her new-found conservative Jewish friends, so she was happy to have her own family together for a festive occasion, even if we were behaving like our usual irreverent selves. I even wore a kippah on my head because I knew it'd make her happy.

It was the last holiday celebration before I left for law school in America. As soon as she saw me, she pinched and kissed my cheeks, told me I was such a "good boy" and that she'd miss me terribly. "Don't forget to say your prayers, and don't ever forget where you come from." I assured her I'd never forget.

"The blacks were utterly fascinating to watch," Gretchen said, pleased to have a story to tell so she could be the center of attention.

Gretchen's announcement immediately reminded me of the time the whole family went to the "human zoo" on the outskirts of Berlin. A certain German explorer was famous for his world travels and his importation of all kinds of exotic treasures and creatures back home to Europe. He primarily wanted to make money with his circuses and exhibits, but he also felt obligated to expose Europeans to the "primitive" cultures of Africans, Asians, Australians, Pacific

Islanders and Eskimos and prove, by comparison, the Europeans' inherent superiority. The black Africans were of particular interest to him and to the patrons
and fans of "human zoos" of which there were several throughout Germany.

⋅⋗▬◉ ◉▬⋖⋅

In the summer of 1923, three carloads of us arrived at the zoo grounds early and
staked out a shaded picnic table, leaving our picnic baskets and red and white
checkered oil cloths with plans to spread out our lunch later after seeing the at-
tractions. Most of the people were there for the "zoo within the zoo" because
everyone was talking about it, handbills and posters were promoting it, the concept
was provocative and they wanted to see the wonders of the world for themselves.
They wanted to show their friends that they were keeping up with trendy ventures
and be able to report that the exhibit was wild and fantastic or that, despite all the
ballyhoo, it was cheesy and boring. Admittedly, our family was curious too, but we
observed with the intellectual skepticism necessary for encounters with snake-oil
salesmen.

The zookeepers had recreated a Sudanese landscape and peopled it with
Sudanese children and adults. A sign attached to a hammered-in stake read
"*Volkerschau*" which translated to "Peoples Show." There were grass huts an-
chored in terra cotta dirt and accented by plastic palm trees constructed to replace the real ones which had since perished in Germany's climate. There were
a few live camels, giraffes, a sleepy elephant, some orangutans, a tranquilized
leopard and taxidermy lions, rhinos and hippopotami. The entire exhibit was
surrounded by a shallow gully, waist-high fencing and chicken wire, just enough
of a barrier to emphasize the fact that the people were on display and required
distance and distinction from the spectators, but not enough to leave the impression that they were imprisoned like the real animals in the other parts of the zoo.

The handlers all stood around looking and acting like carnival barkers in
their pinstripe, cutaway suit coats, tipping their top hats and using their pointers to focus attention on the African people and away from the cheesy setting.
Our family found space amongst the throng of Europeans surrounding the

Volkerschau waiting earnestly to be "educated" by these carnival men who fancied themselves as Darwinian scholars.

"Behold the Nubians!" they cried. "Instead of going on safari in the Sudan, that vast, dusty desert, that unfortunate wasteland, *Herr* Hagenback, the great German explorer, has brought the safari to you!"

"This is a zoo too?" Gretchen asked one of them.

"Not a zoo. This is an 'ethnographic exposition' specially created and authenticated for your edification." He spread his arms wide to take in the entire acre of a transplanted "Sudan." If you're also entertained, so be it, you just get more for your money. You can only see these shows in select European cities. You're fortunate to have one right here in Berlin."

Some of the Africans started beating drums, the women began what was called a fertility dance at the same time as a group of "spear chuckers" pretended to slay a stuffed boar.

"When Emperor Wilhelm II visited a *Volkerschau* in Hamburg several years ago, he was very impressed, admitted that he learned a lot."

It was a bizarre scene and I was struck by the absurdity of putting real African people in a fake African village with fake fauna and fake flora in the middle of Germany in order to exploit their exotic nature and demonstrate their alleged inferiority. It was the unfamiliar dark skin, the fleecy hair and flashing eyes that made ordinary activities like sitting, walking, dancing and singing seem strange and scary. Some of my cousins lost interest after watching for a few minutes. They were ready to go looking around for the real apes, the big cats, the carousel and the ferris wheel. But Gretchen, who'd been about six, was transfixed. The lure of popcorn and cotton candy couldn't get her to take her eyes off the black girls with the cotton candy-and popcorn-reminiscent hair or the bare-chested black woman with the braids encircling her scalp like a coiled-up cobra and the large copper plate distending her lower lip who was stirring something in a smoky cauldron.

"These people have cannibalistic instincts," said one announcer, "but do not fear, this is a controlled environment." On cue, some of the African men snarled and growled like bears. The crowd reacted predictably. "You're safe. There are men milling around with Lugers in their waistbands just in case things get out of control. Nevertheless, men, hold onto your wives and daughters."

There were little boys in loin cloths scratching themselves, rolling around and wrestling with the orangutans.

"See how they love to frolic without a care in the world."

The squatting, evil-eyed warrior-man sharpened his knife on a rock and looked as if he'd pounce any moment. Though I was one of hundreds huddled around the exhibit, his eyes seemed to be following only me like one of those ancient forefathers in a creepy portrait. But his eyes bespoke resentment and not anger or violence.

"The Africans are predatory by nature, so try not to rile them. But, again, this particular exhibit has built-in protections. No guests will be harmed. We guarantee it."

"They say some of these same things about Jews," my father whispered.

"I know," Uncle Erik said. "Predatory and cannibalistic. My word!"

"Needing to be controlled. Hmmph!"

"Some people are so quick to label other people sub-human."

"This reminds me of that traveling 'freak show' we saw that time in Leipzig, but without the freaks," I said, thinking about the carnival we once went to that featured a bearded lady, sword-swallowers, fire-eaters, Siamese twins, humpbacks and people the barkers claimed to be the fattest or tallest humans on earth. There'd been other living people and animals with a myriad of physical oddities. There were enlarged photos of the severely deformed "Elephant Man," Tom Thumb, who'd been the world's shortest human, and Sarah Baartman, better known as the Hottentot Venus, a beautiful South African slave who presumably had the larg- est buttocks ever known. There were jars that supposedly contained a dragon's tongue, an ogre's eyeballs, a unicorn's horn, a werewolf's fangs. I looked at the Africans. "These are just people pretending to be back home in Africa."

My father said, "You're right, my son." He draped his arm around my shoulders.

"So you say," said the barker. "They may not be freaks in the usual sense, but they are a curiosity. They don't live how we live, think how we think. Look at these poor, primitive creatures. They can't live in civilized society. You think you can just let them have a flat in Berlin and they'll adapt? They wouldn't know what to do with themselves. And they'd make a mess of things. The place would need to be fumigated, probably condemned."

"They'd starve and perish," another one said.

"Survival of the fittest. That's what Darwin said."

"That doesn't make sense," I said. At twelve years old, I'd had enough biology to know that that was a gross misstatement of Darwin's theories.

"No, son, it certainly does not," my father concurred.

An orangutan pushed one of the little boys to the ground and the boy began to cry. People laughed.

"He'll be okay. They play like this all the time. They're like brothers."

"So are they humans or are they apes?" the barker asked. "Evolutionists think they may be the missing link, somewhere on the continuum between man and monkey. They're about 2000 years behind the European in terms of mental development."

"Wow!" several spectators exclaimed.

Each of the barkers summoned a young African male to their side to use for their demonstration. "Notice the knotted up hair, the thick, broad, flat noses – just like an ape's." What I noticed instead were the colorful, beaded jewelry, the studded noses, the leather headbands.

"The jaw is longer, relative to width, and retains a vestige of the 'simian shelf', the bony region right behind the incisors – just like an ape's. This feature is absent in Europeans. The jaws are stronger than ours are and jut out – like an ape's."

"The neck is larger and shorter like an ape's. The ears are small, round and high up on the head like apes."

People oohed and aahed as if they could plainly see this. To me, their jaws, ears and necks looked like anyone else's.

"Arms and legs are much longer than the European's; they have a shorter trunk and the cross-section of the chest is more circular than Europeans'. The pelvis is narrower and longer – like an ape's."

They continued to take turns explaining the differences between blacks and whites and the similarities between blacks and apes. They used their pointers to emphasize certain things and the Africans obliged by turning their heads, opening their mouths, wriggling their hands and wrists, running and high-stepping in place.

"See, the eyes have a large black iris and large orbits with a yellowish sclerotic coat over it like that of a gorilla. The mouth is wide and has thick, protruding lips."

"The skull is thicker and the brain is smaller, as much as twenty percent smaller than the European's, and it weighs less. Because of this, they've been unable to contribute anything valuable to the advancement of civilization."

I looked at all the things they'd made that were strewn around them. If they were so lacking in intelligence, I wondered how they were clever enough to create such intricate weaving patterns in their cloths and baskets, to realize that a rhinoceros horn would make a good handle for a dagger and that if the dagger is embellished with tigers' teeth, copper inlays and feathers, it could be unique and attractive as well as functional.

"The biggest difference between black people and monkeys is that the blacks do have the opposable thumb. This of course allows them to manipulate tools and grab things easier. This is an adaptation that allowed the Africans to exceed their simian cousins in evolutionary progress because they could make fire, clothe themselves and build shelter to protect against the elements which allowed them better chances to survive. The only other animals that have anything like an opposable thumb are the possum and the giant panda."

One of the barkers noticed Gretchen's saucer-eyed fascination and asked, "What do you think, little girl? Are they humans, apes, or something in between?" But she was either too awed or too confused to respond.

"They're not all the way evolved like you and me. That's why we had to take care of them for so many years. But we brought them this far. You'd think they'd be grateful." He spoke as if he himself were the epitome of the ideal Homo Sapien, missing teeth, reeking breath, hairy knuckles and quivering, unshaven jowls notwithstanding.

All around the periphery of the exhibit, you could see people clapping with delight and encouraging the Africans to dance and perform tricks.

"Okay, you little bugger, let's see how high you can jump," One British man insisted. The African teen, who evidently did not understand English, looked confused and the man who wanted to entertain himself as well as the people around him, made wild gestures so that the young African could understand. Eventually he jumped like a seal going for an anchovy dangling from a zookeeper's fingertips, and the Brit, with his self-satisfied grin, patted him on the head.

Then there were people throwing peanuts the same way we throw crusts of bread to pigeons in the park. Some were feeding the African kids and some of the African women pieces of banana, gingerly holding the offering up to their mouths. The barker bent down and told Gretchen "If you have a penny, you can buy a banana to feed to the little ones." He had bags of peanuts and bunches of bananas on a stick to sell.

Gretchen looked at another young child holding up a banana to one of the little black girls under the watchful eyes of her parents. "Oh, *vater*, may I have a penny? I want to feed a banana to the little ape-girl too."

The adults in our family had been silent to that point but I know they'd have plenty to say in private when we got home. "No," Uncle Erik said. "I don't think I approve. Of any of this." He grabbed her hand in his. "Come along, Gretchen. Let's go see a real gorilla."

"Were these people kidnapped?" my father asked.

"Heavens no! They were ecstatic to leave that wretched continent and come to Europe where they can prosper. They all receive a handsome salary and are free to leave when their contract is up."

"I can just imagine what's in this so-called contract," my father said, his voice dripping with skepticism. "Let's move on." We left in search of the big cats, turning to look back over our shoulders at the pitiful-looking African villagers in the ridiculous, make-shift habitat.

One of the barkers called after our retreating figures. "Be sure to tell your friends and neighbors that you've seen the 'missing link'. They'll be so envious. Tell them to come see with their own eyes. We'll only be two more weeks at this location."

We were on the opposite side of the zoo, contemplating the king of the beasts, the lionesses and cubs, when Gretchen slipped away. The zoo was teeming with visitors and Aunt Ava, her mother, fainted thinking her daughter had met a terrible fate, and had to be revived with smelling salts. It was almost an hour before the police found her back at the "ethnographic exposition" feeding banana to one of the "ape girls." In retrospect, it should've been the first place they looked.

CHAPTER 32

"So where were these black people you saw?" Gabriel asked his sister.

"We were touring the Pergamon Museum since we'd never been before. My friends and I were admiring the Athena statue and the reconstructed Assyrian Palace. We were still talking about how spectacular it all was when we turned a corner - and there they were. A whole group of them, at least ten. We practically stopped in our tracks."

"What were they doing?" another cousin asked.

"I guess they were looking at the Pergamon Altar."

"What else would they be doing in a museum?" I asked.

"I don't know. Looking for white women?" She was looking for laughs but didn't get any.

Since Gretchen didn't know anyone who was non-white, she filled in the blanks with the vilest stereotypes promoted by many foreign press reporters who managed to remain "neutral and detached" about the attitudes and behavior of American whites towards Negroes and did little editorializing about how wrong it all was. So people like my cousin relied on undisputed "facts:" Black people are criminally inclined, so they deserve to be lynched; they are stupid, so don't deserve to have schools and decent jobs; they are fat, ugly and poor and deserve all the ridicule they get. They had no neighbors or friends to put a human face on the "Negro," nothing to invoke an empathetic response when reading or hearing about race riots or brutal enforcement of Jim Crow laws.

Gabriel and I'd been educated in some of Berlin's finest public schools and enlightened by a decidedly more cosmopolitan environment where we played football with Kenyans and one of our best friends was Bakari, a Nigerian musician. The *Bejte* Ethiopian Restaurant is near the university, my Calculus professor was an American Negro, and a concierge at the Hotel Excelsior was from Ghana and had the crispest English I ever heard.

Gretchen lived at a provincial boarding school in Switzerland where there was a kaleidoscope of nationalities to the extent that one could readily discern British from Flemish, Danish from Spanish, Lithuanian from Albanian. Our trip to the *Volkershau* had a lasting influence. She still regarded blacks with cautious wonderment, believed the entire continent was one huge mass of unevolving dark and wild jungle, and that there was one, all-encompassing black culture. She thought the people all had war-painted faces and bones through their noses – customs more associated with Indians and other cultures – but the promoters of the human zoos, in their zeal to be crowd pleasers, cobbled together as many ethnic peculiarities as they could into a single exhibit.

Gretchen's studies at the fancy boarding school hadn't taught her much about the "dark continent." She'd be shocked to learn that many African countries had modern cities with vibrant commerce and rich, natural resources. Oddly enough, I learned this in a business class because the professor was always telling us about Africa's gold, silver and diamonds just waiting to be had for the persons bold and resourceful enough to finance mining expeditions. My friend's father said "Blast that fitful stock market!" and actually sent a group to Nigeria looking for diamonds. After two years, an influx of hundreds of thousands of dollars, tons of dynamite, the rape of hundreds of miles of virgin terrain, and the tragic deaths and maiming of several of their hand-picked crew and many more penniless and desperate Nigerian guides, they jackpotted and found petroleum instead. All had been fortune-hunters, but only the capitalists profited. My friend's father was a multi-millionaire now. I'm told they have mansions all over the world.

I also learned from my Nigerian friend Bakari that many of the people working the *Volkerschau* were actors and students pretending to be Sudanese villagers steeped in a culture and a lifestyle that was actually alien to them. Most were modernized Africans, but some were American Negroes, and all of them were in need of a job. In their real lives, they didn't walk around with pails of water balanced on their heads. They had to practice so they could do it without spilling a drop at show time. They had to get used to being in close proximity to wild animals. They had to learn to weave baskets, carve wood and pretend to cook, eat and savor antelope meat which was really some kind of pre-made beef jerky. But Gretchen, like most of the *Volkerschau* patrons, marveled at what they thought was fascinating cultural authenticity.

The *Volkerschau* performers received tips in addition to their regular pay, peeled off from a gigantic roll of cash, when they hammed it up by grinning wider, grunting louder, running around on all fours like a chimp just to delight the crowd. Bakari said that when the show was over, they went to their trailers and smoked cigarettes, ate sausage sandwiches and German spice cake, drank beer and milk, played cards, wrote letters home, stuffing money into the envelopes, and read newspapers and books. They probably also got a good belly laugh at European gullibility as they counted out their extra money.

Gretchen fancied herself to be well-read, but she read the magazine articles that were tainted by the subjectivity of unenlightened and agenda-driven reporters. She read American literature like Twain's *Huck Finn* and Stowe's *Uncle Tom's Cabin* at her book clubs that failed to take the discussion beyond a superficial level. They talked about what happened in the plot, but not about Huck's conflicting feelings about race or whether Uncle Tom's faith made him physically weak and passive or spiritually strong and hopeful. And being stowed away in the insular Switzerland and a tucked-away boarding school nine months out of a year disconnected Gretchen from the goings-on in the rest of the world. So Gretchen wasn't prejudiced. *Nein*, our family is far too tolerant to harbor bigots. But she was young and naïve and sometimes made insensitive comments.

"Gretchen, you're incorrigible." I threw a sofa pillow at her.

She laughed. "You know I'm kidding. You know I'm smart enough to know the difference between stereotypes and real people."

"I don't know. You worry me sometimes. You know how we hate it when people stereotype *us*."

"Julius, don't lecture me. I know that. I've been called a greedy Jew too many times to do that to other people."

"But you *are* greedy," Gabriel said. "You ate a whole blueberry pie once."

"Did not," she said. "It was only half. And I was only five years old and didn't know any better."

"It was the whole pie. And you were ten."

Our cousins laughed and Gretchen blushed. She loved food and it showed.

"But, listen," she said, "these people were fascinating to look at. Their skin was so dark. It looked like velvet. Or like that rich fudge *Oma* Zip likes from that chocolatier in Geneva – LaBonbonniere. I really wanted to touch it. And their teeth were so white. I've never seen teeth so white. But their French was so crisp and pretty."

"So these black people were more fascinating than seeing the excavated ruins of a Greek altar?" I asked.

"Almost."

"Let me get this straight. There you were surrounded by two-thousand-year-old empires assiduously extracted from the bowels of Asia Minor and you're distracted by the gleaming, white teeth of some black people. Gee, Gretchen, you need to get out more." She threw the pillow back at me.

"I can't help that they're so … interesting."

"Well staring is rude."

"I couldn't help it. But I wasn't the only one. Lots of people were staring. They caused quite a stir."

"That doesn't make it right," Gabriel said. "I'm sure they felt uncomfortable."

"Probably, but they took it in stride. I'm sure they'd stare at us if we were in Africa."

"That's beside the point. And you just assume they're from Africa. Maybe their native country is France."

"Or Belgium," said another cousin.

"They speak French in Senegal, Algeria, lots of countries in Africa."

"The point is that you can't just assume things. That's what's wrong with our country. Our government doesn't even think *we* can be true Germans."

She thought about this for a minute. "You're right."

"This reminds me of the time you got lost at the zoo."

"I remember. I wanted to see the ape people."

"Except they weren't ape people, just ordinary people with black skin."

"Of course I know that *now*, Julius. I was, what, four? I'm not an imbecile."

"I don't know. You believed every fairytale."

"Right," Gabriel said. "You still think the Frog Prince is real."

"Very funny."

My grandmother Zip, wearing her traditional Rosh Hashanah all-white garb, came in from the kitchen before we could start trading embarrassing childhood stories and argue about who was misremembering and who was just making things up. She is somehow aware of every conversation that takes place in the house, and she added her two cents. "The most important thing to remember is that we all hurt and bleed the same."

"It takes all kinds to make a world," a little cousin chimed in. We all agreed.

"Gretchen, everything is just about done, but I need your help cutting up the apples. Our guests will be here soon."

I followed *Oma* Zip and Gretchen into the dining room where she'd set a beautiful table. Everything shimmered – some of the candles that had already been lit, the spotless, gold-trimmed plates, silverware and glassware, an array of golden mums in a prism-crystal vase, the golden, homemade, honey-glazed, raisin challah bread braided into perfect orbs to symbolize the continuous cycle of life, and the honey-filled glass bowls into which we would dunk apple slices to symbolize hopes for a sweet and prosperous new year.

Of course *Oma* Zip found a way to ruin it. She brought in a gold platter and sat it down in the middle of the table. "*Oma* Zip, what in the world is that?"

"What does it look like, you little *nudnik*?" she said lovingly. My father came in from where he was smoking with the other men in the library. "*Mutti*, what on earth?"

"A sheep's head so we may be at the *head* and not the *tail* in the upcoming new year. And also, we need a visual reminder for the children that God provided Abraham a ram just in time so he didn't have to sacrifice his son Isaac."

"I know what it means," he said. "But why in God's name is it on our table?"

It was a grotesque sight. The over-roasted, tough-looking flesh stretched over the sloping skull with its filmy, intact eyeballs, a pronounced snout and a protrusion of broken yellow teeth. It wasn't made more appetizing by the bed of leeks, garlic cloves, carrots, potatoes, squash and beets on which it nestled. The goat's head broth was still simmering on the stove. Appropriately enough, however, the goat's head was right next to the *shofar*, the ceremonial ram's horn that would be blown to rouse the spirit of God in the souls of the celebrants and remind everyone about Isaac and the ram in the bush.

"I had to go all the way to Grenadier Strasse to get this sheep's head. None of the kosher butchers in Wilmersdorf had any." She turned the dish this way and that, looking for the most attractive angle. There wasn't one.

"For good reason," I said, and she swatted me with her dish towel.

"What happened to the smelly fish heads you used to serve?" my father asked. "Even that would be better than this. And why can't we just dispose of this antiquated custom altogether? The Sommerfeldts have never had a sheep's head. That's a Sephardic Jew tradition. *Mutti*, you are certainly not Sephardic. What's gotten into you?"

"We skipped the fish heads altogether for the past few years and look what happened. You aren't a judge anymore. Symon's no longer a professor. Whole careers down the drain. Family members going away. Innocent people getting beaten up and arrested for no reason. Too many funerals, too many suicides. Times are bad and getting worse. From now on we will honor our traditions, have a proper *Seder* at every holiday. I've been basting this sheep's head for two days and I want everyone to have a bite, at least some soup. You too. So hush up."

"I just don't understand why…"

"Cousin Rivkah is bringing the gelfite fish because Lord knows we need to be fruitful and multiply."

"We need to maintain the people already living." My father sat down, folded his arms and mashed his lips together.

"Come on, *Vati*, *Oma* Zip," I pleaded, "this is supposed to be a joyous occasion."

"I doubt things would've turned out differently if we'd just had the head of some animal on the dinner table." My father was adamant that religious faith and strict adherence to traditional rituals do not guarantee that prayers will be answered and that all will be well.

"Well, we'll never know now, will we?"

I knew my father wouldn't be partaking in the sheep's head "delicacy" which smelled strange and looked disgusting. No matter the taste, he spurned anything that was "too Jewish." He was respectful of the heritage, but preferred to assimilate into the dominant culture. He'd never wear a kippah outside of a synagogue and always did some kind of work on the Sabbath. I'd try some of the sheep's head, peel away whatever little meat there was, because *Oma* Zip would see to it, and because I liked to hedge my bets anyway.

"Julius, go wash up and help Gretchen with those apples."

"Okay, *Oma*."

We sliced red, green and yellow apples into perfect eighths and arranged them on *Oma* Zip's best crystal plates. Guests started to arrive, bearing more food and bottles of kosher wines. They came in hugging, kissing and wishing everyone a happy and blessed new year. "*Shana tovah!*" they exclaimed.

"*Shana tovah!*" I returned the salutation to friends and relatives I probably wouldn't be seeing for quite some time.

A few minutes before sundown, our celebration began. The rest of the candles were lit. We said the *Kiddush*, the blessing over the wine, and the *hamotzi*, the blessing over the round challah bread, essentially thanking the Creator for the fruit of the vine and the bread from the land.

"*L'Chaim!*" *Oma* Zip exclaimed, extending her elaborately engraved, silver Kiddush cup to everyone.

"*L'Chaim*," we all repeated, toasting to everyone's life and taking a sip of the sweet, kosher wine.

We broke off pieces of the honey-drizzled challah and passed it around. We dunked our apples into more honey and hoped for a sweet year to come. Platters of vegetables were passed around and we creatively incorporated their literal translation into our prayers. The black-eyed peas, or *rubiyah*, (similar to *yirbu* – to increase) is for God to grant us increase; carrots, or *gezer* (similar to the Hebrew word *g'zar* – to decree), represent a decree and we want all negative decrees against us to be nullified by the act of their consumption; the leeks, or *karsi* (similar to the Hebrew word *karat* – to cut down), were eaten so our enemies would be cut down and destroyed; the beets, or *selek* (similar to the Hebrew word *lesalek* – to remove) were eaten to eliminate our adversaries. I ate lots of leeks and beets just in case there was any mystical truth to any of it. We also partook of the "first fruit" of the season, pomegranate seeds mixed with rice and dates. *Oma* Zip prayed, "May we be as full of good deeds as the pomegranate is full of seeds."

I ate some of the goat's head which tasted sweet, tangy and gamey; it was rather interesting, something I wouldn't eat more than once a year and only on a special occasion. It was no lamp chop and I loved lamb chops. My Uncle Mordecai started telling one of his rambling stories about when he was in the service, in the German army, and it was a good fifteen minutes before he got to his point. "When I was in Greece, I had supper with some villagers. A goat's head was served and the special guest got to eat the eyeballs. It's considered a delicacy."

"Were you the special guest?" Gretchen asked.

"I was. I found eyeballs to be quite tasty. Very spicy. Not at all what I expected."

"Why in the world did you do that?" Gretchen asked.

"In some cultures, it's considered extremely rude, sometimes dangerously insulting, to decline any food or drink that is offered."

Oma Zip said, "Mordecai, if you wanted the eyeballs, all you had to do was ask."

"No, they should be offered to a special guest. Follow along, Zipporah."

"Everyone here is special."

"Aunt Hagar is the eldest," Gretchen offered.

"No thank you," she said.

"The Eislers came the farthest," Gabriel said. "All the way from Spreenhagen."

"We're still working on this tasty tongue. Enough body parts for us already!" Mr. Eisler said.

"Well, it's obvious," *Oma* Zip said. "My grandson Julius will be leaving us soon. Going to America to become a big-time lawyer. So *he* is our special Rosh Hashanah guest."

"Yay!" Some of the younger children cheered.

"No, no," I pleaded.

"Julius! Julius! Julius! Julius!" They got everyone to start clapping.

"I'm stuffed."

"Don't be silly," *Oma* Zip said. Eat the eyeball. Is good luck."

"Who says?" my father asked.

"I say," said *Oma* Zip. "Is good luck in some culture somewhere in this world. Who couldn't use a bit more luck these days?" She turned to my father. "You should eat the other one." There were chuckles at the thought of Alexander Sommerfeldt doing something totally unconventional.

"Not even if it was the only morsel left on earth."

Uncle Mordecai came around to where I was sitting and carried over the platter with the leftover goat parts so that it was in front of me. He put a fork in my hand and gave me instructions. "Okay, Julius, it's easy. Just poke, twist, pull, pop into your mouth and chew."

"Julius! Julius! Julius!"

My little cousin, Joseph, was riveted, looking at me with such admiration, just waiting for me to do something astounding. Gretchen looked at me daringly, hands on her ample hips. Gabriel was amused. My father's expression said, "Go ahead, you have the spotlight." *Oma* Zip wanted me to maximize my luck any way I could. I was curious – not about how it would taste and feel in my mouth – but what I was capable of doing when I put mind over matter. I did it. I poked the filmy eye that looked like a marble from a set I once had. It stared it me.

I twisted it, tugged it, and tugged it some more. Uncle Mordecai actually was there with a knife to dislodge it from its sinews. I popped it into my mouth. It felt rubbery, a little briny. I bit down and there was resistance. When it broke open, it was bloody and gristly, nothing like the half-shell oyster I'd imagined it'd be like, and I almost gagged trying to swallow it.

"Ewww!" the children said, covering up their own mouths with their tiny hands.

I washed it down with some of Uncle Mordecai's homemade plum wine, actually drained my glass in one, great gulp.

"Aah!" I said. "Tastes like chicken." Everyone laughed.

Oma Zip said, "Now you will have all the luck."

Uncle Mordecai popped out the other eyeball and chewed it up without a second thought. "Not all of it," he said.

After our meal, we went out to the backyard pond to celebrate *tashlikh*, the casting off of sins, by emptying our pockets and tossing bread crumbs into the water. *Oma* Zip thumped and shook a tambourine which I'd never seen her do before. I was surprised she even owned a tambourine. I regarded her curiously. She had one surprise after another.

Uncle Mordecai quoted from the book of Micah, "God will take us back in love and cover up our iniquities. Hurl your sins into the depths of the sea." The crumbs represented misdeeds, bad habits and poor choices made throughout the year and were to be consumed, vanished, nullified, by the giant, golden koi. The pond was soon strewn with challah crumbs and chrysanthemum petals and the thirty-odd people standing around singing actually felt lighter, having had our sins expunged for yet another year.

From the corner of my eye, I saw someone move quickly. I turned toward the splash. *Oma* Zip had jumped into the pond. She was wailing, beseeching God to forgive us, to help us, to save us from our enemies. This was a woman who'd been the spoiled daughter of a banker, the pampered wife of a judge. A few years ago, she'd been a white-gloved, high-heeled, Chanel suit-wearing society maven, very private about her religion, haughty in the presence of Bible-age piety, long, shaggy, matzo-catching beards, and the unfortunate, dull-colored *sheitels* covering up beautiful, tumbling hair. She'd have clutched her pearls and shaken her head at what she'd call "grotesque demonstrations of religiosity." Some old-world Jews had regarded her as a vile assimilator.

My father waded into the pond in his good loafers, demanding that she come out of there. He grabbed her by her elbow to pull her out. She refused at first, splashed around some, then came out willingly, looking stunningly refreshed, the white dress and pond scum plastered to the broad contours of her body.

"*Mutti*," father said, "if you're not careful, I'm going to have you committed to Bernburg."

Someone got an overcoat and put it over *Oma* Zip's shivering shoulders, but she shook it off. She retrieved her tambourine and began banging it again. It was a bizarre scene, unlike any of our traditionally staid family celebrations. For the second time that day, we were treated to the musical blasts of the *shofar*. It was a very meaningful part of Rosh Hashanah commemoration and had to be blown in a certain, precise way to ensure the awakening of people from their spiritual slumber.

Family and friends made their commitments for the upcoming year. We basically vowed to be more helpful, because even though we were going through difficult times, there were so many who were worse off. There were vows to be more industrious and enterprising even though the Nazi government quelled our efforts. We re-committed to thrift and industriousness, especially in the wake of lost jobs and sabotaged businesses. We vowed to stay strong during this time of adversity, to stay proud, have steely resolve, remember our roots, and to cling to family and community to blunt the impact of the Nazi onslaught. There were more prayers, more singing, more Old Testament recitations.

As we walked back into the apartment complex, Gretchen said to me, "I think I have a new idea about how to extend charity and compassion to others in the new year." Self-reflection, self-improvement and doing good deeds were part of the holiday commemoration.

"How?" I asked.

"I'm going to reach out to black people."

"Gretchen, you don't know any black people and you hardly ever see any black people."

"Well, when I do, I'm going to get to know them. There is this one girl in my class. I think they say she's from Egypt. She wears a veil, keeps to herself."

"Probably a nice Muslim girl."

"I'll try to get to know her. It should be interesting. I may even learn something. And if I see some other black people, I won't act like they're from outer space. I'll treat them nicely like they actually belong."

"They *do* belong, Gretchen. But that's a good idea. Good for you. I'm sure they'd appreciate that. I think I'll pledge the same thing. I'm sure there will be many blacks where I'm going. I believe Boston is pretty cosmopolitan."

And I was in great need of a change of scenery, a new perspective, some remarkable experiences, and some unique, new friends.

CHAPTER 33

THE EMCEE CONTINUED the presentation. "And this year I have the distinct pleasure of awarding the 1936 Spingarn medal posthumously to Mr. John Hope." The crowd stood again as members of John Hope's family went to the stage to accept the award in his honor. Mr. Hope, who'd died in April, had been president of an Atlanta college – Morehouse – and a tireless advocate for Negroes and higher education. There was a picture of Dr. Hope on an easel and it was evident that he'd been a very distinguished gentleman. His resume was very impressive and it was several minutes before the applause died down and people resumed their seats.

Having been the victim of discrimination in my own country, I was better able to appreciate the creation of schools for the exclusive education of the Negro race. I was devastated upon learning that I was no longer welcome at the same universities that had provided me a first-rate education since I was five years old. But good schools were becoming obsolete since critical thinking was discouraged and true knowledge was being replaced with outlandish, spoon-fed propaganda. The quality of education had declined dramatically since Hitler took over and the whole country was dumber for it.

One of Mr. Hope's relatives held the medal up, shook Joel Spingarn's hand, hugged him and everyone on the stage, thanked the committee for selecting him, stated that it must've been a difficult decision since there are so many great people to nominate, and that Mr. Hope would've been extremely honored.

The medal was beautiful. It was a gold, engraved disk with a navy and gold satin ribbon so it could be hung around the recipient's neck. It was much like the medals that were awarded at the Olympic games. This brought to mind the telegram I received from my cousin Gabriel that day. It read "Need to know if you're coming home for the Olympics. Things have gotten better. Miss you and need you here. –Gabriel".

I'd love to see home again and was giving it serious thought. Uncle Sy said I should go. Everyone back home said all evidence showed that Hitler was de-escalating his persecution of Jews, mainly because he wanted to project a more agreeable image since the whole world would be watching him and his regime as international athletes competed in his capital city.

America had abandoned the idea of boycotting the Games after US Olympics head, Avery Brundage, who admitted he didn't care for Jews and belonged to a country club that excluded Jews, conducted a "fact-finding" mission in Berlin and concluded that Jewish athletes were perfectly content and being treated fairly.

A former girlfriend of Gabriel's, a swimmer, said she'd been interviewed by Brundage with a German translator and hovering Gestapo officers:

"As a Jewish athlete, you're able to enter the facilities and use the pools and equipment to practice for the Olympic trials?" Brundage asked.

"Yes," she answered.

"You fully believe sponsorship and selection will be based strictly on merit and not race or creed?"

"Yes."

"Do you or any other Jews feel threatened or mistreated by the present administration?"

"No."

"Good! And I understand the synagogues are packed and unimpeded."

"Yes."

"Would you agree that any suggestions by American Jews that the Games be boycotted is foolish and, in all likelihood, a Communist plot to keep the United States out, discourage other nations from participating and undermine the Games?"

"Yes."

"And that would be an embarrassment to your President Hitler?"

"Yes."

"Because any problems between your government and the Jews is a political one and irrelevant to friendly athletic competition?"

"Right."

"Fine. Might I get your photograph?"

"Yes."

"Smile brightly. You can do better than that. Okay. Dismissed."

"What a bastard," Gabriel said. "I'll bet your knees were shaking the whole time."

"Literally. I was surrounded by both German and American Nazis."

She said all her answers had been total lies but, under the circumstances, she felt intimidated into giving those responses. She'd been one of many Jews to provide Brundage with the "evidence" he needed to convince the Amateur Athletic Union that there'd be no racial or religious discrimination since that went against Olympic ideals. The boycott was narrowly rejected. Regardless, Gabriel's friend didn't "qualify" for the Olympic team even though she had a three-minute, 200-meter breaststroke. The only Jew allowed to represent Germany was Helene Mayer, a German-born, half-Jew fencing champion who lived in America and adored Hitler and swastikas.

Germany was awarded the Games before Hitler came to power and was now relishing the opportunity to showcase "Aryan superiority." They'd spent the past two years constructing a world-class stadium and couldn't wait to flaunt this titanic symbol of the "new Germany." For the time being, Hitler would stop the saber-rattling and show tolerance towards Jews and other "degenerates." Everyone was hoping that the worse was over. Even with the passing of the Nuremburg Laws that stripped the Jewish people of their German citizenship and excluded us from virtually every aspect of civic life, people were still breathing a sigh of relief. As King Solomon said, "This too shall pass."

We'd just have to live with discrimination, marginalization and the bouts of random and systemic violence. Other groups did. It must've been terrifying being a protestant while the Catholic church was torturing millions of heretics. The Ottoman empire massacred over a million Armenians. The Islamists hate the Hindus, the Japanese detest the Chinese and vice versa. Men want to subjugate women and, in America, whites continue to tyrannize blacks and have a history of murdering and forcefully removing the Indians from their own land. Undoubtedly, even the meek would step up to cast stones at a revealed homosexual. It's *all* irrational and reprehensible.

Living in the margins, always flinching from anticipated violence, was nothing new to Jewish people. So, figuratively speaking, we've been pushed onto remote reservations; our homeland in Berlin has turned into a big, ruthless southern plantation. It was our turn to suffer, to be vilified and victimized. Again.

The Jewish people are constantly having to hearken back to our heritage, to remind ourselves that we're an eternally put-upon, yet proud, sturdy and resilient group. Now many Jews were returning to the fatherland where their families, synagogues, businesses and bank accounts were although anything could be suddenly shuttered or seized arbitrarily. I knew I'd be returning to Germany at some point. Although I hadn't seen Hollywood or the Grand Canyon yet, the coming of the Olympics seemed like as good a time as any.

CHAPTER 34

Justinia

I FOUND A telephone booth near the Sharp Street Memorial Church and made my daily scheduled call home to Highand Beach. Immediately, Mother wanted to know the exact time I'd arrive home on Sunday after the convention's closing session. She was hosting a dinner party and wanted to plan it accordingly.

"We must make up for that disaster of a party from last week," she said.

It was not Magdalena's fault the last gathering, a boxing match listening party, did not go well. The food was delicious, the alcohol was plentiful and the right combinations of guests had been assembled. There was a radio hooked up to speakers outside on the terrace where the party was held. Everyone was excited about the fight. Nobody had expected Joe Louis to lose.

I happen to think boxing is violent and pointless, yet even I got swept up in the preparations. Mother asked me to make flower arrangements and help frost cupcakes even though my father said that was ridiculous because people weren't coming for a champagne brunch or a formal dinner, they were coming to eat barbecue and listen to the fight. Fresh-cut roses in Waterford vases and pink, cherry-topped cupcakes did not go together with a pig roasting on a spit in the backyard and a keg of beer. But my mother said that style and class are appropriate for any occasion and of course my father just chuckled and shook his head. There were several listening parties going on in Highland Beach and my mother aimed to have the most talked-about one.

The boxing match was a very big deal. The newspapers were calling it the "fight of the century" and the "Brown Bomber" was undefeated and favored to beat Max Schmeling, the German heavyweight who was said to be way past his prime and a Hitler "puppet." People still remembered him as the Nazi who got embarrassed by the Jewish boxer, Max Baer, who wore the Star of David on his trunks and carried the yearnings of the entire American Jewry on his shoulders. When Baer knocked Schmeling down in the tenth round, he yelled at him, "That one was for Hitler!" The papers were all saying how the Baer victory was a victory for the Jews and for America and a defeat for Hitler and Nazi Germany. As Negro people, we could commiserate.

"So how are things at the convention?" my mother asked me.

"I'm really enjoying it. I met a really nice...."

"Have you seen the Chandler twins yet? Their mother assured me they'd be there by now. They were to be a little late coming from California where they just graduated from Stanford. You do remember them from Camp Atwater, don't you?"

"Not really, mother. It's been ten years since I've seen them. I have no idea what they look like now and there are hundreds of people here."

Actually I did remember the Chandler twins. They were the most obnoxious campers at Atwater, a summer camp created for privileged Negro children. The Chandler twins laughingly pointed their arrows at people during archery class, pushed weak swimmers into the pool and heckled the brown-skinned kids, telling them they should stay out of the sun before they got blacker. They caught a garter snake and put it in my suitcase; it scared me half to death when I opened it to retrieve some stationery. They sent everyone into a panic by swearing they saw a bear in the woods. They spoke rudely to the counselors who said those twins were out of control; they dreaded their arrival with all their mischief and special dietary needs and couldn't wait for them to leave. Now in their early twenties, I wouldn't be surprised if they were still insufferable brats.

"Well ask around," my mother urged. "It's important to stay in touch with quality people. Your father and I sent you, Charlotte and Emery to Massachusetts for camp so you could forge lifelong friendships with children from good Negro families from all across the country. It's time to start capitalizing on those connections. They may even know some good men."

"Mother, please. I certainly don't need their help finding a man."

"Well you haven't settled on one yet. Vincent, Tristan, Bradford, Griffin – you let all of them slip through your fingers." Yes, all of them were smart, Greek-lettered and well-to-do, but had the personality of white wallpaper.

"People might begin to wonder if you're a lesbian."

"Mother!"

"Well, dear, it happens; just like some Negroes get the sickle cell. Look at Paul Laurence Dunbar's wife, Alice. And DuBois' daughter Yolande, poor thing, didn't find out about Countee Cullen until *after* their fabulous nuptials, when he used his Guggenheim Fellowship to go to Paris and took their best man with him. Alice and Countee both hid it very well which, in retrospect, is good *and* bad. It must be something about poets. And, quiet as it's kept, your idol Josephine Baker is also suspect."

"Mother, please. This conversation is ludicrous. And I like *men*."

"But you're never satisfied, Justinia. I keep telling you that you'll never find everything you want all in one package. What's important is that he be nice, well-bred and able to keep you in the lifestyle to which you are accustomed. Speaking of which – how is Xavier?"

"Xavier is Xavier."

"You know he's extremely fond of you."

"Yes, I know."

"Anyway, the twins' mother says they're both going to study Business at Penn. Those two are still two peas in a pod. For the convention, they're staying with a prominent Creole family at a quaint brownstone uptown. Try to locate them."

"I'll try," I said as if a "quaint brownstone uptown" was enough of a clue, but I had no intention of looking for them anyway. And if I saw two people with the can't-miss big, round manila faces with hazel eyes and frizzy, blond hair, I'd turn around and walk briskly in the other direction.

"You do that. And be sure to tell them to tell their parents that we send our love."

"Fine. By the way, I did meet this one guy – very charming – and he, Millie and I might be participating in a public protest."

"What guy, what kind of protest?" Her voice trailed off as if she were distracted by something. I heard her tell Lily that she'd be right there.

"Justinia, I must go. Lily needs my direction for something."

"Okay, mother, I'll call back tomorrow to let you know what time to expect me."

"Alright, but I'd like to serve the cheese course no later than five. Try not to be tardy."

"Yes, mother."

"Find the twins."

"I'll try."

CHAPTER 35

I CAUGHT UP with Julius after the Spingarn Award Ceremony. We'd spoken several times since our first encounter. The two of us took a picture together with the remarkable Mary McCleod Bethune. He, Millie and I took another one with Thurgood Marshall and Professor Charles Hamilton Houston. Millie gushed over Thurgood, told him how he is inspiring her to become a civil rights lawyer. She asked him to autograph her *Crisis* magazine and he obliged, joking, "It's times like this, meeting good people like you, young lady, that I'm glad I decided not to become a dentist." We all laughed.

"But then you get all those courtroom doors slammed in your face, literally and figuratively, and pulling teeth and filling cavities doesn't seem so bad." We laughed again. "But I'd just be bored and unfortunately, good dental hygiene doesn't change the world." He said his brother was a heart surgeon and that cracking open patients' chests seemed far easier than cracking some of these hard-hearted judges.

"Well thank you for not becoming a dentist," Millie said.

"You're welcome."

In his spare time, Julius said he'd done some volunteer work for Houston and Marshall while they worked on the Murray case which really impressed me. He did anything from extra research to making coffee. He was one of the top graduates at Georgetown Law School and decided to work for the Legal Aid Society which was fitting because it was initially created to provide free legal services to German immigrants and now helped hundreds of indigent clients of all nationalities.

However, Julius could've been at any of the white-shoe, silk stocking law firms that were all over Washington and to which Xavier aspired to be the one exotic, back-office associate who was allowed to surface only when the firm needed to demonstrate their commitment to racial progressiveness. I knew several other people with law degrees who savored the idea of being "the first," did not mind being a "token," and were perfectly content sitting in a stuffy library, doing research, writing briefs and never meeting clients, going to court or getting credit for their contributions. And they did it for a fraction of what was paid to white associates. It was still prestigious and paid better than the government and most struggling Negro firms.

Daddy says there were fewer than 1300 Negro lawyers in the entire country and, in most states, they could be counted on one hand. The majority of Negro lawyers who hung out their own shingle were held in high esteem in the community but, with the exception of my father and some of his friends, lived hand to mouth. Xavier's eyes grow large at the prospect of making lots of money, and he was not really concerned whether his work would have any utilitarian impact. He was convinced that he'd be one of those "chosen" Negroes who wouldn't be hidden, but showcased in one of the larger, front offices, be welcomed into the dimly lit, paneled Good Ol' Boys' club room where he'd join in the jovial back-slapping and have a thick cigar thrust into his fingertips and lit by a snooty Negro attendant. Between puffs, they'd discuss ways to prevent their client from paying a settlement to a plaintiff who was run over by a corporate van that had a lead-footed driver and bad brakes, or how to convince a jury that a deformed baby was the fault of the mother and not the medication that the obstetrician should've never prescribed. It was Xavier's dream to be part of those equations and calculations.

If anyone could pierce that tough racial shield it was Xavier. He'd already accepted a position as a summer intern – a glorified errand boy according to my father who said Xavier could learn some *real* law by clerking for *him* – at Preminger and Price which had penthouse offices in Washington's august Munsey Trust Building. But Xavier was excited about taking the elevator to the top floor, walking through the mahogany and brass double doors and being greeted by the humorless, blond receptionist who was instructed to greet him as *Mister* Brathwaite.

After talking to Julius, however, it was evident that *he* was more interested in helping people and, although it sounds cliché, making the world a better place to live for everyone. He happened to believe that if qualified applicants wanted to go to a particular college or graduate school, that they should be able to go, regardless of their religion or skin color. He thought that if someone spent their life savings buying a car, that it should run, that if a retired railroad worker was entitled to a pension, that the company should pay it.

"Call me crazy," Julius would say, "but at the very least, I think everyone should be allowed to vote, get health care and live in a decent home, not those severely overcrowded alley dwellings where most of my clients live without plumbing or garbage collection right in the shadow of your United States government."

Chapter 36

It was true. There was unspeakable poverty in D. C., including the Foggy Bottom section near George Washington University and the White House. Entire communities of extended families, mostly blacks and a sprinkling of whites, lived in makeshift shelters in the alleyways behind middle and upper-class homes that faced the street. Since before the Civil War, there was an influx of German and Irish immigrants and, later, former slaves who transformed old storefronts, silos, horse stables and carriage houses into multi-generational homes with uncredited resourcefulness and ingenuity. The alley slums were supposedly breeding grounds for disorder, depravity, disease and death and Eleanor Roosevelt was appalled when she toured them and was fighting to eliminate them and establish a decent public housing system.

Despite the deplorable conditions, pristine white sheets flapped on clothes lines like flags of truce, surrender, or offers to negotiate with whatever oppressive entities that were limiting the progress or egress of the residents. Outdoor church services were still held regardless of the proximity to trash, drunks and junkyard cats and dogs. Columns of collards, turnips, tomatoes and onions thrived right next to yellowed, spring-popping mattresses and mounds of ashes emptied from coal-burning stoves. People laughed, cried or showed stoic resignation. Cheeriness and hopefulness existed side by side with despair and melancholy.

I saw this firsthand when, after church one September Sunday, my father drove us all to Goat Alley so he could pay the eight dollars he owed to a man who had, earlier that week, chopped and delivered firewood to our home and stacked it in the shed because my mother, prone to chills and with an affinity for ambiance, insisted on a brightly lit hearth everyday in autumn, winter and spring. My father also wanted us to see how blessed we were by seeing how poor people lived. He said the children hungered for food as well as knowledge, the women worked harder than men and the men worked harder than mules when they could find work. They cared about their families and wanted the best for them, just as he and Magdalena wanted the best for me, Charlotte and Emery. They deserved better, he said.

"Look," someone yelled as we pulled up. "Them some *rich* niggers!" Daddy gave him a salute.

We did not get out of the car – my mother would've vehemently objected – but the visit was eye-opening enough from where we sat in our plush, Italian leather seats. There was so much activity, a virtual hive of Negro survivability, in one long alley that was no wider than thirty feet across. At the end of the alley, behind some trees, the rotunda of the United States capitol loomed large – a farcical snapshot. Daddy tooted the horn. People looked up from their Bibles, dice games, whiskey bottles and nursing infants to stare at us.

"Church" was in session and one of the men who was haggard but handsome, noticed us and unhooked himself from the pray-moaning, standing-room-only congregation, and came up to our car. He was holding the hand of a little boy dressed in a clean but tattered shirt, too-short, patched-up pants and no shoes or socks. The man removed his hat when he saw Magdalena in the passenger seat, acknowledged her with a polite "Ma'am," but avoided eye contact with anyone but my father. The boy, who I assumed was his son, looked at us like Daddy was Santa and we were a sleigh full of elves. He rubbed the exterior of our burgundy Buick only to have his little hand smacked by his father who then wiped the finger smudges off with his shirt tail. My father gave him his money, plus a generous tip, and the man my father called Leon looked very pleased.

"Thank you, sir. Rent due. Wife tryna buy a chicken to go with the okra and dumplins she makin' for supper." He sounded so excited. Lily says that when poor people get chicken, they eat it all – the giblets, the neck, the skin, even the tail – and sucked every bit of flavor out of the feet. Leon's grin was snaggle-toothed. "We 'bout sick to death of squirrel."

"Squirrel!" said Emery, horrified as one scampered by. "Yuk!" Charlotte pinched him before he embarrassed everybody even more.

The little boy looked at Leon and asked excitedly, "We gon' have us some chicken tonight, daddy?"

"Hush up, Junior."

They chatted briefly and my father told Leon that he'd have more work for him at one of the rental properties sometime next week.

"'Preciate that, Mr. Treadwell. You know where to find me."

"Gotta job for *me*, massa?" an old man sidled up and asked.

Leon shooed him away and walked back to join the church service where the preacher was leading everyone in singing, *a cappella*, "What a Friend We Have in Jesus." We'd sung the same hymn in church that morning, only we relied on crisp, new-smelling hymnals rather than memory, and it sounded less rustic; the voices were smoother and our classically-trained organist added a nice, ethereal aspect to it. We watched for several minutes before my mother said softly, "Okay, Jasper, we should leave." I found both versions to be nice and heartfelt.

We observed for another five minutes because that's how long it took for my father to put the Buick in reverse and, hand over hand over hand, maneuver it 180 degrees out of the tight spot at the end of the alley so we could go back the way we entered. The alley people stared uninhibitedly at us and we watched them surreptitiously from the sides of our eyes because mother taught us it was impolite to stare. But it was difficult to tear our eyes away because there was so much to see and digest and my conscience was being indelibly marked.

"He seemed nice," I said.

"He's a good guy," my father said, "a real hard worker who supports his wife, two babies, his parents and in-laws — at least eight people — all living in a one-room hovel. Imagine having only one room to sit, sleep, eat, cook and bathe in. Some people have been here forever, have never even seen the White House a few blocks away — never mind any place outside of Washington."

"That's awful," I said. As children we went to the White House every year for the traditional Easter Egg Roll on the lawn.

"Times are incredibly hard for most people. They're tired, cramped, sick and starving. Remember that the next time you refuse to eat your liver or complain about your allowance."

"Yes, sir."

Charlotte, Emery and I were quiet for several minutes as we contemplated how that many people could live in roughly 300 square feet, share one scrawny chicken, and make twelve dollars stretch until Leon got paid again. It was incomprehensible. In one shopping trip I spent more than twelve dollars on a bunch of shoes I hadn't even worn yet. At home, Cornish hens awaited us, and Reverend Crawford and his wife would be our Sunday guests. I vowed only to eat the vegetables. Life most certainly was not fair.

The tune stuck in her head, my mother hummed "What a Friend We Have in Jesus" as we left Leon and his alley neighbors and headed back to our brick, tri-level, eight-room house on sunny, tree-lined T Street in LeDroit Park. It was down the block from the home of Mary Church Terrell and the late Judge Robert Terrell, who also owned a beach home near ours. It wasn't far from where Paul Laurence Dunbar and his wife integrated the area in the late 1880s and was within walking distance of a legion of clergy, teachers, Howard professors, professionals, business leaders and government office workers.

Years after delivering the money to Leon, the alleys were still teeming with poor, unemployed, uneducated inhabitants. These were the people who made up a large portion of Julius' client base and whose children might be in my kindergarten class when school started in September. Their problems were complex and manifold and the people in a position to ease the pain were, for the most part, uncaring and unmoving.

But Julius was not deterred. He got a judge to grudgingly order a landowner to stop cheating sharecroppers by claiming they owed "miscellaneous fees" that were arbitrary and unsubstantiated. That Julius cared about people so alien to his own existence was admirable, oddly alluring. It was unfortunate that Julius had to leave behind his family and home in Germany, but many people were blessed by his sojourn in America.

CHAPTER 37

AFTER THE PICTURE-TAKING and glad-handing at the NAACP awards ceremony, there was still time before we were expected back at the boarding house where we were staying during the convention. Many conventioneers had to be resourceful when scouting out a place to stay because all the decent nearby hotels claimed to have no vacancies. There were some sympathetic whites, however, who went out to some of these "at capacity" hotels, registered as the guests, then snuck their Negro friends in through utility doors in the back. The hotel staff eventually caught on and kicked some people out. When some NAACP operatives complained, they were told that the people were "removed" because they had "perpetrated a fraud" and not because they were Negro.

Other people stayed with friends and relatives or in dormitories at the Negro colleges of which there were four – Morgan State, Bowie State, Coppin State and the University of Maryland - Eastern Shore. Some people even bunked in the basements of churches.

The place where Millie and I were staying was airy and comfortable. The little Negro woman who owned it, Mrs. Tuttle, had apple cinnamon tea simmering all day and it made the entire house smell delectable, like the autumn holidays. There was a creaky swing on the front porch and I took every available opportunity to enjoy it. Two at a time, we took turns on it with two other girls from out of town.

Magdalena said socializing on the front porch, especially barefooted with our skirts hiked up around our thighs, like we were doing, was "uncouth." Getting my hair brushed in full view of the dog walkers and the night shift workers walking to the bus stop, calling out to them "How ya doin'?" and answering "Just fine, thank you" when they asked us back, would be considered conduct unbecoming a woman of my station. But such a simple thing was liberating. Millie and I and the two young ladies from Philadelphia had the best time trading stories, catching lightning bugs, swatting mosquitoes, chewing Juicy Fruit gum and slurping syrupy lemonade from Mason jars which would've sent my mother over the edge had she been there to see it.

We talked about why we joined the NAACP. Leddy said she was drawn to its commitment to education. She'd gone to an across-town school with out-of-date, hand-me-down books and inadequate heating and cooling systems when there was a brand new segregated school for whites right around the corner from her house. She knew she had to fight to change things. Shirley joined after doing a current events essay for her Composition class; she'd learned much about lynching and couldn't rest until she was part of the movement to eliminate it. Millie told them she loved how they used litigation in tandem with such things as noose demonstrations to make change and how she wanted to be an agent of change. I agreed. The four of us talked about the convention, movies, men and our families. I couldn't have asked for better company. And I was sure our accommodations were better at Mrs. Tuttle's boarding house than they would have been at those segregated hotels.

The only problem was that Mrs. Tuttle wanted all her boarders in by ten. So much for my temporary liberation. I wondered if I'd ever get to come and go as I pleased. "The only folks out past nine o'clock are bums, pimps, whores and crooks," she said as she took the two ten-dollar bills Millie and I gave her and stuck them down in her bosom.

Returning to the couch and her needlepoint project, she said "I'll allow an hour grace period since you girls are here for the convention and I 'preciate what the NAACP does, but the house is locked up tight at ten sharp. That's a house rule. Don't say I didn't warn you. You'll find yourself sleeping on the porch swing."

"Yes, ma'am."

"If you want dinner, it's at six. The kitchen closes at seven but I'll leave you some plates in the oven if you let me know in advance."

"Well we appreciate your hospitality, Mrs. Tuttle and you have such a pretty home."

"My late husband and I raised thirteen chil'ren in this house. All successful. All got they own businesses or good government jobs. NAACP helped with some of that. They are a very useful organization. Of course maintaining a good Christian household is the main reason we're so blessed."

"Indeed."

"Don't forget. Ten sharp!"

"We won't forget."

CHAPTER 38

I WANTED TO make the most of my time in Baltimore and we still had a couple of hours before Mrs. Tuttle's curfew so I said, "Let's go get some frozen custard. There's a place not too far from here. I believe it's the same place my father took us when we were kids."

"I'm game," Julius said. "Let's go."

As Millie, Julius and I were walking out, Xavier came up and asked where we were going. I told him we were in search of some good frozen custard.

He looked as if I'd just said the Easter Bunny was real. He pulled me aside. "Two unchaperoned women in an unfamiliar city?"

"Baltimore is not that unfamiliar and we are not 'unchaperoned.' Julius will be with us."

"Julius? You don't know that man. He could be another Jack the Ripper for all you know. I was going to go have a drink with some of my fraternity brothers. But I guess I'll go with *you* now."

"Suit yourself." He went over to a group of spiffily dressed gentlemen to tell them to go on without him. Annoyingly, he was back by my side a minute later. His fraternity brothers, curious, watched us walk out into the muggy air.

"Glad you're joining us, Xavier," Julius said.

"No you aren't," Xavier responded.

I gently elbowed him in the ribs. "Be nice."

We walked several blocks, chatting amiably about the weather, the awards ceremony – safe topics to keep Xavier and Julius from having disagreements.

Lauren Cecile

We finally sidled up to a little shop that said "Vogelsang's" on a candy-striped awning. It looked so welcoming. "I think this is it," I said.

"Ah, a German establishment," Julius noted.

We looked inside; the patrons were all white. We walked in, got in line and looked at the menu on the wall behind the counter. The place was air conditioned and felt wonderful. We were grateful for the coolness after all the walking we did in eighty-five degree heat.

Julius said, "Oh, it feels so good in here."

"I could sit in here forever," Millie said.

I didn't need to read the menu, my palate was ready for some super-rich vanilla frozen custard swirled into a warm waffle cone. I remember it being sinfully delicious.

"Sounds good," said Julius. "I think I'll have the same."

"We're closed." A prune-faced woman with no lips came out of nowhere wiping her hands on an apron.

"You don't look closed," Julius said.

"Well we are."

"We'll take our custard to go," Xavier said. "We have no intention of staying here."

"No to-go orders," she said. To underscore her point, she went to the door and turned around the *Yes, We're Open* sign to the opposite *Sorry, We're Closed* side.

The other patrons eventually realized that something was going on and got quiet to watch the drama unfold. I couldn't believe it. Even in our tailored silks and gabardines, we weren't good enough to be served a scoop of custard; but those donning loose-fitting, washed-out, rough-hewn gingham were greeted with wide smiles and gifted with extra whipped cream or double the nuts merely because of their white skin and not because they'd done something good to deserve it. I was wearing Bulgari pearl earrings – heirloom – and this woman looked at me like I was lower than a toad.

"So you're refusing to serve us?" Millie asked.

"I'm saying we're *closed.*"

"I see what's going on," Julius said. "As a German citizen, you shame me."

"You're no German citizen," she said, dropping all pretenses, her thick German accent suddenly evident. "You're just another nigger-loving Jew. Now get out, all of you. Just because that NAACP is in town doesn't mean you get special privileges this week."

The soda jerk and the man wiping off tables looked mortified, as if they were just learning that their employer was a Nazi racist. One man stood up and applauded the woman who must have been the proprietor, Mrs. Vogelsang.

A middle-aged woman raised her hand and shouted "You tell 'em Elke! They tryna take things way too far! Those people will never be my equal." She looked around for confirmation and only saw vacant expressions. They were mostly quiet and obviously uncomfortable.

One young woman worker shrugged her shoulders apologetically at us and the customers at another table got up and pitched their barely-touched sundaes into the garbage. "We're terribly sorry," they said to us as they brushed past us and left the store. A few others followed.

"Look what you're doing!" Mrs. Vogelsang said. "Your antics are costing me business. Leave now or I'll call the police."

"You will lose more," Julian said, "once everyone realizes that you're a detestable Nazi."

"*Ich hoffe Du stirbst!*" she yelled at Julian who looked like he'd been slapped.

"*Ich hoffe, Sie finden ein Herz!*" he replied.

Millie said, "I'm sure we can get much better custard elsewhere."

Xavier looked at his pocket watch. "Let's get out of here," he said. "I haven't any time for this."

We walked out. "This was foolish," Xavier said to me. "We're supposed to be very careful about which establishments we enter so we can avoid scenes like that. Someone should have staked it out first. Have you forgotten those endless D & D lectures?"

He turned to Julius. "Did you convince her to do this? To go to some random German place? With all that's going on in Germany, we should be avoiding anything remotely German."

Julius said, "The fact of the matter is that there're more Germans than any other ethnic group in Baltimore. There are many German businesses in this area so the odds were good we'd end up at one." He kicked a pebble out of his path, still reeling from the encounter.

"I've been here three years and have seen most businesses treat Negroes kindly and very few with hostility. That lady back there, though, takes the cake. I guess if there's no firsthand knowledge about a particular place, it can be a crap shoot."

"You sound like you think you're some kind of expert," Xavier said. "You have no idea what it's like for Negroes here or anywhere else. That's like me going to Berlin and telling a Jew that most of the Nazis I've met seem to be friendly and...."

"I certainly don't mean to imply..."

"It was my idea," I said in an effort to stop Julius from digging himself into a deeper hole and from Xavier throwing more dirt on top of him. "I *know* my father has taken us here before. That's how I know about the custard. I remember the awning."

"It's a common awning, Justinia," Xavier said.

"But it *has* been several years. Maybe it was a different owner back then."

Regardless, I was shocked at the degree of malevolence expressed by this Elke Vogelsang woman, that her hatred was so much stronger than her business sense. I wondered if the tailor to her left or the wig shop owner on her right felt the same way she did. Would Meuller's, the print shop directly across the street, have agreed to print NAACP pamphlets? If not, would Mr. Meuller have just shaken his head and calmly sent the messenger on his way or would he have angrily flung the originals across the room? How did segregationists, integrationists, fence-sitters and stoics, coexist on one short, little block? This was an iteration of the problem that Lincoln admonished against – that a house divided, a country that was half-slave and half-free, could not stand. It was vexing.

"Most Germans are good-hearted people," Julius said. "Both here and abroad. But like I said inside, I'm embarrassed to be German right now."

"You don't have to apologize for all the hateful Germans," I said.

"I guess not," Xavier said. "I certainly don't apologize for all the ignorant, shiftless Negroes hanging about in shadowy doorways, with their boozy breath, waiting to rob you of your property."

"Wow, man," Julius said.

Millie elbowed me. "What did that awful woman say to Julius?"

"She said, 'I hope you die.'"

"And what did he say?"

"He said, 'I hope you find a heart.'"

We walked in silence for a long time.

At some point, Julius hailed a cab. We got in. The cab dropped us off at Mrs. Tuttle's house at 9:00. I thought it was a wasted night.

CHAPTER 39

THE WEEK BEFORE, everyone in Highland Beach was anxiously anticipating the Schmeling-Louis bout. It had been another opportunity to prove that good was stronger than evil, that democracy was better than totalitarianism. It was these hopes and burdens that the "Brown Bomber" carried with him into the ring. Every Negro in America, rich or poor, boxing fan or not, stood to benefit from a boost in morale and pride if Louis beat Schmeling just as Baer had beat Schmeling. Maybe it was too much for one man to bear.

My girlfriends, including Georgine and Millie, and I were in the parlor listening to Duke Ellington records. We lost interest in the fight after the first couple of rounds, preferring to dance around the room in our stockinged feet to "Showboat Shuffle" and "Echoes of Harlem" played over and over, wearing out the grooves in the album. We pushed the sofas against the walls and rolled up the Oriental rug so we could really move. We were having a great time until Georgine started making snide remarks about Millie's dance moves.

"Where'd you learn to dance like that?"

"Like what? We're both doing the lindy hop."

The two of them had been dancing in tandem. Georgine stopped abruptly and just watched, arms folded like she was disgusted. Millie kept going. Rock, step, left-right-left, step, step, right-left-right, then turn! She was an excellent dancer and was enjoying herself, being Millie.

"When you do it, it just looks so...vulgar."

A friend of ours, Bonnie Blackshear, said "Georgine, you're just jealous because Millie's a better dancer than you are."

"Well, that may be how they dance in D. C. slums, but in DuPont Circle, we don't do all that hip shaking and finger popping."

"What an unkind thing to say," I told Georgine.

Millie was unfazed. "I guess we just have more spirit in the 'slums' than you do in your little uptight, utopian cocoon."

Dahlia, who always echoed Georgine's every sentiment, said, "I'm with you, Georgine. Bernard would never approve of my dancing that way in public. It looks *orgasmic* with your eyes all closed and everything. It's so uncouth."

"If that's orgasmic, that doesn't say much for your love life," Bonnie said. "But then you *are* engaged to Bernard." We laughed.

Bonnie explained to Millie that Bernard (known affectionately as That Old Widowed Accountant Who Finally Got Himself A Young Redbone) was as exciting as a wet noodle." Everyone but Dahlia laughed.

"I can imagine what *else* is a wet noodle," said Caroline Carter. We doubled over in laughter.

Bonnie went on to say that since Georgine had spent four years of her life at Wellesley, one could only expect the stiffest, most lackluster dance steps. "You know those white girls couldn't dance."

"As if Dartmouth was any better."

"It was co-ed. There are men there. Keeps a girl on her toes. Seriously, what can you do with a Bing Crosby song?"

Everyone, including the "white school" graduates, continued to laugh, enjoying the chance to tease Georgine who was usually the teaser.

Millie never missed a beat, she got fancier, doing twirls that would make Georgine, and most of us, feel dizzy and fall down. A couple of the girls followed her lead, executing clumsily, but having a good time nonetheless.

Bonnie said, "Have mercy on her, Millie, teach Georgine how to *really* Lindy Hop."

"She knows the steps. The rest is intuitive. It can't be taught."

"Like the Duke says," Caroline added, "It don't mean a thing if it ain't got that swing."

"Doo-wah, doo-wah, doo-wah!" a chorus of us sang and started laughing all over again.

Georgine, miffed, went over to the buffet, got a cupcake from the silver tray and proceeded to lick off the thick, swirly coat of icing. I could tell she was thinking of something scathing to say.

"I'd rather be rich and a mediocre dancer than a good dancer who's poor."

"Really, Georgine!" I said. "That was uncalled for." I hated when she forced me to mediate.

Millie stopped dancing. For a minute all you heard was the signature muted wah-wah trumpet wails and the tinny cymbals from Ellington's band. She went and stood nose to nose with Georgine. "Who're you calling poor?"

"Poor, blue collar, no collar, take your pick."

"Just because I don't live in a mansion and get every stupid thing my heart desires doesn't mean I'm poor. You disparage my daddy's name when you call me poor. My daddy is the hardest working....."

Georgine put her finger up like she was scolding a two-year old. "Your daddy scrubs floors at the hospital....."

"My daddy does lots of things...."

"....I've seen him, had to tell him he missed a spot."

"Her daddy does *what*?" Dahlia demanded, standing up with her hands on her hips. She looked at me as if demanding to know why someone like Millie was undeservingly basking in rarefied air.

"Mumsy says her daddy might still have a halfway decent job if he weren't such a trouble maker, stirring up the workers to join unions and such."

"This is insane!" Millie sat down and began putting her shoes back on; she'd dance no more that night. "My father warned me about being around people like you. All sham and tinsel, and no substance. Money isn't everything."

"Money makes the world go 'round," Georgine said. "And if we depended on your father, the world would come to a screeching halt."

"How dare you."

"I didn't make the rules. I just live by them."

Millie was headed to my bedroom to listen to records by herself. She turned around and said, "By the way, those same rules you love so much encouraged Wall Street greed and are responsible for the mess a lot of people are in today."

"Sure," said Dahlia. "Blame the system."

"Ignore them, Millie," said Bonnie who was definitely not just sham and tinsel. "You're absolutely right."

Bonnie's grandfather, John Blackshear, owned some kind of coal-energy plant and was richer than all of us. Most of us were wealthy, but the Blackshears were actually *rich* – somewhere between Vanderbilt-rich and Madame C. J. Walker-rich. While my family and many of my friends' families were counted among Washington's "premiere 400," Bonnie's family was in the "upper tens," the elite of the elite – predominantly pale, pedigreed, moneyed, and accomplished – heirs of Washington's original Negro aristocracy. The Blackshears had also been one of a handful of Negro families actually listed, alongside the all-white political elites, diplomats and captains of industry, in the D. C. social register during the Reconstruction era. Her charcoal-black uncle was on President McKinley's Inauguration committee – scandalous! More importantly, the Blackshears were also some of the most down-to-earth, charitable people one could ever meet. Despite not needing a paycheck, Bonnie was a guidance counselor at Dunbar.

"They're spoiled brats," Bonnie continued.

Georgine ignored Bonnie, continued to shake her finger at Millie. "Just because my father is a successful physician does not make me ignorant or spoiled – only blessed."

Millie stood back up and slapped Georgine's wagging finger away, launching the cupcake into the silk brocade curtains. "Ooooh, let me tell you a thing or two about your precious daddy, Georgine..."

I got between them, stretched out my arms to keep them apart, and I didn't want Millie to say something she might regret.

"Georgine, everyone knows that your father is held in high esteem," I said, "but you also know full well that Mr. Thomas is a respectable man."

"I don't know that. Do respectable people go on relief?"

"We are not on relief," Millie snapped.

"Oh no? Did you or did you not get free bread and cheese at the Y?"

Millie seethed, refusing to respond and Georgine said, "See, it must be true and she's too embarrassed to admit it."

"Not that I feel I must dignify your ignorant comments, but I'm a community relief volunteer and was passing out loaves of bread and hunks of cheese at the Y. But even if we did get relief, so what? Would you prefer people starve? Is that respectable to you – being so proud that you'd allow your family to starve?"

"Yes, Georgine," Bonnie said, "as usual, you don't have your facts straight. What do you say to that?"

Before she could respond, my brother Emery and some of his friends walked in at that exact moment, right before it got uglier.

"You all need to come outside quick. Wait, are you guys arguing?"

"No Emery. Just a little disagreement. What's going on?"

"Joe Louis is about to lose. The announcer says he's getting woozy, on the ropes, about to hit the mat. It's looking bad."

There was a horrified collective "What!" None of us followed boxing, but we did read the *Afro American* and the *Washington Bee* religiously. We read *Crisis* magazine and the *New York Times* quite often. We listened to the radio for hours a day. The consensus was that this match would be a walk in the park for the "Brown Bomber," that he would elevate, at least temporarily, the Negro race in the eyes of the world. We ran outside where everyone else was. I could barely hear because people were groaning and yelling. Georgine's father was screaming at the radio as if it were a living being.

"Get up, nigger, get up!"

The announcer was saying he didn't think Louis was going to get up, that he was too wounded after being stunned with two of Schmeling's right jabs to the body and the jaw.

Abigail Brathwaite, Ann Kirkwood, my mother and some of her associates from The Girl Friends were stock-still, aghast by Dr. Kirkwood's epithets and the fact that Joe Louis wasn't getting up. The radio announcer then said the referee called the fight, that it was a great upset and that the German underdog had just won the biggest fight of his career. Yankee Stadium was in a tizzy.

"No, no, no, no, no!" one of my father's friend said. "This cannot be happening."

"Goddamn it!" Dr. Kirkwood threw his glass at the radio and jumped out of his chair, overturning it. "That nigger ain't shit." The glass shattered when it hit the ground. The radio droned on about how Schmeling just had more heart, more stamina, had been better prepared, used his head and fought "smartly."

My father said, "I was *waiting* for one of those announcers to imply that a white guy's intelligence trumps a black guy's brute force. As if Louis doesn't have brains *and* brawn."

"Damn!"

Daddy reached over and switched the radio off. "Simmer down, Clarence. He had an 'off' night. You can't win them all."

"He was 23 and 0."

"23 and 1 now."

The women were quiet. The crickets were chirping an uncannily orchestrated cantata. We heard the waves off the Chesapeake lapping the shore. Mrs. Blackshear, Bonnie's mother, had tears running down her face. Millie, her altercation with Georgine forgotten, collapsed on a step like she herself was defeated. She covered her face with her hands. The rest of us stood with our mouths wide open. Inside the house, I heard Lily and some of the servers crying like someone had died. There was a tremendous clanging of pots and pans in the kitchen.

The emotional outpouring continued. My mother allowed everyone to lament a few minutes more, then tried to salvage the evening.

"Now, now, it's not the end of the world." She picked up a deck of cards. "Bridge anyone? Whist?" No one was interested. "More sangria?"

There was a barrage of no thank yous and we'd better be goings. We thought it'd be dawn before the party ended and the last guest departed, but the sun had barely set.

Abigail Brathwaite did not give up that easily. She still wanted to have a good time. "Come on, everyone, the night is young. Nobody died. We're all still fabulous people. Let's play charades."

"Hush, Abby," Dr. Brathwaite said.

"Yes, mother," Xavier said. "People obviously don't wish to be cheered up."

"We still have Jack Johnson and Joe Gans to be proud of," one of my father's friends said. "Remember how white folks went crazy looking for a 'Great White Hope' to beat Johnson. They never could find one. And we still have Jesse Owens to look forward to at the Olympics. He's sure to embarrass those Germans in the track and field events."

"Excellent point, William," my father said. "This was just one match. There'll be a lot more contests to come. And as for Mr. Owens, I can hardly wait for that victory. Hitler thinks Germans are the best at everything. He'll have to change his tune when Jesse wins."

"Yes, that Negro is fast! Heard he outran a horse."

"The NAACP wrote a letter to Jesse asking him to boycott, but changed their mind and didn't send it."

"Why should he boycott? He's got everything to prove."

"Who cares about the past or the future?" Dr. Kirkwood asked. "What about right now? I think the Jews conspired with Louis to throw the fight. Think about it. Baer beat Schmeling. Louis beat Baer. Louis should've beaten the stuffing out of Schmeling. Baer, who's a big, international hero to the Jews, looks even better if he beat someone even the undefeated Brown Bomber couldn't beat. Damn Jews probably paid him a pretty penny to take a dive."

"No, Clarence, Louis simply lost. Why would Louis want to tarnish a perfect record and a good reputation for a few lousy bucks?"

"Because money makes the world go 'round. Money is everything. Does your *reputation* pay college tuition, or buy your wife a nice piece of jewelry? Or a decent vacation? Atlantic City is the pits."

"I think it's fun," someone said.

"For the hoi polloi."

"True."

"Monte Carlo, hell – even the Caymans! – call for *real* money. And who has all the real money? The Jews!"

"A good reputation gets me clients which gets me more money," my father said.

"Well you'd get *more* clients except for the fact that most people want a Jewish lawyer because they know a Jew will do *anything* to win."

Bonnie's father said, "Clarence, you're way too cynical and hateful for your own good. And you sound like a gosh-darn Nazi! If you'd just read the papers, you'd have known that Louis spent all his time on the links when he should've been training in the gym."

"Yes," said the husband of one of the Girl Friends. "I'd heard that he was obsessed with playing golf. Understandable. Everyone here is equally obsessed, but we know business comes first. That may have been his undoing. He didn't put business first."

"Yes, all the newspapers had just written this Schmeling guy off."

"Jewish propaganda," Dr. Kirkwood said. "So it wouldn't look like a conspiracy when Louis lost."

"I'll admit there are some shyster Jews out there," my father said. "Hell, there are some shyster Negroes and even shystier Orientals; but I have to lay this loss squarely at Louis' feet. I think he's a pretty straight arrow; he wouldn't take a bribe. He was just caught flat-footed because he took that Kraut for granted."

"That's right," said Mr. Blackshear.

"I lost two grand," Dr. Kirkwood muttered.

"Daddy!"

"Clarence!" Georgine and her mother exclaimed in unison. "You promised!"

"Ooh whee!" my father whistled. "No wonder you have all these crazy theories – you're looking for a scapegoat."

"Look in the mirror," said Mr. Blackshear.

"I can't stand sorry Negroes!" He kicked another lawn chair, sent it toppling. "Fuck Joe Louis!" That was as much as my mother's proper lady friends could tolerate.

"Really now!" Dahlia's mother, Astrid, exclaimed.

"May I remind you, Clarence, that there are ladies present!" said Mr. Blackshear.

Astrid, the rest of The Girl Friends and other guests began gathering up their purses, shawls, fans and husbands. "Magdalena, thank you for your hospitality, but we're going to go." And thus began the exodus. "It's such a barbaric sport anyway. We shouldn't even be so keen to listen to such a thing."

"I agree," said Marjorie Duncan who tried hard to ingratiate herself with the Girl Friends' membership in hopes that she'd be asked to join. But according to Abigail Brathwaite, she would never be asked. "Two brutes trying to beat each other to a pulp should not be considered entertainment."

"Oh, get off your high-horse!" said Georgine's father. "Both of you enjoyed every barbaric minute of it."

Bernard took Dahlia's wrap and draped it around her shoulders, even though it was still balmy, to signal that they should go too. One by one, people extended their apologies, kissed the air by Magdalena's ear, and left.

"Lovely party, Magdalena. Too bad it had to end this way. Joe Louis made us all look bad with his incompetence."

"Well, Victoria, that's why his comeback will be all the sweeter."

"We'll have to get together again soon, Magdalena. Without the men. Sometimes they can be so crude."

"Yes, Jewel, I'll be sure to give you a call."

"Magdalena, we love the new piazza. You must have used Amish carpenters; it's a finely crafted addition. Thank you for having us. We'll be reciprocating in the very near future."

"I look forward to it, Dottie."

"Magdalena," said the stylish Deirdre Hobbs, "will I see you at the planning committee meeting for the Freedmen's Hospital benefit on Tuesday?"

"But of course. Two o'clock at Cordelia's house. I'm having Chauncey drive me into the city just for the occasion. "

"Well since you're going to be in D. C. anyway, we may as well go shopping. I can arrange for Todd, the manager of The Magic Thread, to re-open the boutique after it closes – just for us – so the white women won't be there to suck their teeth and stare at us. Todd will lower the shades and we can shop until our hearts are content."

"Splendid idea, Deirdre. I need to break in my new Charg-a-plate anyway. I noticed a gorgeous purple opera coat in their display window last month. I hope it's still there."

"It would look divine on you. And I'm going to try on fifty dresses and twenty pairs of shoes just to spite those white women who think they'll catch some kind of disease from us."

They both tittered, allowing themselves a rare moment of impishness. "We're more likely to catch something from *them*, but I'll risk it."

"Anything for fashion!"

My mother waved as Deirdre Hobbs walked off with her husband, Dr. Cyril Hobbs, a renowned orthodontist.

Marjorie Duncan walked up to my mother and grasped her arm conspiratorially with both hands. "Magdalena, remember you promised to have your Lily come teach my Katy how to make that oxtail soup before the summer is over. I've never tasted anything so delicious. Not like those pickled pig's feet Marvella Brown served at her last book club meeting. Some of the ladies are still talking about that. Slave food? No class at all."

"I think some people consider it a delicacy."

"Really? I wonder what Abigail thinks. But anyway, Lily must share her gastronomical acumen with Katy."

"Well Lily is delighted to do it. She learned to make oxtails as a little girl growing up in Tennessee. She says the secret is a fresh herb combination."

"I thought I tasted tarragon. Maybe some ginger?"

"Could be."

"Katy is a terrible cook. She can't make any of those good, traditional Negro dishes, not even a decent pot of greens. If she weren't so good with the children, I'd have gotten rid of her long ago."

Lily always wondered why the Duncans didn't hire a *real* cook and just let Katy be a nanny. Especially since, according to Lily, Katy did the job of three or four servants and the Duncans, who owned a construction company, barely paid her enough money so she could send a few dollars to her little sister who was a student at Tuskegee Institute.

"If you like," my mother said, "I can have Lily pack you some soup in a Thermos to take home with you. It's even tastier the second day."

"You're a peach. Tell her to fill it to the brim. Thank you, Magdalena."

My mother asked me to convey the message.

"Certainly," I said.

Mrs. Duncan turned to me where I was standing with Millie, Georgine and Bonnie. "Thank you, Justinia," she said. "And ask Lily to wrap up a hunk of that chocolate cake for me too. Good-bye, girls."

"Good-bye, Mrs. Duncan."

My mother called Chauncey. He came out; he was totally crestfallen. "Chauncey," she said, "when you compose yourself, please go retrieve the Brathwaites' car."

"Yes, ma'am. I'm alright, Mrs. Treadwell. Just disappointed is all."

"We all are, Chauncey, we all are."

"Yes, ma'am. I'll get that right away." Chauncey was totally dispirited. His head hung low as he walked down the rosebush-lined pathway to where the cars were parked on an adjacent gravel lot.

Soon everyone was gone but Millie who was staying over because she didn't have a ride back to D. C. and the Kirkwoods, including Georgine, who'd gone inside to sit forlornly in the dining room and wait for my parents to offer them some thirty-year old, single-malt scotch from their special stash.

"What a night," said Georgine's mother. She took out a pink, clamshell compact, checked her complexion, powdered her nose. Georgine joined her parents at the table and leafed through the latest issues of *Crisis* and *Vogue* while Millie and I helped Lily and the outside help collect dishes and tidy up.

"Did you see that awful dress Francesca had on? It looked like something from the 1920s. I don't think she's been to a seamstress since the stock market crashed. She and Otis must be going through some really hard times. I hear their barbershop empire is crumbling because there's too much low-end competition. I mean, do they really need a saxophonist and crystal chandeliers? Do these men really need Courvoisier and a shoulder massage when they go for a cut and shave? Yes, I peeked in one day. And who knows what's going on in those private rooms. Clarence comes back reeking of that sandalwood musk and it's positively suffocating.

"And what was going on with Cordelia's hair? It looked like a bird's nest, must've been a wig. And could Abigail's makeup be any thicker? She looks like a ghost, especially with those ruby-red lips. Isn't she pale *enough* without all that pancake? Speaking of which, do Walt and Tabby still have that black lawn jockey with the fat, red lips in their front yard? I don't care about the 'historical integrity' of the original structure, that thing is hideous. I need a cigarette."

Mrs. Kirkwood paused, opened my mother's carved ebony cigarette box and took out a Lucky Strike and a silver holder. Georgine took one too. Most of the ladies we knew seemed to have switched from the "palate-cleansing, digestion-aiding" Camels to Luckies because they were "toasted" and ads said that most doctors agreed they were "less irritating to the throat, lighter, milder and good for maintaining a nice figure." I wouldn't know. Though smoking was very chic, cigarettes made me cough and wheeze, so I abstained. Dr. Kirkwood struck a match and lit cigarettes for his wife and daughter and one of my father's hand-rolled Cuban cigars for himself.

"And I cannot believe that Richard and Astrid are letting Dahlia marry Bernard. He is old enough to be her grandfather. I hear he's got a lot of money socked away, but even so. And I assume Bernard is taking that child back to her parents' home. I know she's not staying with him in his Georgetown house before they've walked down the aisle. How scandalous would that be? I don't believe I even received my wedding invitation yet. I would never allow Georgine, Claudia, Audrey *or* Miranda – even if she *is* cross-eyed and pigeon-toed – to marry a man that old. Even though the competition for the best young men from the best families is so fierce these days. I heard the Patterson boy just gave Fred and Mona's daughter a two carat diamond and sapphire ring that he found in a Paris boutique after his graduation from the Sorbonne. Who saw that coming? She's a little dark-complected for the Pattersons' tastes. Yes, eligible bachelors are going fast. I tried to link Georgine with Cordelia's nephew, but he's in a rebellious stage, out there chasing some big-behind, kinky-haired girl he met at Howard."

She took a deep breath, continued like I wasn't even hovering nearby. "So Justinia and Xavier are both going to Baltimore next week for the NAACP convention. Are they still courting? People are wondering when in the world they'll get engaged. They've been friends since birth for God's sake. So what's the word? Because if Justinia isn't interested, there are plenty of girls who are. Magdalena, are you listening to me?"

"I hear you Ann," my mother said. "Forgive me. I'm trying to figure out what we're supposed to do with all that leftover pig? I don't want that thing staring at me in the morning."

"Forget the pig," Georgine's father said. "Where's Jasper with that single malt?"

CHAPTER 40

At Mrs. Tuttle's house, I made a collect call to my mother. I didn't mention the custard store incident, just that I should be back home in Highland Beach about 4:00 and that I wanted to invite the young man I met at the convention. She asked why it had to be this Sunday. "He sounds like a nice young man, and I'd love to meet him, but the guest list has already been finalized. The place cards have already been calligraphed. Every seat at the table is accounted for." While our dining table in D. C. comfortably seated 18 with two leaves, we've squeezed in twelve at our table at the cottage.

Magdalena was a stickler for having the perfect mix of guests. One wrong person could spoil the whole arrangement. Things should be fun, interesting and lively, not awkward. She didn't want two ruined parties in a row. There was a strategy to putting together just the right group of people. For instance, you couldn't have Cyndra Clark at the same table with certain women because she flirts with their husbands and the Palmers were too outspokenly suspicious of really light-skinned Negroes.

The Sterns, of Stern's Fine Catering, frowned and were quiet the whole time if the Duncans or any other couple considered *nouveau riche* were at the table. But when the Duncans left, Dovey Stern groused that everything about Marjorie Duncan was gaudy, including her husband's pinky ring. "Who, besides old-time gangsters like Al Capone, wears a pinky ring? Or has tacky, whitewall tires? And everything about her is just too big – the dangly earrings, dangly necklace, dangly bracelets. Even her lips and nose are too big. All that jewelry made an annoying racket every time she moved. Not to mention the fact that the humongous charms on her bracelet dragged across the butter and plopped into the gravy boat. It made me lose my appetite. Her husband laughs too loudly and they asked to take food home! They are vulgar. She thinks she's 'high-class' and is always gossiping about somebody. But what can you expect from people who aren't used to having money? They'll be bankrupt soon. I hear they spend too much trying to fit in, and that their construction company had a nice, little run but it's failing because who's building anything larger than a garage nowadays? All the lawyers we know and they aren't even incorporated. What more can I say? The Duncans simply are not meant for polite company. The Brantleys introduced them to us, didn't they? Never trust their judgment again."

Some Lincoln republicans and some Roosevelt democrats couldn't be in the same room as they would get into loud and heated arguments. My father liked impassioned political debates, but my mother usually overruled him and kept the most antagonistic guests away from one another. Both the Sheltons and the Endicotts owned funeral parlors and accused each other of stealing clients. The Stewarts were angry at Professor McCreary who taught Biology at Howard because they didn't like the grades he gave their son. Heloise Giles was allergic to horses and would break out in hives around the Brinsons who owned and operated a horse farm that spawned a Derby champion.

The Pruitts, with their little corner doughnut shops, were too *middle* class for the Brathwaites, the Kirkwoods, the Sterns and some other of Magdalena's snobbiest friends and were dismissed as "hapless strivers" and "voracious social climbers." There was no telling what the Brathwaites or the Kirkwoods were liable to say on any given day, so you could never invite any sensitive people when they were coming. And Nanette Coventry thinks Abigail Brathwaite blackballed her from the Girl Friends although Abigail denies it.

The DeJongs always bragged that an African ancestor arrived in Jamestown with the Dutch, a year before the Mayflower Pilgrims, as an indentured servant, settled his debt and went on to become a famous cabinet maker whose skills and business acumen were passed down to the current generation. This declaration irritated some guests who demanded to know if the DeJongs thought they were somehow better than everyone else, more entitled, more authentically American, and argued that indentured servants were no different than emancipated slaves.

"No," said Faye DeJong. "Indentured servants were a better class of people."

"Well," said Maurice Overstreet, "if it makes you feel better to think so, then. . . whatever butters your bread."

"Well technically," said Virgie Harper, "the Indians are the *original* Americans and weren't enslaved or indentured."

"Some were," said Maurice.

"Well my husband's great-grandparents were all free, full-blooded Cherokee. People don't even see Negro traits in my daughter Inez. They think she's 100% Indian squaw."

"*But*," said Faye DeJong, "can you trace *any* of those Indians back to a *specific* individual or family in the early 1600s? I think not. Allen is a direct descendant of Babatunde from Holland by way of Nigeria. Babatunde was employed by the DeJongs for three years."

"*Actually*," Maurice said, "another black man got here *way* before Allen's ancestors. Pedro Nino actually navigated one of Columbus' ships, the Santa Maria, in 1492, a century earlier."

"You just made that up," said Faye.

"No *ma'am*, I learned that from Professor Hathaway at Howard, freshman year."

"Is he still living?" someone asked.

"He's ninety and walks to Carnegie Library on campus every morning," said Maurice's wife, Lorraine.

"Research it yourself: Pedro Nino, called *El Negro* – he was African and Spanish."

"One drop rule," my father said.

"That's right. But I've seen his portrait – he's got way more than a drop of black," Maurice said. "Pedro and his three brothers were legendary but Western Civilization conveniently omits this fact – among many other facts."

"*But*," said Faye, not to be outdone, "technically Columbus didn't get to the mainland. They ended up somewhere in the West Indies. Last I checked, that's not *really* America."

"Right," Allen said, "and Babatunde was in Virginia."

Maurice took a sip of wine. "As I said before – whatever butters your bread."

"*But*," said Virgie, not giving up, "even if that's true, the Indians were still here first. And nobody gives credit to the Indians for inventing canoes or toboggans."

"I believe," said Maurice, "that was the Cree tribe who lived in coastal, colder regions. Perry claims a Cherokee bloodline."

"Technicalities, Mr. Know-it-all Hair-splitter. And he *is* Cherokee. Look at those cheekbones, all that good hair." She took her husband Perry by the chin and moved his head side to side. "You people are so jealous. And lacrosse, what about that? It's an Olympic sport. And they saved the Pilgrims from starvation. What about that? White people might've become extinct if not for the Indians."

Everyone just looked at her. "Virgie," Faye said softly, "that's ridiculous. And you're not Indian."

"My husband and daughter are."

Eventually the discussion deteriorated into heated arguments about legacy and culture and whether whites and Jews conspire to whitewash history to benefit themselves. They debated indentureship versus slavery, Africans versus American Negroes, Negro self-hatred and whatnot – until the mood was ruined for everybody and Mother told Lily to cancel dessert and coffee.

A person who entertained as often as Magdalena did had to be aware of everything that was going on with the people in the community. She said there was an art to knowing everyone's secrets, predilections, peccadilloes and their complicated relationships with others. Magdalena took great pride in keeping abreast of this important information and piecing together the perfect jigsaw of a guest list. The Treadwells got along well with everyone, a cross-section of society, even though the majority of their friends and associates were listed in the Negro social register.

They liked some people for their intellect, humor or charitable nature, others because they were just nice people with interesting stories to tell; they tolerated others merely because they were considered pillars of society and protocol dictated that they be regularly hosted, wined and dined, to remain in their good graces. Similarly, my parents' social calendar was abloom with dinner commitments and party invitations which they accepted without fretting about whom else would be there.

⋅→⊨◉ ◉⊨←⋅

Magdalena went on and on about the inconvenience of an extra guest for Sunday. "Besides," she said, "I need to know this Julius person would fit in with the rest of the guests already coming. What if his parents are on bad terms with some of the other guests? That could be very awkward. Remember when the Lancasters and the Guthries almost came to blows over their disagreement about Booker T. Washington?"

"Of course. The vase that Nana brought from Tuscany got smashed." Both parties had apologized and agreed to replace it, but Mother told them it was irreplaceable.

"What an embarrassment that was. And since then they cannot even bear to be in the same room together."

"I know."

"The Lancasters even left St. Luke's to join the Methodists over at Mount Zion."

"So you've *said*."

"Don't be fresh, Justinia. It's unbecoming. No man wants a sassy wife."

"Well, mother, it's an old story."

"Anyway, you understand fully why I'd really like to meet Julius first. He can call on you Monday."

"Mother, Julius won't cause any trouble."

"One never knows. And you are so tight-lipped about him. It makes me wonder if you're trying to hide something. You're sure he's not a musician?"

"No, mother."

"Living some rootless, bohemian lifestyle?"

"As I said, mother, he's a lawyer; he graduated from Georgetown and lives in D.C. He's mannerly, intelligent and handsome. And I doubt very seriously that anyone we know knows him or anyone in his family."

"You'd be surprised who knows whom, Justinia. The world is smaller than you think. And even though he sounds wonderful, you really haven't had time to get to know him that well. He could be a Communist, or worse yet, one of those die-hard Garvey-ites. You know I support the NAACP, but it does have its share of Communists and people who still believe Marcus Garvey is some kind of royalty while he squanders people's hard-earned money on ridiculous get-rich-quick, back-to-Africa schemes. I won't have another dinner party ruined by tension or fighting guests. So no, we'll have Mr. Sommerfeldt over some other time."

"Fine."

I was 100 per cent sure that no one coming to our house knew Julius Sommerfeldt or his family. I didn't care if he was a Communist or not and was pretty sure he had no idea who Marcus Garvey was, although he surprised me with the things he knew. He was nice, sincere and interesting and that was what mattered to me. Julius told me that he'd be going back to Berlin soon for the summer Olympics, and maybe for good. So I wanted to spend every available moment in his company. The fact that he was white and Jewish was inconsequential.

Of course most of our friends and associates were Negro but my parents had friends who were white and friends who were Jewish. They also knew whites and Jews they didn't care for at all. My father will never forget how a Jewish business partner left him to sleep in the car in Berlin, Maryland while he took a room at the inn. The man should've camped out with him; daddy would've let him have the spacious back seat while he made do in the front with the steering wheel and the gear shift poking him all night long. Daddy said the man had to be bigoted, had to have viewed him as "less than" to have left him alone in a car without so much as a look back or the promised pillow or blanket. The business deal panned out and they made a lot of money, but Daddy never forgot what the man did, or how other Jewish associates had him cursing and slamming things. Yet he tried not to hold the actions of individuals against an entire group.

"Maybe he was just an idiot," Charlotte had commented.

"You're probably right," said Daddy.

A medley of people have sat at our table, visited in our parlor, sunned on our stretch of private beach. We've had Dr. DuBois; we've had the Maryland governor and the mayor of Annapolis; we've had Harold Ickes from the Roosevelt administration. We've entertained the cream of Negro society. We've had Lily's nieces and nephews over to splash around, go tadpole hunting and roast hotdogs. Likewise I've borrowed sugar from Joseph Douglass, Frederick's grandson, and his wife Fannie and stayed to hear Civil War stories and to hear them play "Amazing Grace" on the violin and piano. When Paul Robeson, singer/actor/ lawyer and Civil Rights advocate, visited a Highland Beach neighbor, Daddy had watermelons – something we'd *never* be seen eating in D. C. – brought over for the crowd who'd gathered for an impromptu concert.

CHAPTER 41

ALL RACES OF people were accepted into our fold, but people balked when it came to romantic interracial relationships. A great percentage of the black-white unions and the miscegenation that created an entire class of mixed-race persons occurred prior to Reconstruction. The lighter-skinned Negroes were able to acquire more education, land, wealth and acceptance than their darker counterparts, much of it bestowed by repentant white rapists – some of whom prayerfully sought last-minute salvation from their deathbeds and bequeathed entire homesteads to their slaves – or from genuinely loving white partners, platonic white benefactors and wealthy abolitionists. The evidence of these arrangements continues to be manifest. Others, my father included, were able to succeed by virtue of pluck, luck and education.

Although our crowd treasured light complexions, and felt there was no such thing as being "too rich or too light," we still preferred to marry within the race. Often those with very light skin became almost a "third race" and were encouraged to shun white people *and* dark people and cling to their "own kind." It was counterproductive to marry dark people because that would nullify all the benefits that accrue to having light skin. Every shade darker meant a loss of advantages – of seeming inherently less threatening, more intelligent, somehow more worthy.

It was likewise counterproductive to marry a white person unless one was ardently in love or deranged by Negro Low Self-Esteem Syndrome or Anything But Black Disease. Whites couldn't give us anything we didn't already have. We already had money and status, but we were still Negro, still three-fifths a person in the eyes of many whites who would resent and resist any intrusion upon their lily-white dynasty. Often the white person was not as established as we were, but if they were, they were likely to be disowned and disinherited for their love choices. And few Negroes wanted to exchange their comfort and prestige in the black community for public rejection by prospective white in-laws. And it was an unwritten rule that Negro wealth should remain in Negro hands and circulated within the Negro community.

As beloved and esteemed as Frederick Douglass was, people still whispered about him behind his back when he married his second wife, a Caucasian feminist, two years after the death of his first wife Anna, a rather dowdy woman who was a conductor on the Underground Railroad. This was according to the surviving local griots – people like "the Countess," the purported once-upon-a-time sweetheart of poet Paul Dunbar, holding court from her perch in Highland Beach, people who watched as the world turned and lurched with both glacial and seismic social change, people who'd been privy to the secrets swirling around Douglass, Booker T. Washington, congressmen, senators, even a President or two.

Not only was interracial marriage considered taboo, but people wondered how Mr. Douglass could purport to uplift the race but ignore the many comely, accomplished Negro women in his private life. Many Negro women felt they would've made a fine wife for the thick-maned Lion of Anacostia, and felt betrayed by his demonstrated affinity for Caucasian women. The "Countess" was said to have warned, "Freddie had better not bring one of those white hussies out here to Highland Beach or he'll have me to deal with! Poor, sweet Anna. What in heaven could she be thinking?" Unfortunately Douglass died before his son had the Douglass Summer House – Twin Oaks – completed for him and, as far as I know, no "white hussy" ever darkened that doorway or entered the balcony, that customized widow's walk where Douglass had wanted to gaze contentedly across the bay to where he'd been twenty years a slave.

Even his own children were supposedly upset about their father's choice of wife. The papers had called it a "national calamity." No whites confronted the great Frederick Douglass who'd made a name for himself by becoming a charismatic orator and pre-eminent abolitionist and fraternizing with Presidents. The

Lion of Anacostia would get a "pass." The Caucasian elite had to suffer at least a few "uppity" Negroes to prove they were sophisticated vanguards standing at the forefront of evolutionary racial attitudes. But behind closed doors, they fumed. Not much has changed in fifty years.

My mother often speaks about a sensational court battle a mere ten years ago involving Alice Jones, the biracial woman who married Kip Rhinelander from one of the richest families in America. Kip's parents were livid and made him file for an annulment and claim he didn't know she was a Negro. Alice testified that he *did* know and was shockingly required to disrobe for the New York jury so they could examine her nipples and the expanse of her skin close-up to determine whether Kip *should* have known she wasn't white. Ultimately, the jury sided with Alice who eventually won a huge settlement.

My mother, who'd followed the case closely, commenting on every *New York Times* article, said any imbecile could tell that that woman, even fully clothed, was Negro. Making her stand half-naked in front of the all-white, all-male jury and allowing explicit testimony and steamy love letters regarding their premarital sexual activity was gratuitous and exploitive. She also said the money that Alice was awarded wasn't enough to be worth the emotional tax, her husband's betrayal or the blow to her modesty and dignity. Daddy said the jury verdict was less about being fair to Alice and more about punishing Kip for being a traitor to his race. The point of her anecdote was that it was just easier to stick with your own kind.

The Negro aristocracy could conceivably become extinct if the goal was to assimilate completely. Abigail Brathwaite didn't want to be white; she wanted to perch on her pedestal on the black side of the color line and look down on the others, and have the others look up at her. To become totally absorbed into the dominant race, to get "lighter and lighter every generation" until the "blackness" was obliterated, would be to relinquish that feeling of special-ness, that ability to flaunt light skin like a status symbol or, for women, long, luscious locks like a badge of honor, and be perceived as the best Negro society had to offer. Such assets were premium in our society. Over the years, too many people to count have remarked, gaily, that I was the "pretty one" and, consolingly, that my sister Charlotte was the "smart one" which was an insult to us both.

Light skin was currency, better than "passing" which promised a lifetime of looking over one's shoulder, enduring enhanced looks and double-takes, being terrified of running into a relative or friend – especially at an inopportune moment – and dreading children and grandchildren because of sneaky recessive genes. And they still might be denied the rights and privileges afforded those whose whiteness was unquestionable. It was worth it to wait, to endure being a privileged black in a whites-only world, until whites decided they wanted to treat us all fairly.

I didn't know Julius well enough to say I'd like to be in a romantic relationship with him, but I couldn't deny I was attracted to him. In four days, I was wooed by his intelligence, candor, affability and empathy and concern for others. I thought his stories about life in Germany, especially after Hitler came to power, were frightening and fascinating and I couldn't help seeing the parallels of being Jewish in Nazi Germany and being Negro in America. It kind of made us kindred spirits.

When I walked into a convention symposium, we'd immediately find each other. We sat next to each other during a panel discussion about "Living Your Best Life Despite a World Full of Racism." One of the speakers, a minister from Pennsylvania, railed against white people in general, said none of them were any good and none could be trusted. He said it was time for Negroes to fight back, using deadly force if necessary, and advocated for an armed militia to protect Negro citizens since the police couldn't be bothered to do it, and to prepare for the imminent and inevitable race war. Only a few people seemed to agree with this viewpoint, but he went on and on getting louder and louder. At times, it seemed as if he was staring directly at Julius, who may have been the only white person in the room at the time. Julius never cringed; in fact, he nodded at many of the statements the angry man made.

Julius visibly seethed when it was discussed in another session, "Negroes and the Economy," that field hands and domestic workers were ineligible for the newly legislated Social Security benefits. The speaker said this was done by design to exclude the majority of Negroes, that it was the "same old, same old," and that "your darling" Roosevelt was complicit.

"And that," said the speaker, "is why we need to dump Roosevelt and support the Communist ticket of Browder and Ford. That way we get someone who *genuinely* cares about equality and a Negro Vice-President to boot."

I could see Julius mull over the possibility – as preposterous as it was. "He has a point," he said.

It impressed me that he was so comfortable in his own skin, that racial issues, especially when he was in the minority, didn't make him squirm. Julius had been easy to spot that first day of the convention. In the NAACP's infancy, there were many involved whites but now, as Negroes began to take more control over the organization, there were far fewer. And amid many other women, of all shapes, sizes and shades, Julius gravitated towards *me*. Just like my parents had somehow been drawn together at the overcrowded black-and-tan party at the Gans Hotel. I found that interesting. My sister Charlotte would say it was prophetic.

CHAPTER 42

It was after ten when the doorbell rang at Mrs. Tuttle's house. I was sitting in the living room with Millie, Leddy and Shirley discussing the evening's sour turn of events. Mrs. Tuttle shuffled out of her bedroom tying the sash around her robe. "Now who in the world could that be?"

She looked through the tiny window in the front door. She gasped. "Lawd, it's a white man at the door. Is one of you gals in some kind of trouble?"

We had no idea what she was talking about.

"When I was growing up in Georgia, a knock on the door by a white man in the middle of the night was bad news. It usually meant somebody was 'bout to get snatched out they bed to be beaten or lynched. Or sometimes they just busted in with guns blazin'." She looked out the window again. "Well, he don't exactly look like a Kluxer."

"May I help you?" she asked. She listened to his response by cupping her ear to the door.

"Justinia, this man says he knows you and wants to talk to you." She looked at me for an explanation.

I joined her by the door and peeked out. "That's Julius Sommerfeldt, Mrs. Tuttle. He's with the NAACP. He's harmless."

"Well, gal, you know my rule."

"I know, Mrs. Tuttle. Do you mind terribly if I see what he wants?"

She looked out the window one more time, sized Julius up and decided he wasn't there to drag anyone out of their bed. "Seeing as how he's with the

NAACP and all, I'll make an exception this one time," she said. She unlocked all the deadbolts on the door and opened it. Julius was apologetic.

"I'm sorry ma'am. Miss Justinia left her scarf in the taxi and I thought I'd return it since I wasn't sure I'd see her tomorrow."

"Well come on in. My daughters could tell you I never allowed gentleman callers past 8:00, but I'll allow you to sit for a spell. Just remember this is a Christian home."

I wasn't sure what she was implying, but I just said, "Alright, thank you, Mrs. Tuttle."

Millie gave me one of her knowing looks and suggested to Leddy and Shirley that they retire to their rooms because tomorrow was to be a busy day. We were doing the noose demonstration. A confluence of past and immediate events and a heartfelt conversation with Julius had convinced me that I should participate.

Mrs. Tuttle gave Julius another once-over. "Would you like a cup of tea, Mr. – what did you say your name was again?"

"Sommerfeldt, madam, but please call me Julius." He offered his hand and she took it. "And if that's what I'm smelling, and if it is not too much trouble, I'd love a cup."

She brought out a highly polished silver tea service, complete with a teapot, cream and sugar vessels, and two china cups with silver spoons and linen napkins on a silver tray. Even Magdalena would've approved. Julius stood to take it from her and place it on the coffee table in front of the sofa where we were sitting.

"How nice," he said. "You should not have put yourself out."

"This ain't nothing but some tea. Don't be so surprised. This is how I do all my guests," Mrs. Tuttle said, then went into her own room, surprisingly leaving the door uncracked.

CHAPTER 43

I'M GLAD MRS. Tuttle was so hospitable. If she hadn't offered tea, Julius probably would have just delivered my scarf and left right away. I'm glad he noticed the pink and blue paisley scarf on the floor of the taxi; it belonged to my maternal grandmother, the mysterious Sylvia Pierce, and was one of the few things I had to remind me that she existed since I only remember seeing her twice or thrice, and every time she stayed in the car, partly shielded by a huge, plumed hat, petting a snow-white Pomeranian who seemed more curious about "the grandchildren" than she was. We were only allowed to say "Hello, Nana," but couldn't touch her, couldn't reach out for a hug or we'd become too "attached." Meanwhile, her valet unloaded elaborately wrapped gifts that Chauncey took into the house to be opened later.

Twenty minutes later she was gone and there was only her nineteenth-century portrait as a blithe, blushing ingénue on the wall leading up the stairs to ponder. There was that and the gifts – Parisian soaps, Venetian lace, Belgian chocolates, Delft Blue ceramics and wooden clogs from the Netherlands, ceremonial masks from Fiji, Brazilian leather clutches, drawings on vintage papyrus from Egypt, a Cherokee tomahawk from Wyoming, framed photographs of her blending in, chameleon-like, with the natives of whatever place she happened to be in at the time. As young children we couldn't truly appreciate the mementos from her extensive travels. Now I loved that paisley pashmina from Malaysia and was grateful to get it back.

If Mrs. Tuttle hadn't allowed the late-night visit, then we never would've sat down and talked, swapping life stories until one o'clock in the morning.

We packed a lot of memories, hopes, dreams and angst into those two short hours. Of course I was aware from radio reports, the newspapers and dinner conversations that a new regime had come to power in Germany and was persecuting the Jewish people and threatening to start another world war, but I didn't really understand how bad it was until I heard Julius' stories. It was terrible what happened to his father the judge and all the other people who'd been deprived of their jobs and careers. It sounded eerily like the Jim Crow nonsense here in southern America – and the rest of America as quiet as it's kept.

And rampant book burnings! Unconscionable. I can't imagine such a thing happening here. Whites can have their segregated movies, concerts and plays, but they'd better leave me to my books. It required no sharing of air or space, and brusque encounters and mean glares could be completely avoided when I was reading a book. Life would be unbearable without books.

In some warped sense it was consoling to know that Negroes weren't the only ones destined to live their entire lives in strict survival mode, striving to be both invisible and visible at the same time. I was weirdly gratified that there were others living with the knowledge that gross unfairness was an inexorable part of life, that one's life, liberty and ability to pursue happiness could be stolen for no other reason than accident of Negro or Jewish birth. I felt strange relief knowing there were people who were equally or even more despised than I was, probably the same way Indians felt about blacks, the way Old Testament prostitutes must've felt about lepers.

To be honest, it was the way the Negro privileged class sometimes viewed the people who landscaped our yards, cleaned our homes and spent hours languishing on milk crates in the alley neighborhoods. We know they took the brunt of the abuse by virtue of their numbers and greater visibility and, because they were mainly service providers, had more interaction with abusive people.

When Chauncey runs errands, he is often stopped by the police for no other reason than the fact that he was driving my father's fancy car. The encounters are rarely cordial but he knows to keep his cool and drop my father's name as Daddy was on good terms with the D. C. chief of police. This way Chauncey has been able to avoid the situation from escalating to the point where he actually got hurt. The worst he's suffered were some torn pants and skinned knees from being thrown down onto the rough pavement for allegedly speeding. Lily was kind enough to dab Mercurochrome on his scrapes, patch up his pants and listen to him rant and curse while Charlotte, Emery and I eavesdropped a room away.

While incidents like the one at Vogelsang's were hurtful, I can't begin to imagine what it's like for people who experienced racist cops, employers and businessmen on a routine basis. I've read enough essays, poems and books by writers like Langston Hughes, scoured enough newspaper reports, and heard enough stories on the radio and from various people to know that pernicious racism as well as abject poverty – a horrible combination – were prevalent.

I saw many unfortunate things when I did my required student teaching at George Washington Carver Primary School. Students were dropped off by slow-moving, thick-tongued adults; they had bad limps, prominent scars and lightless eyes and I wondered what had happened to them. Was it just the travails of daily living, the realization that the forty acres and mule would never materialize, or had there been an altercation with a violent racist, a recalcitrant mule or a malfunctioning circular saw? Many of the children already had jaundiced, lightless eyes and permanent scowls and I wondered what they'd seen, what had been said or done to them, to cause this affliction. Did the light start to dim when they saw their parents being continuously disrespected or when they realized there would be more drudgery than amusement in their young lives? Did a fist knock out the tooth of the mother of one of the students, or did it rot and fall out on its own? Was the grandmother stooped from the weight of the world or calcium-starved bones? I didn't know how they could help their children when it seemed they could barely help themselves.

A ten-year old boy named Danny, an off-again, on-again student, came to school one day "for good," he announced, because his mother told him someone in the family needed to get an education to help out with all their problems.

"I need t'be a lawyer and a doctor," he said. "Like quick."

"And if you work real hard," I said, "you *can* be."

"Cuz my mama got sugar and my daddy finna lose his truck. How long it gon' take?"

He had absolutely no idea and I didn't have the heart to tell him that it could take twenty years. "You have some catching up to do. First you have to learn English, math and science real well."

"That's easy. H2O means water and 'vaporates when it rains."

"Good! Then there's college..."

"I'm smart and a fast learner, Miss Treadwell. I can read the Bible and already know my times tables. I know lotsa stuff. Adam was the first man, Abraham Lincoln was the world's greatest Pres'dent. Fo' coters make a dolla."

"Very good."

"Clorox makes plants green."

"Chlorophyll."

"That's what I said."

"Well, you're well on your way."

"Toldja."

I playfully pinched his pudgy cheek. "Be here bright and early Monday morning. Don't forget to brush your teeth and your hair real well."

"I won't."

"It's Negro History Week. We'll be discussing Frederick Douglass. As a special treat I'm bringing scones and raspberry jam from a fabulous Negro bakery."

"Stones?"

Danny, his smiling face greased-up with Vaseline and wearing a grungy shirt and tie, was the first one there Monday. I gave him a big hug and my heart ached for him to do well. But after a couple months of struggling through *Dick and Jane* books and counting on his fingers to figure out math problems, he left and never returned. After approval from Mrs. Lane, my teaching supervisor, I found out where he lived and had Chauncey take me to see what happened. Their apartment was dark and tiny and Danny explained that, even though his mother drank gallons of vinegar and cinnamon-dandelion tea as instructed by the neighborhood herbalist/root doctor/midwife, she still lost her leg to "the sugar" and his father still lost the pickup truck he was $10 away from owning, so going to school was now pointless. I was deeply saddened by his sense of hopelessness, the stench of mold and mildew, and the sight of his mother lying on the couch, mute, handicapped, and eyeing me with suspicion.

Mrs. Lane, writing a bell work assignment on the chalkboard, said she wasn't surprised. "Justinia, this school is full of 'Dannies.' They don't have adequate food, clothing or transportation. It's hard to concentrate when you're tired and hungry."

"I can imagine."

"Some walk miles to get here and many parents send their kids reluctantly because they prefer they be *working* somewhere. They're taking care of younger siblings and have other adult responsibilities. They have short attention spans and don't have goals for the future. They just want to make it through the day."

"That's so sad."

"I was like you when I first started, idealistic and wanting to save everyone, uplift the race and coax the brilliance from their fertile minds. It's the hardest thing I ever tried to do. They just can't get a foothold on life. It's not our fault or theirs, just the way the cards were dealt."

"Right."

"I love the children, but honestly, I'm applying for a transfer to Dunbar."

I don't know why Mrs. Lane's words bothered me so, but they did, especially after she left Carver and went to Dunbar to replace a pregnant teacher. I felt pangs of envy and guilt because I'd love to launch my teaching career at Dunbar where the students were brighter, had better parental support and fewer distractions. Mrs. Lane was replaced by a harried white woman who couldn't understand some of the students' raw dialect. "What did she *say*, Justinia?" she'd ask, always assuming I could translate.

Georgine and Xavier were uninterested in the lives of anyone outside our tight, little circle; and I understand that because it's much more comfortable being oblivious to the suffering and needs of others. Twice a year Georgine boxed up her old underwear, had it delivered to the Y or the Ionia Whipper Home for Unwed Mothers and thought that would secure her place in Heaven. She'd never talk to a "Danny," let alone touch him because dirt-poor people gave her the "heebie-jeebies."

Eventually I too would retreat into my own world, obsessing over hem lengths, how to perfect my tennis serve, or deciding whether or not to cut my bangs. Sooner or later I'd get yanked back again when Lily told me about her sister and her five children being evicted from yet another run-down tenement or when Chauncey would re-tell the story about the time he had to help his brothers cut their father down from a weeping willow tree back home in Georgia once the Klan rode away on their horses. Or I'd remember the little, brown moon face of Leon's son delighting over the prospect of eating a scrap of chicken. And I'd remember how Reverend Crawford is always saying, "There, but for the grace of God, go I."

Lily's eyes and Chauncey's eyes were somewhat dim, but the light hadn't completely faded. They had a good life working for our family, but they still had family members and close friends to worry about. I wondered how long it took for one's eyes to reach a state of perpetual dullness – was it a few incidents, one really bad one, or did it take years, a virtual death by a thousand cuts?

Did the Jews in Germany have lightless eyes yet or was it too soon? If so, would the glimmer ever return? Was it worse to never have been able to go to school, own property or start a business, or was it worse to have known freedom and prosperity but have it snatched abruptly away? Was it better to have never had an opportunity to be a lawyer or a judge, to only dream of becoming one although, in oppressed minds, it was the same thing as dreaming of pots of gold at the ends of rainbows? Or was it preferable to have dreamt and achieved it only to be dragged out of the courthouse in the middle of a trial, in the middle of a stellar career?

I'd have to ask Julius if there were any good essays or books about people whose lives changed for the worse when the Third Reich came to power. I'd love to read them, especially one condemned by the Nazis because it probably contained truths and insights they didn't want the masses to know about. People might revolt. That's precisely why southerners didn't want slaves to read and why they punished those who defiantly taught them anyway. Like Frederick Douglass said, "Knowledge makes one unfit to be a slave."

Julius says the Germans blame the Jews for everything – from the loss of the war to the weather. That ascribes a lot of power to them. American segregationists thought Negroes were inherently inferior and used the Bible, the law and tradition to justify that attitude. They hesitate to credit us with the ability to influence the country as it would undercut the notion that we were virtually inconsequential – only good for servicing them, entertaining them, reminding them of their higher place in the social hierarchy – and unable to do anything collectively to ruin, or save, the nation. But the Nazis must have viewed the Jews as being quite exceptional if they had so much impact on German society. And since much of Germany's professional and business class was Jewish, it seemed the Nazis were primarily driven by resentment and jealousy and were just being vindictive.

But contrary to common belief, Negroes were exceptional too. I was fortunate to have grown up with Carter Woodson as a neighbor. He was an educator and historian who established Negro History Week. When he spoke, Dr. Woodson could keep his friends, Dukes & Duchesses, strangers – anybody – captivated for hours. He said Negroes have had a positive, significant impact on economies, wars and the evolution of the law. He claimed that a Negro slave, not the slave owner, Eli Whitney, conceptualized the cotton gin and that Benjamin Banneker, a free black astronomer and mathematician, helped survey and design blueprints for Washington D. C. Garrett Morgan invented chemical hair straighteners, the gas mask and traffic light and others invented useful things like door knobs, curtain rods, egg beaters, lawn sprinklers and folding chairs. He said that an influx of slaves and free Blacks, soldiers like my great-grandfather, helped the Union beat the Confederacy and win the Civil War, that our contributions are trivialized or ignored. The "talented tenth" did not originate with DuBois; it existed long before, there just was no name for it.

Julius and I could've talked all night, like old friends reunited, but we didn't want to bend the house rules any longer than we did. At the door he tucked a wayward strand of hair behind my ear and kissed me on the cheek.

"I'll see you tomorrow, Miss Treadwell."

"Yes you will, Mr. Sommerfeldt." My cheeks burned and I felt the hot sensation of his lips the rest of the night.

Over the course of the week, we'd discovered how much we had in common. Both of us enjoyed cinema, insightful poetry and a good, thick novel, and we both liked to record our thoughts and experiences in a diary. He loved American literature, was partial to Faulkner and Sinclair Lewis. When I told him one of my favorite books was *The Blacker the Berry* by Wallace Thurman, and told him it was about a very dark-skinned Negro woman trying to exist in a color-conscious world, he amusingly said, "Well darker berries *are* the most delicious."

He encouraged me to try my hand at writing something more substantial than diary entries – a memoir or novel in the vein of a Nella Larsen or other Harlem Renaissance writer. "You have so much to say," he said. "I find your life fascinating in every way."

At the Baltimore Public Library where Julius and I spent one especially hot evening, I wanted to introduce him to other Negro authors but their one volume of Wheatley poems was checked out so I had to share her lyrics from memory: *"Twas mercy brought me from my pagan land…"* And the librarian had never even heard of Langston Hughes, Jessie Fauset, Countee Cullen, Zora Neale Hurston or the Harlem Renaissance.

"Zora who?" she asked, frowning. "Is that a colored writer?"

"Yes," I answered. "She's a very popular *Negro* folklorist and author. She wrote *Jonah's Vine Gourd.*" There was no flash of recognition. *"Mules and Men?"*

"You need to try the D. C. branch. They cater to a much larger colored clientele."

Surrounded by books, sitting in a back corner of the library and ignoring all the curious glances, Julius cooled me off by fanning me with a magazine and we chatted about our favorite writers. He already knew the poetry of Emily Dickinson and we recited in whispery unison and mutual delight, *"I'll tell you how the sun rose; a ribbon at a time…"*

I told him I enjoyed the imaginativeness of Hermann Hesse's novel, *Steppenwolf,* and have admired the captivating, surrealistic art and poetry of Max Ernst since learning about him in my German class at Howard. Julius told me about Heinrich Mann whose scathing social commentary about Germany caused him to flee the Nazis who burned his books and about Hayyim Bialik, the most renowned Jewish poet who wrote dark and disturbing verse in Hebrew and Yiddish. It sounded lovely when Julius read his famous poem in seemingly flawless Hebrew:

After my death mourn me this way:
There was a man-and look: he is no more;
He died before his time,
The music of his life suddenly
stopped.

A pity! There was another song in him.
Now it is lost forever.

Sad, but I still found it lovely even after he told me the meaning in English. Julius said it reminded him of his paternal grandfather, a brilliant, fair-minded jurist, accomplished cellist and wonderful family man who gave up the bench and a charmed life to go fight in the war where he died.

"I still miss him," Julius said. "But he'd be sickened to see the cesspool that Germany has become.

The stories of a grand and glorious Germany before the Nazi takeover were interesting and the lurid tales of Nazi domination were both disturbing and fascinating. I realized again the significance of Max Baer, Joe Louis and Jesse Owens and the pervading controversy over Berlin hosting the Olympics. There was so much irony, so many American parallels, so many social and political implications. It made me seriously consider going to Berlin to witness living history up close. I realized that the very charming Julius Sommerfeldt would be a perfect companion with whom to share such a spectacle. We appreciated the same things. So I spent a lot of time trying to figure out exactly how to tell Jasper and Magdalena Treadwell that I wanted to do just that. I knew it would be difficult.

CHAPTER 44

Julius

"WHO'S THAT YOUNG lady you've been spending so much time with?" my Uncle Sy asked me.

"You must be speaking of Justinia Treadwell, a charming, remarkable young lady."

"And quite fetching."

"Indeed. And smart and cultured. She speaks French and German, plays piano and a little harp. She can quote from memory verse from Phyllis Wheatley as well as Emily Dickinson."

"Phyllis Wheatley?"

"She was an 18th century slave, the first Negro woman to ever have her work published. I hadn't heard of her either before Justinia told me about her. Apparently there are a good number of Negro literary prodigies that I had no idea even existed."

"Yes, their history is very rich."

"Nothing like what we've been taught to believe growing up in Germany."

"Or even what they lead one to believe here in America."

"I'm pleasantly surprised every day that I'm here."

"And unpleasantly reminded of the dishonorable way they are regarded and treated."

We'd had a taste for some authentic German cuisine and were sitting in the Eichenkranz in the Highlandtown-Canton section of Baltimore and waiting for the waitress to bring us our veal schnitzel. The *Eichenkranz* was a restaurant that evolved from an eighteenth century German social club, singing society and dance hall. The food there was delicious and transported us back home to Berlin where Helga would've been toiling at the kitchen stove and scolding us when we dipped a finger into the pan for a taste. The restaurant also provided live entertainment; an award-winning women's choir would be gracing us with their talents shortly.

"Do you know what the young lady's father does for a living?"

"He practices law and owns a lot of real estate."

"So they're wealthy Negroes?"

He put a *kluntjes*, a crystallized lump of sugar into his teacup, poured the hot tea over it so that it began to melt slowly, then poured a cloud of cream over that. It was to be drunk without being stirred so that the layers – sugar, tea and cream – would manifest separately and gradually and complement each other. This was the way we took our tea in Germany, and Uncle Sy, who was my father's older brother, preferred this style of tea service to the American version where tea was bought in filtering pouches instead of bulk leaves; then lemons were squeezed and teaspoons of sugar, perhaps a splash of milk, are stirred into the tea-steeped water which was often overpowered by the sweetness. I, however, was beginning to get used to drinking tea like a Yankee but without as much sugar and many times I drank it with ice in a tall glass. But the cinnamon-apple tea that I had at the home of a woman where Justinia was staying during the NAACP convention was delicious without any add-ins at all.

"Well I certainly did not ask outright, that would be crass, but I get the impression that her family lives very graciously."

Uncle Sy sipped, pinky out, his curiosity about Justinia Treadwell and her family fully aroused. "A rich Negro attorney with the name of Treadwell. Sounds vaguely familiar. Is he involved in the NAACP?"

"Justinia may have mentioned that he has some involvement. I gather that he's very civic minded."

"Many affluent Negroes are. But they usually limit themselves to financial and intellectual participation. The elitists let the lower classes go into the trenches and do the dirty work."

"You sound a little disdainful, uncle. Did you have a run-in with one of those 'elitists'?"

"Not exactly. But affluent Negroes are quite an interesting group – lots of entitlement issues."

"Justinia has a friend – he's a student at the law school – and he can be quite pompous, but not so different from those filthy rich bungholes we knew back in Berlin."

"Who's her friend?" He took another sip, looked at me over his cup.

"Xavier something or other."

"I had a Xavier in one of my classes last year. He was a pain, tried to tell me that property rights were more important than civil rights. Can you imagine a Negro saying such a thing?"

"I can imagine *him* saying it," I laughed. "Although I think he enjoys being contrary. I know everything I say seems to be wrong. We probably have the same person in mind."

Uncle Sy had come to the states only a couple of years before me and developed much insight into American sociology. He found socioeconomics fascinating, even more interesting, at times, than the law. And he loved the law. Before his wife died, he liked to say the law was his mistress. Now he was obsessed with studying how people acted, thought and interacted with different people in different environments as well as how Americans differed from Germans.

As a German of Jewish descent who sought refuge in the States after losing the university job that he held for nearly thirty years, his feelings about Germany were bittersweet. 1932, the year before Hitler took over, was a bad year for my uncle. It all started when one of his favorite students turned him into the university dean for teaching "subversive" and "socialistic" ideas.

To hear Sy tell it, it was a tremendous betrayal. He'd mentored this student since his first year when he, along with many others, arrived at school eager to be instructed by the esteemed Symon Sommerfeldt, engage in rigorous Socratic dialogue and pick his brain for information, wit and hypothetical meanderings. Sy would meet with any of his students at all hours of the day, even invited them to his house for tea and to discuss the finer points of law or how to write a more compelling legal brief.

But one day during his Weimer Constitution class, this worshipful student went rogue, bringing a real, direct, public challenge to my uncle and his forty-year scholastic career of teaching, lecturing and authoring books.

"You've been lying to us."

"I beg your pardon?"

"You claim Article 109 says all Germans are equal under the law."

"Not a claim, it is fact!"

This student, the one he'd bestowed the honor of being his research assistant, stood at his seat and demanded that Sy repudiate the notion that under Article 109 all Germans were equal before the law.

"I'll do no such thing," my uncle told him. "That's precisely what Article 109 says and there are no exceptions. If you've allowed yourself to think otherwise, then you've been bamboozled."

This spunky student, who'd shared meals at my uncle's kitchen table and who helped ponder research angles in Sy's paper-and-book-crammed office, walked down the classroom aisle to where Sy was standing behind his desk.

"Article 109," he said, "was put in place to eliminate the supremacy of people with nobility titles, so princes, barons, lords and knights are no longer better than average, untitled citizens."

"It addresses that, sure, but its primary purpose is to affirm that all Germans are equal in all respects."

He took another step forward and said, "That's your communistic interpretation."

"Balderdash! What's wrong with you, Lars?"

"And everyone who *lives* in Germany is *not* a true German."

"What do you mean by that?"

"You know exactly what I mean. Equality under the law doesn't extend to Poles, gypsies, homosexuals, Jehovah's Witnesses or... Jews because they are not *true* Germans. They are an abomination to the German heritage."

"It was a slap in the face to me," Sy told me when he originally recalled the episode.

"Repudiate!" the student demanded again.

Obviously, Lars had been corrupted by some Nazified professor, one who'd probably never taken a stressed-out 1 a.m. phone call or reviewed a paper he was preparing for another class. Or else he was some perverted inside agent.

"You're a malignancy," Sy told Lars. "And you disgust me. Get out!" Lars went straight to the dean to tell him that Professor Sommerfeldt was teaching subversive material. With no due process, the dean gave my uncle 24 hours to vacate the premises.

As he was boxing up his things, he noticed a note attached by a dagger to the inside of his wooden door. It stated, "This is *your* fault. You had the chance to *repudiate!*" Sy vowed to give the kid "what for" if their paths ever crossed again. Sy said the administration had probably been looking for an excuse to get rid of him anyway; they thought he was too comfortable with socialistic ideas and Sy felt they'd become too fascist for him. It was time they parted company.

But then they also blackballed him so he couldn't get another teaching position anywhere. Not in all of Bavaria, not in Hamburg, not in Cologne. No one wanted to hire a subversive who was obviously a socialist and quite possibly a communist. This was all before Hitler ascended to totalitarian power, but the Nazi influence was already pervasive. So Sy came to America and discovered that finding a teaching job in the states was just as difficult. The schools he applied to evidently had enough Jewish professors and didn't need or want any more, especially cantankerous, wrinkly, old Jews with thick German accents – his words.

The only places that would have him were some Negro schools and that's how he came to be at Howard Law which became a second home for him, and, as in Berlin, he went that extra mile and it was appreciated. The prevailing culture throughout the entire Howard campus, as promoted by Dean Charles Hamilton Houston, was that students and instructors both were expected to let their reach exceed their grasp, so Sy fit right in.

The Howard students came to his home for potlucks and to prepare for exams, papers and moot court competitions. Out of politeness, they tasted his borscht and he gobbled up their gumbo and sweet potato pies. They became very close and he didn't have to worry about them complaining to the deans that his talk of equality under the Constitution was subversive thinking.

Now Sy planned on staying put, perhaps even applying for American citizenship as was our fellow Berliner, the much talked-about physicist, Albert

Einstein, who he'd never met in Germany but did meet through the mutual acquaintance of Dr. W. E. B. DuBois who'd known my great-aunt. Dr. Einstein was an NAACP member in New Jersey. Naturally, Sy became involved in the organization too. With his new career, his new associations and his new friends, Sy was content. Unlike me, Sy was completely disillusioned about Germany. He didn't care if he never went back.

"I'm an old man now. There's no reason to go back there. They could elect a Jew as president and I wouldn't return to that blasted place," he said on more than one occasion. Sy now viewed himself as an American, saying "Jim Crow has migrated to Germany and people like you and Gabriel must defeat it. Prepare and educate the children. There might even have to be an armed revolt."

"I certainly hope it doesn't come to that."

"Me either. But you have to be ready for anything."

"I'll certainly do my part. Sommerfeldt men are no yellowbellies."

"Damn right."

I leaned back in my chair. "So how's Howard?"

Although we lived in the same house, rarely did we get to sit down and have serious conversations. We were both so busy that we were virtually two ships passing in the night. When we did talk, it was usually about Germany, family, Jewish issues and current events. Seldom did we discuss the Negro people who we worked with everyday.

"Ninety percent of my students are first-generation and their family members are hanging all their hopes on them. They invest meager savings so that their darling can become a lawyer even though it's unlikely they'll be hired anywhere and private practice will probably yield them less money than some menial jobs."

"Hmm."

"They do this knowing they could very well end up being a frustrated chauffeur. All that time, effort and money wasted. But at least they can brag that there's a lawyer in the family."

"That's still a great thing."

"One of my students, Humphrey, is a very impressive young man. He told me his grandmother had forty dollars frozen in a block of ice that she was saving for the right occasion. She didn't believe in banks after losing the little bit she had on Black Tuesday. She wanted to keep up with her own money but she didn't want easy access to it, what with all the Fuller Brush salesmen coming around looking for easy prey to buy their overpriced cleaning implements when vinegar and a sturdy rag or an old toothbrush would do nicely. The forty dollars was all she had to her name, all she'd been able to save after doing laundry for years after the crash. Every time she got a whole dollar, she'd wet it and plaster it to the block of ice. When Humphrey told her he still needed law books after his family already pulled together four hundred-plus dollars for tuition, room and board, his grandmother let the ice melt in the sink and used an ice pick to free the bills and, three days later, presented the dried and ironed bills to him stuck in a shiny new Bible. Right smack in the book of Job, he said. He never would've found it had he not cracked the darn thing open. I suppose there's a moral or two in there somewhere."

"That's a good story."

"It would be had there been a happy ending."

The waitress brought our food and Sy tucked his napkin into his shirt collar, rubbed his hands together in anticipation.

"*Danke schon*," we said.

"*Bitteschon*," she answered with a smile.

"Where's Humphrey now?" I asked, pouring the burgundy-mushroom sauce over my schnitzel.

"Working as a busboy at the Diplomat. It broke my heart to see him. He looked bitter. He always fancied himself as a David who'd slay all the Goliaths in the D. C. courtrooms. It was the vision that got him through my class, through law school. I almost wish he'd never even tried."

"If I didn't know you better, uncle, I'd say you didn't think Negroes should become lawyers."

"To the contrary," he said to me, "but they'd be better off going into medicine or dentistry because at least there'd be a steady supply of patients. A person might spend their last dime to stop their tooth from aching but not to hire an attorney to placate some grievance. Even white folks will go to a Negro doctor if they're desperate enough."

"True."

"It's different with affluent Negroes. They don't carry the hopes and dreams of hundreds of people on their backs because others have walked the road before them and left it well-paved. They can take much for granted. They have connections that enable them to get attorney jobs. And if they fail, they have family to fall back on. They'll rent out space, put their name on the door and play golf and tennis everyday. Someone might have them draw up a contract or contest a will from time to time. They won't have to chip away at a block of ice and they won't be bussing tables at the Diplomat. But still it's not easy."

"I guess they have the same complex problems as everyone else."

"Same, but different. For most white people, success is determined by their own actions. But even the most intelligent, industrious Negro has external barriers they may not be able to overcome. I just don't want to see them disappointed, their hopes dashed."

"Sure," I said, "but law and medicine are not interchangeable. I, for one, couldn't see myself as a physician. Blood and guts is not for me."

"Yes, but you still have to eat. Unless there's a trust fund, you need good, paying clients to enjoy a certain lifestyle."

"Maybe they want to be a lawyer to fight to make the world better, not for the money."

"I'm sure there are many who feel that way. But you can't be a fighter without food, shelter and some kind of cushion. The law of diminishing returns dictates that, at least for now, law school may not be the best investment for Negroes. And if medical school isn't possible, they can save a whole lot of money and heartache by just getting a civil service job."

I nodded. "I also cannot see myself alphabetizing files when I really wanted to practice law. What a dilemma."

"That's what I'm saying."

"There's no guarantee they can even get a civil service job. I hear they're hard to come by."

"Not as hard as a job in the law. You work in the courts, Julius. How many Negro government attorneys do you see? How many prosecutors?"

"No prosecutors. Very few others. Maybe two or three?"

"Exactly. Probably less than half a dozen in a city filled with Negroes and with a Negro law school to boot. And don't even get me started about the women. Their law careers are even more improbable."

"But at some point, one has to just try, take a risk. It's about personal fulfill-ment. You don't want to have regrets. "

"No, but I happen to think it's more practical to wait until an opportune time, when society is more receptive to the idea of Negro lawyers."

"You raise some good points. But then I see lawyers like Thurgood Marshall breaking down barriers and it gives me hope for everybody."

"I just don't want them going broke buying hope and no future."

"I understand. I just think it'd be terrible to deprive the world of a genera-tion of Negro talent. There're some smart Negroes out there – even the un-schooled ones. They may be the ones to convince the world that opportunity belongs to everyone."

"It will take the Humphreys of the world to make that happen. People like your friend Xavier take too much for granted. They won't fight for the masses. They'll write a check, but they won't fight." He tasted the veal schnitzel, smacked his lips. "Now having said all that, Howard University is a wonderful institution and I'm proud to be affiliated."

Sy signaled to the waitress, exclaiming *"das war köstlich!"* I agreed; the schnit-zel was delicious, almost as tasty as Helga's. He asked her if the chef had made any of his famously scrumptious rum balls.

"He did indeed," she said.

"Rolled in hazelnuts and powdered sugar?"

"Of course, just for you!"

"Wunderbare! Bring us a plate of them for our dessert."

The women's chorus, ladies of all shapes, sizes and ages, came into the dining room and began exercising their vocal chords for their performance. Even their warm-up sounded good. It was evident how they won so many competitions.

"You know," I said, "maybe we Jews have been too entitled and complacent too. Maybe if we'd been more vigilant, Hitler would never have gotten a foot-hold. Maybe *we* wrote a lot of checks, looked out for ourselves and hoped for the best too."

"No, Hitler is a result of circumstances beyond our control, The war, stock market failure and economic depression caused a multitude of hungry, unemployed and disillusioned people to flock to a charismatic speaker with fistfuls of golden promises and propped up by gangsters and money. You know this, Julius."

"Of course, but you and I both know some 'assimilated' German Jews who are embarrassed by the orthodox *Ostjuden* – by their poverty, the way they look and smell and walk and talk – because they make us *all* look bad and encourage anti-Semitism. Nobody fights for them. Even *Vati* says they're from the Dark Ages."

"Because they've contaminated our mother with their antiquated habits and ideas. But what's your point?"

"We looked the other way when they were mistreated. Some of our leaders have called for their deportation or a moratorium on their immigration from eastern countries. Some don't allow them to vote in community elections because they're not German nationals. Aren't we guilty of being a little anti-Semitic ourselves?"

"Bah!"

"And Aryans think Communism is a Jewish movement. We distanced ourselves, looked the other way when both Communists and *Ostjuden* were brutalized. Didn't that contribute to the hatred? Shouldn't we have seen this coming and done something to stop it?"

"Absolutely not. We cannot be blamed for what is happening in Germany. First, Hindenburg was a damn fool for appointing Hitler Chancellor knowing that when he died, he'd be leaving the country in the hands of a maniac. And second, never underestimate the capacity for people to be stupid. They support ideas that sound good but are really against their best interests, just jump on the bandwagon and don't realize their error til its too late, when the hidden agenda is revealed, until their own ox is gored."

"I know."

"Then why are we even having this conversation?"

"Xavier, for example, disdains Negroes who aren't wealthy and sophisticated like he is. Perhaps that attitude contributes to the overall prejudice. It just made me think of how we regard *Ostjuden* back home."

"Interesting. Well, regardless, we're all the same under the skin. Does your friend Justinia have the same attitude as this Xavier?"

"Not at all. Justinia is compassionate."

"She sounds like an exceptional human being."

"She is."

"If I didn't know better, I'd say you're smitten."

I smiled. "I think she's a delightful *fraulein*." My uncle just looked at me long and hard. After several seconds, I turned my attention to the singers.

"Well you just be sure to tread cautiously." He continued giving me a look that was almost chastising. "Don't lose your head."

"Definitely not. You know me."

"I know you too well. You're impetuous like your grandfather was. Like the time he joined the German Alpine Club, tried to climb Hochkalter Mountain, got stuck half way up and had to be rescued."

I chuckled as I remembered hearing the story when I was a lederhosen-clad lad with aspirations of becoming a professional mountain climber, of scaling the heights of those alluring peaks that I saw in the distance during countryside hikes.

"He was trying to impress *Oma* Zip," I said.

"She told him he was a damn fool."

"But he still got the girl in the end."

"Wonder what he'd think of her now."

"He'd be just as enamored."

Hot, potent rum balls were placed on the table and we dug in. "*Perfekt*," we exclaimed.

The chorus began singing their first song, *Ein Freund, ein gutter freund*, which translates to "a friend, a good friend." It was a hit tune from a German musical and was very catchy; it would be in my head for the rest of the day. I couldn't help but tap my foot. One of the dancers winked at me and I winked back. Her alto voice was strong and prominent.

It really brought back memories of home where we often went to choral concerts. This Eichenkranz women's chorus was a great accompaniment to a great supper. For awhile, I was transported to the Germany I knew before Hitler took over, when Jews and Aryans could work together in the halls of law and justice, when we could sit side by side on bar stools and discuss football and beer brands without being uneasy.

"Anyway, my boy, Berlin awaits your return. Go and make a difference."

"I'll try."

"In the meantime, keep your head."

"I will, uncle, I will."

"Good! Now let's get the waitress for more tea."

"Lets."

CHAPTER 45

I<small>T IS UNFATHOMABLE</small> to me how someone could take a length of rope and fashion it into a noose, a fancy slip knot designed to kill. They had to wrap the rope six to eight times around a head-sized loop so that the coils formed around the rope and slide down to deliver a heavy blow to the side of the neck when tightened. It's uncomfortable to imagine the noose fashioner standing there admiring his handiwork, having his buddies and fellow posse members hold it up, caress it and remark on what a beaut' it was, knowing that it would soon be placed around the neck of some man or boy, sometimes some woman or girl, untried by a judge or jury, but fated to die for some subjective offense.

I wondered if the makers of the noose made them one at a time or several at once, stockpiling them in case they wanted to kill many at one time or just wanted to have some lying around in the event there needed to be a quickie hanging. A noose was a peculiar thing to have around. A rifle could be used for tin can target practice or to down a buck; a pitchfork lifted and turned hay; a knife could clear brush, trim tobacco, or whittle a block of wood into a toy; but a noose had only one purpose – to kill someone. I certainly wouldn't want to run into the man whose barn or tool shed had one or more ready-made nooses, a man who probably tipped his hat to passersby and masqueraded as a civilized gentleman instead of a psychopath. And it was more sadistic to hang someone than shoot them. Shooting took much less time and planning, but it didn't cause the same psychological terror or leave the same gruesome messages.

These thoughts came to mind as Justinia and I sat in the church basement with many youth committee members and helped turn twine into thin nooses so that NAACP activists could wear them around their necks to draw attention to the lynching crisis. It was a sobering activity. Justinia had decided that she would participate in the protest. The incident with the woman at the custard shop was apparently the impetus she needed.

Initially she wasn't sure she wanted to participate in this provocative demonstration. But then she said she could easily imagine Mrs. Vogelsang being part of a crazed lynch mob, shaking her fist and yelling, "Hang'em high!" Hatred would contort her face just like it did when she refused to serve us and kicked us out of her establishment.

Anyone who showed that much hate toward people they didn't even know was dangerous. Her customers might think of her as the nice, little custard lady, but if someone came along and said, "Hey, Mrs. V, let's go hunt down a nigger or a Jew," Justinia and I knew that she'd go along cheerfully; or she'd dispatch her husband or son, some male representative to show the family's support for the mob and their mission. People like that needed to be stopped.

So there we were at the quaint but stalwart Promise Baptist church making nooses while others made signs: "Stop the Lynching" or "Congress Act Now." A little girl customized her own message, "Negroes are people too," complete with a backwards "r" and a face with an upside-down smile and a big, fat teardrop. I wasn't going to be a part of the actual demonstration because even though some non-black people like the Jew Leo Frank had been lynched, my presence with a noose around my neck would be a distraction and I didn't want to complicate the operation in any way. But I'd be helping to transport participants to the selected location.

The room was brightly painted with framed pictures of a yellow-haired, blue-eyed Jesus plastered all over the walls, just as they were at the homes of my Negro clients. This same depiction of Jesus was on the wall calendars, the colorful covers of the Sunday School kiddie Bibles, and the cardboard-and-popsicle-stick fans. Upstairs in the sanctuary, light shone through the stained-glass images of angels, shepherds and assorted biblical icons traipsing through Middle Eastern deserts with milky white skin. I thought it was peculiar that white Jesus was everywhere in this gorgeous black church even though Jesus was Semitic and most Mid-Eastern Semitic peoples, like Sephardi Jews, unless they mixed with "whiter" Europeans, are dark. It wasn't surprising to see a blond Jesus at Georgetown University and in the European Christian churches, but I was surprised that Negroes didn't prefer to worship a Jesus rendered in their own image, one that reflected historical, geographical and biblical realities.

I don't recall ever seeing a picture of a blond Moses or a blue-eyed Abraham. Admittedly, most of the time they were shown as old men with white or gray beards so their younger selves were left open to interpretation. But I'm certain my childhood rabbi would have ripped out the pages from any book that depicted them as anything remotely Nordic. I didn't understand why Negro Christians accepted the portrayal promoted by their oppressors.

This needled me because this is exactly the paradigm Hitler wanted. He wanted everyone to think fair coloring was superior to all else and that it invariably determined the person's societal worth. The irony was that Hitler himself could be visually perceived as Jewish, and perhaps he was and was fooling the world because, with the exception of his ridiculous moustache and humorless visage, his dark hair and smoldering eyes made him the spitting image of one of my uncles who died in the war. Yet he held up the blue-eyed blondes to be the epitome of the Master Race, the ideal Aryan.

I'd love to know why Negroes were so accepting of the classic European-created, Nazi-perpetuating images, but knew this wasn't the time or the place. I'd ask Justinia her thoughts at a later time. Right now, it was best to stick to safer topics. I didn't want every conversation to have a politicized or racialized aspect. But it wasn't meant to be. It was hard to avoid controversy in mixed company. Innocent comments get misconstrued and, alas, I managed to stumble into another touchy subject.

While inside was yellow and sunny, outside was hot, gray and rainy. Rain streamed down from blackened skies and steam shimmied up from dusty sidewalks. Justinia, Millie, Shirley, Leddy and I were chatting amiably while seeing to our appointed tasks. Leddy, a young lady from Pennsylvania, who was carefully stenciling one of the signs, said she didn't think she was going to participate in the protest.

"Really, why not? I thought all of you were going. My car will fit six."

"I paid two whole dollars to get my hair pressed and marcelled and the rain will just ruin it." She put her marker down and patted her hair which had lots of waves. "This style has to last me at least another two weeks."

"If you carry an umbrella, how can it get ruined?" I asked innocently.

"It's really not nice to question Negro women about their hair. It's like asking movie starlets their real age. But since you asked..."

"I'm sorry, but I was curious. Your hair is so pretty. Very Greta Garbo."

"I prefer to think of it as very Nina Mae McKinney."

"Nina McKinney! Yes, I saw her in *Hallelujah* and *Safe in Hell*. In Europe she's known as the black Greta Garbo, although I think she's more beautiful than Greta. Nina McKinney is a cinematic sensation in Europe."

"Right, the first Negro movie star. You certainly know Hollywood trivia, Julius."

"I'm obsessed. Next to books, movies are my favorite pastime. I've wanted to visit Hollywood for three years but have never gotten the chance."

Leddy said, "Well, I love Nina Mae and told my hair dresser, Lurlene, to replicate her hairstyle in *Hallelujah*."

Justinia said, "I like Nina Mae too, but I *adore* Josephine Baker. Maybe I'll cut *my* hair to look like she did in *Princesse Tam-Tam*, slicked down curlicues and all."

"Don't forget the banana skirt," Shirley said.

"Her mother would have a heart attack," Millie said.

"Yes, she would," Justinia said, laughing. "Just from the haircut alone. Her eyes wouldn't even make it down to the banana skirt."

I blushed at the remembrance of seeing that eight-foot poster of Josephine Baker in the banana skirt when I was a teen and she and her troupe brought their Paris act to Berlin. And that banana dance! All I could say was "Whoa!" *Mutti* tried to cover my eyes with her hand as we passed the wall with the large poster advertising *La Revue Negre'* at the Titania Palast, but she was too slow. I'd already gotten an eyeful. And I saw more than that when some friends and I snuck into the auditorium and saw most of her first act until the manager caught us wolf whistling from the cheap seats and threw us out. As in Paris, she was a huge hit in Berlin. Multitudes of people, especially those who were into jazz, swing and the whole gay and glitzy cabaret scene, loved Josephine Baker, the Black Pearl.

Nazis hated Baker, "degenerate Negro music," the Jewish musicians who liked to play it and the homosexuals who reveled in it. They closed down the gay clubs, like the famous Eldorado, where many of their own used to carouse. They chased away Eldorado's most captivating performer, the bisexual, androgynous Marlene Dietrich, because the Hitler regime was as sanctimonious and hypocritical as a pontificating, bacon-eating rabbi – *and* she'd called Hitler an idiot. I was reminded that Berlin used to be fun and free, a magnet for American expatriots, a mecca for people from all over the world looking to meet interesting people and have one hell of a good time.

"Look at the bright side," said Shirley. "No amount of rain could mess up all that gel. You'd need a chisel."

"Justinia has nothing to worry about anyway," Leddy said. "She has good hair. She can just pull it back into a ponytail and still look great. Me, on the other hand, the humidity alone will make me look like a wet poodle in twenty minutes flat."

"Well, poodles are cute," I said.

"Believe me, there'll be nothing cute about it," Leddy said as she stenciled the "L" in "lynching."

"I know I can feel a little self-conscious when the barber clips my hair too close."

"It's hardly the same thing, Julius," Leddy said.

"But people will remember that you stood up for something important, not how your hair looked."

"I can appreciate that. But remember, you're speaking as someone for whom hair isn't an issue. You're not judged by it."

"Well, if you don't mind my asking, how is it an issue? My cousin Gretchen lays her head on a board and has her friend press her hair with a clothes iron to try and make it look sleek like Katharine Hepburn whom she absolutely adores. A few hours later, she's back to looking like Albert Einstein."

"Who?"

"He's a physicist, a good acquaintance of my uncle who fled Germany because the Nazis were after him. People say he's the smartest man in the world and that he has the secret to making an atomic bomb. Every time I see the guy, he has the most bizarre, wind-whipped hair. It suits him, but not Gretchen."

"I think I've heard of him," Millie said.

"He was on the cover of *Life* magazine," Shirley said. "A brilliant man, won a Nobel prize, but he did look like he'd stuck his finger in an electric socket."

"That's hilarious if your cousin really looks like that," Leddy said.

"She does."

"It's still not the same thing though. The world won't judge her six ways to Sunday. But me? My hair will stay puffy until I get another two dollars and a three-hour appointment with Lurlene. You have no idea what a tedious process it is to put in marcelle waves. I'm still a train ride to Philly and two city bus rides away from home. I have to look respectable. People watch you and make all kinds of assumptions. So I want to preserve what I have. I need to have something going on."

"What do you mean?" I asked. "You've got a lot going on. You're an NAACP young adult delegate. That's a big deal. And didn't you say you're studying to be a nurse?"

"Yes, but the people on the train won't know that. They only know what they see – just another nappy-headed colored girl."

"Is that so bad?"

"Yes, because I'll be stereotyped, never given the benefit of any doubt."

"Really?" I wanted to say more but didn't because I didn't think it would be helpful.

"It's even more complicated, . . .let's just say I'll never get into a paper bag party."

"What's a paper bag party?"

"Ask Justinia to tell you about that later. That's a whole other can of worms."

"Plain foolishness," Justinia said and left it at that. "And Leddy, you're beautiful."

"Why thanks, but let's tackle one thing at a time and focus on this lynching thing." Leddy began to fill in the "Y."

I was compiling quite a list of subjects I wanted to talk to Justinia about. She was a font of information, a vessel of charm, an exotic bloom. This was our last full day at the convention. There'd be no one in Germany to abide my unbridled curiosity about Negro issues. I'll feel like I closed the book or left the movie right when it was getting interesting. Hopefully this wouldn't be the last time we were together. I was going to have to stay in America longer or she'd have to come visit me in Berlin.

"Alright."

Justinia smiled at me and asked me to pass the scissors. Our hands touched and something inside me sizzled. I smiled back and turned my attention back to finishing up my noose. I threw it on top of the growing pile. It was a macabre sight.

Leddy said, "I'll wait here at the church but will be with you all in spirit."

⊷═◉ ◉═⊶

"May I have everyone's attention," said a tall, distinguished man in a gray, pin-striped suit and a cleric's collar. "We need to go over some things before the demonstration."

Another man, much shorter, with a big, heavy gold cross hanging from a gold chain said, "Listen up, this is important." Juanita Jackson went to stand next to them but let the men address the demonstrators.

People paused in their tasks and gave their full attention to the pastor and his associate. As if scripted, they alternated speaking parts.

"We're going to Federal Hill," the pastor said. "For those of you from out of town, it's at the end of Charles Street which separates the east side of Baltimore from the west side."

"Many of you may have explored Charles Street," the other man said. There're many businesses with friendly proprietors. Barbecue shacks, crab shacks, some bakeries, ice cream parlors, things of that nature. It's a major thoroughfare, lots of foot and vehicle traffic." That's where we should've gone, I thought.

"This is to be a *silent* vigil."

"Many of the NAACP's protests have been vocal marches down the street with bullhorns blarin', marchers clappin' and sangin'. We aren't gonna march, clap or sang. Won't be no speeches. We'll just stand there and let the spectacle speak for itself."

"Yes, it'll be a powerful statement."

"This has been done before and it always has great impact."

"There will be some people who won't 'preciate our presence or the message we're conveyin'. They may shout, call us names and what have you. Your duty is to ignore them."

"That's correct. Do not engage! This is about delivering a message using visual stimuli only. If someone feels antagonized, their reaction only serves to underscore the problem. No need to bring additional negative attention to it. It could backfire."

"Don't give ignorant people the satisfaction of making *us* look like the agitators."

"So we're just supposed to stand there no matter what?" someone called out.

"Yes."

"That's going to be difficult." It sounded like something Xavier might say, but it wasn't him. Xavier had said he had other plans.

"Well, young man," the second man said, "maybe you aren't cut out for this kind of demonstration. We don't want anything to detract from our message. So if you don't think you can control your emotions, we'd 'preciate it if you'd just wait here at the chu'ch." Juanita nodded in agreement.

"Just wondering," said the young man. "But that's still a tall order."

The pastor explained the philosophical reasoning. "We're embracing the concept of *satyagraha*. In Sanskrit it means 'insistence on the truth.' *Satya* meaning truth and *agraha* meaning force."

"It's the policy of non-violent resistance advocated by the Mahatma Gandhi in his continuous struggle to win India's independence from Great Britain."

"Yeah, and how's that going?" someone else asked.

"Last I heard, they were still exploited British subjects," another person responded.

"Well, as we all know, progress is a slow process, 'specially when you're asking the oppressor to give up power, land or money. The object here, as it is over there in India, is to *convince* or *convert*, not to *coerce* those with the power to do the right thing."

"Exactly. And for any protest to work, utilizing *satyagraha*, the demonstrators must adhere to a non-violent strategy. And they must be fearless. And they must have faith in a living God and respect for all religions."

"They must believe in the inherent goodness of humankind and be obedient to the laws of the land."

"We must represent the NAACP well," Juanita said.

"Yes, and the *Baltimore Afro-American* will prob'ly be along to take some pitchers. If any reporters ax you anything, just say that the NAACP is dedicated to ending lynching and that we're calling on the President and the Congress to help accomplish this. Any quer-stions?"

There were none.

"Then let us pray."

Juanita wanted everyone to gather in a circle and hold hands while the minister led a prayer. Justinia and I grabbed each others' fingers before being instructed to. The circle ringed the entire circumference of the room. There were quite a few people. It should be a good demonstration. It was a nice prayer, asking God to watch over everyone and keep everyone safe and focused, to soften the hearts of even the most hardened segregationists and to rid the enemy of its lynch mob mentality. The prayer went on for several minutes before everyone finally said "amen." Then there was singing, the final preparation before departing for the protest venue and heading into battle. The short minister burst into song and the people followed instinctively. His voice was a smooth baritone.

Swing low, sweet chariot. Coming for to carry me home.
Swing low, sweet chariot. Coming for to carry me home.

I looked over Jordan and what did I see
Coming for to carry me home.
A band of angels coming after me,

Coming for to carry me home.
Swing low, sweet chariot. Coming for to carry me home.
Swing low, sweet chariot. Coming for to carry me home.

If you get there before I do
Coming for to carry me home.
Tell all my friends I'm coming there too.
Coming for to carry me home.
Swing low, sweet chariot. Coming for to carry me home.
Swing low, sweet chariot. Coming for to carry me home.

I thought it was a nice song and easy to learn but I wondered about its message. I whispered to Justinia, "Nice song, but isn't it about dying?"

It seemed like a strange song to sing before going to a silent protest where people would be wearing nooses around their necks. It seemed to anticipate danger and the chance some people could die for expressing their anti-lynching beliefs. It worried me because I was hoping that the entire episode would be just a peaceful symbolic gesture and that no one would get hurt. Justinia put me back at ease.

"On the surface the song *is* about going to Heaven. But this is an old Negro spiritual and, like many of them, it had a hidden meaning to the slaves who were trying to escape."

"Oh really? What was the message?"

"When slaves sang that song, it meant that a conductor of the Underground Railroad, someone like Harriet Tubman who's famous for leading over 300 slaves to freedom in Canada, would be arriving soon, and that those planning to escape should be alert and ready to go."

"I read about Harriet Tubman. Her roots are right here in Baltimore."

"Yes, after *she* escaped she went back nineteen more times to free all her family members and many others."

"Incredible!" I said. "And singing in code – how ingenious!"

Millie said, "White people thought slaves were dumb and couldn't possibly come up with coded messages. That would be admitting they were clever. The slaves would sing these songs right in the cotton fields, right out there with the overseer listening, and he'd be none the wiser. Then the next morning, half a dozen slaves would be missing."

"I get it now," I said. "The 'chariot' is the railroad conductor, and instead of heaven, they're singing about going north to freedom."

"Exactly," Justinia said.

"So the song was actually about hope and vigilance."

"Right again," said Millie. "So it's appropriate to sing it now."

"And sometimes," Justinia said, "the slaves weren't so cryptic. You've heard the song, 'Go Down, Moses' in your culture?"

"Not in Germany, but it was sung during a Passover Seder I attended last year." I recalled it vividly:

When Israel was in Egypt's land: Let my people go,
Oppress'd so hard they could not stand, Let my People go.
Go down, Moses,
Way down in Egypt's land,
Tell old Pharaoh,
Let my people go.

The parallels hit me. Harriet Tubman was called the Black Moses.

"Yes," Justinia said, reading my mind. "'Israel' means 'Negro slaves' and 'Pharaoh' is the 'slave master'. So they sang the song in the overseers' presence and they still didn't connect the singing – let my people go – to their intentions to escape. So who are the real dunces?"

I laughed at the irony and the profundity of it all.

"And get *this*," Millie said, feeding on my enthrallment., "My father says that abolitionists stitched codes into the patterns of their quilts and hung them in windows and on laundry lines to help slaves find hideouts, tunnels, food and water on the Underground Railroad."

"That's brilliant!"

"Sometimes it's smart to just let people think you're dumb."

I couldn't believe the education I was receiving in America. My studies at Georgetown were only academic, the tip of the iceberg of knowledge and discovery. I was amazed at how much more expansive my world view had become, how much keener my insight was becoming. Everyone should have the opportunity to travel, to meet new people and experience other cultures. If more people were to immerse themselves in an alternative existence, I believe there'd be more empathy and understanding and less indifference and hatred. Hitler should spend some time in Harlem, New York. Better yet, he should go to Queens which had a large population of Jews. He could get to know the people he hates so much.

People began gathering up the signs and nooses and went up the stairs where we would walk out the door to get to the parking lot. We followed suit. I was ready.

CHAPTER 46

Justinia

I DON'T KNOW if it was the prayer, the singing, or the finger-crossing that Millie and I were doing, but when we walked out of the church, the rain had stopped and the sun was shining. I was so glad because I knew that Leddy really wanted to participate in the protest and I hated that she had to choose between doing something meaningful and memorable and feeling she had to keep her hair from getting messed up.

After knowing her for a week, it was painfully obvious that Leddy was very self-conscious about her looks, confiding that because she was dark, she at least needed to have pretty-styled hair. Neither I, nor Millie or Shirley could convince her that she was a lovely young woman regardless of how her hair looked.

"That's easy for you guys to say," she said, pointing out that I was light with "good" hair, Shirley was dark with "Indian" hair all down her back and Millie was medium-toned with shoulder-length hair that could just be gathered into a rubber band if it wilted.

Leddy had her straightening comb heating up on Mrs. Tuttle's stove every morning to straighten her edges because the hot sun and perspiration caused her hairline to "bead up" and she couldn't abide that. A tiny, orange tin of "Sweet Georgia Brown" hair pomade was on the counter nearby to aid in the "de-beading" process. And I know beauty has its price, but Leddy, with big, silver hair clips all over her head to keep the waves in place, slept sitting up in bed, her back against pillows which were piled up against the headboard. Shirley and I stopped teasing her when we realized she wasn't joining in our laughter. Her hair was serious business.

She said when she was eight, her grandmother taught her to make lye soap to straighten her naturally coiled hair. "All you need is some woodstove ashes, rain water, some lard and an egg. It burns like the dickens but, in a pinch, gets your hair real smooth." I tried not to turn up my nose. Most of my friends and I just went to the beauty parlor or bought some G. A. Morgan Hair Refining Cream. "But you girls are lucky," Leddy said, "and wouldn't know anything about that."

In the kitchen, Mrs. Tuttle fussed at her, telling her to hurry up so she could scramble the eggs and put the tea kettle on. "I don't want hairs gettin' in the food."

"Almost done, Mrs. Tuttle."

Mrs. Tuttle then told her that if she weren't careful, she'd burn her hair clean off. "If God wanted your hair to be straight, he woulda made it straight Hisself."

"No disrespect, Mrs. Tuttle," Leddy said, "but is *your* hair naturally straight?"

"No it's not, child," she said, patting her own grease-shined-and-pressed locks, "but that don't make my point any less valid."

But Leddy was obsessed with her hair and no one could change her feelings about it. She reminded me of the protagonist in the book "The Blacker the Berry," except Leddy was more self-conscious about hair than skin color.

"What if it starts raining again in the middle of the demonstration?" she asked, looking out of the window of the church to see if she could read the clouds. Leddy didn't want to get her hair wet, or let the humidity cause her salon-created waves to disintegrate. She wanted her hair to look like Nina Mae McKinney, a popular Negro actress who was known worldwide as the black version of Greta Garbo, though she had Bette Davis' eyes. Looking outside, there were no clouds; they were drifting away fast towards D. C. Her marcelle waves should be safe.

"I think you'll be fine," Millie said. "Look, the sky is clear and the puddles are drying up. It looks like it never stormed."

Shirley peered out to see for herself. "You're right. Okay, it's an obvious sign. God wants me to do this. Let's go."

We got into Julius' car and drove to a park-like setting on Federal Hill.

CHAPTER 47

HALF OF US stood on the sunny side of the street and half stood on the shady side. I was in the shade because Magdalena would be peeved if I came home too suntanned. Millie and Leddy stood on either side of me. There may have been thirty of us standing around wearing slender nooses representing past and future victims. We were a sight to see.

There was a little boy, about six, with no noose, holding a sign that said, "Why do you want to hang me?"

His sister, a tad younger, wearing no noose, held a sign that read, "Negroes are people too!"

I don't see how anyone's heartstrings could remain untugged after seeing something like that. My own mother, though, would've been unnerved had she been walking by. The whole thing would've been too graphic for her delicate constitution. She'd much prefer hearing a speech, reading a *Crisis* article or writing a check.

It was an emotionally-charged thing putting that noose around my neck. This was just a symbolic gesture and the strands of twine could easily be cut with a good pair of scissors, but it made me tense. Still it was incomparable to the real-life terror a victim must feel when he knows that no amount of clawing or pulling would remove it, that it would be the instrumentality of his demise.

I can only imagine what those last few moments were like, how dread must have caused their heart to bang vainly against the rib cage, how any protestations must have become more gravelly and guttural as the throat tensed up in anticipation and the rope tightened. I pondered how difficult it must be to remain stiff-lipped and stalwart for the benefit of hysterical family and friends who were watching from behind closed or wide-open hands because it was important to minimize the manifestations of the suffering; or maybe they wanted to deprive the killers of the pleasure of seeing them tremble, whimper or scream. It was futile anyway. There would be no mysterious, white-hatted hero on a white horse riding in to save the day. That only happened in Hollywood. One may as well show audacity instead of panic and fear. So when the story was told fifteen minutes later or fifteen years later, it could be said that the condemned had been brave and defiant til the end. Or maybe they looked forward to death, to being in Heaven, which I assume is peacefully integrated.

These were my thoughts as I stood, just as they said we should, wistfully contemplative like the Statue of Liberty, barely moving with my eyes straight ahead, ostensibly oblivious to the spectators who were passing by. I was resolute but self-conscious; I'd much have preferred to be one of hundreds instead of one of dozens, but there I was. Some singing, some bongo-beating and some pamphleteering would've been nice to diffuse the focus and help me feel less conspicuous, yet there I stood. Mary Church Terrell would be proud.

Julius sat on a nearby park bench, on the sunny side. He could've been doing anything else, yet chose to drive me, Millie, Leddy and Shirley to the demonstration and stay, observe and take notes so he could write about it later on. I was conscious of his eyes, shaded by the cupped palm of his hand, on me. Or maybe it was my imagination or my hope that they were.

There was a luncheon and a boat ride taking place, but Julius thought this was more important. I had to agree. I'd been on plenty of boat rides – paddle boats, sailboats and yachts on the Chesapeake, riverboats and motorboats on the Potomac, canoeing with a lackluster blind date on the Howard University Reservoir. Last year my family and I cruised to St. Barts for a cousin's island wedding. I'd gone to countless luncheons, had dined on chicken and potatoes re-created in the most imaginative ways, had a closet full of hats I'd donned for such occasions, and the "we can be victorious if we all stick together" platitudes delivered by many a luncheon speaker would reverberate in my ears and in my mind in perpetuity. Yes, I could forego another tour of the Inner Harbor, a mere binoculars' view away from where we were, applauding another distinguished dais, sugaring another cup of tea, or running into the Chandler twins.

I finally saw them at the previous night's outdoor gospel concert which featured special guest and rising star, Mahalia Jackson. They were sitting right behind me on the lawn. "If it isn't Justinia Treadwell," they said during the intermission and free will offering. "In the flesh. We've been looking for you."

"Hello, twins. Mother told me you were here. It's been years. You look exactly the same. How are you?"

"Peachy! We were magna cum laude from Stanford after spending the last month studying in Oxford. We met the Crown Prince of Ethiopia while there. We became friends and have a standing invitation to his palace in Wollo. Those Ethiopians, especially the coastal ones, are so gorgeous, it's hard to remember that they're African; they're like Europeans with just the right amount of caramel coloring. Mother tells us you finally graduated Howard, that your little brother is at Morehouse and Charlotte finished Spelman, got married and is in Liberia of all places. How does she find the Liberian people to be? Are they properly westernized? We may visit Ethiopia before we start classes at Penn in the fall, the Wharton School of Business to be precise. An Ivy League Master's Degree should take us far. We plan to own corporations one day. One day you'll be reading about us in *Crisis*, and before you know it – *Fortune* Magazine. Father has already arranged the purchase of a nice row house for us; it has rental units attached so it will pay for itself, and it's not far from campus. We're all set. As Father says, 'The sky's the limit.' So how are you? You look the same too. And who, pray-tell, is this?"

"I'm well, thank you. This is Julius Somerfeldt from Germany. He's here for the convention." They shook hands. The twins eyed him with suspicion; he eyed them with astoundment.

"Well I'm in Baltimore for the NAACP convention, but I've been living in Washington D. C. for three years." He rubbed his handsome chin. "Wow, you guys are buddies with African royalty. That would be Haile Selassie's son? How utterly fascinating."

"We didn't say we were *buddies*. We met him and he invited us to his compound in the Ethiopian mountains as soon as the army ousts the Italian occupiers. So how do you know Justinia?"

They didn't wait for a response. "You two look pretty cozy together. Are you seeing each other? Mother would be very interested to know this. Do Mr. and Mrs. Treadwell know about your...friend?"

"There's nothing to know. We just met and are enjoying each other's company. Nothing more. Isn't that correct, Mr. Sommerfeldt?"

"Yes, we only recently made acquaintance."

"And are you a big fan of gospel music, Mr. Sommerfeldt?"

"Please call me Julius. Yes, I'm a fan. I think Mahalia Jackson will be an American treasure."

"Is that so? Well, we suppose that if *we* can be fans of the Gershwin brothers and their *Porgy and Bess*, then *you* can be a fan of Mahalia Jackson and 'Precious Lord, Take My Hand.'"

Turning back to me, they continued with, "As you know, Father runs an engineering division at Boeing, so we took a plane all the way to New York to see *Porgy and Bess* on Broadway. It was a bit stuffy and very bumpy but clearly flying is the only way to travel nowadays. Only eighteen hours, twelve passengers."

"Lindbergh would be impressed," Julius interjected.

"The trains are too slow and ...racial...when crossing certain states. The whole thing was Mother's idea. It was midterms, but Mother thought this was an important cultural experience. We sat next to Celestine Greer – well, it's Kennebrew now; she married a psychiatrist – he trained at Yale and Meharry. You remember her, Justinia."

"Not really."

"Well you should. Her mother was the first Negro woman to play in the orchestra at the Met. Celestine is at Juilliard, mastering the strings like her parents. She has about a million freckles."

"Oh yes, Celestine. I remember she loved to ride the horses and refused to bait her own fishing hook. And she always cheated in freeze tag." She was also a notorious hair flipper but many of the girls were guilty of that annoying habit so I omitted that part. Charlotte curbed me of the habit many years ago when she said that excessive hair flipping and fluffing, especially in the presence of Negro women with stiff, untossable hair, was as obnoxious as wearing diamonds and furs to go teach poor people to read.

The twins just gave me blank looks.

"But I'm sure she's remarkably talented."

"Absurdly so. The weekend was *tres* expensive. They roped off a section of the Rainbow Room so we could dine – in private. Sixty-five stories up and the dance floor revolves. Stunning views. And of course we paid homage to Nana and Papa, who are ailing and live in Harlem – but in the *good* part, Sugar Hill. They were the second Negro family on the block. Papa's been retired twenty years, but his insurance firm is still going strong. So. . . have you ever flown before, Mr. Sommerfeldt?"

"So far I've only ridden old-fashioned locomotives and steamers. Fortunately ones that proved much more seaworthy than the Titanic. Or the Lusitania – of course it couldn't help that it was torpedoed. Other than that, I travel exclusively by secondhand automobile with a dented fender. I do, however, look forward to enjoying a Zeppelin flight one of these days. Preferably one without a swastika emblem."

Again there were the blank expressions. Evidently no one was permitted to be joking and sarcastic in their presence. Julius said later that he didn't think flying was for the claustrophobic. The idea of many people jammed into a small space and being unable to escape, feeling trapped and vulnerable, was unappealing to him.

One of the twins said, "Well the Broadway show was everything you could imagine. The music, costumes, scenery, everything was superb. We loved it."

I was waiting for them to say George Gershwin himself invited them to come on stage and sing along with the cast but, surprisingly, no further embellishment was forthcoming.

"Well, good for you," I said. "I had to wait until it came to D. C."

"Me too," Julius said. "It's an outstanding opera. And I believe it was the first time the National Theater ever had an integrated audience."

He and I looked at each other. We could add *Porgy and Bess* to the growing list of things – fine prose, good cinema, strong, flavorful tea, an abiding sense of social justice – we already had in common. We may have attended on the same night, might have brushed shoulders or stood in the concessions line together during intermission. No, I definitely would've noticed him. But I wonder if the downy hairs on the back of his neck became erect when the high notes were sung in the "Summertime" aria, just as mine did. We most certainly read the same newspaper articles about how the lead actor of the all-Negro cast, a former Howard professor, had refused to go on stage unless every seat was available to every theater patron regardless of race, how the management capitulated, how the shows were still sold-out and well received, and how the National went right back to being segregated after *Porgy*'s swan song.

"It proved Negro and white can intermingle and still enjoy themselves," I said.

"We suppose."

"And while we're on the subject, I understand Paul Robeson is magnificent in the film version of Oscar Hammerstein's *Showboat* though I've yet to see for myself. Apparently," Julius said evocatively, "the collaboration of Negro and Jewish talent is a great thing."

"He razzes us, twin. My, my. It's all so very... interesting." The twins, subtly chided, looked at me, Julius and back at me again.

"Please excuse us," I said, gathering up the picnic blanket. "I see someone I need to speak to before the concert resumes and they bring out Miss Jackson. It's been wonderful seeing you both. Mother sends her regards."

"Will you be at the prayer luncheon?"

"Yes."

"We'll save you a seat at our table. Or will you be needing one for Mr. Sommerfeldt...Julius... as well?"

I pretended not to hear as I ferried Julius off to another spot, away from their grandiose stories, their opportunistic segues, their prying, their audacious assumptions.

"They're more insufferable than you said they'd be, Justinia," Julius whispered to me as we walked away feeling the twins' eyes boring into our backs. "I see why you wanted to avoid them."

"I warned you." We shared a private laugh as we squeezed in with Millie, Leddy and Shirley on a narrow patch of lawn.

Millie mumbled into my ear. "We were trying to give you two some time alone. What happened?"

"Those crazy Chandler twins."

CHAPTER 48

OUR EXPERIENCE AT the custard shop had shaken me up. It had been a long time since I'd been refused service or kicked out of an establishment. Looking back, there was the time that a deceptively welcoming restaurant deliberately over-salt-and-peppered our food, rendering it inedible, then threatened to call the police when my father refused to pay the bill. This latest incident made me remember the pain of seeing the fabulous Magdalena, pregnant with Emery, humiliated from soiling herself when Barrington's Department Store refused to let her use the public restroom even after spending thirty minutes and twenty dollars at the perfume counter. Even then, her head was up, as if willing the world to ponder on what could cause this classy, high-stationed woman to have tears streaking through her studiously applied blush. I remembered how sad and helpless I felt.

My father, who was litigious, sued offending establishments but mainly got dismissals, symbolic, one-dollar verdicts or "piddly nuisance settlements" which was fine with him because at least he got to make a point. He said he may not win, but wanted his opponents to know they'd been in a fight and expose their nastiness to the world. There was a genteel segment of society that very much disapproved of conspicuous racism. "It's the principle," Daddy says. "And even small money adds up."

If Julius didn't think he'd be a distraction, he'd be standing right next to me, his neck in a twine noose. Listening to his stories about Nazi Germany also helped conjure up those memories I wanted to forget – like gagging on salty spaghetti and Emery's coughing fit unabated by my father's slaps on his back, like my mother ambling out of Barrington's smelling of *Quelque Fleurs* by Houbigant and bowel movement. Like drinking Coca-cola that a server spat in. It was almost half gone before another server, also white, could warn me.

"Don't drink that," he whispered to me. "Bea hocked a loogie in it." When I realized what that meant, I was immediately ill. He wiped up my vomit with a towel. "She thinks you're high-falutin', but she's just white trash." I composed myself and thanked him.

I'd blocked those things from my conscience because my parents thought a new toy, a new outfit or a party invitation would eclipse the indignities and soothe the hurt. Now there was this custard incident and I'm sure the proprietor, Mrs. Vogelsang, at a different time and place, would've thought nothing of siccing a lynch mob on us. This helped me decide to participate in the demonstration and Julius was my battle muse. I felt emboldened and reassured in his presence. It was unbelievable how close I felt to him. I flipped my hair over my shoulder and tried to concentrate on feeling like a victim which wasn't as difficult as I'd thought.

It almost felt as if we were animals in a zoo or some abstract artwork at the Smithsonian. People would walk by, stop, cock their heads, move sideways to observe us from a different angle as if searching for something to undermine the demonstration. Mothers pulled their curious children as if they might be morally corrupted by the sight of us. Many of the men ignored us completely. Many of the women looked offended as if we were advertising pornography and not realizing that lynching was another version of pornography and that they should be outraged at the practice, not the complaint of it.

"Not all them bastards is innocent," someone said. "They were probably all guilty of *something* and deserved exactly what they got. Animal justice for animals."

We ignored the woman who said this. She yelled some more bigoted propaganda but got discouraged when she couldn't bait anyone into an altercation. She left in a huff, pulling her wide-eyed, inquisitive children behind her. But there were many vocal supporters and empathizers.

"George Armwood was innocent!"

"So were Henry Woods, Claude Neal and the Smoak brothers. And all those people in Rosewood. I've got postcards of some of these incidents, sent to me by relatives in Jacksonville. Sick stuff! Folks think Alabama is bad but Florida has the worst rednecks of all! They are certifiably crazy."

"Yes, the lynching has got to stop. We're a better country than this."

"Is this stuff still happening? I had no idea."

"What about all the police brutality? That's contemporary lynching."

"Amen!"

"If the lynch mob don't get'em, then the 'lectric chair will. Ain't no 'scapin' the white man's vengeance."

"You people are brave to do this. I couldn't put a noose 'round my neck, even pretendin'."

"I'm so glad someone is standing up against this. My cousin was lynched in Texas last week and the police are trying to say it was a suicide. How could it be a suicide when his hands were tied behind his back? How? And he had everything to live for; he was a successful cattle rancher, had a wife and three little ones."

"I'm so sorry," I said to her softly. Others, to maintain the integrity of their roles, expressed their condolences with their eyes.

The woman nodded, then proceeded down the boulevard cursing those "lying, murdering Texas crackers."

About an hour into the demonstration, an important-looking man walked up to us, a photographer in tow. "Who's in charge here?" he asked. The coordinator of the event who was the co-pastor at the church that was the base of our operation stepped up.

"I'm the coordinator. How are you, Senator Wagner? I'm pastor of Providence Baptist Church, undersecretary of the Baltimore City chapter of the NAACP. This here is Juanita Jackson, leader of the Youth and Young Adult section. How can I help you, Senator?"

They shook hands. "I'm in Baltimore for a meeting just down the street. I heard what you people were up to so I came on over. I want you to know that I appreciate the message you're trying to convey."

"Thank you, Senator."

"As you know, I've been trying to get the Costigan-Wagner anti-lynching bill passed."

I could tell that all the demonstrators' ears perked up when they heard "senator" and "anti-lynching." Eyes darted in the direction of the senator from New York and curiosity briefly edged out the sorrow, feigned and real. But everyone stayed in their role as instructed.

"We know," Juanita said. "We've been following along. It's a shame the southern senators blocked your and Senator Costigan's efforts."

"Even the President didn't back it. He was afraid of losing southern voters too. It's that whole 'states' rights' argument. And they really didn't like the idea of the sheriffs getting prosecuted for failing to protect their Negro prisoners in the jailhouse. And the number of lynchings is way down due, in no small part, to the activism of individuals and groups like yours."

"True, but even one is too many."

"Well I just wanted to tell you to keep the pressure on."

"We will. Thank you for stopping by." They all shook hands.

"Godspeed, Reverend."

"Godspeed, Senator."

It was a privilege to be acknowledged by a sitting United States senator. It was a shame that his fight to eradicate lynching ended up in a puff of smoke. The number of *reported* lynchings was on the decline, but Juanita Jackson reminded us that there were still many that went unreported. We were happy the senator stopped by and, even though it was supposed to be a silent vigil, someone thought this was a good time for a song. One of the women who was carrying a big, thick Bible started humming softly; then people started singing softly.

"Jesus loves me, this I know
For the Bible tells me so,
Little ones to him belong,
They are weak, but He is strong.
Yes, Jesus loves me, Yes Jesus loves me.
Yes, Jesus loves me,
For the Bible tells me so.

There was a white man pacing back and forth in between the two lines of demonstrators. He wore a newsboy cap, his shirt was half-tucked and he was clearly agitated. He either didn't like our demonstration or he didn't like our song. He looked at us all accusingly.

"One of y'all killed my daddy." We ignored him. "Stabbed him in the gut and let him bleed out like a mangy, old mutt. Few nights ago. Not even a mile from here. Which one of y'all is responsible?"

The singing turned into humming.

The pastor came forward again. "Sir, I'm awful sorry 'bout your daddy, but no one here is responsible. We're just tryna have a peaceful demonstration here. We'd 'preciate you just letting us be."

"Well you covering for somebody. I think it was one of these here Negresses. Always complaining about being harassed and pawed on by decent white men. Yet they continue with their sinful, trollop-y ways. Temptresses, all of 'em."

"I'm askin' you nicely to leave."

"I'll bet it was you!" he yelled into the face of this pretty girl from Chicago who was nice to talk to. "Prob'ly shook your tail, led him into the bushes and sliced him with your razor. Didn't you!" She did not flinch.

"Leave her alone. Get out of here. We'll be leaving soon."

The man ignored the pastor. "How 'bout you?" he asked another girl. She was tall and from St. Louis. She glared at him. "You look like you've led many a good man astray."

He went up and down the line screaming into the faces of the young ladies. "Did you leave him before or after his guts spilled out onto the sidewalk?" Nobody answered.

"Well?"

The male demonstrators were tense, wanting to pounce and defend, but honoring the instructions to stay calm. The humming petered out. He was coming closer to where I was. The pastor hurried off, saying he was getting the police.

"Brang'em! Brang back the whole durn precinct. And tell 'em to brang some *real* rope with 'em, somethin' that'll choke a horse."

He was upon me before I realized it. "Yeah, you're definitely the type – when your mama and daddy made you it was bestiality. You're no purebred. Your daddy was a big, black beast that prob'ly forced hisself on your mama." He was two inches from my face.

"Yeah, you did it, just stuck him and left him. Then you show up here acting all innocent. Well, I got your numba, ya little filly."

His whiskey breath was practically strong enough to be intoxicating and suffocating. Even so, his eyes were cold sober and determined, his teeth were gritted and he pulled on the cord around my neck, started twisting it so it got tighter. I looked at the man in disbelief. Was he really trying to strangle me? Was his wraith-like visage the last thing I'd see before succumbing to a horrid death that I had minutes ago just pondered? If I could breathe, I would've laughed at the horrible irony of it all. People got out of line and rushed toward me. I was aware of Millie and others trying to pull me away from this awful creature.

Then I saw Julius. "Get off her, you creep!"

There was a swishy-pounding sound and the creature's face collapsed in a tumult of blood, bones cracking and teeth shifting. The creature crumpled at my feet and Julius, my very own Max Baer, socked him a few more times for good measure, then stood there shaking the pain out of the hand that had been the fist that had vanquished my attacker. People swirled all around me. The demonstration had officially ended.

People asked me if I was okay. Juanita Jackson and Millie led me over to the nearest park bench to sit down. I watched as a beat officer came on scene, assumed Julius was in charge and directed all inquiries to him, not the pastor, Juanita Jackson or any of the other NAACP operatives or participants who he ignored. Never did he ask me if I was okay or needed medical attention. I don't even think he looked my way, just jotted notes on a little pad.

Julius had to be the one to convince him that yes, he was the one who'd punched the man, that no, he wasn't covering for the real culprit, that no, no one knew anything about the stabbing incident he'd been yammering about, that no, no one else had attacked the man, that yes, he thought my life was in danger and why was he more concerned about the wicked, crazy, drunk man than about me; yes, it was supposed to be a peaceful demonstration, but should he have just let the man strangle me to death; that the man would be fine, but he needed to be arrested for assault, probably even attempted murder and that he would file a complaint if they didn't follow through; he told them yes, he was a lawyer, yes, he was with the NAACP, and no, we had no permit but that we were exercising our First Amendment rights and that as an officer of the law he should know that a permit wasn't required under these limited circumstances, and that yes, he should enjoy the rest of the day too.

I'd never experienced such a thing before in my entire life. I'd been mortified and terrified. Yet there was triumph and vindication. One could almost say it was a Hollywood ending. Maybe next week when I was back at Highland Beach rehashing the week's events and updating my diary, I'd assess myself as foolish and impetuous, someone who played a game in a league that was much too advanced for my skill level because I must've done something to make that man think I was a weak link, the one with wee or faltering faith in our cause. But at the moment I had no regrets.

CHAPTER 49

Julius

I HAD ONE last criminal case to handle before I left to go home to Germany. I'd already transferred the rest of my case files and tendered my letter of resignation. The director, supervisors, colleagues and clients at the Legal Aid Society had already expressed their disappointment that I was leaving. I'd miss the work and the people although many of the assignments had been long, arduous, uphill battles. The four-year old agency was still trying to garner respect and influence in the legal world and the indigent people we represented required the most advocacy but were considered unimportant in the grand scheme of things. However, it felt good knowing that, as an intern and a rookie lawyer, I'd done some good or at least tried to.

Even helping to "dot an I" or "cross a T" for Thurgood Marshall was gratifying. I was fascinated with his efforts to integrate the University of Maryland Law School. Marshall, Professor Houston and Nathan Margold, a Jewish lawyer, designed the strategy to attack the "separate by equal" doctrine. As a Jew who was turned away at Harvard and went to a Catholic school instead, I commiserated with Donald Murray who was poised to be the first Negro to get a Maryland law degree. I wanted to be part of this history-making effort and would sweep floors and empty wastebaskets if it meant I could be close to the operation. I understood that Marshall was swamped with cases, had practically no legal staff, did most of the work single-handedly, typed briefs in his car that doubled as a mobile office, and could always use some good volunteers. So I wandered into the Baltimore NAACP office one day to see if I could help in any way.

The office was busier than a bucket brigade at a forest fire. Guys with rolled up shirt sleeves and loosened ties stood around bouncing ideas off one another, pointing out passages in huge, dusty law books and drinking coffee and Coca-cola like it was going out of style. Oral arguments in the Maryland Supreme Court were about a month away and all were deep in preparation.

"I called last week about volunteering for the Murray case. Julius Sommerfeldt." I stuck my hand out. "I just drove here from D. C."

A brown-skinned man with a triangular-shaped head shook my hand.

"Hi, I'm Paul." He was a Howard graduate and knew my uncle, called him a "good man."

"Thurgood and Professor Houston are out right now. Interviewing some potential litigants for another case. It never ends." He patted me on the back. "Follow me."

We walked and he talked and, clearly, he was excited about the law and his tasks; he was practically breathless as he explained some of the strategies.

"Right now we're briefing the argument that the *Yick Wo* case should've been the controlling precedent when the Supreme Court decided *Plessy* because race-neutral laws resulting in prejudicial effect are still unconstitutional. And of course we're studying Justice Harlan's brilliant dissent in *Plessy*..."

"Profound." I said. "Colorblind constitution, no superior class of people, no arbitrary separation of citizens by race to inflame mistrust and hatred." My Constitutional Law course was still fresh in my mind.

"Exactly, but we need to contrast that with his perplexing decision in *Cumming versus Richmond* where Harlan allowed the kids of Negro tax payers to go uneducated because the district couldn't afford to build a separate school for them, and also *Wong Kim Ark* where he basically said the Chinese can never be perceived as true citizens because they're too different."

"Harlan was a little schizo," another guy offered as he barreled past us in the narrow hallway laden with papers and books.

"To say the least," Paul said. "Then we need to pick apart *Gong Lum versus Rice*, another school de-seg case where the white school refused to admit a Chinese student and the Supreme Court applied the *Plessy* doctrine."

"So many Chinese litigants."

"And many of their cases go all the way to the high court."

"I didn't realize they faced such discrimination."

"Yes, Chief Justice Taft even refers to them in his opinions as the 'yellow race.' But their blues are not like ours." He looked at me pointedly. I understood implicitly.

"Then there're hundreds of state court cases that we can comb for favorable dicta which can come in handy when crafting comprehensive oral arguments. Check out *Alvarez versus Lemon Grove* where the judge found that requiring a separate school for Mexicans was wrong."

"But as I recall, they rationalized the ruling by saying that Mexicans were Caucasian."

"Right, but it's still relevant precedent."

A list of cases and rulings rolled off Paul's tongue effortlessly. He was knowledgeable and passionate. Donald Murray had a good team grinding in the trenches for him, for American Negroes everywhere. And there were a thousand things to do, to check and double-check, before the big day.

"Thurgood wants to be prepared for whatever curve balls the Maryland justices throw at him." We stopped at a long table covered with overflowing ashtrays, partially-eaten sandwiches, more coffee cups and Coca-cola bottles. "He doesn't expect to win the case, just appeal and get the issue before the Supreme Court. That way a desegregation ruling will apply to the whole country, not just Maryland."

"Right."

"Excuse the mess," he said, gathering up debris.

"No problem. I do my best thinking in chaos."

"Then you'll be much inspired. So, chop-chop! Thurgood will want answers when he returns. First he'll regale you with some of his stories, then turn serious and go all Socrates on you."

I was there all weekend, and because I'd heard Thurgood had a sweet tooth and a fondness for good liquor, every morning I brought in strudel from a German bakery and a bottle of Four Roses Kentucky Straight Bourbon Whiskey to bestow as a token of my admiration. I hoped to meet him and the Professor before I went back to Washington. In the meantime, I read, underlined, took notes and sparred good-naturedly with the others.

They were all very intelligent. Some worked on the Murray case, others researched unionizing, equal pay, the death penalty, voting rights and other social justice issues. They were learning the Constitution, inside and out, because Thurgood Marshall preached that it was the "Bible," that it answered all legal conundrums. I spent the weekend shepardizing cases to determine if they'd been upheld, overturned, questioned or cited elsewhere. It was tedious but I enjoyed every minute and basked in the camaraderie.

I met Thurgood on my last day. I heard him, laughing and back slapping, before I saw him.

"I hear we've got another fella here to help us kill Jim Crow." I stood to meet him.

He was tall, handsome, debonair, about my age and already iconic in the eyes of his interns and peers. He was influential and bigger than life with a cunning gaze as if he had some third-eye knowledge that he would use to smite those not as intellectually swift.

"A pleasure," I said, shaking his hand.

We spoke for a few minutes and he told me how he used to watch court trials with his politically aware, blue-eyed father, about how they used to get into loud, boisterous arguments at dinner about different issues, and how those experiences and memorizing the Constitution as punishment for pranking a teacher fueled his interest and passion in the law. He told the little group that had gathered round that, believe it or not, he'd been against integrating the faculty at Lincoln University where he was a student until classmates – poet Langston Hughes and bandleader Cab Calloway – ("one professor asked if the three of us were triplets – not even brothers, but triplets! – with our light skin and what we black folks call 'good hair' because you know we all look alike or have to be related somehow") – talked some sense into him. He told how his civil rights work was long, hard, frustrating and often dangerous, but that you had to roll with the punches and never give up.

"When I was in college," he said, "I got a summer job working for the railroad and they issued me a uniform that had pants that were about a foot too short. When I complained, the boss said, 'boy, it's cheaper to get another nigger than another pair of pants. You want the job or not?' I rolled with the punches and took the job. You don't give up, you do what you have to do. It's not always pretty."

"It's hard," someone said. "The world's against us."

"Evil never sleeps."

"But we can change things," I said. Everyone murmured agreement.

"We try every day," Paul said. "It takes legal eagles working behind the scenes *together* with the brave foot soldiers who protest and boycott."

"It'll take both to change hearts and minds."

"It'll happen one day."

"Now," Thurgood bellowed, "did anybody find me some law that says racial discrimination violates the Thirteenth Amendment? Just one goddamn case."

"Still looking," Paul said. "So far, no luck."

"Separate but equal is a 'badge of slavery' and the Thirteenth Amendment abolished that shit seventy-odd years ago. Surely some judge somewhere made that analogy. I need a quote, something I can use."

"Preaching to the choir," said Paul. "If a case exists, we'll find it."

I wished Thurgood luck with the Murray case. "If the courts aren't there to protect the weak and vulnerable from the strong and powerful, then what good are they?"

"That's gospel. Take care, my German Jewish friend," he said.

One cold January day, I found out Thurgood had won the Murray case when I walked by a news stand on my way to work and the headlines of the victory leapt out at me: "Maryland Law School Ordered to Integrate;" "Negro to Attend White-Only Law School;" "Negro Lawyers Win in Court; An End to Segregation in Maryland?" I made like Fred Astaire and clicked my heels in the air.

CHAPTER 50

I'D LEFT BERLIN more than three years ago demoralized and filled with acrimony and uncertainty. I was being run out of my home country just because a brand new government, one less than a year old, decided they didn't like my ancestry, how we looked or where and how my family worked and lived. They hated that we worshipped at a synagogue instead of at the imposing St. Mary's Lutheran Church – *Marienkirche* – or, like many Germans, no place at all. They hated the ground we walked on and I hated being hated. At least I'd had the wherewithal to take a breather and reclaim my humanity elsewhere.

As much as I enjoyed America, I missed my home and family. When I got back, I would miss walking around Berlin, carefree and whistling, arms swinging, the way I did in Washington D. C. But I'd trade that freedom if it meant I could have my mother muss my hair, play a game of Chess with my father and get into deep, philosophical discussions with Gabriel. I longed to soak up *Oma* Zip's classic wisdom, tell little jokes at Gretchen's expense and bask in the admiring eyes of all my young cousins because I was the one who'd gone away for three whole years and learned to be a lawyer in the vast and wondrous United States of America.

A steady stream of letters and postcards from abroad kept me abreast of all the goings-on at home. The family was trying mightily to hold on to Kempner's Furniture. Aryans rarely shopped there anymore and the Jews, many of whom had been stripped of their livelihoods and professions, couldn't afford to. Many had to sell what they had and weren't trying to accumulate more. There were no regular store hours anymore; Kempner's operated on an appointment-only basis. Every once in a while, a tourist or some foreign national would stop in. They walked past the empty flag shaft because Jews could no longer display the German flag, and ignored the big, yellow "*Juden*" painted on the windows which was required on all Jewish shops. They came because they heard we had extraordinary inventory and didn't care who sold it to them.

The store which had once been full of light, color, curiosities and classical music – especially Brahms – had been vandalized several times and some nice items had been stolen. It no longer looked like a specialty store, more like a dim, cobwebby thrift store. The insurance companies didn't pay our claims and we couldn't sue them because the courts refused to file our complaints. Or if they did get filed, it was because the clerks knew that some judges derived much pleasure in summarily throwing them out or ruling against us with all the disdain and vitriol one might expect to be reserved for the rapists and murderers on the criminal docket. It seemed inevitable – the family would end up selling the century-old business, sooner rather than later and, like pawning a wedding ring you knew you'd never get back, that'd be a sad day indeed.

Helga, the house helper we've employed since she was twenty and I was in knee pants, and who made schnitzel like nobody's business, was gone. *Mutti* wrote that she hung on as long as she could but finally left because she kept getting threats of prosecution and jail. Helga was an under-45-year old German Aryan woman working for a Jewish family and that was a violation of the Nuremburg laws. Helga was like one of the family and everyone wept as she packed her suitcase and removed all the photographs from her room. She moved to Heidelberg where she had a sister and planned to land a position as a governess or a hospital cook. According to *Mutti*, Helga blamed the Dreschlers' housekeeper for telling the authorities that she, Helga, was not Jewish. "Otherwise, how would they know? Because I look just like your Aunt Rivkah. I never should've gotten close to that *yenta*. Snitch, snitch, snitch, that one. Watch out for her." *Mutti* also wrote, "Helga said to tell you good-bye, that she loves you, and hopes to see you soon." I'll miss her.

The family was worried about Gabriel who was thought to be involved in some underground activities with some shadowy group that might prove dangerous if the Gestapo got wind of it. The Gestapo had eyes and ears everywhere.

I'm told things were such that one couldn't trust the shopkeepers, the newsboys, the little kids shooting marbles on the sidewalk, or the little old lady sweeping outside her doorway. So no one conversed, no one exchanged anything other than the pleasantries of *guten tag* and *auf wiedersehen* – Good day and Good-bye – lest the most innocuous small talk get misconstrued and reported. The simple question, *Wie geht's?* – How are you? – could be a trap, could cause the unsuspecting to say something worth reporting and a Gestapo officer might appreciate such a tip and reward the informant in some way. Someone could inadvertently reveal that they'd purchased goods from an Aryan if they were Jewish, or from a Jew if they were Aryan when neither was supposed to be patronizing the other; or they could get too comfortable and let loose a Hitler joke.

If Gabriel was involved in something dangerous, he could disappear, be taken to that dreaded building located at No. 8 Prinz Albrecht Strasse, better known as the Gestapo Headquarters, where people were taken to be interrogated, imprisoned, tortured or killed. People say agonized screams could often be heard coming from the basement.

The family wanted me to talk some sense into him, and when I communicated with Gabriel through letters or telegrams, he tried to convince me that I needed to join him, but he was never specific about what the group did. One of the goals was to prepare people to immigrate to Palestine, to teach them to adapt from an urban to an agrarian lifestyle and learn some Arabic and the Islamic culture but, according to my father, Gabriel and his affiliates huddled in the backs of cellars to kibbutz about other things too. It was those *other* things that had us worried. Gabriel said it was time for drastic measures, that the indignities were getting worse, that he'd heard Nurenberg Jews were herded into the sports stadium to cut the grass with their teeth. But that had to be an outlandish lie. I didn't believe it for a second. I had to speak to Gabriel, who always had just a touch of madness and who *Mutti* says paints beautiful masterpieces then defaces them as soon as they dry.

My father was becoming more and more morose. Unable to practice law himself, he found himself relegated to being a notary (for Jews only) and ghostwriting lawsuits for Aryan lawyers who now found themselves with much more business than they had prior to the Jewish expulsion from the profession. He was paid a tiny fraction of the amount that the attorney of record received from his Aryan clientele. But even that work was tapering off. No one wanted to risk backlash for doing anything to enhance the livelihood of an erstwhile Jewish lawyer. Everybody was in self-preservation mode and my father was trying to figure out another way to make a living.

He and another brother, also a lawyer, thought about going somewhere else for a while, but *Vati* was "much too German" and France was "much too French" and he had neither the time nor inclination to assimilate. By the same token, he eschewed the United States because it was "grossly uncultured" and what little culture it did have was "purloined from Europe." Italy had the fascist Mussolini who tortured and killed his own people, let them suffer and rot in the Gulag labor prison, and was just as dangerous as Germany. Hungary, Poland, Romania and Greece were too underdeveloped for everyone's cosmopolitan tastes. Spain, where emperors Ferdinand and Isabella burned Jews for refusing to convert to Catholicism, was still blatantly anti-Semitic.

They thought about Copenhagen or Amsterdam, but found out things were no better than Germany there. The Danish and Dutch people, not unlike Europeans everywhere, were nervous and resentful of the influx of Jews and the stiffening competition for precious available jobs. And they didn't like the idea of their sleepy, little towns and burgs becoming more conspicuous because of our increased presence, and hence a shiny target for Hitler's ubiquitous Nazis. Latent prejudices bubbled to the surface and made it difficult for migrating Jews to feel comfortable. It seemed the whole world was twisted so it was better just to stay put – with the devil they *knew*.

Also there was the 25% Reich Flight Tax and a limit to how many reich-marks Jews could transfer out of German banks. The German economy would completely crumble if all the Jews withdrew their holdings from the country's banks. My family, at least my father, didn't want to leave the vast amount of their wealth behind for the Nazis to plunder. They didn't work, earn, save and invest all those years just to cede their fortune, such as it was, to Hitler. It was hor-rendously unfair but there was no magistrate, judge, arbiter, burgermeister or any other intercessor who would, or could, do anything about it. And they'd need an adequate amount of money if they decided to relocate to another country or regain our comfortable lifestyle when things finally returned to normal.

Most importantly, who was Hitler, this *Austrian*, this profoundly Jewish-looking creature, to encourage, even demand, Germans who'd lived in Germany for generations, who'd served and died in its stupid wars, to leave the country because they were Jewish? The thought made my father's blood boil. It made him even more determined to stand his ground, to wait them out. The Nazis had stripped him of job, title and status, obliterated decades of personal and professional accomplishments, banned him from sitting on a park bench and patronizing the theater where they'd banned all Jewish actors and directors. They barred him from the sports clubs where he played squash twice a week, forcing him to patronize what he considered to be the ghettoized, all-Jewish equivalents; but he refused to be banished from the land of his forefathers. We understood that the Nazis wanted to starve us out, take everything so we'd leave and they could have the whole country to themselves. Well *Vati* wouldn't give them that satisfaction.

So they stayed. Sadly, he, this former esteemed jurist, was now conditioned to venture out only in daylight, to keep his head down, walk real fast, avoid speaking to his friends and associates in public so as not to be accused of conspiring against the fuehrer. If he had packages, he hid them in his coat, under his hat, stuffed inside his undershirt or in his socks to avoid an impromptu stop and search by a bored SA officer.

It was hard to believe that only a few, short years ago, men tipped their hats and shook his hand. "Your Honor!" they'd call out – when they saw him on the street. He was one of Berlin's finest judges; he had clout and discretion and would, upon great deliberation, affect people's lives and livelihoods with a pen stroke. His opinions were published in newspapers and professional journals. He'd received many accolades from the German Bar Association, the same organization that disowned him and hundreds of other Jewish lawyers and judges. *Vati* says he wouldn't be surprised if they sent someone to confiscate all his awards, erase all evidence of previous affiliation. The plaques and certificates wouldn't be there. He'd trash them first. He might trash them anyway seeing as how they came from people who so easily turned their back on him just because Hitler told them to.

So he stayed. And worked, harder than he ever had before. The idea of being destitute, of becoming like those sad-eyed gray-beards and their pear-shaped, kerchief-and-apron-clad wives who showed up at *Juedische Winterhilf,* or other welfare agencies groveling for food, clothing or shelter was repulsive to him. Such a predicament would be worse than shoveling coal, cleaning and deboning fish or performing any of the other odd manual labor jobs my father would occasionally pick up because he was going stir-crazy just sitting in the apartment all day and, even with *Mutti* taking shifts as an aide at the Jewish hospital, we still needed money, some income source, to balance the outgo. Also, he didn't want to be accused of being "work-shy" and sent to a camp in Dachau.

As he stated in his many missives to me, it was very easy to wallow in despair and be paralyzed by third-class citizenship, to be seen as *untermenschen* – subhuman – lower, it's professed, than the scorned gypsy, the despised homosexual or Eve's treacherous serpent, but nevertheless one had to be ready for the future because this oppression, too, shall pass.

Meanwhile *Oma* Zip was obsessed with this deranged individual who claims to be a prophet and is predicting the eradication of all European Jews and how this will be the beginning of *Olam Ha-Ba*, the "end-times," or "the world to come." This will be immediately preceded by a "new exodus," because Jews, according to legitimate prophets like Ezekiel, Jeremiah and Daniel, would be leaving Germany and other parts of Europe and migrating to the holy land, going to Palestine to reclaim Israel and live securely without walls.

Oma Zip invites this person, this fraud, who actually walks around with a pikestaff and sandals like he's Moses, into her home; and apparently the two of them go on and on about earthquakes in India, famine in China, wars in South America and the Orient, despotism in the persons of Stalin and Hitler and the rumor of wars closer to home and how it all portends the coming of the *Mashiach*, the Jewish Messiah, some righteous and extraordinary man who's a direct descendant of King David.

It's said that the *Mashiach* will rebuild The Temple and forty years after His arrival, the dead will be resurrected in the Promised Land and Israel will rise again. Eventually there'll be no other faith but Judaism, all humans will accept Talmudic law, and there'll be no more jealousy, hatred, greed or political strife – only goodness, kindness and peace. Then we'll have *Olam Ha-ba* which apparently is the exact opposite of the Christian concept of Armageddon which, as I understand it, promises the mutual destruction of the forces of good and evil.

I learned a lot of this in Hebrew school but thought nothing more of it. And our family, including at one time, *Oma* Zip, who now loudly sings *"Ani Maamin,"* which is about believing with complete faith in the Messiah, has always been more concerned with *HaOlam HaZeh – this* world, the here and now, rather than the afterlife.

Cousin Gretchen says the family is quite alarmed that *Oma* Zip is keeping company with this charlatan, shaking tambourines, quoting Old Testament Hebrew prophets and even the mysticist Nostradamus who some say predicted Hitler as the anti-Christ, and claiming that the end-times prophesies were beginning to come to pass. I'm certain that anyone who knew the Zipporah Ilsa Schmidt Sommerfeldt who went to piano bars with her fox-head stole and drank sherry with her pinky extended while the pianist played her requests would think she'd officially lost her mind.

She could draw the attention of one of the too-eager Hitlerites who were constantly on the lookout for anything "irregular," including the handicapped and mentally infirm so they could be toyed with, denigrated, physically abused, thrown into a camp or forcibly sterilized. *Oma* Zip was too old for sterilization, but not too old to be violated in other ways. The Nazi lieutenants were demented and always pleased when their protégés brought them fresh prey.

Oma Zip bought my first suit, took me to *Sparkasse* bank every Friday to deposit fifty pfennig into my account, made her entire Skat Club come to my bar mitzvah where she'd hired a beautiful, popular local songstress to serenade me after I'd chanted the *haftorah* and before the dancing bear act that an uncle had arranged much to *Oma* Zip's displeasure. The girl sounded heavenly and both the bear and the argument surrounding it were hilarious. Dear, old *Oma* Zip – I don't think I could handle seeing her mistreated; I'd feel murderous. The first thing I'd do when I got to Berlin would be to give her a long, tight embrace.

CHAPTER 51

It was my last case, and the judge looked at me, impatient, his mind seemingly already made up. I could see it in his eyes, detected it in the way he drummed his fingers on the bench top and looked at his watch. I aimed to change his mind, to persuade him to grant probation instead of sending my client to prison. I was up late preparing a passionate plea that I thought would help mitigate his penalty. I looked at my client, Rutherford Nash, and patted him on the shoulder.

The day before, a jury had convicted Rutherford Nash of burglarizing the painters' union headquarters and stealing $100. It was his first serious conviction and the judge wanted to know if I had anything to say on his behalf. I did. I stood. Rutherford stood.

"If it pleases the court, in mitigation, I do have a few words to say. Rutherford Nash throws himself on the mercy of the court. He's a 28-year old husband and father of seven whose chosen profession is a house painter. Of course, ever since the Depression, he's had very few employment opportunities, especially since he's not protected by a union. They won't even let him in the union. Rutherford – his parents named him after a President because they had high hopes for him and he's been trying to live up to those expectations. Contrary to how the prosecutor has portrayed him, he's not lazy and shiftless. He wants a steady job but can only find spot labor, barely enough to keep a roof over his family's head or food in the pantry.

"Add to that the societal pressures of seeing billboards advertising restaurants that he can't eat in, vacations he can't take, cigarettes, refrigerators and gas ranges he can't afford to buy even though he's a hard worker who plays by the rules. Then they're all those ads with the smug, smiling faces touting the 'American Way' which are taunting to *anyone* who is unemployed or broke.

"What's your point, counselor?" the judge said.

"My point, your honor, is that my client is constantly besieged with subliminal messaging and personal affronts that make him feel like a failure as a husband and father, as a man, as a human being. People like that do desperate things to get ahead. Rutherford stole out of *need*. He needed money because the lights were out at his house, his roof was leaking and his children needed shoes. It's not an excuse, just an explanation.

"So when Rutherford was walking the five miles home from cleaning stables – a filthy, grueling task by the way, and the shiny Pierce Arrow came zooming by, spraying him with dirty storm water, he was angry. And when the occupants stuck their heads out the windows and laughed, he recognized them as former union bosses, the same ones who told him there were no jobs but sent younger, less experienced *white* painters on many assignments, he went into a rage."

"I heard the testimony, counselor, you don't need to rehash it."

"I just want Your Honor to understand the psychological motivators that caused my client to double back, break into the union office and take the money. Society deprives certain people of opportunity, does everything to stifle their progress, puts them in positions where they feel they have nothing to lose, then wonders why they remain poor, angry and desperate. Not to mention the whole slavery thing. It's a wonder the whole country's not on fire.

"Understandably, Rutherford was blinded by his rage. It made him think irrationally. It made him feel vengeful which was very uncharacteristic of him. Rutherford is a mild-mannered, church-going man. And, mind you, he only took $100 of the cash, just enough for his immediate needs. He left behind over a thousand more. He wasn't greedy. . ."

"Mr. Sommerfeldt, I couldn't care less about his reasons or the fact that he didn't take all the money. The fact is, he's a criminal, pure and simple. He broke the law. And the district doesn't take kindly to law breakers."

"Again, I don't mean to condone. I just want the court to understand..."

The judge tapped his watch. "Not only are you interfering with my tee time, counselor, but your dime store, psychological analysis is condescending and of no interest to me."

"But studies show…"

The prosecutor, a short, pudgy man, butted in. He spoke while keeping his teeth firmly around the pipe he was smoking. "Statistics *prove* that Negroes are prone to be criminals. If they weren't so lazy and shiftless, they wouldn't find themselves in the position of having to commit crimes so they can pay their bills and support the litters of children they all seem to have." He took a long draw of his pipe, held the smoke in his mouth for several long seconds, then released it through his nose. "That's precisely why the Negro will always be poor. And being poor evokes criminal behavior, a vicious cycle. So, you see, it's also a character issue. Of course, Your Honor knows this already."

"That's a load of bull," I said. "You can't just generalize an entire race of people." He probably also thought that all Jews are greedy, neurotic misers who conspire to control all aspects of society.

"You're naïve, counselor," said the judge. "I know that kind of claptrap you're spewing is typical from you liberal Jews or people suffering from 'white guilt', but this court is about law and *order* and anything else is immaterial. Without the law, there'll be no *order*. The citizens demand and expect *order*."

"Exactly," said the prosecutor, gesturing with his pipe. "We can't just allow these people to continue taking stuff that doesn't belong to them. Most of our criminal docket is cases about Negroes stealing, raping, or just out there acting a fool."

I wanted to call him out for the *putz* that he was but decided to maintain decorum. His head would spin if he saw Justinia and her family and friends, Negroes who were richer and more polished and poised than anyone in that courtroom, including the judge. He'd have to readjust his whole conception of the Negro race just as I had to readjust mine once upon a time.

Granted, the Treadwells were in the upper echelon of Negro society, but there were lots of middle class and lower class blacks who would defy his cherished stereotypes. This was Washington D. C.; surely he's seen laborers, teachers and government employees going to work, families going to church, conscientious restaurant waiters serving his food and pouring his wine. Most likely, he knows that Negroes are as civilized and cultured as anyone else, but refuses to let facts stand in the way of sending a person to prison for as long as possible under the guise of law and order.

"Rutherford is *not* criminally inclined. And negative traits can be applied to *all* races."

The prosecutor stood up to add another two cents worth of crap. A cloud of smoke surrounded his bald, shriveled up head. "And may I remind the court that the defendant committed a *felony*. He broke a window and crawled inside. The broken window created shards of glass that could've been used as a weapon against the upstairs tenant had he come downstairs to investigate. Plus he used a large rock to break open the locked drawer. Another weapon – Exhibit B." He picked up a medium-sized stone from the trial table. "Hence the first degree Burglary conviction."

"Good point, Mr. Prosecutor."

"It's a good thing McGillicuddy is such a sound sleeper. Otherwise the defendant might've slit his throat or bashed his head in to avoid detection. Same thing if the union stewards came back and surprised him. Then he'd be facing murder charges too."

I just looked at him, astounded. This man, with his absurd arguments, was a disgrace.

"The prisons are full of Nigg-ro convicts who murdered out of panic." This prosecutor just wouldn't stop. "They're childish that way – impulsive and unable to think things through. Real men throw their hands up and say, 'Okay, you got me, I give up.' But not these people. They can be caught with their hand in the cookie jar, deny it, then kill you so you won't tell. Negro psychology proves my scenario is not far-fetched.'"

"Your scenario makes no sense as it relates to this case. Everything you're saying is racist and ridiculous."

I despised guys like him, smug conservatives with a fondness for regressive ideas, policies and politics to insure they'd always remain highest on the totem pole. He was probably a cocky, young teenager around the time that Reconstruction ended, already infected by rightist influences and spouting off about race-mixing and states' rights. Had he lived in another era, he would've argued that Dred Scott was *property*, not a citizen and that the Missouri Compromise was unconstitutional because it infringed upon the property rights of slave owners.

He reminded me of William Jennings Bryan arguing for the prosecution in the Scopes Monkey Trial that a teacher should be convicted of the crime of teaching evolution because it was contrary to the fundamentals of the Bible. But he also could've been one of those people, like Hitler, who claimed evolution *validated* racial superiority and eugenics. Both interpretations scared me.

If this guy were living in Germany, he would've been part of the council advising Hitler to enact the Nuremburg Laws because Jews were an abomination and shouldn't be allowed to be doctors, lawyers or municipal window washers, let alone German citizens. If he lived in the future, this *putz* or his progeny would be arguing against anything that would bring equality or comfort to "lesser" human beings; they'd defend the status quo, their privilege and imagined superiority til their dying breath. I had nothing but scorn for those who deign to be on the wrong side of history for ignorant, selfish reasons.

"Close your eyes to the truth if you want, Mr. Do-gooder." The prosecutor grinned at me and winked. "Rutherford Nash has the propensity to be a cold-blooded killer. Lying leads to thieving which leads to killing. There are plenty of examples of this kind of escalation. Just look at all those alley dwellers who went from petty thief to throat slasher. Those people love their razors and cutting people up. Yes, best get Rutherford Nash off the streets now, judge, before he really *does* kill." He turned his back to me and went back to sit at the government's table.

I was flabbergasted. "This is preposterous, and everyone in here is more ignorant from having listened to you."

"Now see here!" he said, popping back up, thinking, apparently, that he should be the only one to levy insults.

"At most, this is a simple burglary with no weapons. Rutherford, who by the way is not an alley dweller, but a responsible home owner..."

"Ha!"

"...would've gladly pleaded to a petty larceny and saved the court some time."

"Counselor," the judge said, "you had your turn. Mind your manners. And may I remind you that your client chose to have a jury of his peers."

"The prosecutor refused to offer my client a plea bargain. We had no choice. And not one of those twelve jurors was Rutherford's peer. You don't allow Negroes on a jury."

"One more word, counselor, and I will hold you in contempt and throw you in jail."

He consulted some papers that were in front of him. "Your client has three prior drunk and disorderlies. Hardly the saint you're making him out to be."

Rutherford and I had talked about that. He'd get drunk with some white co-workers at a nearby bar, things would get rowdy, and usually he'd be the only one arrested.

"Alcohol eases pain, your honor," I said. "Many people seek refuge in a bottle of whiskey. Times are tough."

"Yet they always seem to find money for liquor."

I was really getting ticked. How obtuse could this guy be? Judges were supposed to be wise.

"Judge, how many poor people do you actually know? Especially poor black people. They come before you every day, but you don't really know them; you barely look at them. Investing in some liquid stress reliever is a small price to pay in order to keep one's sanity." I looked around the courtroom. "I'm sure everyone in here can attest to that fact."

I looked at the prosecutor sitting there like a contented walrus. "Mr. Prosecutor, you're a Cavanaugh. Isn't that Irish? Should I assume you're a mean, sloppy drunk? Maybe you're drunk right now. Your arguments suggest that you are."

"I object!" He looked to the bench as if searching for a lifeline, then swiveled toward me. "How dare you! I'm not on trial here! And neither is the judge."

The judge banged his gavel and looked at me like I'd made advances on his wife. "Enough! Rutherford Nash, I sentence you to eight years of hard labor on the chain gang." He banged the gavel. What?! Last week I saw him give a white guy six months in the slammer for stealing a milk truck.

Rutherford's knees buckled and his wife shrieked "Ruthie!" before she fainted. His seven children began crying and his mother cried, "Lord, Lord, not my son!"

"Order!" yelled the judge. The bailiffs grabbed Rutherford and began to lead him away.

"And I'm adding another year for going to trial when he knew good and damn well he was guilty." He banged the gavel again with finality and doom.

"Nine years!" I said. "That's insane!" I was floored, but trudged on, channeling my new, favorite idol, Thurgood Marshall. "He has a constitutional right to trial. Chain gang? That's slavery. You're essentially repealing the thirteenth amendment by putting my client back in chains and making him work for free. This is Washington D. C. This sounds like a sentence from a court in the Mississippi swamps. What about the Eighth Amendment's rule against cruel and unusual punishment? Does the Constitution not apply here?"

The judge was now banging the gavel like a maniac. His face was red as a sunburn. I'd really hit a nerve. But this was my last stand. Rutherford didn't deserve this. My Legal Aid supervisor had cautioned me about getting too emotionally involved with the clients if I ever wanted to have a restful night's sleep again. The court system was not known to be very sympathetic to the kind of people we represented and I was setting myself up for disappointment unless I maintained a "clinical detachment."

The best we could ever hope for was not *stopping* an eviction, but getting a short reprieve; not having a debt *forgiven*, but arranging some kind of payment plan; not getting a former employer to pay *all* the unpaid wages, but agreeing to a *portion*; not winning an *acquittal*, but trying to get the defendant probation or at least a minimal jail sentence after the inevitable conviction. Meanwhile, people who were well-connected and had better resources got all sorts of leeway, special dispensation, benefits of the doubt, and second chances.

The Nashes were very nice people and I'd grown fond of them. Rutherford was one of my favorite clients. I'd spent hours at his kitchen table with his family discussing baseball and case strategy. At a wobbly, oil-cloth-topped table on hairline-fractured dishes, I ate rabbit stew and Jell-o at his wife's insistence even though the meal had to be stretched about a dozen ways. I explained to the children that a lawyer was someone who helps people with their problems and two of them expressed a desire to become one. They begged their parents for an extra five minutes so they could sing the "Star

Spangled Banner" for me before bedtime. They sang in three-part harmony and it was delightful. No one in the Nash family deserved this terrible outcome.

So I soldiered on. "Better yet, this is what I'd expect from the kangaroo courts back home in Germany that were created to kill and incarcerate people they don't like. The accused aren't even allowed to defend themselves. Everyone is found guilty and everyone has the book thrown at them. There, the judges work for one person – Adolph Hitler. They do his bidding and *screw* the people. They kill people or put them in camps for the smallest, most insignificant things." I stepped closer to the bench.

"You," I said, pointing at the judge, "are no better than they are."

"How dare you!" he said to me, then turned to Rutherford. "Rutherford Nash, I'm adding another year to your sentence because of the insolence of your attorney! That makes it an even ten. You can thank him when you get released in 1946. Take him away!" Rutherford looked at me helplessly and I looked back at him helplessly.

"Enslaving him for ten years for stealing $100 is outrageous! Eight was bad enough. You may as well sew a green triangle to his uniform and throw him in Dachau labor camp with the other so-called criminals."

"I don't even know what you're talking about. This is *America*, this is how we do things *here*. And I find you in the utmost contempt." He stood up and banged the gavel insanely.

"It's mutual!"

"Bailiffs, get him the hell out of my sight!"

I was livid. This a travesty of justice, and I started thinking about all the stories from home about neighbors caught stealing bread only to be arrested, "tried" and convicted in the *Sondergericht*, a "special" court, within an hour and taken away to Dachau; about a former classmate who was caught distributing a subversive, anti-Hitler newspaper, taken before a judge at the *Volksgerichtshof* – the ignoble "People's court" – labeled a Communist, convicted of treason, and taken to Dachau where he was killed a month later. *Mutti* said his family had to bury him without his head which the Nazis said they couldn't find and didn't bother to explain how it got separated from his body in the first place.

It took four bailiffs to remove me from that courtroom, each holding on to a wriggling limb. It took me five minutes to wish I hadn't antagonized the judge and that I could take back everything I said. My colleagues evidently were right when they said this judge was hardened, and that I shouldn't expect leniency. It took three hours for Uncle Sy to come down to the courthouse and pay my $80 contempt-of-court fine so I could be released from the stifling holding cell with the stained mattress and cracked commode, which was probably nicer than Rutherford's cell in the Negro section. Five minutes later, Sy had assessed the situation and told me that I'd overstepped, that by trying to make what I thought were some valid points, I'd succeeded in making things worse for my client and in the process, helped to reinforce the stereotype of the whiny, arrogant Jewish lawyer.

"Eighty dollars is a steep price to pay for the privilege of calling a judge a Nazi to his face," Sy said. "That's practically three house notes. Was it worth it?"

"Yes, it was and I'll pay you back every penny."

"Well, nephew, just don't pull that stunt in Germany because they'll probably just take you out back and shoot you."

"Fortunately for me, I guess, they won't let me anywhere near a courtroom. So I don't have to worry about that."

"Sometimes you're just too smart for your own good."

"Maybe."

"And perhaps you cater to your ego a bit too much?"

"Perhaps." And this latest act of bravado was fueled by the knowledge that I probably wouldn't be practicing in that court again.

"I'm guilty of it too sometimes. So is your father. It must be an inherited quality."

I admitted to myself that I was probably more interested in being *right* than in doing what was best for my client. I'd done Rutherford a disservice and had to figure out a way to correct the situation.

"I'm done with my classes for today," said Sy. "Let's go to Biergarten Haus for some schnitzel. Your treat."

He gave me a back slap and led me out the courthouse doors – to freedom, leaving Rutherford behind to be taken to some chain gang overseen by someone channeling Simon Legree from *Uncle Tom's Cabin*. I agreed to go but my heart wasn't in it. I'd go because Uncle Sy might have some ideas about what I could do to resolve matters.

I was leaving for Germany in two weeks and had to convince this judge to reconsider Rutherford's sentence. Rutherford was a victim of stereotype and *my* audacity. He was too nice a guy to be forced into striped pajamas and made to dig ditches or work on a railroad at gunpoint while chained to another inmate, essentially providing free labor to boost the estates of multimillionaires like Cornelius Vanderbilt, Jay Gould and other infamous past, present, or up-and-coming robber barons. The idea was detestable and I didn't want to have his fate, such an unfair, disproportionate punishment, on my conscience.

My second task was to convince Justinia Treadwell to sail away with me to Europe, to experience the eleventh quadrennial Olympiad with me in Berlin and see my crazy world. She told me that she was ready to do something different, to put her job and everything on hold and have a unique and memorable experience. I could deliver that. I hoped she'd give me the chance.

CHAPTER 52

JUSTINIA HAD GIVEN me her Washington address as well as her Highland Beach address and I threw caution to the wind and dropped in on her at her summer home under the pretenses of returning her Montblanc pen – a splendid tool of fine German craftsmanship, by the way – that she'd lent me to make the entries in my address book.

After asking around, I learned that Highland Beach was remote and had many unpaved roads, so leaving my car on the edge of the city, I took a cab to the place Justinia had called an Eden for prominent Negroes. The cabbie dropped me off in front of the Treadwell cottage on Douglass Avenue.

"You know there ain't nothing but colored in this neck of the woods," the driver said, leaning his head out of the window as if I were embarking on a dangerous path.

"I'm aware," I called back.

"You want I should wait?"

"Come back in an hour."

"Suit yourself. No street lights in these parts. It'll be black as the ace of spades in less than an hour. You won't be able to see a one of 'em lessen they smile nice and wide. Hee-hee!" He turned the taxi around and was gone in a trail of dust.

Justinia's place was nestled in thick foliage in this little beachfront hamlet that reminded me a little of a summer getaway on Warnemuende, the Baltic seaside resort island, fishing village and artists' colony that's popular with vacationing Berliners. My family and I visited many times as I was growing up; it was where my grandfather taught me to sail.

I took it all in. Manicured red, yellow and white roses exploded from dozens of bushes, black-eyed Susans rose with abandon from the sides of gravelly roads and Spanish moss draped itself over surrounding oaks and gave this little patch of Eden a surreal quality, like a scene from a German fairytale by the Brothers Grimm. Behind the house, the expanse of grass sloped into groves of oaks, maples and poplars. Encircling a patio structure were strands of twinkling white lights draped between Polynesian Tiki torches which were very chic and Hollywood and so unlike the menacing torches wielded by the Hitler Youth, storm troopers and other brainwashed jackboots during their incessant parades. The ambience was serene, beckoning. There were late model cars parked in neat parallels and light laughter and white, fluffy curtains billowed from open windows.

I went to the back of the house, crossed the terrace and rang the bell. A woman in a maid's uniform answered. I smiled and introduced myself. My smile faded and my heart sank when I saw the man behind her. He had a champagne bottle which he almost dropped when he saw me. It was Xavier.

"What the hell are *you* doing here?" he asked, so discombobulated that the cork he was unstopping popped out and flew across the room like a bullet, knocking over a champagne flute in the butler's pantry.

"What on earth?" came a woman's voice from an interior room. There was the scraping of a chair against the floor so someone was undoubtedly coming to check out the commotion.

"Justinia forgot her pen." I told Xavier. "It looks expensive so I'm returning it."

"Likely story."

"I'm sticking with it."

I opened the door and stepped over the threshold like an overbearing landlord.

The maid had begun sweeping up the glass. I leaned down and took the dustpan from her. "Let me help you with that."

"Who are you?" The woman was gorgeous with a fussy hairstyle full of luxurious, auburn curls. She must have been Justinia's mother. "And who's responsible for breaking my Waterford crystal?"

"Julius?" It was Justinia, looking radiant in white with wildflowers in her hair. She stopped short at the threshold between the dining room and kitchen. I couldn't tell if she was rattled or elated, or both.

"*This* is Julius?" her mother asked.

"You've heard of him?" Xavier asked.

"You've heard of me?" I asked.

CHAPTER 53

Justinia

AFTER ENDURING A hot and muggy train ride and an even hotter taxi, I arrived at Highland Beach with an hour to bathe and change from my traveling clothes into something "cute and nobby."

Georgine was waiting for me when I arrived, talking a mile a minute and following me into the house, past the hustle and bustle of the kitchen, and up to my bedroom where she lay herself across my satin duvet. "So, were there any interesting men at the convention?" she asked.

"A few. You should've gone."

"You know that kind of stuff bores me."

"Desegregation and civil rights are important, Georgine."

"It's all a waste of time. Nothing will ever change. Not in our lifetime. We should just resign ourselves to that fact and make the most of it."

It was pointless to remind her of the progress already made. Slaves probably thought there'd always be slavery, the country probably thought all blacks would be downtrodden forever. The idea that one day there'd be Negro elected officials, successful professionals and prosperous business owners was dismissed as the fanciful musings of the drunk or delusional. The sight of a *white* man holding an umbrella over the heads of a tuxedo-wearing Negro and his jewel-laden wife as they walked toward the National Theater to experience *Ziegfeld Follies* could cause a person to drop dead from shock.

The *Washington Bee* reportedly ran a story where something like that actually happened in the early 1900s. A Mississippi congressman was driving down Pennsylvania Avenue, saw such a glamorous couple and their Caucasian valet, lost control of his Model T and ran into a gaslight pole. Legend further claims that this Negro man, a respected, well-known doctor, raced across the street in the pouring rain to administer aid and comfort, and that his black face leaning over the injured man asking, "Where exactly does it hurt?" was the final straw; the man groaned, turned his head away and died.

Georgine's comments were a mirror reflection of her father's beliefs. NAACP affiliates say having a defeatist attitude is often just a way of disguising one's refusal, be it from laziness or selfishness, to participate in the struggle. They just couldn't be stirred from their complacency or sidetracked from their daily responsibilities. They sit back and wait for *others* to desegregate the schools, trains and all other aspects of public life, to prove there was nothing inherently threatening about integration and that we could be different yet assimilated at the same time.

After the convention I had a renewed appreciation for people – black and white, named and unnamed – who fought and died to end slavery, create unions and acquire women's suffrage and civil rights for all people. Without them, we all could be sharecroppers, but Georgine fails to realize this. Daddy says, in the baseball game of life, she and Xavier were both born on third base and think they hit a triple.

"Georgine," I said, "you should come to at least one local NAACP meeting. It might change your outlook."

"How did you become so militant in one week?" she asked, reminding me that I needed to write a letter to the Baltimore library about them stocking more books by Negro writers.

Georgine fanned herself with a fashion magazine. "No thank you, my outlook is just fine. I'd rather watch grass grow."

"There are some interesting men there."

"A bunch of laborers, porters and clerks."

"Reverend Crawford says they're the salt of the earth."

"We're 'above the salt,' Justinia, a reality you've always failed to grasp. And I, for one, can't abide a poor, uneducated man. Think of what people would say."

They'd say she must be undesirable to men of true quality, that she was damaging the Kirkwood name and weakening the bloodline. They'd also disregard the fact that many laborers, porters and clerks had college degrees and unimpeachable character. At some point though, we had to disregard what others thought and just follow our hearts.

"You're incorrigible. Goby Richards, for instance, is a handsome, unmarried teacher and a really nice guy."

"Goby? What kind of asinine name is that?"

"Really, Georgine...."

"Teachers and preachers, I'll pass."

"I give up."

"Well why aren't *you* with him?"

Lily's six-year old niece, Dixie, helping out for the day, knocked on the door. She came in and asked me if I wanted lilac or rose-scented bath salts in my bath. "I think lilac. Thank you, Dixie."

"Oh," she said, "I made you something 'purty' for your hair." She handed me a wreath made of grapevine, daisies and buttercups.

"I'll wear this tonight," I said, "with my white eyelet dress." I gave her a hug. She left and I went behind my dressing screen to change into my bathrobe and came out tying the sash.

"You're not actually going to wear that thing," Georgine said, referring to Dixie's gift.

"Absolutely. It's cute and I would never hurt Dixie's feelings."

Before I could escape, Georgine tried to lasso me into a commitment for the next morning. "A group of us are meeting by Black Walnut Creek to go berry-picking. Birdie, the Toussaints' maid, is going to teach us how to make cobblers because men love a good cobbler. You should come. Doesn't Xavier like cobbler?"

"He prefers cake." I told her, "Georgine, you're never going to make cobbler. You'd simply ask the cook."

"Mumsy says men appreciate it when the wife can whip up their favorite things in a pinch. What if the cook is off that day and he's craving a berry cobbler? And men apparently find it sexy when the wife is in the kitchen with flour on her face and her hair is all awry. It shows she's making an effort to please him."

"Georgine, you can't even boil water."

"That's beside the point. Birdie's teaching me everything tomorrow. The countess' great-great-grandson is coming to visit next week. He's an engineer at IBM. I hear he loves pretty women, especially ones who bake. I plan on inviting him over for coffee and cobbler." Unless that flirt Inez Harper gets to him first, I thought.

"Someone should alert the volunteer fire department."

"Very funny."

Georgine was devoting the entire summer to getting a husband. She and her mother hatched all kinds of schemes to spot and lure the "right" kind of man – pretending to love golf, shoehorning herself into church pews next to eligible bachelors while wearing the biggest hat, dilly-dallying at Robinson's Haberdashery and Leather Shoppe. She sometimes threatened to move to "greener pastures" like Philadelphia or Chicago which had a thriving Negro upper class and many young Negro professionals. Because if Cleopatra Billingsley could go to Pittsburgh and snag the Harvard-bred son of a banker, surely *she* could go somewhere and do just as well if not better. Georgine's younger sisters were already beginning to date, so as the eldest sister, if she didn't have an engagement ring by the end of the year, she'd really start to panic.

Everyone knew Georgine was desperate when she dove for the bouquet my sister Charlotte tossed over her shoulder at her wedding reception. She actually leaped in front of a stunned Penelope Coleridge who fiercely believed the superstition that the catcher would be the next to marry. Penelope had already ordered a "princess" gown from Milan and just needed a groom.

Despite her efforts, there was a chance that Georgine, with her mean, persnickety ways, might still be destined for spinsterhood. She could be like several women we knew who lived their entire lives with just their sister or a cat as a companion. They died childless, leaving thousands of dollars to Negro colleges and charities. It was a fate we all feared. After about thirty years old, people stopped asking about marriage prospects and just shook their heads pityingly.

"Well, I have to get ready for dinner."

"Yes," Georgine said, "caterers, caviar, gold-plated silverware. Magdalena is really putting on the Ritz this evening. What's the occasion?"

"You know Magdalena. 'Just because' is reason enough."

"Why wasn't I invited?"

CHAPTER 54

CHAUNCEY MADE ME this trendy drink, a Shirley Temple, named after a white, six-year old actress who tap-danced and made movies with Bill "Bojangles" Robinson, a Negro entertainer. The drink is ginger ale and grenadine with a maraschino cherry floating on top. It was created for children and Chauncey made one for Dixie too, though she was technically "on the clock." I told him to put rum in mine. I needed fortification before rejoining the guests who'd already begun peppering me with marriage questions. As I sipped, Dixie looked at me and said, "I wish I could be fancy like you, Miss Justinia."

Dixie was such a sweet girl. I see her sometimes trying to imitate me. She squares her shoulders, straightens her back and picks up her feet instead of shuffling them. I've seen her sliding those little feet into my shoes, caught her gazing in the mirror patting and smoothing ungainly plaits as if they were long, silky tendrils, pretending to apply one of my lipsticks or squeezing atomizer bulbs to spray perfume. She replaced her "ain'ts" with "am nots" and "is nots," pronounced the "g" in her "-ing's." But if Lily caught wind, she would say, "Quit it, Dixie. Folks at home won't cotton to you puttin' on airs."

Whenever Lily brought Dixie along to help and "gain work experience," she abandoned the dusting and gravitated to me. "Whatchoo readin'?" she'd ask.

"No, say: what *are* you reading?"

"What *are* you read*ing*."

"It's a book called *Passing* by Nella Larson about a mulatto woman who passes for white, marries a racist white man and comes to a tragic end."

"She die?"

"Sadly, she did."

"How she die?"

"She fell out of a window."

"That's terr'ble! But that's what she git for bein' shame of who she is."

We'd talk until Lily told Dixie to stop bothering me and handed her the lemon oil and a chamois. Dixie was never a bother. I enjoyed her, appreciated that she was inquiring and precocious. I told my father he should set up a college trust for Dixie – she was too smart to keep house all her life – and he agreed. In twelve years, there'd be enough money for four years at Howard.

I sat my drink down, leaned down and told Dixie, "If you do a good job helping your Aunt Lily tonight, you and I will have a private tea party afterwards."

"Yippee!"

I hadn't seen Uncle Jett and Aunt Esther in several months and gave them both big hugs.

"Justinia," asked Aunt Esther, enveloping me in her bosom, "where's your beau this fine evening?"

"I don't have a beau, Aunt Esther."

"Still no steady beau? How can that be? You're too beautiful to not be somebody's bride yet. What about that nice, young man – Xavier?"

"We're great friends."

"Well listen honey, the son of one of my new customers is a sales executive at a pharmaceutical company. He's single. A little on the short and wide side, but other than that, he'd make someone a fine husband. Can I give him your telephone number?"

"No thank you, Aunt Esther."

Lacey Russwurm stopped feeding herself caviar long enough to grab my hand and underscore the fact that, at the ripe old age of twenty-two, I was still unmarried and childless. "Daphne married her college sweetheart in '33 and is already pregnant with her second child. It'll be born around the time Edward finishes dental school."

"I know. I was at the wedding and the shower tea."

"Hmmph." She stuffed some grapes into her mouth. Her daughter Daphne went to Dunbar and was in Dukes and Duchesses with me. "Well I know

Magdalena wants grandchildren. You and Xavier would make beautiful café au lait babies."

"Well, my fair child," Aunt Esther said, "your knight in shining armor will come. When you least expect it. I was already twenty-seven when I married your Uncle Jett."

As if on cue, Uncle Jett sidled up, kissed Esther's cheek, and asked the Russwurms if they'd heard the story about his escape from the Kentucky KKK even though Magdalena keeps telling him that many people find Klan tales to be sleazy. But Uncle Jett disagreed, saying most people were fascinated. All eyes and ears were on him as he recounted his sensational tale.

"My goodness," said Natalie Shayle, a sophomore at Spelman and the granddaughter of Reverend and Mrs. Crawford who brought her to meet my brother Emery. "Your story reminds me of the legend of Henry 'Box' Brown, the slave who mailed himself in a crate to abolitionists in Philadelphia."

"Yes," said Uncle Jett. "Only he didn't have a reeking dead body on top of him." He drained his glass. "I barely moved a muscle for *hours* until we got to Charleston, West Virginia. Then I peeked out, saw the coast was clear, went inside the depot and bought myself a ticket to Arlington."

"How on earth did you breathe?" Natalie asked.

"I used a screwdriver to poke holes in the sides, just large enough to keep from suffocating."

"Amazing," said Dr. Russwurm.

"The Klan! You must've been scared to death," Natalie said.

"A little," Uncle Jett admitted. "But, mind you, I could round up a posse just like they could, but leaving was the better option at the time. A few years before that, those crackers thought they'd teach a lesson to a friend of mine for acting 'uppity.' Well as soon as they got close to his house, we were waiting for them. About thirty of us were around the perimeter, long guns at the ready. They hightailed it out of there and we didn't even have to fire a shot. My friend had no more problems after that. And there were other incidents. Right, Jasper?"

My father simply nodded. He didn't talk much about his life before he became a lawyer.

"But I'll leave those stories for a more appropriate time."

"Thank you," my mother said.

"All these stories – and there're some doozies – are just part of our oral tradition."

"Yes," said Aunt Esther. "We must pass them down to the next generations. We learn from the triumphs and tragedies, the good and the ugly, all our collective experiences."

"That's right," said Reverend Crawford. "It's important to appreciate all aspects of our history."

"Bottom line though," Uncle Jett said, "– don't mess with Treadwells." He punched his left hand with his right fist like he was about to do battle right then. "They burn our bait shop, we burn down their feed store. They burn a cross in our yard, somebody wakes up to red splattered paint everywhere. They rob our speakeasy, we hit two of theirs. Talk about vigilantism…"

"Okay, Jett," said my mother in her warning voice.

"Wow," said Natalie whose eyes were wide with wonderment.

"But," said Uncle Jett, "all those experiences, especially that casket ride, helped mold me into the man I am today."

"A great man who will always defend a lady's honor!!" said Aunt Esther, raising her aperitif glass. "God, how I cherish my hubby!"

"One day I hope to have a man like that," Natalie said, looking slyly at Emery who didn't seem to notice.

Me too, I thought, thinking of how Julius defended me just the other day.

"Well bravo!" said Lacey Russwurm.

Mrs. Crawford said, "Every time I hear your stories, I get goosebumps."

"Better than listening to the radio soaps," said Dr. Russwurm.

We all agreed.

Everyone gobbled up appetizers, chatted and mingled until the doorbell rang and the last guests arrived. I was astonished to see the Brathwaites walk in. I hadn't asked Magdalena who all was invited – I knew to be charming and sociable regardless – but she normally would've mentioned they were coming. I'd just spent a whole week with Xavier and frankly I'd had my fill of him.

My parents greeted them, then Xavier came toward me. "Are you alright, Justinia? Millie told me what happened at the protest."

"What happened?" Magdalena asked. "Why wouldn't she be alright?"

Xavier related the story secondhand, keeping his arm around me as if I needed consoling. "Had I been there, it never would've happened. I'd have removed her from that volatile situation immediately. Mr. and Mrs. Treadwell, you know I'd never let anything bad happen to your daughter. She means the world to me."

"Awww," said Natalie.

"By the way," he said, "I brought these for you." He presented me with a paper bag which I opened to find two beautiful mangoes that smelled delectable. Usually I'd be delighted, but for some reason, I was just annoyed.

"Thanks," I said.

"Awww," said Natalie.

Magdalena asked if perhaps Dr. Russwurm should have a look at me, make sure everything was okay, but I assured her and our dumbfounded guests that I was fine, that another man intervened, beat my attacker down, caused him to be arrested.

"A foreigner," Xavier said. "Some Jewish guy."

"Ah," Dr. Russwurm said, as if that explained everything.

Thankfully, before he could bring up the Vogelsang incident, the white-jacketed, bronze- statue of a man that was the steward from Stern's Fine Catering, came in and told Magdalena, "Madam, dinner is served."

We reconvened in the dining room. Chauncey freshened drinks then went to the gramophone to replay the Beethoven album of piano sonatas because Abigail demanded to hear *Fur Elise* again. Dixie helped Lily bring out baskets of croissants and the Stern staff brought finger bowls and warm towels so we could dip and dry our hands.

Each course was announced by the steward. "Baked brie in puff pastry with pistachios and figs. . . accompanied by a noble Chardonnay from Tucker's Vineyards – Ahem! Another stellar *Negro* establishment . . . Shredded radish and cucumber salad with chive vinaigrette. . .French onion and wild mushroom soup with grated gruyere and pumpernickel croutons.. . .Oysters Rockefeller and crab croquettes with remoulade sauce. . .Lamb chops with spearmint jelly. . .String beans with slivered almonds. . .Sweet potato chutney. . .And for dessert, angel food cake and chocolate-drizzled strawberries." The steward offered a mahogany cigarette box of Camels or a demitasse spoonful of lemon sherbet to cleanse the palate between the savory courses.

Even for Magdalena this was too sumptuous for a no-occasion summertime dinner regardless of last week's Joe Louis fiasco. While everyone chatted and ate, Xavier leaned toward me, poking my flower wreath. "What's this for?" he asked.

"Dixie made it for me."

"Kind of silly, don't you think?" I swallowed an oyster so I wouldn't be able to respond.

Right before the dessert course, Xavier stood up, cleared his throat and asked for everyone's attention because he had an announcement to make. I looked at him curiously, wondering what he had to say that required such pomp.

"This past week has brought Justinia and me even closer. We've gone through a lot together over the years, have had good times and trying times. But I can't imagine a future without her." He pulled something out of his pocket. It was a ring box – Tiffany blue. He flipped it open and reached down and took my hand.

"Justinia Treadwell, will you marry me?"

I gasped. Everyone gasped. My mother and Abigail beamed. Daddy and Emery looked blasé. Natalie said, "So romantic – I think I'm going to cry."

They all looked at me for my response.

"This was Grandmother's ring," Xavier said like that would convince me to say yes.

How dare he do this! A public proposal! Gutsy.

"Father wanted to bury her in it," Abigail said, "but we said absolutely not, a diamond that valuable should be bequeathed. Justinia, you've no idea how lucky you are."

"Wow," Aunt Esther said, "my parents got married with matching cigar bands." Abigail coughed, grabbed her water goblet. "They were together 73 years."

"My parents had *no* rings," Dr. Russwurm said. "Married 81 years." Abigail finished her water, downed her Chardonnay, then raised the glass for the steward to refill it.

"What a blessing! But my how far we've all come," Aunt Esther said. "So what do you say, Justinia? We were just talking about this."

I could strangle Xavier. After all our hollow marriage discussions. But I'd look like a heel if I said no. I was steamed. But at some point I must have said yes because there was applause and Xavier went into the kitchen to uncork the bottle of Dom Perignon he'd presumptuously brought along.

The congratulations were profuse, the admiration for the diamond flashing on my finger was profound – Natalie really was in tears – and I accepted it all graciously, wondering how I'd ever extricate myself from this predicament. I needed to call Millie.

"It's about time," Mrs. Russwurm said.

"A match made in Heaven," said Reverend Crawford.

Then there was a crash and Magdalena excused herself to the kitchen to see what happened. I followed, grateful for a reason to leave the table and to give Xavier the "evil eye."

I stopped short. Julius was standing there. He was a sight for sore eyes.

CHAPTER 55

WHO KNEW THAT when I purposefully forgot to retrieve my pen from Julius that I'd see him so soon afterwards? Either I wanted him to have something to remember me by or knew instinctively that he'd track me down to return it, like he did with my grandmother's pashmina. We must have a cosmic connection because I willed him to do the latter and there he was.

It was an awkward situation. Upstairs in her bedroom, away from prying ears, Magdalena accused me of being deceptive, omitting critical details about "this Julius character."

"And then," she said with dramatic hand flourishes, "he just *swoops* in here out of the blue in the middle of your engagement party."

"I wish I'd *known* this was supposed to be an engagement party. You never mentioned *that* critical detail. It appears, Mother, that *you* are the deceptive one."

She bristled. "What has gotten into you, Justinia? You never speak to me in this fashion." She paused. "Besides, it was Abigail's spur-of-the-moment idea. Xavier wanted to propose before he began his internship next week because he knew he'd be busy."

"But you knew I was keeping my options open. I told you about Julius, how we had a lot in common and how we were having such a good time together. You said you were happy for me."

"Well, like many of your other relationships, I didn't think it would actually develop into anything. And you could've just told Xavier no, or that you needed time to think about it."

"Right, that would've gone over well."

"And even if Julius is as wonderful as you think he is, you don't need those unnecessary complications." I wanted to tell her how much I *really* liked him, but didn't know how she'd react.

After a brief verbal tit for tat, we returned downstairs and proper introductions were made so the guests could stop wondering who this white man was and why he was there. Julius apologized for the intrusion and for startling Xavier so that he broke Mother's crystal. My father said "no problem" and thanked him for saving my life.

"I've heard so much about you all," Julius said.

"Well," said Magdalena. "Justinia *mentioned* you. I must say, you're not what I expected."

"You thought I'd be taller?" Everybody laughed.

Daddy told Chauncey to make Julius a drink. "Chauncey here makes a mean Manhattan." He told Lily to slice him some cake and asked Dixie to find an extra chair. "There's a rocker in the sitting room." He lifted the needle from the Beethoven record, but not gently enough, so it scratched. "Enough of that. Let's hear the Duke." Julius was delighted and, on the inside, so was I.

Good manners dictated that the conversation be steered away from potential "race talk" – Joe Louis, Jesse Owens, Thurgood Marshall and the Maryland law school, the upcoming presidential election and what it all meant. Instead the topics were pedestrian – the weather, sporting events, food, drink, whether Julius had trouble finding the place. It was Julius who brought up the NAACP and how great the convention was, about how John Hope was a great choice for the Spingarn medal, about how he'd never comprehend the mind of a racist. "As my grandmother always says – we're all the same under the skin."

"Hear, hear!" said Reverend Crawford, raising his champagne flute.

Xavier sulked while we blithely discussed world peace and racial harmony. His mother finally looked pointedly at Julius and said, "Pardon me, but this is supposed to be Xavier's moment. He just proposed to Justinia. And she accepted."

Julius turned to me. "Well this is news indeed. Congratulations!" A few minutes later, he made his excuses and left. I didn't know if I'd see him ever again.

CHAPTER 56

"BERLIN?" MY MOTHER exclaimed. Laden with shopping bags and hatboxes, she'd just returned from D. C. where she'd had socialite errands and was now catching up on family business. "Berlin, Maryland?"

"*Germany*, Mother, I'm going to Germany." She sat down on the sofa because my announcement evidently made her feel faint.

"Treadwell women do not chase men, Justinia. And you're engaged to be married – to a man most women would kill to be with." She looked at my father who'd come into the room. "Did you know about this, Jasper?" He nodded.

"And you approve?"

"She's not chasing anyone, Magdalena. She's going for cultural enrichment. She has the gift of German gab, let her utilize it. Consider it a graduation present."

"We docked in Frankfurt during our honeymoon cruise. Remember, I found it to be mediocre and overrated, unable to hold a candle to Paris. Why not go to Paris, Justinia? Or London?"

"Maggie-dear," my father said, "Berlin is far superior to Frankfurt."

I explained to her that I was going to Berlin to attend the Olympics. "It will be fascinating."

"No," Magdalena said, "Edgar Bergen's ventriloquism act is fascinating. A television receiver console is fascinating. Germany is just the scourge of Europe."

I'd never been to Europe and wanted to see another part of the world before I inevitably settled down into the role of teacher, wife, and – eventually, ugh! – mother. There'd be no turning back from that life, no digression for the next fifty years. Julius had sent me a letter formally inviting me. He said he'd meet me at the New York Harbor where he'd booked himself on the *SS Bremen* – first class passage to Hamburg – and from there he'd take a train to Berlin. He said he'd show me around Berlin and take me to meet his family. Depending on how long I stayed, we could take a jaunt to Warnemuende, a seaside Berlin resort, explore castles in Prague, or go to Munich to see the clock tower encasing the famous Glockenspiel. He promised I'd have fun but understood if I declined.

It sounded like a fantastic distraction. I could either go to Berlin or stay in Highland Beach and attend dozens of clambakes, garden parties, fundraisers and teas and see the same fifty people over and over again. I chose Berlin. I gave a postcard to the postman just that morning. It was addressed to Julius and it said, "I'll meet you at the dock."

"It's inappropriate," my mother said. "Engaged women do not frolic with other men."

Daddy said, "That's why Emery is going with her. I contacted a tourist agent to make arrangements for the two of them. I offered a bonus if they could also get tickets to some track and field events. They can't go all that way and not see Jesse Owens."

My little brother was to be my "chaperone." Emery, who was always reckless with his exploding chemistry sets, constantly mischievous with his rubber snakes, plastic spiders and whoopee cushions, was to be my shadow to assure that my aura of respectability was not compromised. Emery – who Daddy had to teach a lesson about the importance of scholarship when he got three C's on his report card in the fifth grade. My parents had been furious, telling him he was fully capable of getting straight-A's but didn't work hard enough or think critically enough.

·+≡◉ ◉≡+·

"Treadwells did not get this far by being average." It was my mother's mantra.

"Okay," my father had said, "I'll show you what happens to Negro boys who get bad grades." He told Chauncey to bring him his shoeshine kit, then gave the kit and a pair of his patent leather opera shoes to Emery.

"Alright, get to shining!" Emery looked confused. "Do it!"

Emery jumped, handled the shoe and the tools awkwardly, like a monkey trying to figure out a telephone.

"Apply the polish to the rag and rub in clockwise circles!. . .Faster, harder. . .More elbow grease!. . .Now snap that rag! Customers like it when you snap it. Snap it!...No, that's a little, *sissy* snap. . . Pop that wrist! How're you going to get a decent tip unless you snap it?. . .And grin, act like you're enjoying it. Customers like those big, wide grins. . .Come on, wider, faster, wider, faster. . .Don't help him, Chauncey. . .Hurry up! There's a line of five men and they all have places to go, people to see!...Say 'be right wit'choo, boss' before they go down the block to Skeeter's stand cuz he's faster and full of flattery and enthusiasm. Competition is rough out there. Jojo by the Greyhound terminal will brush the lint off your jacket and do a rendition of 'Ol' Man River' if you ask. . .So say it: be right wit'choo, boss...Say it!...Snap that rag. . .Smile wider, rub faster. . .Now spit on it. They like those spit shine finishes. . . Good! Now the other shoe. . ."

This went on for about twenty minutes and it was painful to watch. Emery was trying to grin through the tears, snap the rag, and my mother finally said, "I can't take it anymore, Jasper. Just spank him and be done with it."

That was startling because my parents did not believe in spanking. They thought it showed a lack of sophistication. Upper-crust families *spared* the rod and withheld privileges when a child erred. Besides, everyone had seen the photograph of Gordon, the fugitive Louisiana slave who became a union soldier. The tree-like scars and keloids crisscrossing his back became a popular propaganda piece for abolitionists. No sane parent would abuse their child to that extent, but *any* corporal punishment was evocative of the brutal treatment Gordon, and other slaves, received from the overseers.

"The only difference," Daddy told him, "between you and a bootblack is opportunity. You have it, they don't. Don't squander your opportunity by being lazy in school. Or *this*'ll be your future."

He finally allowed Emery to go to his room where he cried for hours. Emery would've preferred a few swats on the behind rather than endure that shoeshine lesson. But he never got anything lower than a "B" again. Even so, Emery was a little absentminded and daydreamy. He'd be an easy chaperone to ditch.

⋯⊶⊙ ⊙⊷⋯

Mother was still unconvinced. "Jasper, Germany is dangerous. Those Nazis are vile."

"No more dangerous than living in America. As a Negro male, Emery has more to fear from these crazy yahoos than those Nazis, especially when he goes back to Georgia."

"Perhaps."

"Remember how frightened you were when Charlotte went to Liberia." He lit a fat cigar, took a puff. "And she's fine."

"Thus far."

Mother did not want to be reminded of that time. It was not her finest hour. She predicted Charlotte would get lost in the jungle, be trampled by stampeding elephants, eaten by lions or cannibals. "I forbid it," she'd said.

Charlotte chuckled at the list of implausible tragedies and the notion that Magdalena could still dictate her life. "You can't forbid me, Mother. I'm a grown, married woman and Calvin and I have decided that our missionary work is paramount. We'll be in a house near Monrovia College, not in the Hinterland."

"You young people think you're invincible and that you know everything. There are places on this earth, not just in Africa, that are still very uncivilized and unpredictable."

"That's the reason we're going – to spread enlightenment to our people."

"I did not raise you to become a quirky evangelist."

"Mother, please, stop exaggerating. We'll be digging wells, building schools, encouraging people to get smallpox vaccinations, all kinds of things."

"Cousin Kirby got mauled by a hippopotamus while trying to imitate Hemingway hunting big game in the Serengeti."

"But cousin Kirby was crazy, and they warned him about the riverbanks."

"Still, the next thing, you'll be coming home with tribal scars and strange piercings and wearing some African get-up just to spite me."

"You're being dramatic, mother. This is our calling. We'd like to have your blessing, but if not, so be it."

"You do not have my blessing," Magdalena said and left the room. She stayed in her room and didn't bid them farewell when they left a month later.

I continued pleading my case, reminding my mother that lots of people traveled after college graduation, that thousands of people from all over the world would be descending on Germany for the Olympics, that there'd be lots of security and that the Nazis were even treating the Jews better. Also, Dr. DuBois, Paul Robeson, Mary Church Terrell, Dr. Alain Locke and Josephine Baker all said that Berlin was exciting and much more welcoming and tolerant than many American cities.

"DuBois," my father said, "will be there for the Games. Berlin is one of the stops on his trip around the world. Arrange to have dinner one night."

"I will," I said.

"But," said my mother, "there was that one black man who the Nazis killed. Remember Mary Terrell told us about him."

"Hilarius Gilges," my father said. "Yes, he was one of the German Communist Youth who went to prison and still continued his activities after he was released. He was a martyr."

"Mrs. Terrell called him an Afro-German Crispus Attucks," I said. "But I assure you that neither I nor Emery will go there acting like Communist agitators."

"You'll miss the Dawsons' annual summer soiree. I hear Paul Robeson is coming again."

"There'll be many other soirees."

"Not like this one. They've hired a French chef, Calypso musicians, Russian acrobats – no cohesive theme unfortunately, but interesting nonetheless. They're even having a bandstand erected as we speak."

"Sounds wonderful."

She crossed her arms. "And what about Xavier?"

"As soon as I get back, you and I can begin making wedding plans."

At this, she brightened a bit. "Good, because we need to book a photo session with Addison Scurlock immediately to have your engagement portraits made. He's always so busy, but I'm sure he'll make time for *us*. Then we'll have to send the photos to the *Bee* and the *Afro-American*. Who knows, maybe even the *Post* will publish a story. It might be a first, but the Treadwells and the Brathwaites are Negro gentry and *all* society people should want to read about this union."

"Okay, mother," I said before we got into a premature debate about details.

"They just ran a story yesterday about the Novak-Pantinelli nuptials and those families are so much less accomplished."

"You're right, mother."

As a traditionalist, I knew Magdalena envisioned me, like Charlotte had, following twenty attendants down the aisle to Pachelbel's *Canon in D* played on the massive church organ, wearing blinding white and carrying the typical, prim spray of tulips, freesia and baby's breath. Butterfly-shaped, origami place cards and the release of a hundred live butterflies upon everyone's exit from the church was initially a little over-the-top for Magdalena, but Thelda Michaels, the wedding planner and cousin to Dovey Stern, had convinced her that it would be enchanting. And it was – until a bunch of them landed in Calvin's mother's hair and she whooped and hollered, swatted and stomped on the poor creatures. The whole thing was a very elaborate affair and Charlotte would've preferred a much smaller, simpler affair, but she let Magdalena have her way because she knew she'd soon be dropping the Liberia bombshell on her and there was only so much stress and dissension our mother could endure.

I thought an *ivory* gown flattered my complexion more. I wanted to glide to the altar to "Here Comes the Bride" played on a harp and carry an armful of showy flowers like gigantic stargazer lilies in my sorority colors of pink and green. Charlotte could be my Maid of Honor and there could be a Best Man. All the musical selections would be played in a sensual minor key. No butterflies or doves. People can throw rose petals which symbolize love and passion – and they're softer than rice. After eating rich cassata cake – not the usual bland, white-on-white cake no matter how layered and prettily frosted – Magdalena would recommend London or Paris as a honeymoon destination, but I hear that the exotic Punalu'u Beach in Hawaii with its sea turtles and lava-created, jet-black sand is uniquely beautiful and must be seen. If my life was careening towards marriage to Xavier, at least I'd fight to have the kind of wedding and honeymoon I wanted. But later – one battle at a time.

Despite assurances to sit down with Thelda Michaels as soon as I returned, my mother sighed deeply, like she had empty cupboards and many mouths to feed. My father went to her, put his arm around her waist, and said, "Don't worry, Maggie. They'll be fine."

CHAPTER 57

Julius

THEY WERE LATE. The ship's whistle was blowing to alert passengers that departure was eminent. In thirty minutes I'd be on my way home and five days later, my life as a non-citizen in my own country would commence. It was dismaying to know that I was leaving behind the freedom to come and go as I pleased, to say what I wanted without fear of retribution. Someday I'd like to return to America though I knew it'd be difficult if war ever broke out.

Meanwhile I would miss baseball, especially seeing the Detroit Tigers' Hank Greenberg – the "Hebrew Hammer" – who I thought was more exciting than Babe Ruth – slugging against the Washington Senators. I would miss hanging out in Chinatown, walking around the National Mall and Embassy Row and seeing people from all over the world. I wish Germany had something akin to Ellis Island and the Statue of Liberty, some symbol to ostensibly welcome all people and not just German Aryans. I would miss the Smithsonian, witnessing real democracy and free elections with more than one political party on the ballot and no reprisals for failure to vote. I still remember the SA going door to door, demanding that people get to the polling stations to retain members of the Nazi Party and beating them up if they refused, which is why there was nearly 100% participation.

I would miss Fourth of July celebrations, Thanksgiving dinners, the cherry blossom festivals and D. C. weather that was sunnier, drier and warmer than home. I would miss Twinkies, corn bread, barbecue and macaroni and cheese – food I'd never find in Germany. All these things made me feel American and I liked that feeling. And I would miss Justinia. But I couldn't ignore the magnetic force tugging me back home.

During my three years in America, I dated many girls, but none of them held my interest for more than a month or two, though truthfully, I was probably the one who didn't measure up. I wasn't Jewish enough for most Jewish girls or their husband-questing families. Some found me to be *too* Jewish. Some said I was too preoccupied with "outside" matters, too opinionated. One girl decided I was just "too strange" and ordered me off her doorstep when I picked her up for a movie.

But many of the young ladies were pushy and forward, only good for temporary enjoyment. And I found them to be vain, self-centered, stuck-up or disturbingly unaware, blissfully ignorant, disconnected from the world and not opinionated *enough*. They were either subtly or unhesitatingly prejudiced. One girl told me she thought Hitler was misunderstood and felt sorry for him because people were constantly defaming him. She said he was a valiant soldier, a gifted author and prolific painter who only wanted the best for his country and the German people. "And," she said, "I think he's handsome in a rugged kind of way." At that point, I asked the waiter for the check, before our entrees even arrived, then put her right into a cab. It was too bad I didn't meet Justinia until it was almost time to go home. We could've had such good times together. And... who knows in what direction we could've gone?

CHAPTER 58

I BADE A frosty good-bye to Uncle Sy back in Washington before boarding my train to New York. He was troubled that I'd invited Justinia to Berlin. She'd be a distraction, he said, and her presence would make me more conspicuous to the Nazis. I assured him there'd be too many people around for anyone to focus on *me* and that Justinia was just a friend looking forward to a trip to Germany and the company of a great guy such as myself. His response surprised me.

"Did you know her father was a notorious bootlegger?"

My stunned look was not because of the revelation but because he'd obviously been digging around for some dirt, hoping it might change my feelings about Justinia. But he should know, unless he discovered ties to Hitler, I couldn't care less. Justinia said her father, unlike her mother, a Negro aristocrat, was self-made, worked his way through college and law school, slowly and steadily built a good name for himself and was considered a "credit to his race." The details of his exact road to success were unimportant to Justinia or to me. And in the grand scheme of things – manufacturing and trafficking hooch, and all that it entailed – was way down on the list of world sins.

"So what?" I said. "Mr. Treadwell, as I understand, has been a respected lawyer for over thirty years."

"Yes, but apparently he was a real hoodlum in his younger years, before Prohibition, in Kentucky, during the temperance movement. Made a fortune selling that 198-proof, gut-busting swill."

"Who cares?"

"Some people do. They talk. And his best friend, a Dr. Kirkwood – did you meet him? – is an abortionist – discreet – for rich, white people – and he's also well-known to the bookies."

I was flabbergasted. I cared even less about Justinia's father's associates. This kind of cheap-shot ploy only worked on the small-minded and Sy knew I was anything but. "Why are you telling me this?"

"You should know the kind of people you're dealing with."

"Gossip. As I recall, back in Germany, you weren't too thrilled about rumors that you were some communist insurrectionist."

"Well, they were *partly* right. Communist, yes; insurrectionist – I wish. Perhaps if I'd been thirty years younger."

"Well, *I* wish you'd kept quiet."

"I thought you should know."

This was the second spat we'd had in a week. When I told him I was giving my car to Rutherford Nash's wife, he got upset, saying Mrs. Nash didn't want what was the equivalent of "blood money," that she didn't have anywhere to go that required such a nice vehicle and that, since her husband would be in prison, she probably couldn't afford upkeep and fuel anyway. I told him I was doing it anyway.

I didn't know when I'd see Sy again. I gazed long and hard at him, told him I loved him but that I was very disappointed. I squeezed his shoulder, picked up my suitcases and disappeared into the crowd.

"You'll thank me later," he called.

"*Shalom.*"

Now I was worried that Justinia and her brother had stood me up. Maybe it was best. Honestly, I didn't know what to expect, how poisonous the atmosphere might be once we got to Germany. Justinia didn't need more racial strife. This should be a vacation from that. Germany was an ironic place to find relief from racism, but the Nazis didn't care about blacks that much because there were so few of them around and no one thought they were conspiring to dominate the markets, the media and everything else. Their focus was primarily and unrelentingly on Jews. But things had simmered down and I expected the Berlin of my youth to come roaring back. Still we'd be cautious because psychopaths were unpredictable.

Xavier must've convinced Justinia not to go, to stay and compile their wedding guest list, select china and silverware patterns. I couldn't believe she was going to marry him. They didn't seem to have much in common except for the fact that they were both Negro and wealthy. She and I were much more similar. Xavier said he didn't like gospel music, didn't even want to go to the "churchy" Mahalia Jackson concert at the NAACP convention. And he refused to dance, preferring to stand against the wall, observe disapprovingly, and check his stupid pocket watch. What a stick-in-the-mud. I love gospel, jazz, blues; even some of those so-called "hillbilly" tunes were catchy. And I could lindy hop all night, especially if I was twirling Justinia around the parquet dance floor while the whole room watched and clapped their hands. I didn't see Xavier making her truly happy; she'd be little more than a fashion accessory. *I* could make her happy.

I know I shouldn't think like that, but I couldn't help it. It was ridiculous, I know, a fairy tale playing out in my head. Society was unapologetic about its aversion to relationships between people of different colors, religions or social classes. It ridiculed other so-called mismatched couples – fat and skinny, attractive and plain, droll and humorless. There was little appetite for couples who weren't opposite-sex, carbon copy versions of each other. How boring and perverse that homogeneity is so valued and that anything else is discouraged, disparaged or delegitimized. A bouquet of red roses is classically beautiful, but adding pink, yellow and white ones makes it prettier, more interesting – at least to me.

Other than the African soldiers and the Rhineland *frauleins* and American master-slave situations, I didn't know about many interracial relationships. In Germany, too, such unions were reviled, but seemingly less controversial than *rassenschande* – racial defilement – specifically, Jews marrying, or having sex with, German Gentiles. The Nuremburg Laws explicitly prohibited this and subjected Aryan violators to imprisonment and non-Aryans to the death penalty. But even before this bigotry became law, the tides were turning, and "mixed" couples were becoming taboo. This growing attitude is what doomed me and my sweetheart Irina from the start.

Irina was an Archaeology student at the university at the same time I was. She was arrestingly beautiful with blondish hair and aqua eyes. She was also an amazing athlete and I could watch her run the track and throw javelins all day. We were inseparable for two years until her father, a prominent Catholic priest of one of those parishes that cozied up to the Nazis, put an end to it. Influenced by the gusting winds of anti-Semitism, he demanded she stop seeing me or risk being "cut off" – no more tuition payments, no more financing her intercontinental digging excursions, no more going home to Potsdam for holidays and breaks. He said our relationship had no future and he wouldn't stand by and allow her to ruin her life by being with a "filthy Jew" and risk having *mischlings* (Jewish-Christian half-breeds) whom he vowed to never acknowledge as his grandchildren. It was a heart-breaking chapter in my life.

Mutti and *Vati* had no qualms about Irina and me. They liked her. They would've liked me to find a "nice, Jewish girl," but were not insistent. They were more concerned that she be from the professional class and not "peasant stock." However, they warned that the "writing was on the wall," the country was changing, that intermarriage would soon not be tolerated. Preexisting couples would be forced to divorce and the offspring would face all kinds of legal and social problems. Families would be torn apart as children faced divided loyalties and parents made mad dashes to get themselves and their kids baptized. They purchased counterfeit birth certificates and other documents from purveyors of a burgeoning business enterprise that purported to remove all traces of Jewish ancestry. But I was certain such a fate would never happen to Irina and me.

Oma Zip at first said, "You can't help who you love," but was furious after learning Irina's father had said those nasty things. She said that when you marry someone, you marry the entire family, so even if Irina was wonderful, her father was a *dummkopf* and not worthy of linkage to the Sommerfeldt clan. "Forget her," my mother said, as if it were that simple. "You can do better anyway."

I think my family and friends would like Justinia, a pretty American girl who was smart, cultured and knew German. They weren't expecting her; I didn't tell them in my letters that I was returning with friends. I know they had no problem with black people, but I wasn't exactly sure how comfortable they'd be seeing Justinia and Emery actually standing in their living room. They were staying at the Adlon Hotel, but I was hoping to show the same hospitality in my home as they'd shown me in theirs.

Things were already tense with the Nuremburg Laws and Nazi agents everywhere. Everything was totally different from three years ago. My family used to love entertaining, serving brisket and the homemade apple-elderberry wine that used to win awards at the Berlin wine festivals before Jews were banned from participating. My younger cousins would play piano or cello, astonishing everyone with their talent, and my father liked taking down his Mauser rifle and re-telling stories about his Great War exploits until a shoulder injury sent him back to his law career in Berlin.

The rifles should've been gone from the house long ago after the Nazis passed a law requiring anyone unconnected to a Nazi organization to surrender all military weapons or be deemed a public enemy. That he kept them, actually displayed one of them openly, was my father's one act of rebellion. He threw out all his "leftist" reading materials – Locke, Kant, Rathenau – just in case the Gestapo came knocking, but being without his guns made him feel naked and afraid. He cherished his war memories, reliving a time when he felt powerful and revered.

One of my family's last gatherings ended abruptly. My little cousin was at the piano, playing a piece she'd recently perfected.

"Is that Wagner?" asked a guest.

"Yes, it's *Fantasia*," said my aunt. "Hilde's been practicing it forever."

"Make her stop."

"But it's beautiful," said another guest.

"Wagner was a notorious anti-Semite. I will not sit here and pretend to be delighted when I'm repulsed. Why not hang one of Hitler's paintings too?"

"Hold on," my father said, rising from his favorite chair. "In this house we are Germans *first*. We celebrate German heritage and culture *first*. You must separate Wagner's politics from the fact that he was a musical genius."

"I might have years ago, Alexander. But how can you possibly have that attitude after all that's going on today, after what the Nazis have done to you?"

"I was a German soldier. In the 8th Army. My father and uncles were killed defending Germany. Do you know how many Russian Jews I shot and killed in the Battle of Tannenberg?"

With swiftness, *Vati* retrieved his unloaded Mauser, pointed it at a window and maneuvered it like he was actually shooting. "Pap, pap, pap! I mowed them all down." We were shocked, speechless. These histrionics were completely uncharacteristic.

"Pap, pap, pap! They shot back. Because they were Russkies. We all wanted our respective *countries* to be proud of us. Pap, pap, pap! But we were too strong. Russia had to retreat."

Hilde stopped playing the piano. A baby, sensing unease, started bawling. "Alexander!" my mother scolded. "Put that thing down." I took the gun from him, hung it back up over the fireplace mantle, under the framed Sommerfeldt family crest.

The offended guest stubbed out his cigar, downed the rest of his drink and gathered his wife and children.

"I was fighting for the *Vaterland*, not Jewry," *Vati* said. "I'll win back the respect I deserve."

"Don't leave, Franz, Ada," my mother said. "Alexander is under tremendous stress."

"No excuse. It's a difficult time for us all."

"President Hindenburg and Adolph Eichmann both promised me my future was secure," *Vati* continued, "that I'd have 'honorary Aryan' status."

"Well Hindenburg's dead," Franz said. "And Eichmann lied. They're all liars."

My father sat down, put his head in his hands. "I'm sorry."

"*Guten nacht.*"

My family hasn't hosted many affairs lately. Too many people were wallowing in misery. Jewish friends were tired of wearing false cheer, telling each other to buck up, that things could be worse. Food and drink weren't as good and plentiful as they used to be. Jews were only allowed to shop at the end of the day when sometimes nothing was left but overripe produce, stale pastry, dented or bulging cans and maggoty briskets so they were doing well to get enough food to make meals for their own families.

But *Mutti* says they still got together occasionally for potlucks and such just to maintain some sense of community and normalcy. Though Gestapo officers monitored the services, our temple was still a place for solace, spiritual renewal and fellowship. But our Aryan friends always made excuses about why they couldn't visit or host. Even the Dreschlers claimed to be overbooked or that their apartment was a "shambles."

Socializing with blacks, who Hitler despised as much as gypsies, Poles and Slavs, would be a new experience for my family. The "blacks" who attended Gabriel's last art show turned out to be Bangladeshi. Upon meeting Justinia and Emery, Gabriel would probably shrug, my cousin Gretchen would be thrilled, though the Treadwells lacked the ebony skin, stark white teeth and beady hair that captivated her. The little kids would have questions. *Oma* Zip would offer them some tea. Everyone would be guardedly polite. Understandable. Most Germans could go years, even a lifetime, and never see anyone but other white Germans or the occasional white ethnic immigrant. But it was senseless to despise something you hardly ever saw. Is it rational to hate, on principle, on sight, Eskimos, cowboys or monks? Notwithstanding Aryans interacting with Jews, there were few occasions for people to practice racial tolerance.

There were people, but no one I knew, who resented the Japanese and their steakhouses and stores scattered throughout the country, but Hitler considered them honorary Aryans for their "racial integrity" and military alliances. No one I knew would ever raise their fist or stamp their foot at an approaching Gypsy, regarding them as they would a stray dog. We might not buy their chintzy wares or tip them for their gyrating dance, though once I did allow a fortune teller to scan my palm and tell me to "be careful," but everyone I knew has occasionally put money into a beggar's tin cup.

Practically everyone I knew admired Josephine Baker, loved the Russian poet Pushkin and considered *The Three Musketeers* by Alexander Dumas their favorite novel and didn't care that any of them were black. No one I knew would ever condone the poor schmuck we saw railing outside one of my favorite restaurants. "That *shvooga* took my job," he yelled, pointing to a black boy peeling potatoes in the alley. *We* didn't say such things. It was the epitome of poor taste. But Nazi hate and propaganda were closing minds and hearts faster than the flu spreads in a crowded elevator. I didn't want my family, friends and acquaintances to become infected. I prayed for them to remain friendly and tolerant.

CHAPTER 59

"JULIUS!"

I was halfway across the gangway and stopped and turned when I heard her voice. It was like music and I forced myself not to sprint toward her. She was waving excitedly, but primly. I walked toward her and Emery to meet them halfway. They stood out like rainbows in winter. They were glamorous, like the models in *Town and Country* except with darker skin. Someone needed to photograph them, let the world see them in their chic, understated outfits – Emery in a smart, Burberry plaid vest, Justinia holding a matching plaid parasol – undoubtedly custom – but not trying too hard like some of these people wearing fur in July, outlandishly ornate hats and practically every piece of jewelry they owned all at once. Justinia and Emery would look great in a feature story about "American Exceptionalism."

Seemingly the only magazine images of blacks were of fire-dancing Africans and naked Pygmies in *National Geographic*. In *Life*, I've seen tenant farmers in Georgia or rioters in Detroit after a cop shot and killed a kid who had a toy gun, but rarely scenes of Negro success and prosperity. The world needed a glimpse of this. Someone should've sent a photojournalist to the NAACP convention in Baltimore to capture the smart, pensive, multi-shaded faces as they tried to figure out ways to achieve equality. Photographs like that should be worth Pulitzers.

Justinia and Emery drew many admiring but curious looks and I, in my wrinkled sports jacket and unbarbered locks flopping into my eyes, felt like a *schlump* next to them when we met midway. Justinia and I hugged.

"I thought you'd changed your mind," I said.

"And miss out on a trip of a lifetime? Never."

"We got waylaid," Emery explained. "The Customs agents didn't believe our passports were authentic."

"Unbelievable," I said.

"That's the way it is," Justinia said.

⋅⇒◉ ◉⇐⋅

We enjoyed champagne and threw confetti and streamers off the side of the ship to the well-wishers teeming on the walks below.

"Bon voyage!" they shouted.

"Thank you," the passengers responded in multiple languages.

A band playing Benny Goodman tunes had people foxtrotting and lindy hopping all across the main deck. It was a fun and fantastic send-off. I was leaving the United States in grand style. I wondered when I'd return.

"All ashore who's going ashore!"

Everyone who was not traveling to Europe disembarked, turning back to give one last wave. Justinia, Emery and I stayed on deck reveling with other passengers until the Brooklyn Bridge, the Statue of Liberty and the entire Manhattan skyline were just specks.

We were on our way to the first-class section when an over-perfumed, over-rouged woman stopped Emery and asked for assistance. "Young man," she said, "I need this footlocker taken to cabin 404."

"Sorry, ma'am, I'm not a crew member. I'm a guest, just like you are," he told her.

"Well!" she said as though he'd insulted her. Emery was wearing no uniform or name badge. Surely she'd noticed he was one of the best dressed men on board and had spent the last hour hobnobbing, sipping Mojitos, and helping himself to the shrimp cocktail being circulated by waiters on silver platters. He's the one who should've been insulted. I was insulted on his behalf.

"What's going on here?" her husband asked.

"He claims he's a passenger."

"Is that so?"

"Yes, sir."

"What's your name?" he asked, offering his hand. Emery shook it.

"Emery Treadwell, sir. And you?"

The man seemed taken aback that Emery was asking *his* name, putting them on equal footing. But he recovered quickly enough.

"I'm Mr. Teague of Teague's Hardware," he said. "I own nine stores and 'bout to open two more in Staten Island and Hoboken."

"That's great."

"I've never shaken a black man's hand that's as smooth as yours. What do you do?"

"I'm a college student."

"Whereabouts?"

"Morehouse College in Atlanta."

"Is that one of Booker T's schools?"

"No, sir, Morehouse is a liberal arts school."

"What're you studying?"

"Biochemistry."

"Really? Well, this is an expensive voyage, you must have a very generous benefactor."

"Yes, sir, my father is very generous."

"Your *father*? Is your father white?" he asked, knitting his brows, trying to discern the Caucasian blood.

"No, sir," he laughed.

"Who is he then, Bojangles, Duke Ellington, someone like that?"

Emery was holding his own just fine, but I felt compelled to end the obnoxious interrogation. "We should get to our state rooms. We need to prepare for the lifeboat drill."

"Enjoy your trip," Justinia said.

I touched Justinia's elbow to lead her away. I didn't want anyone picking on my friends.

CHAPTER 60

August 1936
Justinia

PASSAGE TO GERMANY was splendid. Emery and I felt like celebrities. We received attention from lots of nice people who smiled and told us that we were attractive, articulate, fashionable and "smelled good." We smiled sweetly, as Magdalena taught us, even though the compliments were inadvertently backhanded. Even when we told them that we weren't related to Josephine Baker or Paul Robeson, that no, we didn't personally know Joe Louis or Duke Ellington and never met them, they still wanted to sit down, have a drink and chat. Word got around and everyone wondered who we were, and they weren't disappointed to learn that we were "nobody." While we still got looks of resentment and disgust – "I thought this was a *luxury* cruise!" – many passengers were excited to get the chance to meet "exceptional" Negroes in a social setting.

We even got invited to the Captain's table. The ship's manifest showed that, of the 2000 passengers, in addition to the movie star Cary Grant and publishing magnate William Randolph Hearst, there were two Negroes, brother and sister, in First Class. In true Magdalena Treadwell fashion, the ship's hostesses strove to put together a scintillating group to have dinner with the Captain and thought Emery and I fit the bill.

We didn't have a *lot* of experience socializing with white people. Our world was extremely insular, but our meticulous upbringing prepared us for any occasion. We understood the art of conversation, were well-informed about past and current events and always used our best grammar and diction. We knew to take tiny sips and dainty bites, to toss our heads back and laugh once or twice – haha! – at anything moderately amusing, to be complimentary, mildly self-deprecating, and a little bit coy, to give good eye contact and smile winningly. I still considered declining the invitation because Julius wasn't also extended one, but he wouldn't hear of it. "I wouldn't invite me either. You and Emery are interesting and fabulous. I'm just a regular Joe. Go, have fun!"

At dinner the Captain went into excruciating detail about the ship, the world's sleekest, and its many modern, technological features. His guests showed polite interest, especially when he talked about the catapult on the main deck which launched a seaplane into the air at flying speed; the plane reached shore in record time to deliver transatlantic mail. I considered taking advantage of that service and send Xavier a postcard to let him think I was thinking of him.

He'd been piqued when I told him about my trip, said maybe he'd go somewhere too, perhaps a weekend getaway to check out the "shenanigans" at the swank Savoy Ballroom in Harlem with his fraternity brothers. I told him that sounded like a good idea and to have fun, which aggravated him even more. Unsurprisingly, his mother was angry too, but Abigail was easily riled.

We'd just said our good-byes to my parents and Chauncey was about to drive me and Emery to the train station, when Georgine walked by with her dogs. I thought she wanted to say good-bye again or remind me to bring her back a bottle of *4711*, the original *Eau de Cologne*, as a souvenir, but she just wanted to tell me that Abigail was at her house the night before at a whist party and told the other ladies that I was being "whorish." I undoubtedly sneered as Georgine acted as if she were vicariously aggrieved. "I thought you'd want to know."

"What did *you* say?" I asked her.

"Well, of course Dovey Stern agreed with Abigail, and Astrid said who'd be so stupid to go to Germany now. Virgie Harper said Magdalena must be so embarrassed! But Deirdre Hobbs said no, she's *livid*. Then…"

"You didn't set the story straight?"

She dropped her eyes. "We tried to explain that the trip was a graduation present."

"Okay sure," I said, climbing back into the car. "Thanks anyway. We have a train to catch. See you soon."

"Bye!"

After the Captain explained the mechanics of the catapult, the diners' fascination turned to me and Emery and we spent a good part of the evening answering questions about ourselves. "What a gorgeous ring," said a woman who'd been eyeing my finger all night. "What is that – three carats?...What does your fiancé do? He must be very smart...I think it's wonderful how Negroes are beating the odds and coming into their own...When's the big day?...How much are you planning to spend?"

"Thank you," I said. "Haha!...Not quite... Haha!... Your Cameo choker is beautiful...He does pretty well for himself...Haha! We're still ironing out all the details, but it should be very nice...." When the sommelier came by with a limited edition Bordeaux from the renowned *Chateau Margaux*, as much as I wanted a taste I said, "Just seltzer with lime for me, thank you," because D & D etiquette taught that even one glass of alcohol can make a lady look like a lush in an intimate, white-only setting.

During dessert, several people confided that they'd be relieved when all this "nasty segregation business" was over and everyone could relax, stop frowning and just be themselves. "It's a lot of work maintaining a racial status quo," said one lady from Mississippi. "It makes everyone grumpy and miserable and I do believe my daddy would be happier and healthier if not for worrying about 'keeping the darkies' – please pardon the expression – in their 'proper place.'"

"Meanwhile," another woman said, "we're all missing out on what could be some wonderful friendships. Here's to making new friends!"

"We can all drink to that." I lifted my goblet. Glasses clinked and the conversation turned to the Olympics.

"I hear this is going to be the grandest one ever."

"And America should do well. We have some great teams."

"So glad we didn't boycott."

It was an enjoyable night. Julius would've really enjoyed it. The other guests would've enjoyed him, would've appreciated his wit, humor and insight. The captain invited me and Emery to visit the bridge to see how the ship is steered. I thanked him and asked if I could bring a friend.

CHAPTER 61

Washington D. C. is a vibrant city, but compared to Berlin, it was a sleepy, little town. The city, especially the heart of it, literally quaked with people. Julius reminded me that over five million people lived in Berlin and there were thousands more from all over the world in town for the eleventh Olympiad.

Walking down *Unter den Linder,* Berlin's main boulevard, I was awed by the Brandenburg Gate, the iconic entrance to the city which is topped by a quadriga – the victory goddess driving a four-horse chariot; but I was taken aback by the flags. I'd never seen so many flags. Berlin was draped head to toe with red swastika flags. Festooned from every window, flagpole and telephone pole, from every apartment, shop and public building, were swastika flags, banners, pennants and signs. It was even difficult to find postcards without swastikas. The Olympic rings were overshadowed by the swastikas. Instead of honoring the Games, it seemed Germany was paying homage to the Nazi Party.

I'm glad Julius told me the real stories behind those symbols and flags. Otherwise I might have marveled at the pageant-y feel, been unaware of the menace they actually represented. I might have dismissed the scene as merely a pretentious but harmless display of partisan zealotry as opposed to perilous omens. After three years away, Julius couldn't have been more surprised than I'd be to return home and see the confederate flag hanging everywhere down Pennsylvania Avenue. "Dogs marking their territory," he whispered to me.

Despite all that, I could see that Berlin was a beautiful city and why so many black and white Americans spoke so fondly of it. I didn't witness any of the rampant indignities Julius told me about. Supposedly everyone was on their best behavior because the world was watching.

In two days Emery and I had seen a lot. Julius showed us the University and the spot where the books were burned. We saw the Reichstag, the Berliner Dom – the city's largest Protestant church –, the American, French and British embassies and so much in between. I could've spent all day at Kaufhaus des Westens, better known as KaDeWe, the largest department store in Europe, that Julius says used to be owned by Jews until the Nazis took it over. I had many souvenirs to buy but Julius said not to get everything in one place as there were so many unique boutiques to check out.

We traversed the city with ease, without feeling we'd be accosted for being brown in a place where everyone was a varied shade of pale. Emery and I took advantage of every blessed moment. Our suite at the Adlon Hotel was regal with the high beds that required a step stool to get onto, the praline truffles on the pillows, turn-down service and the plushest bathrobes we've ever felt. Of course Jim Crow laws meant we weren't welcome in most luxury hotels (or shabby ones, for that matter), and we hadn't been born when the historic, Negro-owned Wormley Hotel – Washington's finest – boasting elite clientele, the first hotel elevator and scrumptious turtle soup, was in existence. So this was a real treat. We rode streetcars and double-decker buses, had doors opened for us, elevators held for us. We walked in and out of establishments without a care, ordering drinks, sampling appetizers, trying on shoes, hats and various clothing items. At KaDeWe I gave Julius an impromptu fashion show.

"What about this one?" I asked, modeling a rhinestone-studded hat with a giant purple satin rose attached at a rakish angle.

"It looks beautiful on you," Julius said.

"Complements your complexion," a saleslady offered.

"You don't think it's too gaudy?"

"Yes," said Emery.

"It's gilding a lily," Julius said. "But you look fabulous."

I wrote a check and had it shipped home.

Later, we were standing on the curb down the street from the Adlon Hotel where we were staying. A marching band and a group called the Hitler Youth goose-stepped by. They seemed mechanical, like the Glockenspiel I hoped to see, singing a victory song by a man named Horst Wessel who Julius said was a Nazi martyr supposedly killed by Communists. They also sang sanitized versions of Nazi songs that deleted references to hating Jews and starting another world war. Hitler didn't want the visitors and foreign press thinking they really *were* evil and imperialistic. Standing next to me were a mother and child who looked to be from some rural part of the country in town to enjoy the festivities. They wore tattered "farm" wear and spoke in the Low German dialect. The boy asked his mother why there were so many flags.

"German pride," she said.

"What was wrong with the old flag? It was prettier."

"That was the Jews' flag."

"We used to wave that flag. Are we Jews?"

"Hell no! German through and through,"

"I think my friend Karl is Jewish.

"Shut your mouth," the mother said, hitting him over the head with her pocketbook. "These troopers will hear and you'll be in big trouble."

"This is scary," he whined. "Let's go home."

"Look! In two years you'll be old enough to join those youngsters coming up the street – Hitler's youth, but the one closer to home, in Hamelin."

"No, *Mutti*, they're scary."

"Hush that stupid talk! Look how fit and trim they are. They'll know how to whip a butterball like you into shape. Meanwhile, no more gingerbread for you."

"*Mutti!*"

I felt sorry for the little boy. His mother was already promising to turn him into an automaton, trained to shun his Jewish friends, to be hateful, predatory and violent because racial bullying was a civic virtue. He'd be like so many white American children who hurl rocks and slurs at Negro children with whom they secretly – deep down – just wanted to play ball and House and Hide and Seek. That German boy would probably rather be friends than enemies with *all* his peers. I was convinced that babies weren't born bigots, that bigotry – like arithmetic – was taught, that altruism and decency were the dominant, default genes.

Yet, this German mother obviously thought she was doing right by her child. So I felt for her too. She was a victim, sucked into a maelstrom of Nazism. Going against the grain was lonely and uncomfortable.

Daddy's contacts were successful getting us three tickets to the opening ceremony and the first two days of track and field competitions in the new Berlin Stadium which was draped with even more Nazi flags and covered with Coca Cola ads, an official Olympics sponsor, featuring smug Aryans sipping Coca-cola like it was God's nectar.

We had the hottest tickets in town. The ticket-less stood around outside hoping to get a sneak peak of the festivities. The opening ceremony was an amazing spectacle. It was the largest Olympiad ever with 49 countries and over 4000 athletes. The *Hindenburg* airship, circumnavigating above, towed the five-ring Olympic banner. There was the torch relay – a Nazi creation – comprised of over 3000 Aryan runners each carrying the flame one mile all the way from Olympus, Greece. The crowd went wild as the last runner completed the relay, ran up the steps and lit the Olympic cauldron where it would burn throughout the Games.

Each country was in the ceremonial procession and I was glad the United States team refused to dip the flag or return Hitler's Nazi salute which evoked some boos from the crowd. It was good seeing the American contingency acting on principle, refusing to show deference to an evil dictator. Though they did a military-style "eyes right" gesture towards Hitler's box, they just removed their hats and placed them over their hearts just as they would if the "National Anthem" were playing.

At the same time, I couldn't ignore the hypocrisy of demonstrating such pride for a country that had a Supreme Court with supposedly the best legal minds deciding that legalized segregation and forcible sterilization for the infirm and handicapped were constitutional because Justice Oliver Wendall Holmes said "three generations of imbeciles are enough," and a Congress that flatly refused to outlaw lynching. Just recently, I'd read in *Crisis* that the government was providing a bogus health care program to poor Negro farmers in Tuskegee and lying to them about treating their syphilis – a new low if it turns out to be true. While Germany was doing everything to exile German Jews, Uncle Sam was ripping half a million Mexican-American citizens from their homes and streets and deporting them to Mexico without due process. Still I was proud because, despite its myriad flaws, I believed the claims that America was the world's greatest country.

I wanted to jump up and wave my arms when I spotted through my binoculars the Negro athletes, introduced derisively as the "black auxiliary," but remembered my breeding and just applauded. I was not just a spectator; I was, like Jesse Owens, representing a race, whether I liked it or not. My mother reminded me of this several times before I left. "Most Germans have never laid eyes on a real-live Negro. Make sure your appearance, and everything you do, is exemplary."

When Chancellor Hitler stood to greet the crowd and officially open the Games, the noise was deafening. "Heil Hitler!" the crowd roared with their right arms extended. Everyone was on their feet. It was bizarre, cultish. Surely there were many genuine Nazi-lovers, but I think some people, especially foreigners, joined in as if it were all in fun, part of an authentic cultural immersion or doing it merely because everyone else was. They'll go back home and conveniently forget they ever went wild over this despot, the enigmatic, little man with the penetrating eyes and odd toothbrush moustache. It would be just one of the memories – like the gray, drizzly weather, the crowds, eating hog head cheese, blood sausage and beer soup, or the poop from 25,000 pigeons raining down on us when they were released at the opening's climax – they'd recall lightheartedly, but with a scrunched-up face, when people asked about their Berlin vacation.

The fervor was palpable, infectious. It was the din of 100,000 Pentecostals glorifying their snake-handling bishop, the delirium of 100,000 teens swooning over the singing star Bing Crosby. President Roosevelt was revered but not deified and, unlike Hitler, I believe few would follow him blindly over a cliff. It was clear why the little country boy I'd seen earlier found it all "scary."

All around me were shouts of "Heil! Heil!" It went on for several minutes. The craziest part was looking over and seeing Julius with his arm outstretched. I couldn't have been more astonished if Hitler came into the stands where we were and shook my hand.

CHAPTER 62

Julius

JUSTINIA AND EMERY fell in love with Germany as soon as we docked in Hamburg, our largest port, Germany's "Gateway to the world." They marveled at all the cruise ships, the beautiful, 17th-century buildings and remarkable red-brick architecture, the bustling train station. The train, known as the *Flying Hamburger*, got us to Berlin in a little over two hours and we were immediately enveloped by Olympic frenzy and a profusion of swastikas.

I took them to the Adlon so they could get settled before beginning a whirlwind sightseeing tour. They said it was the nicest hotel they'd ever stayed in since American segregation laws barred them from the Ritz Carltons and Waldorf Astorias. I'd visited the Adlon numerous times and wondered if I'd be allowed in after the Olympics were over and the Nazis remembered they were supposed to be ostracizing Jews. The Adlon has hosted everyone from Russian tsars, the Maharaja, FDR and other heads of state to Josephine Baker, movie stars and many other prominent individuals. Most Germans like and respect Americans, and were really impressed by ones who, like Justinia, spoke fluent German. At check-in, the hostess didn't even blink, just smiled and gave her the room key.

On the way to the elevator, someone called, "Justinia Treadwell?"

Justinia turned around. "Dr. DuBois!" They hugged. "My father mentioned you were a guest here. I was going to have the clerk ring your room later."

"Well, I'm glad I saw you. Fortunately we're easy to spot around here. But I'm off to Bayreuth soon, must escape this Olympics madness. Tonight it's Courvoisier, Beethoven and Tolstoy. At the week's end I'll be in Japan as the Ambassador's special guest." He exhaled. "How are you, my dear?"

"I'm well."

"And Emery, you've grown into a fine, young man."

"Good to see you again, Doctor."

Justinia introduced me to this great man and I was exultant. He was quite a dandy with his Van Dyke beard, polished walking stick, sharp, smoking jacket and silk ascot. I asked if he remembered my aunt who was an NAACP organizer.

"Of course! What a small world this is."

I suggested we all go into the salon for some tea but he was on a tight schedule. I would've loved to talk to him longer, explain how I read *The Souls of Black Folks* and was particularly moved by the parts where he talked about "double consciousness" – viewing oneself through the eyes of others – a concept I as a Jew found relatable, and also the part where he mourned his first-born baby son who died from diphtheria thirty-odd years ago because Atlanta hospitals wouldn't treat Negroes and pondered if the child wasn't better off dead although his wife was inconsolably heartsick. I admired his intellectualism and wanted to hear his assessment on the state of the world. Justinia asked him about his wife and daughter.

"Nina has good days and bad days. Yolande's still teaching social studies in Baltimore and caring for her new husband and baby."

"How have you enjoyed your stay here?" I asked.

"I'm amazed at the economic progress, the autobahns, stadiums and such. And just like forty years ago when I was a student here, I'm treated with the utmost respect. But I'm concerned about all the hatred against the Jews. Are you Jewish, son?"

"All my life."

"Be careful. These Germans are obsessed with your people. I know they're downplaying it now. But I've seen some things and, as a persecuted minority myself, I sense they mean you no good in the long run."

"I certainly hope you're wrong."

"So do I."

It was good seeing my family again. After all the hugs and kisses, *Mutti* and *Oma* Zip attempted to "fatten" me up with all kinds of food and drink because they thought I was too skinny.

I laughed. "I *gained* twenty pounds. American food is delicious."

"Well it can't be better than this veal schnitzel," *Mutti* said.

I took a bite. "Tastes like Helga's," I said.

"Ah! I've been practicing. Just for you."

We chatted about everything, even the stories we'd already written each other about because they were better told in person. I tried to figure out how to tell them that I wanted to bring Justinia and Emery to the house for them to meet. There didn't seem to be an ideal time.

"You've got that American... swagger," my father said, playing Patience, a German card game similar to Solitaire. "Be careful with that."

"What do you mean?"

"A little too confident and carefree. You're in Germany now."

"I know *Vati*."

"They treat us worse than Americans treat their Negroes."

"It's pretty bad over there."

"Yes, but *they're* used to it. *We're* used to freedom and prosperity."

"Moses suffered," *Oma* Zip said. "And all his followers."

"Contemporary Jews don't suffer unless they choose to," *Vati* said.

I continued eating my schnitzel, unsure how to respond. "So how are the Dreschlers?"

"Who knows?" *Mutti* said. "They avoid us like the plague. Wolfgang joined the Party. Eva claims it was only to save his job. The reason doesn't matter. They're a disgusting party."

"It's a fast-moving bandwagon," said Gabriel.

"A pox on them!" said *Oma* Zip.

It seemed like only yesterday that the Dreschlers defied the boycott, came into the store and bought things. They were the last people I expected to yield to Nazis.

"*Verdammt!*" my father yelled. "My luck isn't changing!"

"It's a silly card game, Alexander," my mother said. "Leave that, come have some cinnamon bundt cake. You've been at it all day."

"I don't want any cake!" I winced. My father never raised his voice to my mother. I tried to pierce the tension with some levity.

"*Vati*, when did you become superstitious?"

"Since they took my country away from me."

Our home used to be so peaceful. Everyone was trying to be normal and upbeat for my benefit. But I sensed they were on edge, that the smiles were forced. The meal, unfortunately, was dry and bland, the tea was weak and tasted like dish water. The pillows hadn't been fluffed and the rugs hadn't been swept in a long time. The light bulbs were naked because no one bothered to replace the lampshades. Mail and government-approved newspapers were stacked everywhere. *Oma* Zip fought off sleep while reading and making notes in her Torah and Gabriel stared into space though I could tell he was ruminating on something. Even the cat scooted away when I tried to scoop her up. Then I noticed something else amiss.

"Where's the Van Gogh?" I asked, pointing to the empty space on the wall.

At first no one responded.

"Well," *Mutti* said, "The Gestapo came by a few months ago. One of the higher-ups in the Party heard we had nice art and sent some officers over with an 'offer.'"

"One they couldn't refuse," Gabriel said.

"Not if we want peace," said *Vati*.

"How did they even know what we have?"

"I think it was the Dreschler's maid," said Gabriel and punched the air. "She's a snitch!"

"And those scallywags will be back," said *Oma* Zip."

"Probably," said my father who'd hidden his trophy military rifle that used to hang above the parlor fireplace. "Now that they've had a look around."

We owned several valuable paintings, including a small Cezanne in my parents' bedroom; and those ignorant, uncultured Gestapo goons missed the Rodin sculpture in the dining room.

I stared at the rectangular void. The velvet flocked wallpaper was much lighter where it'd been covered up by the Van Gogh for many years. I loved that painting, loved its short, squiggly lines that Gabriel said was a "stippling" technique. It made the picture seem alive and in motion.

"Put one of Gabriel's paintings in its place. It'll be just as nice."

Gabriel let out a short scream – "Agh!" – and left the room.

This was not the same place I'd left three years ago when everything was fastidiously kept. I was having second thoughts about whether I even wanted Justinia to see this dreary place but she was eager to meet my family. While outside was glossy and clean in a contrived, artificial way, inside was dull, gloomy and void of laughter and energy. Of course Helga is gone, but a Jewish girl comes in once a week to do some light cleaning. My parents are now burdened with grinding jobs they needed just to pay special taxes and keep from looking slothful. My mother, a successful businesswoman and bookkeeper, would change linens, clean shit and empty bedpans for eight hours at the Jewish hospital, coming home as my father went out to pluck chickens at a poultry factory. Actually, *mutti* had a night shift and was about to leave.

"There's more schnitzel, Julius," she said, grabbing her purse and sweater.

"*Danke schon.*"

I didn't even share that I was going to the Olympics the next day. It would elicit too many questions and I wasn't ready for the interrogation. I'd find an excuse for my disappearance and explain everything later.

It may have been my imagination, but, despite everything, it still seemed some people were looking at me funny, as if I didn't belong. To borrow a phrase from my former client Rutherford Nash, I felt like "chitlins at a White House supper." Perhaps I shouldn't have. There were plenty of people with dark hair and questionable heritage – people from all over the world – walking around with a carefree nature, completely oblivious to Germany's anti-Semitic reputation. Everyone acted as if Berlin never had "*Juden Verboten*" signs posted everywhere. I suppose that was easy to do. Anti-Semitic newspapers like *Der Stürmer* had been removed from the kiosks. Jewish shops didn't have the Star of David scribbled contemptuously on the windows and no one was publicly humiliated or beaten. They didn't see storm troopers slapping old ladies for failing to give the Hitler salute, spray painting graffiti on churches and synagogues, or ordering

Rabbis to scrub the sidewalk in front of the temple, kicking them in the behind when they knelt down, then laughing hysterically.

The streets were swept, flowers and trees had been planted and businesses and home owners had all spruced up their edifices. The trains ran on time. Bookstores were allowed to sell banned books. Butter and eggs had been rationed for months so there'd be plenty for "intrusive, judgmental foreigners." Even the cabaret scene was revived. I passed by taverns and heard jazz riffs wafting out. Tourists could discreetly hire prostitutes and engage in homosexual activity without fear of consequences. The local military presence was toned down and no one spoke of the troops dispatched to the demilitarized Rhine region, a blatant violation of the Treaty of Versailles. Everything seemed normal.

When I left in 1933, the global Depression was raging. Germany, because it had to pay reparations for the war it started, was hit the hardest. Six million people were unemployed, many were homeless, and panhandlers were everywhere. People tried to sell anything to earn a pfennig – dirty shoe strings, pieces of soap, cigar butts, cardboard boxes, single bullets, yarn and thread unraveled from moth-eaten clothing, old, worthless banknotes that were good for wallpapering or lighting stoves. Any street was a virtual beggars' bazaar.

Now those people were nowhere to be seen. Gabriel says all the beggars, drunkards and Gypsies had been rounded up and put into detention camps. The homeless and hungry who'd scour the streets for discarded apple cores, rotten fruit and morsels of bread had all been arrested for stealing food meant for the pigeons. The economy had strengthened and unemployment was allegedly at an all-time low. Many shop windows had portraits of Hitler looking like Charlie Chaplin except Hitler was wearing a frown instead of a smirk and a halo instead of a bowler. Presumably Hitler was Germany's lord and savior. I wanted to gag.

I could tell visitors were impressed. This was nothing like the Germany they read and heard so much about. Tourists will go back to their respective countries and proclaim that all the terrible things they heard about Germany were lies or exaggerations. Berlin was flourishing, Hitler was charming and charismatic, and the Jews were happy and mingling. Goebbels was genius. He created a "Potemkin village" – someplace deceptively attractive – and transformed a brutal dictatorship into a benign administration. The only question was how long the civility would last.

I realized the natives were under strict orders to be charming and hospitable to *everyone*. But I was still aware of trained, narrowing eyes focusing on Semitic-looking people. I detected some sinister smiles and a festering attitude of disappointment that prejudices couldn't be acted on, that random abuse could not be unleashed. Perhaps newspaper and radio reports and letters from home had made me somewhat paranoid – or just very perceptive. Jews and anti-Semites were all hiding in plain sight.

As we approached the stadium's box office, I was half-expecting to be assessed up-and-down and told that Jews weren't allowed, to be arrested for even trying to get in. I might be relegated to watching the games in some warehouse on *Telefunken* – a German television system which would broadcast live sporting events for the first time in history. I applauded the trailblazing effort but rued the fact that it would be used for more Nazi propaganda and to further legitimize Hitler as a world leader. But I really wanted to see the festivities and contests in person, in the moist, open air. I crossed my fingers. And I relaxed and grinned when the ticket takers and ushers wished me *"Guten tag!"* because I'd gotten in and maybe they weren't being sarcastic, maybe things *had* changed and maybe they really did want me, as well as my Negro friends, to have a good day and enjoy ourselves. I was still cynical, but we did.

When I went to see the Senators play at Griffith Stadium in D. C., the announcer said the sell-out crowd numbered 32,000 and I thought "wow." This Olympic stadium was gargantuan, almost four times larger. From the highest bleachers, I imagine the athletes looked like guppies in a swimming pool. Fortunately we had decent seats. Hitler evidently thought he needed this monstrosity, this phallic symbol, to demonstrate "Aryan superiority." As a proud German, I still hoped our teams, which excluded all Jews but for the self-hating American Jew Helene Mayer, would be defeated. I didn't want Hitler's promises of Aryan dominance to come to fruition.

I didn't find it adorable when a little blond girl curtsied and presented Hitler with a bouquet of flowers. I didn't tap my feet in time with the marching bands or hum along with the choirs. I didn't think the Hindenburg – shaped ominously like a torpedo – flying above was an awesome sight. I thought the swastika symbol stitched onto every piece of cloth and engraved into everything metal was obnoxious, repugnant and presumed perpetuity.

Though I still felt conspicuous as a Jew whose countrymen were being impelled to hate me, I didn't care. So when the whole crowd stood up and gave the Hitler salute, which Jews were really not supposed to do because we were non-citizens, I was caught up. Last month I saw a New York Times photo showing a man, August Landmesser, who was the only individual in a huge crowd refusing to give the Nazi salute at some Hitler function. Not only was he not saluting, but his arms were folded and he had a defiant posture and a look of perplexity. I loved it, loved the audacity of it and couldn't stop staring at it. I snipped it out and put it in my billfold although it'd be considered subversive material in Germany and people got killed for little nothing-things like that.

Standing in Olympic Stadium during the opening ceremonies when everyone was, unthinkingly, "Heil"-ing Hitler, I channeled *Herr* Landmesser's *chutz-pah* and stretched my arm forward too. It was no kowtow. I was saying "*Fick dich*" to Hitler, Goring, Himmler, Goebbels and the whole Nazi entourage, including US Olympics Chair, Avery Brundage and Charles Lindbergh who flew himself in for the occasion and was a special guest. Maybe some random camera angle would zero in and catch me in the act too – *Jew Dares to Perform Nazi Salute at Aryan Olympics*. If so, I hope I look brash and stalwart in the New York Times so my American friends and associates will say, "That's Julius. He's a righteous guy." Unfortunately for Landmesser, after that photograph was published, an arrest warrant for racial defilement was issued because he had a child with a Jewish woman whom he, an Aryan, couldn't marry due to the Nuremburg Laws. Who knows what could happen to me.

I was glad when the Hitler-Nazi Party glorification was over. It was almost as obnoxious as ancient Colosseum spectators cheering on the slaughter of gladiators. I caught the attention of a roving vender and bought a tiny "star-spangled banner." I cheered wildly for Jesse Owens and America. And I cheered wildly because I was so happy to be home and because Justinia was there with me.

CHAPTER 63

Justinia

I REMEMBER SOME of the proudest moments I experienced as a Negro. When the debate team at Wiley College, a small, obscure Negro school in Texas, beat the University of Southern California, reigning national debate champions, I was elated. When Roosevelt appointed William Hastie, a D. C. lawyer, to a federal judgeship in the Virgin Islands, he became the first Negro federal judge and our community came out in full force to celebrate his inauguration. When Lucy Slowe Diggs, an educator and a founder of Alpha Kappa Alpha Sorority, became the first Negro to win a national tennis championship, members of our sports club danced, ate, drank and played doubles all night.

Then Jesse Owens won four gold medals for two sprints, a relay and the long jump, broke three world records and tied another. I was thrilled. Julius, also delighted at the American victories over Germany, lifted me up off my feet and kissed my lips. I wondered if the electric sparks I felt were visible to anyone else. I looked at him and blushed. He blushed and Emery blushed.

"Sorry, I got carried away. He left those guys in the dust!" It *was* amazing how Jesse breezed past his opponents with effortlessness and grace, how he leapt gazelle-like almost twenty-seven feet. The obvious chemistry between Julius and me was even more amazing.

"That's alright," I said.

Four gold medals in one Olympiad was a record in and of itself. I couldn't have been prouder if a Negro were elected President. It more than made up for Schmeling beating Joe Louis. Jesse's stunning victory wasn't expected to happen. *Schvartze*, inferior mortals, were not supposed to best those Nordic, Aryan gods.

It was great seeing Jesse standing at the top of the winners' podium, wreathed in laurel, thanking the audience for its support. He had a great smile, showed class and humility, and was so well-spoken to be a poor cotton picker from Alabama, that I didn't cringe when he spoke during his on-field radio interview. He talked about individual excellence and perseverance, how he loved running, and how it was such a great sport for poor kids because there were no swimming pools or ice rinks in their neighborhoods and all you needed to run was the "strength of your feet and the courage of your lungs."

He thanked his team mates, all the people who helped him get to that point, including his high school track coach in Cleveland, his mentors at Ohio State University and his German opponent, Luz Long, who gave him the advice he needed to barely avoid getting scratched from the long jump competition. Long won the silver medal and they both embraced like brothers afterwards, giving Hitler another reason to fume. Owens represented our people, *all* people, well. It was a great moment in time.

Germany loved Jesse and the entire "Negro auxiliary" who dominated the track events. "Jesse, Jesse, Jesse!" they'd shouted, waving tiny American flags. But Chancellor Hitler seethed. He'd been greeting the other medalists, but now refused to shake Jesse's hand and was subsequently told by the Olympic Committee that he had to greet every winner or none at all. He elected to greet none at all, conveniently slipping out of the stadium, rather than shake hands with a Negro and be photographed for posterity doing so.

Before it was over, American Negroes had won fourteen medals and a returning black Canadian physician won his fifth bronze. After all the bragging he'd done, all the predictions he made, these feats were a poke in Hitler's eye. I think the foreign press was secretly delighted. This kind of controversy was grist for the mill and sold lots of newspapers, garnered lots of ads for the radio shows. Although their coverage had to meet certain Nazi parameters, the headlines of at least one newspaper offered a mild gibe – "Jesse Spoils Hitler's Party." Hitler's response was that Negroes should be disallowed from the Olympics due to their sub-human physical strength. He didn't have an explanation for the thirteen Jewish medalists.

CHAPTER 64

EMERY COULDN'T STOP grinning. Everywhere we went, people stopped him, saying "Jesse! Jesse Owens!" though they looked nothing alike. People wanted to shake his hand and buy him a beer. After the first dozen acknowledgments, he stopped telling them he wasn't the Gold medal sprinter and just grinned and pumped their hand. Some people had cameras and took pictures with him. We'd be long gone by the time the pictures were developed and someone with discernment told them "I don't think that's Jesse Owens." When he emerged from the Olympic Village, the real Jesse Owens was met with much fanfare. Reportedly, huge crowds surrounded him everywhere, wanting just a touch or glimpse of him.

"It's like," said one observer, "he's the Pope or someone."

"Yes," said another. "Or Hitler."

While dining at a nice French restaurant, several "fans" came up to me thinking I was Josephine Baker and asking for my autograph. "Josie Baker!" they screamed. Not wanting to disappoint, I chuckled – "haha!" – and signed my own name – "Justinia T. (USA)" – and they beamed with satisfaction. I only hoped no one asked me to do the banana dance. But a few drunken men performed it for *me*. They bent over, shook their hips and moved their arms like they were doing the hula to the raucous amusement of other diners.

People bought Emery so many drinks that he became slightly inebriated although Julius did his best to help them disappear while I sipped Chablis and nibbled on foie gras on brioche. The restaurant owner was so pleased with our presence that he served us flaming crème brulee "on the house."

"*Merci*," we said.

Julius and I were planning to go on a carriage ride through the city, but we first had to make sure Emery got back to the hotel okay. My little brother was having a wonderful time in Germany. For the first time, he was able to move about without trepidation. He always had to be wary, especially as a student in Georgia where several of his classmates had been hassled, beaten or arrested for no reason. In Berlin, we were met with indifference, curiosity and sideways glances, but mostly congeniality – phony or not. No store, eatery, pub or attraction was off-limits.

With no invitation, I was even emboldened enough to crash a party that the American Ambassador William Dodd was hosting at the Kaiserhof, the Olympics' official host hotel. I'd never seen so many stiff-backed, heel-clicking, Hitler-heiling Nazis in such close proximity. A short, older woman had one of them cornered. "You people are violent, greedy and really, really mean!"

His voice dripped with condescension as he humored her. "Don't believe everything you read and hear, little lady. We're not so bad. We just want what's best for Germany just as you want what's best for Canada."

But she wasn't easily swayed. "I don't think so. *We* want peace and harmony, not all this unnecessary aggravation." I wanted to applaud her as we sashayed by.

"You think Hitler will be here?" Emery whispered as we descended the red-carpet staircase to the second floor and navigated the line between the black velvet ropes.

"No," Julius whispered back. "He's way too insecure to go where people aren't fawning over him and he knows Americans detest him."

"Well it'd still be fascinating to see him up close."

"Justinia Grace Treadwell of the Washington D. C. Treadwells," I announced to the social secretary stationed at the ballroom door. I pointed to Emery and Julius. "My brother and guest." Magdalena always said to act as if you belonged even if you didn't. The secretary just nodded and we walked in, shook hands with Ambassador Dodd and his daughter who was rumored to be of "loose morals" and, grossly enough, to have had a fling with the head of the Gestapo. The press had had a field day.

"Enjoy yourselves," she said, batting her eyes at Julius.

There were lots of Americans in the room and it was refreshing to hear English being spoken. Everyone was still excited about the Olympic victories. They couldn't stop talking about Jesse Owens and rising stock prices, and the mood was joyous and fun. Ambassador Dodd was known for being frugal, and while the band played fun and swingy music, the food and drink were rather uninteresting. They said down the hall the British ambassador was serving hot food and champagne, but here it was mostly beer, trays of crudités, cucumber-cream cheese-and-salmon finger sandwiches and almond cookies – all of which were tasty but made at least one couple walk away in a huff, complaining about "Jew food" and "crappy Jew music." Julius and I looked at each other, shook our heads and helped ourselves to another canape. Then he pulled me onto the crowded dance floor where we shimmied until our feet ached.

There were clusters of elegantly-dressed people – haughty, white-jacketed American men with flag pins, suave, satin-lapelled Frenchmen and courtly German men in crisp Nazi officer uniforms deceiving a coterie of silk-swaddled, feather boa'd ladies with their superficial charm. I heard someone introduce Heinrich Himmler, SS commander and chief of German police, to some American admirers. "Welcome to Berlin," he told them.

Through them all, I didn't see Hitler, but I could've sworn I saw my Nana. My eyes locked with the glamorous older woman's and she cocked her head which was piled high with cascading silver tendrils and fastened with an antique barrette like the one I had. She smiled at me wistfully as a distinguished younger man bowed and kissed her extended hand. *Was it my imagination or did someone speak her name – Sylvia? No, maybe I heard "silver" or "civil."* I lost track of her as Julius was spinning me around and a few minutes later saw the plunging back of her gold sequined dress exiting through the door. I thought of following her if only to luxuriate in her presence for a few precious moments, but realized that could be a disastrous idea; and it probably wasn't her anyway.

Our travel planner had arranged us to have a tour of the Black Forest near Stuttgart. Julius had friends at a Jewish-owned travel agency that was still doing a booming business because it was being "fronted" by an Aryan friend. So he accompanied us since he'd been fortunate enough to finagle tickets and lodging reservations even though it seemed the whole world had descended upon Germany which was smaller than the state of Montana.

"Providence," he said. "And friends who can pull strings."

We didn't even need a professional guide since Julius knew the area so well. We spent a whole day strolling, window shopping, browsing antique stores and checking out cuckoo clock stores and some of the artisans at work. I bought a lovely clock for Millie and her family. Often the forest, in spots, was so dark and dense, even midday, that it was like traipsing through another era, experiencing the Underground Railroad or some bedtime fairy tale, *Hansel and Gretel* or *Rumpelstiltskin*. I almost expected to see whip-cracking slave catchers, a gingerbread house, Little Red Riding Hood or a talking wolf, maybe witches, werewolves or dwarves that were the stuff of Black Forest myths. We did see lots of deer, some foxes, a boar. My imagination was running wild. Maybe Snow White and Prince Charming would appear on the trail around the bend, though I was traveling with my own Prince Charming. Julius arranged a picnic by the Danube in Donaueschingen, taught me to skip rocks over a gurgling brook. He climbed some twenty yards up a mountain to pick some flowers for me, came down and placed one behind my ear.

"They're beautiful. What are they?"

"Alpine roses."

"They're the most intense orange I've ever seen,"

"A rare shade – vivacious and fiery like a sunset... bewitching. I knew you'd like them."

"I *love* them."

Julius made everything more fun and interesting. Even Emery, who didn't mind being a third wheel, enjoyed his company. Of course we tried the legendary Black Forest cake with all the Kirschwasser liqueur-soaked cherries and whipped cream. Fabulous! And afterwards, since we were supposed to make the most of our stay, we detoured to Munich and saw some old churches and palaces and the Glockenspiel which features 32 colorful, mechanized, life-size figures enacting sixteenth century historical events. It was as riveting as Julius said it would be. Looping back north, the tour bus took us to see more old churches and palaces and we surveyed baroque architecture in Dresden, a city known for its china.

At a Dresden boutique I ordered two porcelain and lace dolls for Dixie and a friend of mine who was a collector. The delicate figurines were molded into dancers, musicians, flower-bearers and daydreamers and the detailing was exquisite. Dixie would know that the doll was to look at, not to cradle or play with. But all the dolls had geisha-white faces. I thought she'd really appreciate one that resembled her. She'd name it, ascribe an elaborate background story to it and gaze at it for hours.

"Do you have any black dolls?" I asked the proprietor.

"*Schwartze? Nein. Das tut mir Leid,*" he said apologizing. Not surprising. One was hard-pressed to find a black doll in America too. I never had one – except for ones Lily made us when we were very young by bean-stuffing and ornamenting old black or brown socks. Charlotte and I thought they were cute and cuddly but Magdalena disliked them because they looked "voodoo."

"But you can special order. It'd be one of a kind, signed and numbered by the artist with a certificate of originality and authenticity." That's exactly what I wanted. Something unique and meaningful that could be handed down and that even Magdalena would admire.

"*Braun,*" I specified. And I wanted them to have soft, black curly hair and fuller lips – a ballerina, a singer and maybe one more for myself – a harpist. And beautiful dresses with layers upon layers of porcelain-dipped crinoline.

"*Wunderschon,*" he said, indicating they'd be very beautiful.

"*Danke.*" I couldn't wait to see them.

As we were leaving, Julius saw a doll he said reminded him of his *Oma* Zip when she was a young, feisty redhead. "I think I'll buy it for her," I said.

"You don't have to do that," he said. "She has too much stuff already."

"Not from me. I'd love to present her with a gift when I finally meet her." He couldn't talk me out of it.

"That's what I love about you – your generous heart."

Did he say love? My heart skipped a beat. It took a few moments for my breath to come back and I composed myself. This man was so wonderful. He made me forget I was an engaged woman. But I knew in a few days, I'd be returning to America and may never see him again. The fairytale setting was making me dreamy, but I wasn't Sleeping Beauty and he wasn't an *actual* Prince. I had to get my head out of the clouds and come back down to earth.

I asked the seller to wrap Redhead in his prettiest paper.

"My pleasure," he said.

Even outside of Berlin walls, far away from Olympics excitement, the cameras and press, we were treated with dignity and respect. Lynch mobs were a hemisphere away. If the Germans hated us, they hid it well. After awhile, we almost felt the luxury of colorlessness. Emery said, "I could get used to this." So could I. It was a trip we'd never forget. Apart from all the sights, smells and tastes, we'd probably most cherish the way people made us *feel*. We'd both miss feeling *normal*, natural and un-self-conscious. I'd miss the way Julius made me feel *special*.

Our two-week trip would be over soon and I still hadn't gone to Julius' home to meet his family. I'd heard so much about them and wanted very much to see the people who helped shape him into the person he was.

CHAPTER 65

WE SAT STARING at each other on sofas on opposite sides of the room. Julius, Emery and I were on one and Julius' parents and grandmother were on the other one. It was quiet enough to hear a butterfly land, a very awkward situation. Julius warned me that his family was upset with him for "disappearing." He spent one day with them, had dinner, spent the night, and was gone the next day. They only found a note: *Will be at Olympic Stadium, then squiring some American friends around the country. See you in a few days. Love, J.*

That was ten days ago. I definitely understood why they were quiet and distant. They probably had a million questions, wanted to know where he'd been, why he left so stealthily and, more importantly, who *we* were. They were surprised when we came through the door. "I thought you'd gotten yourself kidnapped," Julius' grandmother said to him, grabbing him in a bear hug and checking to see if he was all in one piece. "I should put you over my knee!"

When Julius introduced us, his father said, "Julius always *was*…. adventurous," and sat back down. His mother offered us a glass of water.

"Your home is lovely," I said, ignoring the dust, clutter, tightly closed blinds, and the empty spots around the room where you could tell something integral was missing. Magdalena couldn't spend two minutes in a room without sunshine, some natural light. I understand. It's gloomy.

"It used to be," Mrs. Sommerfeldt said.

"She's being modest," Julius said. "Our house and garden were photographed for a huge spread in *Berlin Today* magazine."

"That was a lifetime ago," said his father.

I'm sure it was difficult having your world turned upside down. It would've been nice to meet the Sommerfeldts in their prime when he was a renowned jurist and she was an upscale store owner and secretary of the Central Berlin Merchants Association, when they both sat on boards and won awards for their homemade wine and community contributions. Instead I was meeting them in the midst of their suffering.

Three years living under Nazi rule had obviously taken its toll because, though they weren't unpleasant, Julius' family were not the fun, vibrant people he'd described and it was obvious they weren't in an entertaining mood. I understood. When our family got "Jim Crowed," we went home to sit in silence and usually never spoke of it again. I intended to keep in touch with Julius but I'd probably never see his family again and didn't want to be remembered as an inconvenient intruder; I wanted to leave a favorable impression.

"Is that a Rodin?" I asked, referring to the sculpture of two nude lovers sitting on a rock. It was cast in bronze on a marble pedestal. *"The Kiss?"*

"It is," Mrs. Sommerfeldt said.

"May I?" I asked, getting up for a better look.

"You may."

I looked without touching. "No other artists have been able to capture the sensuality of movement like Rodin did."

Julius' father walked over to where I was admiring the work. "So right," he said. "And this is no posthumous reproduction. It's a first edition cast from the Rudier foundry and is hand-signed."

"I can tell. The later editions don't have the texturized detailing that depicts light and shadow and the gentle cleaving and pull of biceps and tendons which let you know this couple is in love even without the kiss."

"You know a lot about art and sculpture. How'd you get so smart?"

"I took a few classes." *It was the way my muscles tensed in anticipation when Julius touched or kissed me.* "My father has a paper weight of *The Thinker* on his desk, just a cheap ceramic replica. He likes it because it, plus a good cigar, helps him solve the world's problems. *He's* a lawyer too."

"Hmmm, a man after my own heart."

Julius came and stood by me, regarded the sculpture as if for the first time. "I'm surprised the SA didn't proclaim it 'degenerate' and seize it."

"I threw my apron over it just in time," said *Oma* Zip. "They'd just add it to their private stash. Especially that pig Goering. "

"We have a Cezanne," said Julius' mother. "Would you like to see it?"

"I'd love to."

The ice was beginning to thaw. After going to the study and beholding the Cezanne, a beautiful, Bible-size still-life of fruit, I presented my gifts – a box of Hershey's Kisses, a carton of Camel cigarettes and the Dresden china doll for *Oma* Zip who took one look at it and said, "That's me!" and gave me a hug.

"A lifetime ago," said her son.

"I haven't had red hair since I met the people who gave aid and comfort to Papa after he got sick during the occupation of Belgium."

"What people?" Mr. Sommerfeldt asked. "This is the first I'm hearing this story. Were they *Ostjuden?*"

"It shouldn't matter, but yes they were."

"That explains a lot."

"Germany did unspeakable things to the civilians and they still cared for your father even as his fellow soldiers raped, pillaged and massacred the villagers. German warriors weren't always the patriotic saints people think they are."

"Who told you this wild story? Papa died on the battlefield."

"He died of the flu and a horrible case of Trench Foot. It was pandemic. I still have the letters he wrote. He had orders to shoot them and burn their house down, but didn't. He sent his troops on, said he'd handle it. The family saw he was sick, took him in, bandaged him up, fed him broth and prayed over him for months but he never fully recovered. When the war was over I looked for them, the Strassbergs, and they were still there, but they refused any payment, said my visit was payment enough."

"That's an incredible story," Julius said.

"I know," said *Oma* Zip. "That got me thinking."

"So that's when you started going a little cuckoo." Mr. Sommerfeldt popped a Hershey's Kiss into his mouth, lit a Camel and took out a deck of cards. *Oma* Zip ignored him.

"*Vati!*"

"But it's still no excuse. She needs medication."

"Alexander!" said *Mutti*.

"She does."

"Your father's still a war hero," *Oma* Zip said. "Even more so."

It felt odd being present while such "family business" was being divulged. It was a little uncomfortable as more of Julius' relatives arrived – having been summoned – excited to see their "prodigal son" Julius and curious about his exotic guests. They came in guardedly, frowning as if they detected a gas leak, ready, it seemed, to hold us liable for their darling Julius going "missing."

At first, the gathering seemed like a wake – low lights, low, slow-metered music. The house was filled with aunts, uncles and cousins. I'd never experienced such a thing. Our family was small and we didn't know most of our relatives. Either they were somewhere trying to "pass" or were down-and-out and too embarrassed to come around unless they needed something. Interestingly, Julius told me his family was actually twice as large but many of them had abandoned Germany or were somewhere "passing" too.

They brought wine, leftover stews, whatever was available for a patchwork meal because they didn't believe in coming empty-handed to family/friend get-togethers, impromptu or otherwise. One of the aunts came in saying, "I made cookies. They're a little flat and hard because at 6:00 no Jewish grocery had baking powder. But they taste good."

"I'm not breaking a tooth on one of your damn cookies," an uncle said. "You know how hard it is to find a good Jewish dentist nowadays?"

"Used to be one on every block."

"Two."

"Has anyone found cream?" someone else asked. "I can't find cream anywhere."

"Or honey."

"Find a trustworthy 'good German' to shop for you during Aryan hours for a small fee."

"I don't know many 'good Aryan Germans' anymore."

Maybe they hadn't been together in quite a while and had lots of thoughts bottled up inside because they all talked at once, starting and dropping several threads of conversation. They spoke about how creepy it was that the Nazis were being so amicable and fretted about their children having nowhere to go when school started. They weren't allowed in the public schools anymore and they weren't impressed with some of the Jewish schools in the area.

"That's why we're organizing our own school – secular," the cookie-baking aunt said. "We're almost fully staffed."

"The Aryan kids start in two weeks. I don't want our kids falling behind."

"They won't and ours are way ahead already."

"Rabbi Regina Jonas is preaching at Beth Israel next week."

"Bah," said another uncle, "I don't believe in female rabbis."

"She's the first one ever – in the world. Aren't you curious?"

"No."

"The Morgensterns left."

"Where'd they go?"

"America. Texas, I think."

"Texas? Are there Jews in Texas?"

"I don't think they plan to be Jewish in Texas. They're changing their name to Morgan, joining a Baptist congregation."

"*Mazel tov!*" said Julius' father, holding up his cigarette like a glass. "But *I'm* not going *anywhere*. *I'm* waiting them out."

"Me too," said the uncle who didn't like women rabbis.

Julius' cousin Gabriel came over balancing a bowl of stew in his palm. "The United States is racist and anti-Semitic too. That's why I keep saying we need to go home – to Palestine."

"There's violence against Jews there too."

"Violence is everywhere. The British troops protect Jews against Arab bandits. Business opportunities are rife. We'd do very well there. It *is* our ancestral homeland. Stop just dismissing the idea."

"I'm a podiatrist. I've no desire to become a wheat farmer in the middle of nowhere."

"The *Mashiach*," said *Oma* Zip, "will lead us all there in good time."

"Hmph!"

Eventually everyone settled down, food and drink in hand, and acknowledged Emery and me, realizing Julius had not been kidnapped and that we weren't walking, breathing stereotypes or part of some Trojan Horse scheme. The floodgates opened and they wanted to know all about us, how I learned to speak German so well, how I got to know Julius so well. They nodded, like I was explaining some academic concept.

They finally asked how we liked Germany and, of course, whether we knew Jesse Owens. We said Germany was magnificent and that it was a shame two Jewish runners on the American team were pulled from competition at the last moment for no apparent reason.

"Oh, the reason is obvious."

They didn't know whether to be proud or chagrined about champion fencer Helene Myers or that Germany won the most Olympic medals – 89. America was second with 56. I said it was a pleasure finally meeting all of them, that they were as wonderful as Julius said they were.

"He lied. We're all nutcases."

"You should meet *our* family," I joked.

Julius' cousin Gretchen was wide-eyed and held on to our every word.

"You have beautiful eyes," she told Emery who smiled.

Another cousin, about five years old, asked, "Can I see your tail?"

"Tail?"

"Meira! That's not kind," said her mother.

"Ida's brother says black people have tails."

"He is *verrückt!*"

Julius said, "Meira, that's a terrible myth. All people are built the same."

"How do you know? Have you seen her *arsch*?" she giggled.

"Meira!"

"Uh, no," Julius said, turning bright red.

"What about horns?"

"Meira!"

I thought I knew all the horrible things people thought about blacks, but hadn't heard this one about tails and horns, though I'd seen drawings of Jews depicted as Satan. Apparently, in addition to sambos, mammies, mandigos, sapphires and jezebels, Negroes were also the devil personified. I patted the top of my head. "Nope," I said. "No horns either. See, I'm just like you."

"Tell Ida her brother is wrong," Julius said.

A few minutes later Emery said, "Well, we'd better go. We have an early train and we still have to pack."

Julius said he'd drive us back to the hotel in the family Benz. "You're coming right back, right?" several people asked him.

"Of course. I promise to be back before you leave."

"Good, because we want to hear everything about your time in America."

"Elza, you don't need to hear it all in one evening," said the uncle who refused to eat the cookies.

"Well can we at least hear about the time he ran into Groucho Marx at the Woolworth's in Washington? My neighbor knew his mother when they all lived in Dornum."

"We *know*, Elza."

Julius laughed. "Sure, I'll be right back."

Everyone told us good-bye, but his *Oma* Zip came and gave both me and Emery a hug. "Come back to visit anytime."

"*Auf wiedersehen!*"

CHAPTER 66

IN OUR HOTEL room, I sat at the vanity looking in the light-up mirror. Emery walked by. "What are you thinking about?"

"Nothing."

"Tell the truth. You're thinking about Julius."

"No, just how much I'll miss Germany."

He sat down on the bed. "I see how you look at him, how he looks at you."

"I'm engaged to Xavier," I said, beginning to brush my hair the recommended one hundred strokes.

"He's a twerp. Run and get Julius before he drives off. Tell him how you feel."

I put the brush down and turned around to face Emery. For the first time I was seeing him as a grown man with mature thoughts, not the annoying brat I was used to. But his advice was impractical. We were leaving in the morning. In five days, after docking, I was meeting Magdalena in New York City to go wedding dress shopping. I had a "private, at-dawn" appointment at Bonwit Teller and Bergdorf Goodman (Thelda Michaels envisions a monarch-length train — at least ten feet, Mother's postcard had said). Then it was lunch at the Russian Tea Room unless they seated us way back by the kitchen or restrooms, then we'd just leave and go to a nice Harlem restaurant that served good, southern cuisine. It'd been a while since I had smothered pork chops, black-eyed peas, buttermilk biscuits or sweet potato pie.

We'd stay a few days in the city, maybe see a concert or play, visit family friend Adam Clayton Powell, Sr., the fair-skinned, dynamic pastor of Abyssinian

Baptist Church which had the largest Protestant congregation in the country. Then we'd take the train back to Baltimore, close down our Highland Beach cottage for the off-season and head back to Washington. A few weeks later, Emery would leave for Morehouse and I'd be starting my job at George Washington Carver Primary School. And there'd be Xavier to contend with. And Abigail. I didn't see how I'd fit Julius into that plan.

"Emery, it's way too complicated."

He stood up. "Yes, it is. Just like when Mother tries setting me up with all these girls I'm uninterested in." He said Natalie Shayle, the Crawfords' granddaughter, told him she loved him before we left.

"Really?" I was excited for him. I can't remember Emery – who used to be small and cherubic and was now tall, slender and handsome – ever really having a serious girlfriend. Georgine's sister, Claudia, was crazy about him but nothing ever developed.

"Well, do you love *her*?"

He hesitated, turned his back to me. "I love Jamison."

"Jamison?"

"Yes, Jamison. I spent July with his family. He's pre-law at Morehouse."

"I know who he is." I was stunned. I'd met Jamison when I was in Atlanta for a Spelman classmate's bridal shower. With his great looks and personality, he seemed like he'd break many girls' hearts in his lifetime, but my friends said he was "queer." Apparently Jamison had corrupted my brother, but I loved him the same. Maybe he'll grow out of it, then again maybe not. If anything, I've realized that love can be involuntary, that the heart wants what it wants.

"I just had no idea you were…" The appropriate term eluded me. "Does he love *you*?"

"He does. You're the only one I've told."

"Your secret's safe with me."

"Thanks, sis."

I got up, went to him and gave him a long overdue hug. "Look at us. Both of us in love with someone we can't have."

He pulled away. "Why can't we? Even Mother says everyone has only one true soul mate. If you're lucky enough to find them but let them go, you'll never find another one."

"And sometimes it's someone totally unexpected."

"Exactly. Anyone else – you're just settling. Is Julius your soul mate?"

"Without a doubt."

"Well, go. Catch that man before it's too late. I'll be downstairs at the bar for as long as you need me to be."

"Thank you."

I ran to catch that man.

CHAPTER 67

Julius

MY HEAD WOULDN'T stop spinning. My heart wouldn't stop racing. I'd been with many girls, but this was the first time I had fireworks go off in my head. A day later, I was more serene than a hedonist in a plush opium den. My soul was on fire, yet I was in Heaven. Her smell clung to every part of me – a combination of vanilla, lemons and mint. I could still feel the softness of her skin and my hands had committed to memory every curve, dip, hill and valley. I'd thought I'd been dreaming, but when I woke up, she was there beside me, sleeping like an angel snuggled contentedly in a cloud.

I was sitting in the lobby when I saw her. I hadn't left yet because I had half a mind to run up to her room and beg her to stay. I had nothing to offer but myself. I had no career, dwindling funds and tenuous plans. I had to help my community, be with my family, do what I could to help them weather the Nazi takeover. But I wasn't ready to say good-bye to Justinia. I think I loved her from the first day we met. I looked up and saw her through a throng of people. It had to be providence because she never would've seen me. I assumed she wasn't searching for a bellhop. I went to her.

"You came for me?"

"You stayed for me?"

⋗═◉ ◉═⋖

I didn't want to wake her yet. I just wanted to watch her a little longer. Emery was gone; he left earlier to catch the *Flying Hamburger*. The *Bremen* sailed at noon.

In the middle of the night, Justinia said she didn't want to leave, that she wanted to stay here, in Berlin, with me.

"I'd love that," I said. "But there's nothing here for you."

"*You're* here."

"You'd be miserable."

"Not as long as I'm with you."

"Let's figure it out then. We'll stay here for awhile, then I'll go back to America with you."

"Will you?"

"I promise."

CHAPTER 68

"LISTEN TO THIS one," Justinia said. We were having tea and looking over my little cousin Hilde's old textbooks and worksheets. "Jews are aliens in Germany. In 1933 there were 66,060,000 inhabitants of the German Reich of which 499,862 were Jews. What was the percentage of aliens in Germany?" She was reading a problem from a homework assignment given when my cousins were students at the state schools. In addition to the math problem, the coursework in Civics, History and Science – race science – all had anti-Semitic themes. "Reprehensible," she said.

Worse, the Minister of Education stated that every child should be educated in Nazi principles, particularly Aryan superiority and blood purity, and that they should all be "swift as a greyhound, tough as leather and hard as Krupp's steel." All boys were trained in the art of war and the girls were trained to be good wives and mothers and bear as many children as possible. And every Aryan student was taught to accept the inferiority of the Jew. As such, Cousin Hilde told us how she was subjected to the grossest humiliation.

"*Frau* Gerhardt made me, Zeke and Fritz go to the front of the room. She pointed a ruler at us and said, 'These are Jews, our misfortune. They killed Christ who was a German waging war on the Jewish money-changers, so they killed him. You can always spot a Jew with their dark, shifty rat eyes, big, crooked noses and earlobes fused to the head instead of separated. The men all have briefcases and chain-wallets and the women are all loud and shrewish. They have flat feet and long, money-grubbing arms.'

"She told everyone to take good notes because there'd be a quiz. She then measured our noses, the distance between our eyes because that's supposed to prove something. She made us remove our shoes and socks to show the soles of our feet. It was awful!

"'Come up here, Johann.' *Frau* Gerhardt said. Johann came up and she talked about how he was so tall, handsome, blonde and blue-eyed, the perfect Aryan specimen. Johann flexed and posed like he was Adonis although he has mousy hair and chicken legs. All the students applauded the lesson even though half of them were brown-eyed brunettes and didn't look much different from us. And who analyzes earlobes anyway?

"Then that loathsome Dirk Bauer raised his hand. 'If Jews are as mean and nasty as you say, can I punch them in the nose?'

"'Yes,' *Frau* Gerhardt said, 'but only outside. We must maintain order in the classroom. Heil Hitler!'

"'Heil Hitler,' all the Aryan kids shouted for about the tenth time that day.

"At recess" Hilde continued, "me, Zeke and Fritz got beaten up. I got blood all over my new blouse – it's ruined. Everyone laughed. No adult helped us. The school nurse, another Hitler freak, wanted to charge me a reichsmark for a bandage. We were terrified to go outside because someone would attack us. I hated that stupid school and that idiotic teacher. I'd hoped *Frau* Fromm would come back but they fired her and all the others because they were nice."

"How could schools treat their students that way?" Justinia asked.

"The people at that g*ymnasium* are the worst on earth," Hilde said. "I know we're not supposed to hate anybody, but I *hate* Hitler!"

Justinia said, "I think God will forgive you."

Justinia and I were appalled at what the public schools had become – a Nazi propaganda machine aided by hateful newspapers, films, youth groups and speeches blaring on radios known as "Goebbels' snouts" which all citizens were encouraged to have. There were even public loud speakers throughout the city that aired even more tripe about the Jewish "enemies." Truth didn't stand a chance. It was no wonder so many Germans were becoming so easily brainwashed.

Justinia has been in Berlin for two months and doing a fine job as a teacher of English and American History and Culture at the Jewish Community Day School my uncles and neighbors created in an old button factory. "Yes," she told the astonished children. "Not too long ago, America enslaved black people, brutalized them and split their families up, and it took the influence of Frederick Douglass, Abraham Lincoln, Harriet Beecher Stowe and a four-year war to end the practice. I know some former slaves." She may as well have said she knew Moses. When Justinia spoke, the students were transfixed.

At first there was reluctance having Justinia participate in the endeavor but she won everyone over with her intelligence, charm and my ringing endorsement. Anyone who objected to her presence sent their children to Eisner-Hirsch two blocks away. The students and parents loved her and once the zillion questions were asked and answered, their curiosity and concerns were placated and we were able to get down to the business of providing an outstanding education.

In addition to her English and History lessons, she taught them hopscotch and how to jump "double-dutch." She translated Br'er Rabbit tales and Aesop's fables and taught them playful songs like "The Itsy Bitsy Spider" and "Miss Mary Mack" with accompanying hand-claps. She ordered five pounds of pink bubble gum from a D. C. Negro candy shop and passed it out as treats for high test scores and good behavior. They'd never had such a confection before and were even more motivated to excel. It was fun watching them laugh and competing to see who could blow the biggest bubble. Many said American History and Culture was their favorite class. Justinia would've been an outstanding teacher in the D. C. schools though the destitute were often harder to teach. But our gain was their loss.

I taught the older kids about law and government. The administration and teaching staff made sure the entire curriculum was thorough and rigorous and even included a class about Zionism for informational purposes. The children had calisthenics and some sports to keep fit. It was truly a unique education. I think we had the best school in central Berlin.

Justinia's mother was devastated when she didn't return home with Emery. Letters from home said that she developed a mysterious illness and was housebound, refusing even to get up for some chichi parties or her goddaughter's cotillion. Justinia said she was just over-reacting and being manipulative, that she'd rejoin society real soon and would "never miss the Girl Friends' Christmas Extravaganza or the inauguration festivities if Republican Alf Landon defeats FDR."

Her father had stopped sending her money a month ago and she was living in one of the unoccupied basement units in our apartment building. Xavier was furious and Justinia didn't respond to any of his letters which were more and more insulting in nature. "I know I owe him some answers," she said, "but I really don't know what to say."

I told her to tell him the truth, that she was breathlessly in love with *me*, though he probably figured that out by now. For the first time, she was doing what she wanted to do and not going along blindly with what was expected of her. She and I were inseparable. If she was out somewhere or out of my sight too long, I got nervous, afraid she went back to the States, to her fiancé and life as a Negro princess.

CHAPTER 69

THE OLYMPIC DUST had barely settled before the Nazis went back to overt persecution of Jews. The "*Juden verboten*" signs returned and they were everywhere. They popped up overnight, like dandelions in freshly mown grass. The same French restaurant Justinia, Emery and I dined in, that had patrons sending over complimentary drinks to "Jesse" and "Josie" all evening, probably wouldn't give me the time of day or a glass of water if I were dying of thirst.

Justinia and I were walking home from the school when an SA officer with a snarling German shepherd asked us where we were going.

"Home, to our apartment building," I answered.

"Who's that?" he asked of Justinia. The dog growled.

"An American teacher." I was intentionally vague. "Doing charity work."

"American?"

"*Ja.*"

"Well, get along. Stop loitering," he said although we'd been walking briskly before being accosted.

It was difficult getting used to being abused and reprimanded for no reason. Justinia's presence made everything bearable. I had to resist the urge to hold her hand or encircle her waist and pull her toward me while walking down the street, because that would just be inviting more attention and confrontation. *Oma* Zip treated Justinia like another grandchild and insisted she come upstairs and have dinner with us every night. *Mutti* didn't know what to make of the situation and pretended not to notice me sneaking down to her apartment late at night. I loved how Justinia could lift *Mutti's* spirits with her quick humor. When *Mutti* reported how she'd been rebuffed by yet another gentile friend, Justinia asked, "You mean the lady with the fat ankles and the fake Chanel suits?"

"Yes," said *Mutti*, cracking up.

"Obviously she was never a true friend."

"You're right." And we all had a good laugh.

Vati scowled when Justinia was around, though he scowled all the time now, so I tried not to attribute it to her presence, but he couldn't help cracking a smile when she said his estranged Aryan squash partner looked and waddled like a penguin.

"How on earth did he chase the balls down?"

"He didn't," my father snorted, temporarily vindicated. "I scored every point."

"I bet you were a formidable opponent."

"I still am."

Gretchen loved Justinia and went back to school in Switzerland, promising they'd be pen pals forever. "Sure," Justinia had joked. "Now you can tell everybody you have a black friend."

"A smart, funny, glamorous one. They'll be so envious. We must take a picture or they'll never believe me."

Gabriel liked engaging her in lively debates. "Why do you think all those Negroes left the southern states and went up north?"

"To get away from the racial tyranny" she said, "and find better – industrial – jobs."

"Right. And are things better there?"

"Better, but far from good."

"Exactly. So will you tell my dear cousin that that's why we need to migrate to Palestine – not ideal but better than here."

"But," Justinia argued, "the Great Migration isn't exactly the same as the Zionist movement because Negroes aren't reclaiming an ancestral home. They mainly left out of practicality."

"Spiritual necessity or simple practicality. Isn't the main objective to escape tyranny?"

"I suppose all those reasons compelled some blacks to embrace the Back to Africa Movement and go to Liberia. They thought the racial climate would be better, but it's not a very *practical* option." Justinia would make a great lawyer.

"Mental and physical self-preservation is more important than practicality."
To me he asked, "Isn't that why you went to America for three years?"

"I left to prepare myself for a better life," I said, "not to embark on some spiritual quest. However, the 'spiritual awakening' I *did* receive was totally unexpected."

"Well Palestine means we can have economic opportunity as well as a place of our own."

"But I still believe there's more opportunity *here* than in a desert thousands of miles away. I feel no connection with that place and the Palestinians don't want us there anyway."

"So you'll stay here forever?"

"Not forever, but for the time being. Justinia and I both feel obligated to do things to make this place more tolerable for our people."

"We'd have to take up arms for that to happen."

"Shh!" I said, looking around to see who was listening.

"It's okay." He looked me in the eye. "So you're leaving again?"

"Eventually."

"Absolutely," said Justinia. "We have work to do in America too."

⊷⊶

"So you believe in God?" Gabriel asked her one day as we sat in a Jewish coffee house having cappuccino and strudel. Kristof's was a popular place for young people to gather, get caffeinated and engage in heavy discussions. We went there often.

Justinia paused, thought for a moment, and said, "I do. Don't you?"

"No," he said. "Not with all the evil in the world. If God exists, why wouldn't he hurl a lightning bolt at Hitler?"

"Well, Gabriel, God did give people free will. Christians believe evil people will have their day of judgment and pay dearly."

"Okay, but what about tornadoes, earthquakes and floods? Disease, famine, train accidents? Many innocent and devout people, babies and children, suffer and die because of these things."

Again Justinia looked reflective before giving her answer. "Reverend Crawford, my minister, would say that suffering is a part of life, that rain falls on the just and unjust, and life's challenges present opportunities for people to do good, to do unto others and carry out God's will to help alleviate suffering."

"Interesting," Gabriel said. "Sounds oddly like a typical Jewish response."

"How so?"

"Jews emphasize good deeds. Christians seem to emphasize rules and the profession of faith. And, correct me if I'm wrong, but Christians could do good deeds their entire life and not get to Heaven if they don't profess enough faith in your Jesus Christ."

Justinia thought about this. "I understand your point, but believe it's more complicated than that."

"Well, that's why I don't believe in a God who would, in addition to allowing bad things to happen to good people, condemn the kind-hearted along with the black-hearted."

Justinia took a few more sips from her drink. "Well my faith is in a God who is loving and forgiving and not the petty, vindictive God some purveyors of organized religion paint Him as being. My God would never admit Hitler or Goebbels or Himmler into Heaven no matter how much they repent and profess a love or acceptance of Christ. That wouldn't make sense."

"Good answer."

"And *my* God smiles down on Christians, Jews, Hindus, Buddhists and Muslims equally. He wouldn't condemn *any* good person."

"I like your God," said Gabriel. "Wish He were real."

"He's real."

Justinia turned to me. "You're awfully quiet, Julius. What do you think?"

I popped the last bite of strudel into my mouth. I was on the fence, still sorting things out. "I think we ought to get out of here. It's getting late and the Nazis will be out on the prowl soon."

Justinia, never judgmental, smiled. I took her hand and kissed it.

Each time we went outside, we never knew what malice we'd encounter. Another day we were walking home and saw an officer beating up an older, distinguished-looking gentleman that could easily have been my father or one of my uncles had they been on that block at that time. It was difficult to watch, impossible to un-see. We kept walking but Justinia turned around and said, "Disgusting! How do you sleep at night?"

The SA stopped stomping the old man and turned his attention to us. "What did you say, you Rhineland bastard *neger*?" The old man retrieved his mangled spectacles and stumbled away.

I grabbed her in a protective clutch though I was no match for these punks with their truncheons and knives and strength in numbers. One-on-one, with no one looking and assurances that the SA wouldn't storm my residence and shoot me and my family in retaliation, I'd trounce his ass mercilessly and send him crying to his mother. The storm troopers were a bunch of poor, uneducated, power-hungry thugs bestowed with the unchecked authority to be street terrorists but whose ranks were chastened and diminished by the assassination of their leaders during the Night of the Long Knives two years ago and whose envy of the more elite Gestapo and SS forces were well-known and embarrassing. They had everything to prove, nothing to lose, and that made them dangerous.

"She's not a Rhineland bastard. She's American." To Justinia, I said, "Speak English, darling. Then say something nice and deferential in German."

He smacked me, then her. Another SA came running and I knew this wouldn't end well. He pulled a riding crop from his boot and started swatting us with it. But nothing hurt more than my inability to protect Justinia.

"Leave them alone," said the arriving SA officer.

"They were loitering and interfering with my official duties."

"I don't care. Back off!"

He backed off. I looked at his face. He was barely eighteen.

"Are you alright?" the other officer asked me.

I looked at him. It was Gunther Hertzog, my book-burning friend I protected from bullies when we were in school together.

"*Ja. Danke!*" I said to him and shook his hand.

"They're off limits," he said to the kid. "Spread the word."

"Yes, sir!"

I took Justinia home. She was badly shaken but thankfully unhurt.

"We must be careful, darling," I said. "We have to survive out here. You wouldn't sass a D. C. cop."

"You're right. I apologize. But I couldn't help myself."

There was only one thing to do after that ordeal. I pulled the tarp off my Windhoff motorcycle, my escape vehicle. "Let's go for a ride."

We put on helmets, obscuring our identities to all the people with the swiveling heads and dropped jaws because they'd never seen a Negro, let alone a Jew and a Negro "together" and thought automatically that we must be "up to something." We'd cruise the autobahns and clear our heads, jettison our anxieties, escape the madness, be faceless and raceless and just cling for a few hours. "Faster!" Justinia would urge. And I'd go faster.

When a little boy came running past us one day because the police were after him for picking a flower in the park, Justinia didn't think twice about hiding him. "In here," she told him and we both stuffed him into a nearby garbage bin and slammed the lid down on top of him. "Don't move and be very quiet."

"Where'd that little thief go?" the office demanded when he got in front of our residence moments later.

"Thief?" she asked. "We've only seen the newsboy." She held up the afternoon edition as proof.

"You'd better not be lying. I'll throw both of you in jail."

"I'd never protect a thief," she said. "I hope you catch him."

The officer ran off. A few minutes later we helped the boy out. He was covered with banana peels and coffee grounds, but the tulip he'd risked his well-being for was fresh and unruffled in his little cupped hands. It was for his sick mother.

"*Danke*," he said and ran off in the opposite direction of the officer.

I looked at Justinia. "Sweetheart…," I began to chide.

"I know, I know."

I couldn't be mad at her. She was too wonderful, willing to endure all the Nazi bullshit, the crazy looks, a drafty, spartan apartment and even one week of nothing to eat but cabbage soup, stale soda crackers and limburger cheese (which she normally refused to eat because it smells like 100 pairs of stinky feet – it does, but tastes delicious) because The Party bought up most of the groceries and provisions for all the shindigs they were having to celebrate Berlin's 700th anniversary. And by the time the rest of the Aryans finished shopping, there was nothing left. So I know she truly loved me. No sane person would put up with that if they didn't have to.

Despite everything, we were happy. The school was faring well. In short order, the kids knew colors, numbers, common objects and several tourist-y phrases in English. I told them there was freedom in America. "You can say whatever you want to say, go wherever you want to go." The children thought the States sounded like paradise and wanted to see it for themselves. "I promise Germany will be like that again too someday soon." But they didn't seem convinced.

There was a group of older kids who Justinia and I especially bonded with and we'd spend hours talking, giggling, venting and crying. We spoke candidly with some kids who confided that their parents thought Jews needed to be stockpiling weapons for self-defense; that the Palestinians needed to emigrate to Jordan or Syria to be with other Muslims and leave the Holy Land – especially Jerusalem with the Temple Mount and the Wailing Wall – to the Jews; that Hitler looked effeminate when he threw his hand back to return a "Heil!" greeting, or that he was secretly Jewish, that his own father was the bastard son of a maid and a Jew named Frankenberger and that, by his own expansive definition, made him Jewish.

We had to be cautious though. One never knew who was watching or listening. Someone could go to a Gestapo agent and tell them about our conversations if they thought it would curry some favor, maybe earn a fresh quart of milk. Not every Jew was a friend. Some were back-stabbing double-crossers. But our American influence made our interactions unique and memorable for the kids. We helped create leaders in a place that encouraged followers; we helped develop thinkers in an environment that valued anti-intellectualism. Justinia and I were gratified to be part of such a Herculean task.

Justinia and I were solid. We couldn't imagine life, especially one filled with daily unknown challenges, without one another. She was my oxygen. I didn't know Irina would come along one day and spoil it. Yes, I used to love Irina, but Justinia was, and will always be, my soul mate.

CHAPTER 70

1938
Justinia

SO MUCH HAS happened since I arrived in Germany almost two years ago. But not much had changed in America. A novel, *Gone With the Wind*, that glorified the confederacy and a self-absorbed female plantation owner, won a Pulitzer and Hollywood was turning it into a movie. Roosevelt was reelected and appointed Hugo Black, a former Klan member, to the Supreme Court, and there was still no anti-lynching law despite the tireless efforts of so many people and organizations, including my beloved Alpha Kappa Alpha sorority. On another note, Joe Louis redeemed himself by knocking out Schmeling in the first round and Negroes, according to letters from Millie, were ecstatic. "Even my father was doing the rooster strut," she said.

Millie, who'd graduated Howard, received a scholarship to the law school and was engaged to a fellow student, also said my mother wore black everywhere because she's in mourning for me. Again Magdalena's being overly dramatic; she's in the "unenviable" position of not knowing exactly what to tell people at church, the investment club, the whist parties and all the other places she needed to be.

Magdalena wrote she'd never live down all the embarrassment I'd caused her, starting with her having to call Bonwit's and Bergdorf's to cancel my "special" appointments. "I'm sure we left them with an unfavorable impression of Negroes." Magdalena said she could barely face Abigail anymore. The "situation's" only saving grace was that at least Julius wasn't a farmer or some bass player, but a lawyer whose father was a judge. "The grapevine is completely out of control," she wrote. People were saying that the Nazis got me, that Julius was keeping me against my will, that I was heroin-addicted and ran off with some Parisian jazz musician. Magdalena's friends and club members from all over the country called or wrote her to get the "real scoop."

My father was uncharacteristically stoic and sent postcards every few months saying I'd "sown enough oats" and that he'd send me a few bucks and buy my ticket home as soon as I came to my senses. I was still "senseless," but I missed my family and friends, as irritating as they could be. At times I half-expected to see Chauncey pop up to drag me back home. "Time to come home now, Miss Justinia," he'd say, "and don't give me any fuss."

Charlotte, who was still in Liberia trying to convert Muslims and pagans to Christianity, last wrote me to say that she and Calvin were recovering from their second bout of malaria, had adopted an orphan girl and, with hundreds of converts to their credit already, were thinking of going home soon. "You should too," she stated, "because Mother and Father are getting older and need family around them. Until then, please be very careful." I wrote back that I was relieved she and Calvin had gotten better, that I couldn't wait to meet little Makemba, that of course I was being cautious and that I'd return home "eventually."

Oddly, it was Millie who informed me that Xavier married Georgine and that she read in the *Bee* and the *Afro-American* that it was "the decade's finest nuptials" with twenty-*two* attendants and a six-foot, bride-and-groom ice sculpture commissioned by Thelda Michaels because of course Georgine Kirkwood had to outdo Charlotte Treadwell. Xavier and Georgine were perfect for each other and I planned to wish them well when I saw them again.

When I first arrived in Germany, there was round-the-clock celebration with an international flair. In a sea of plain suits, neckties and proper, pleated skirts, I saw people wearing turbans, Islamic hijabs, jilbabs and thobes and caftans made of lovely, hand-woven fabric called kente cloth, according to the Ghanaian woman whose outfit I couldn't help but compliment. The East Indian women with their saris and the red 'bindi' dots on their foreheads were very beautiful and drew both curious and appreciative looks. Everyone was friendly and, for two weeks at least, the heart of Berlin was just one, big, happy intercontinental party.

Now the torch was extinguished, the Olympic village was deserted and all the "colorful" people had gone home. Practically everyone left was pasty-white and German. I don't know how they readily distinguished Aryans from Jews because, as Julius pointed out, there were dark-featured Aryans and fair-colored Jews. Yet the "No Jews Allowed" signs went back up, Jews began "walking on eggshells" and the malice and menace returned.

Mistreatment of Jews and friends of Jews escalated. It was common to see them being frog-marched from their homes and thrown into mysterious armored vehicles, being verbally or physically abused. I saw Aryans made to wear humiliating signs saying they defiled themselves with a Jew. One "mixed" couple were stripped down to their underwear in the middle of a busy intersection, had their heads completely shaved and rotten fruit hurled at them. I saw crying children snatched away from their crying parents to participate in the Hitler Youth which was now compulsory.

There was so much cruelty that after awhile, I almost became numb. As did many Aryans who didn't seem to show alarm that all this was happening under their noses, by their government, under the guise of German nationalism and pride. Germany – Berlin in particular – used to be the jewel of the continent, and now it had devolved into something ugly and primitive. It was a vibrantly contemporary place transformed into some bizarre nether world that could've been imagined by the minds of Poe or Kafka where men and children lose their minds and souls and spend a good part of their existence literally marching in lockstep, saluting a crazy, paranoid man-god and carrying out his misanthropic ideas. It was a Hollywood science-fiction movie pitch. Yet Julius remained hopeful. I should've gone home. I thought about it several times, but just couldn't leave Julius. I couldn't get enough of him. It would be like leaving a piece of myself behind. I'd be incomplete. Nobody else existed who could satisfy my mind, body and spirit.

Despite all the bad things, there were many bright spots. Julius and I could always find quiet enclaves to picnic, chat and read to each other. I met his Nigerian friend, Bakari, who invited us to some of his "jam sessions" in damp tavern basements and was pleasantly surprised to see so many Germans who knew how to swing dance. We discovered there was a whole underground, anti-Nazi swing culture and we loved it. We took long motorcycle rides through the countryside and on the autobahns which would've had Magdalena clutching her pearls and pressing imaginary brakes had she seen us. I'd never flown a kite before, but Julius taught me, standing close behind me, his hands caressing mine, as he released more string. "Higher," I said, and he made it go higher.

Neither Julius nor I had ever done laundry before, but we had fun laughing over torrents of bubbles, shrunken blouses, lost socks and Julius' pinkened skivvies until we learned to get it right. Then there were the potlucks, talent shows, concerts, plays, movies, dinner dates, academic lectures and sporting events sponsored by the *Kulturbund* at the few Jewish facilities that were left because, after all, life goes on.

Julius and his handsome cousin, Gabriel, took me to a comedy show where a friend of theirs was performing. Everyone needed a good laugh and Saul was hilarious: "My mother gave me two sweaters for Hanukkah. When I visited her the following week, I made sure to wear one of them. She took one look and said, 'What, you didn't like the *other* one?'" Everyone laughed and someone crashed cymbals. "My cousin brought her fiancé home to meet her father. The father questioned him about his career plans. The man said he was a Torah scholar. When asked how he would afford the big house, clothes, jewelry and vacations that his daughter so richly deserved, the fiancé said God will provide. When the man left, the daughter asked her father what he thought about him. The father said, 'He has no job, no ambition, and he thinks I'm God.'" The cymbals crashed, the audience was bowled over and Saul kept the jokes coming.

I even enjoyed going to temple services from time to time, especially during Rosh Hashanah and Hanukkah which were joyous and fun. *Oma* Zip loved to light the menorah during the eight-day Festival of Lights and frying enough of the traditional latkes and jelly doughnuts "to feed David's army." The extended family gathered together and everyone loved watching the children spin their dreidels in a German gambling game where they tried to win money, pecans and gelt – chocolates in gold foil designed to look like coins. The child with the most prizes at the end won the game. Julius' cousin Meira took her dreidel spinning skills very seriously and usually won. On the eighth day of Hanukkah, some revelers gathered around a bonfire, an old custom among Jews in Germany, but Julius didn't want to do that.

One evening during my first Christmas season in Berlin, Julius and I were walking down the street looking at the lights, decorations and carolers commemorating Julfest – the winter solstice and Hitler as the "messiah." Instead of fat, jolly Santa Claus, there was the tall, slim, white-bearded, stern-faced Odin with his harpoon, flying horse and sack of presents for good Aryan children. The lights and sounds were fascinating, but I was completely turned off by Christmas without Jesus, swastikas on "yuletide" trees and a malevolent-looking gift-giver. It all made me wonder if my family was celebrating any differently because of my absence, or if they still took a sleigh ride through the tree farm to pick out the perfect ten-foot Douglas fir while sipping hot cocoa from a thermos and watching Chauncey and his helper chop it down. I wondered who my mother went shopping with, who she took to marvel at the famously festive department store windows, whose opinion she'd get while deciding whether my father would like the sweater vest and driving gloves she was thinking of gifting him with. I wondered if anyone would mention me by name during the special prayers at St. Luke's Christmas Eve service.

Turning onto *Wilmersdorferstrasse*, Julius and I saw a special Julfest-inspired merry-go-round filled with laughing Aryan children. Signs saying *"Juden Verboten"* kept lots of Jewish children on the sidelines watching yearningly and seemed to make the carousel riders exaggerate their joy so the Jews felt worse. It made me think of the time when the parents of a "Duchess," Mr. and Mrs. Tiberius Blake, rented a Tilt-a-Whirl for their backyard the day after Negro children were denied entrance to a springtime carnival. The Blakes welcomed *any* Negro child as well as the little Caucasian boy who lived next door, and everyone had a ball. D & D lawyers were stationed in front of the house to handle the police officers who'd responded to "a disturbance" or, as was overheard, "uppity Negroes with they own amusement park." Daddy, ready to quote chapter and verse from the city code book, told them nobody was breaking any laws and that they could do what they wanted on private property and, in this case, private, *unmortgaged* property. The cops hung around anyway waiting for someone to litter, fight or get drunk so there'd be an excuse to shut it all down, but they left disappointed and my father thanked them for their free security services. But on *Wilmersdorferstrasse* on this particular Julfest day, there was no "Jewish" carousel, and soon the police came by throwing rocks and snowballs and yelling, "Get out of here, you cockroaches!" The children scattered and Julius and I walked away stealthily. We had Hanukkah gifts to wrap anyway.

I liked going to temple. It was interesting how the men and women had separate seating and that there were no statues or paintings of Jewish icons -- Abraham, Isaac, Moses -- inside. Julius explained that the Second Commandment forbade idolatry, particularly in houses of worship. But there was a lot of standing up and sitting down, hymn singing and call and response prayers just like at St. Luke's. The Episcopalians sprinkled Latin phrases throughout the service and the Rabbi and the cantor used liberal doses of Hebrew throughout the *Shabbat*. Julius taught me a little Hebrew which became easier once I got used to reading right to left. I learned the holiest place in the synagogue is the Ark where the Torah is kept and it is only opened when the scrolls are presented during the most important prayers.

The thoughtful sermons were in German so I understood them, and when they were over I joined the congregation in saying, "*Amain.*" The message was usually inspiring but "safe," nothing like the one Reverend Crawford gave years ago after the Armwood lynching, because some Nazi was usually standing in the doorway listening to every word. The Gestapo looked for any reason to bring in a substitute rabbi or shut the whole thing down. A post-worship *Oneg Shabbat*, where people got to *nosh* and *schmooze*, was like an informal, expanded version of Christian communion with wine drinking, bread eating and socializing.

Going to temple was a nice, occasional respite and the people were pleasant enough, though one congregant insisted on referring to me as a "daughter of Ham," Noah's "cursed" son and alleged progenitor of the black race. Julius wanted to demand an apology, actually grabbed him by the shoulder and when the man spun around, told him eye-to-eye, "Her name is *Justinia.*"

"Okay," the man said, "Justinia, who has the mark of Cain." He laughed and popped a piece of challah bread into his mouth.

Julius was about to argue, but his mother said, "Let it be, Julius. He's just a crusty, old coot. Have some more Manischewitz." She refilled his glass.

"It's okay, darling," I said. "I've had much worse said about me."

Julius was not really religious, but he believed in concepts like retribution, atonement, justice and karma which were rooted in theological teachings. When the swastika-emblazoned Hindenburg passenger airship crashed and burned in New Jersey as it attempted to land, Julius said it was karma for Germany's misdeeds. We were sorry for the passengers and crew who died, but felt it was a sign from God that Hitler needed to keep his Nazi propaganda and goals of expansion out of North America. A sane leader would've been introspective.

But the Chancellor had grandiose ideas and when he achieved *anschluss* – the annexation of Austria – many Germans were pleased to have broader borders but wondered if that imperialist move was bringing the world closer to another war. Julius and I certainly hoped not because it would make it much harder to leave the country. We weren't ready to leave our students yet – we'd grown close and were having such a positive impact on them – but we had to think of ourselves and also of little Julius who was a year old and looked just like his father – only tanned.

Juli, as he was called, was a godsend. He made everything more tolerable, yet more challenging, at the same time. At Julius' insistence, I took him to a Catholic church to be baptized and told the rector, hospital and government authorities I didn't know who the father was. "You poor dear," a nun told me. They may have labeled me a prostitute, but at least my son wouldn't be classified as a Jew in Nazi Germany. His bouncy curls and omnipresent smile even lifted the spirits of Julius' father who'd come home calling, "Juli, Juli, where's my Juli?"

The Sommerfeldts accepted me and my child unconditionally now. Years ago, this wouldn't have been the case because they, like the Treadwells, didn't approve of pre-marital "dalliances" or out-of-wedlock children. But with everything that was going on, Juli, with his butterfly kisses and baby laughter, was a much-needed balm. And to think I almost went home to pay a visit to Dr. Kirkwood so he could dispose of "it." I may have gone through with it too if I didn't think Julius would jump off a cliff. Keeping Juli was the best decision I ever made. I loved his father with all my heart. Juli was a blessing, not my shame. Magdalena wouldn't think so. I fully expected to be disowned.

CHAPTER 71

November 9, 1938

IT HAD BEEN a good day, sunny but brisk, no power-drunk SAs bothering us. Julius and I were walking home, Juli in his stroller, from a soccer scrimmage between our school and Eisner-Hirsch. We'd beaten them 4-3 and were happy about that. We passed a park bench that had "*Juden Verboten*" painted on it. I'd always wondered what would happen if *I* sat on one of those benches and read a book like this pretty, blond woman currently was. Julius said it wasn't worth the risk finding out.

The blond woman was reading a storybook to some children and she looked up as we walked by. I could see by the book's cover that it was that awful *Der Giftpilz* which translates to *The Poisonous Mushroom* and had a drawing of a "Jew" with the face of a toadstool. The title referred to Nazi propaganda that Jews were as toxic as poisonous mushrooms and each illustrated tale was about how every Jew is a menace – a child molester, a thief, a swindler – and that German children need to be wary of the danger they posed. When Gabriel showed us a copy, we were aghast. It brought to mind a nursery rhyme book I saw at the D. C. library once – "Ten Little Nigger Boys: A Counting Book ("Two little nigger boys sitting in the sun; one got frizzled up, then there was one...")

"Julius?" called this bench-sitting woman who was warped enough to corrupt little children with anti-Semitic filth.

We stopped and Julius looked over at her. "Irina?"

They both stared at each other as if they were seeing ghosts. She composed herself, got up and approached us. She was tall. "Who's this?" she asked.

"Irina Graf, this is Justinia Treadwell from America," Julius said.

"*Wie geht es dir?*" I said, extending my hand which she ignored. On second thought, she wasn't that pretty; she looked like the little Dutch boy on the paint can.

"Still audacious, I see. Another charity case?" she said, presumptuously pulling back the canopy and looking in the stroller where Juli was sleeping. I let the insults go.

"No, this is my family, our son, Juli." I was surprised he was divulging so much information. He was usually so careful. He didn't want people besides relatives and close friends knowing Juli was half-Jewish.

"Unbelievable."

"Julius," I said, "who exactly is this woman?"

"I was his wife."

"Wife?!" I looked at Julius, demanding answers. I felt sucker punched.

"Not true!" he said. Our marriage was annulled years ago!"

"So you were married? And you didn't tell me?"

"Because it was *annulled*, like it never happened. I wanted to put that chapter out of my mind."

"But you lied!"

"No."

"By omission!"

"Listen, darling," he said. "There was no point." He grabbed my shoulders, pulling me towards him as I was about to storm off with my child. Irina looked on, rather amused. Her children looked curious but impatient, eager to get back to the book.

"We eloped and were married for three measly months. It was a 'mixed' marriage. Her father was furious when he found out. He gave her an ultimatum and she chose him over me."

"Else I would've regretted every second," Irina said. "Being with you would've brought me nothing but misery. I was insane to marry you. You see what's going on. They might've tarred and feathered me." Julius was a good judge of character. What had he possibly seen in this awful woman?

"You used to say love conquered all," Julius said.

"No, *you* did. I just went naively along."

I couldn't believe what I was hearing. And it got worse.

"Maybe Juli would like to meet his brother," Irina said. *What!?* She snapped her fingers at the older child and he came over. Closer up, I saw the resemblance immediately. He, like my Juli, had the same keenly perceptive, onyx eyes and longish, floppy hair in a lighter hue. He was the spitting image of Julius who I thought would faint.

"Julius," she said to the boy, "meet Mr. Sommerfeldt." *Julius?*

Julius bent to embrace the boy who looked about six, but Irina said (in English), "Don't. He'll be confused. He thinks Sven is his father."

"Sven?"

"Yes, Sven, my husband of five years. He's high up in the Party. I'm Irina Graf Hanssen now." She pointed to the other two children who had straight, blond hair like Irina. "And that's Ivan and Ingrid."

Ingrid called out, "*Mutti*, are you talking to a Jew?"

"*Nein! Halt die klappe!*"

"You can't drop this bombshell on me and just expect me to walk away."

"Yes I can," she said. "And I do."

"What's happened to you? You're a totally different person."

"The old Irina was young and stupid. My life is easy now. I want it to stay that way. Pretend you never saw us."

"I can't forget my son!"

"If you don't, you put him in danger. Why are you still here anyway? All the *intelligent* Jews have left the country."

"Please, Irina, I can't just forsake my flesh and blood."

"Yesterday you didn't even know he existed. Leave now," she said, pulling the other little Julius back to the bench with his half-siblings and that disgusting book. "Or I'll find an SA officer and tell him you're bothering me."

"Irina!"

"Go, be with your *schwarze*."

I couldn't take anymore. Devastated, I turned the carriage in the direction home and jogged all the way there.

CHAPTER 72

JULIUS' MOTHER MUST'VE heard the racket in my apartment because she came down, knocking on the door.

"Is everything okay?"

I was emptying out drawers, pulling dresses off hangers and stuffing everything into my suitcases. *Why didn't he come after me?* Juli was crying. I was crying. I opened the door anyway.

"What's going on?" *Oma* Zip walked in behind her. They followed me into the bedroom where I was packing. I explained the situation to them.

"That Irina is a *dumme schlampe,*" said *Oma* Zip.

"There always was something about that girl I didn't like," said Julius' mother. "She only named the boy Julius to spite her father. Now this. How dare she dangle his son in front of him and snatch him back. It's cruel, which is why we never told him about the boy because a relationship was unattainable."

Minutes later Julius walked in. He'd overheard the conversation and confronted his mother and *oma.* "You *knew* I had a child and didn't tell me?"

"We thought it best," his mother said. "We'd see her around occasionally and she was always so nasty, saying she wanted nothing to do with any Jews, no matter who they were. We wanted to spare you the heartache."

Julius sat on the bed, his head resting in his hands. My anger dissipated somewhat, turned into compassion. When Julius loved, he loved hard. He wasn't tepid or faltering when it came to family and people he cared for. It was his Achilles heel.

His mother and *oma* took Juli and went back upstairs. I sat down next to him, laid my hand on his knee. He looked defeated; the week-old stubble which I'd always thought made him look lusciously virile now made him look scruffy and tired. He glanced around at the disheveled room.

"Darling, what are you doing?"

"Packing. We're leaving. Come with us or you'll never see us again. You won't have either of your sons."

He groaned. "Please, let's talk."

"There's nothing to say except, 'yes I'll come.' Remember you promised."

He paused, remembering that day at the Adlon years ago and all the times since then. I needed him to make a choice. I needed him to choose me over everything else. It was a good minute before he answered.

"Yes, I'll come."

"And we'll get married?"

"Right away."

"I can hardly wait."

"But no chuppah or breaking of the glass; no communion, sermons or un-necessary candle-lighting."

"No."

"Just you, me and the Justice of the Peace."

I paused. "Well, we can discuss that later."

"We'll honeymoon in Hollywood."

"Palm trees and movie stars."

He took my hand and looked at me with a wistful smile. "Maybe we'll even get discovered."

"Gary Cooper better watch out." I reached up and smoothed his hair back. "And we'll stay in the states and never come back here, except maybe to visit after Hitler is gone and forgotten."

"Yes. I want to be an American citizen and your loving husband. Together we'll make a wonderful life for Juli."

"Then get your suitcase and let's go home."

⋆⊰⊱⋆

I had to borrow money from Julius' father to purchase my tickets home. It might be several days before my father could wire money from overseas and I wanted to leave immediately. The idea of sharing a city with Irina and Julius' other son made me ill. I needed distance. If he was going to obsess over his other son, I'd rather he be in Washington than Berlin. The Sommerfeldts had cash and jewelry sewn into their mattresses; other valuables – Julius' impressive stamp collection, silverware and such – were secreted in the inoperable dumbwaiter because they particularly didn't want Goering (who reportedly fancied himself a philatelist) to get his hands on those stamps and, contrary to what the law required, the Nazis didn't need to know about every pfennig, every asset.

We could be at the train station first thing in the morning. We'd have to make a detour to the emigration office because the government had recently canceled Jewish passports and to re-validate them they'd have to get stamped with a "J" and have "Israel" or "Sarah" added to their names so there'd be no mistake that they were Jewish. We could be on the *Flying Hamburger* by noon, setting sail by evening.

That was the plan. But Mr. Sommerfeldt wasn't cooperative. "You can't take Juli with you," he said.

Julius and I looked at each other. "*Vati*," Julius said softly. "He's *our* son." Judge Sommerfeldt was delirious if he thought I'd leave Juli behind. Everybody yelled and cried for hours.

"Go ahead. Leave me with nothing. I have nothing else. You're taking the only thing that brings me joy."

"Alexander, that's not fair," Mrs. Somerfeldt said. But he went into the bedroom and slammed the door. He came out a few minutes later throwing money at us. It rained down on the floor like confetti. "Here, take it all! Nothing matters anymore."

We took what we needed to travel third-class and went to finish packing.

Chapter 73

April 1939

It'd been five months since I saw Julius. The last I saw him was November 10th, the day we were leaving to go back to America. Julius had just been released by some SA officers who were assigned to round up and arrest Jewish men. It was a continuation of chaos from the night before when uniformed Nazis as well as civilians vandalized Jewish shops and burned down synagogues while police and firemen stood around watching. It was a virtual war zone, but we had to leave. The Sommerfeldts felt we should wait until things simmered down.

"What's a few more more days?" Gabriel asked, peeking through the blinds and sticking a handgun back down into his pants.

"I have to get Juli out of danger and he needs his father. *I* need him."

"It'll calm down," Julius' mother said. "The madness ebbs and flows."

"It's a hornet's nest out there," I said. "I can't take that chance."

"Right, I've never seen it this bad," *Oma* Zip said. "The *Mashiach* will come soon. The signs are clear."

Outside a taxi was waiting and the driver honked the horn impatiently. We hugged everybody, cried, promised to contact them soon, and left them peeking through the blinds until the tail lights were out of sight.

Block after block, we whizzed by overturned cars, burnt-out delivery vans and people weeping openly. There was broken glass everywhere, fires still burned, buildings smoldered and church bells pealed the "Hallelujah Chorus." The air was thick with smoke. People were shrieking and running around mindlessly. There was a column of nuns carrying huge crucifixes and signs saying "*Frieden fur Juden*" – peace for Jews. We saw cigar-puffing police officers laughing and shooting dice against the torched exterior of a tobacco shop. A Jewish furrier had just finished boarding up his broken-out shop windows when a group of Hitler Youth came by with crowbars and ripped them open again. There were SA officers shooting guns into the air for fun. It was truly dystopian, H. G. Wells-ian.

Turning a corner we passed a piano store where beautiful Steinways had been pushed out onto the street and axed to oblivion. The cab couldn't get around the wreckage. "This is as far as I go," the nervous driver said.

"Thanks anyway," Julius said, giving him a big tip. We got out of the car.

"We should leave the bags," I said. "It'll be too hard to walk with them and carry Juli too."

"Are you sure?" Julius asked. "We'll be at sea for five days without any 'stuff.'"

"We'll manage."

"You're right, they'll slow us down."

Slamming the car door shut, I told the cabbie he could keep our bags, including my velvet-lined Vuitton luggage. He looked perplexed. "You don't need?"

"Give the clothes to your wife," I said. The steamer trunk was stuffed with silk lingerie, couture dresses and skirt-suits, my favorite pair of Ferragamo slingbacks.

"*Danke*," he said.

We heard more gunshots, startling Juli who burst into tears.

"*Viel gluck!*" the cabbie told us, and took off in reverse with tires screeching. We called after him to wish him luck as well.

"Let's go," Julius said, cooing to Juli to soothe him.

We began walking as quickly as we could past more mayhem and despair. We were just blocks away from the emigration office when we were accosted at gunpoint by three brownshirts.

"You!" one said to Julius. "Come here!" Julius handed me our baby and the brownshirt pushed him up against a brick wall with several other men who looked like they were waiting for a firing squad. I panicked.

"What'd I do?"

"Other than being a *schmutzig Judin?*"

"I'm on the way to get my passport renewed, then I'm leaving Germany. One less Jew you'll have to worry about."

An SA officer jabbed him in the throat. Juli started crying again.

"Stop!" I said.

"*Halt die klappe, neger*!"

I had to think fast before these horrible men did something horrible to my man. I scrounged through my purse, found my engagement ring from Xavier and tried appealing to their greed.

"Leave him alone and you can have this." It twinkled even in the gray, lightless atmosphere. He could easily have snatched it and refused to let Julius go, but he didn't.

"Where'd you steal that?"

"It's mine."

He glared at me. "Alright," he said. "Go on, *schmutzig Judin*," he said, reaching for the ring.

Julius got up, coughing, still clutching his throat, and rejoined my side.

I pulled the ring back, pressed my luck.

"Let them *all* go," I said, referring to the six terrified men who were still facing the wall. Surely somewhere their loved ones were praying for their safe return. Their reprieve might be minutes, hours, days or permanent, but I wanted to extend their freedom, however long that might be. "This ring is very expensive. You gentlemen can go to that pawn shop right there, divide up the proceeds three ways and still go home with a lot of money."

The SA officer looked at me with eyes full of hate and the haze of alcohol.

"*Geh jetzt*!" he commanded. The men scattered and the officer snatched the ring.

"*Geh jetzt*!" he said to us. "And don't let me see you again." We ran, pulling our coat collars up to look as incognito as possible.

"Listen, darling," Julius said hoarsely, a block later. "You go on. I'll join you when I can."

"No!"

"Don't argue. You need to leave now. Berlin is not safe. I think the emigration office is jam-packed. Who knows how long it'll take or how cooperative they'll be in light of what's going on."

"I won't leave you."

"I want you and Juli on that train. Don't worry. I'll see you soon."

"Promise?"

"I promise. Keep your head down and walk very quickly."

"I will." I'd go as fast as I could and prayed I wouldn't get robbed amid all the commotion. With no purse, without the pearls around my neck or the rubies in my ears (a birthday gift from Julius), I'd have nothing left – no money for trains or boats, no bargaining chips at all.

Julius kissed Juli, then me.

"I love you," he said, backing away. He was beautiful.

"I love you too." A tear rolled down my cheek. He took off down the ravaged street, looked back once and waved.

That was November, five months ago. It'd been *Kristallnacht*, or the Night of the Broken Glass, a horrifying event presumably precipitated by the shooting death of a diplomat by a teenage Polish Jew at the German embassy in Paris. Death and destruction were nationwide. I read there'd been almost 100 deaths, 1000 temples and 7000 businesses burned, and over 30,000 men arrested and interned in camps. Cemeteries were desecrated and private homes were looted. And the Nazis were making the Jews clean up and pay fines and restitution for all the damage! Hitler had long ceased caring about bad press or what the world thought about his ruthless regime.

I hadn't seen or heard from Julius since that fateful day. My letters and post cards went unanswered, long distance calls wouldn't connect. I didn't know whether to be worried, dejected or furious. Had I been betrayed? I had a recurring dream of him being on a carousel with Irina, the other little Julius, Ivan and Ingrid. They went round and round, laughing, eating ice cream cones and reaching for the brass ring. Julius nabbed it, confetti fluttered down, the calliope played louder and when the ride stopped, they all jumped off and walked away holding hands. My heart was as shattered as the store windows had been. But I thanked God I'd gotten Juli out of that wretched place before it was too late.

Then the letter came. It was postmarked in Amsterdam. Close enough – it had to be *him*! Finally, after months of meeting the postman day after day at the curb and seeing him shake his head that there was nothing from overseas, only bills, magazines and domestic correspondence.

I ignored the letter opener and literally ripped the envelope open. It was from Julius' mother. She said it pained her to have to tell me that Julius had been killed.

My heart stopped. The scream got caught in my throat. I felt trapped in another dimension with invisible walls and exits. I must have looked completely horrified because even little Juli stopped playing with his fire truck and said, "Wha's wrong, mommy?" I grabbed him to my chest and squeezed him tightly. "Ow, mommy!" But I couldn't let him go. It was several minutes before I could re-orient myself so I could resume reading.

Mrs. Sommerfeldt said that Julius had been able to bribe an emigration officer, go to the front part of the endless line and get his passport re-validated, and it still took all day. He was planning to leave the next morning, but Nazis came to the house that night just as Julius was trying to stuff Juli's favorite toy giraffe into another small suitcase. We'd left it behind in our haste to leave and Juli wanted it. He cried for his toy and his daddy. He'd get neither. The SS came to the house to look for weapons and arrest Gabriel for alleged "treasonous" activities; they took Julius away too when he demanded to know where they were taking his cousin. They were both taken to a concentration camp in Dachau where they were treated inhumanely, made to do back-breaking labor, sometimes just moving cinder blocks from one end of the camp to the other. They were there about a month before a guard shot Julius for complaining that another prisoner didn't get his rations and was starving to death. He and Gabriel would've both been released soon too since a ransom had been paid but apparently the envelope full of cash didn't reach the proper "authorities" in time.

The family was devastated. After their apartment house was raided and ransacked, the rest of the family fled to Amsterdam and Mrs. Sommerfeldt provided the new address so I could send pictures of Juli. She didn't know how long they'd be there though because they were trying desperately to cut through the red tape so they could get to Switzerland. She said she was walking with a cane after getting knocked over by some Jews being chased by Nazis in an armored truck and her hip hadn't been properly set. Gabriel was crazed and dangerous; the judge refused to talk – never said a word at all to anyone, and *Oma* Zip wouldn't stop singing. "Just remember" she said in closing, "Julius loved you very much and you brought him so much happiness. Give a hug to Juli from me, *Oma* and the judge and stay safe. Love, *Mutti*. P. S. I'll send you his ashes when I can. He'd want you to have them."

I cried all day, sobbed myself sick. I couldn't believe Julius was dead. The poem he recited to me in the Baltimore library years ago during the NAACP convention jumped into my mind: *The music of his life suddenly stopped. A pity! There was another song in him...* His death – his murder – was so unceremonious, so mind-numbingly senseless, and I couldn't get the conjured image of him slumped cold and alone in a barracks or lying in the middle of a barren courtyard, and I agonized over how long he may have lain there. Did the guard who shot him even know his name? Did he look him in the eye when he pulled the trigger? Couldn't he have made his point with a simple pistol-whipping? Did he give him a second thought later, feel any remorse whatsoever, or was it just all in a day's work? Did he eat heartily, sleep peacefully, that night? Would he recall this murder in years to come? Would there be a reckoning in this life or the next? What causes a person to get that way, lose all sense of humanity? Are they pre-programmed or *re*-programmed? I wracked my brain but couldn't understand it. For a few fleeting minutes, I was angry at Julius. *Why couldn't you have just stayed out of it, kept your mouth shut? Why did you have to be everyone's hero?*

But it was his nature. He couldn't help it. His savior complex was one of the things I loved about him. But it was so painful. My mother tried to console me. She even shed a few tears for the man she said had "ruined" me for any "man of quality" who might step into my life. She brought me a hot toddy and rubbed my back, something she'd never done before. She asked if I wanted Dr. Russwurm to come by and I told her no. I'd be fine the next day. I had a child to take care of.

CHAPTER 74

THREE DAYS LATER was Easter and Millie, Juli and I were going to see the contralto Marian Anderson sing outside on the steps of the Lincoln Memorial. She was supposed to give a concert at Constitution Hall but the Daughters of the American Revolution refused to accommodate mixed audiences or Negro performers, even one of international acclaim who'd performed at the White House and Carnegie Hall. Mrs. Eleanor Roosevelt arranged the special recital right after resigning from the DAR with a scathing letter to its president. Tens of thousands of people were expected to attend and millions more would listen on the radio. I hoped to get a good spot so I could clearly see this enchanting, iconic figure. I knew Julius would've been at that concert, Juli on his shoulders, but that he'd be looking down at us, humming along in Heaven when she sang "He's Got the Whole World in His Hands."

But first Juli and I, dressed in pastels, went to Millie's Morningside Baptist Church for Easter services. Magdalena said it'd be absolutely scandalous to go to St. Luke's Episcopal Church with an illegitimate child ("I can hear the whispering already," she said), so I stayed away. It would be awkward anyway, having to see, Sunday after Sunday, the Brathwaites and the Kirkwoods, Xavier and Georgine, who was pregnant. Supposedly Xavier's ritzy law firm was feting them with a huge baby shower because they were "like family."

I enjoyed Millie's church more anyway. I liked how they sang, instead of recited, the Lord's Prayer. The music was better, people clapped, the choir swayed and the minister was always passionate. But there were still a fair amount of whispers and judgmentalism, which I imagine was par for the course. Millie told her fellow parishioners that my "husband" had died, but no one believed her. I was notorious throughout D. C. and beyond. People gawked, open-mouthed, at me. I chalked it up to their questionable upbringing and held my head higher. I sang, full-throatedly, – "Onward, Christian Soldiers" – ignoring all the pivoting heads. I thought about having Juli re-Christened, but decided I'd let him determine what religion, if any, he wanted to embrace when he got older. I still made Millie his honorary godmother but spared Magdalena the additional angst of having a Baptist in the family.

I was still living at home and my parents made us feel welcome. It took a few weeks for them to fully accept Juli, but then Magdalena was telling me he needed a jacket, I was feeding him too much, that I shouldn't pick him up every time he cried. "Don't let him suck his thumb, Justinia," she said. "He'll develop an overbite." It was annoying but I was happy she was taking an interest. Before long, even Magdalena was picking him up and accepting his slobbery kisses unless he was poopy. She offered to babysit while Millie and I went to see a new movie, *The Wizard of Oz*, a musical fantasy in Technicolor, at the segregated theater. My father adored Juli, loved sneaking him cookies when my mother wasn't looking. I was happy to be home, but my heart ached for Julius, my first and only true love.

Epilogue

THE WORLD WAS at war. Poland was already conquered, and the same year that Germany invaded Belgium, France, Luxembourg and the Netherlands, Hattie McDaniel, the daughter of slaves, became the first Negro to win an Academy Award for Best Supporting Actress in *Gone With the Wind* which won Best Picture. My family was excited for her, even though she won the Oscar for playing a loud, sassy house slave named Mammy. But we were disturbed that she had to use the freight elevator at the Ambassador Hotel and was seated at a table far away from her co-stars and the other white actors and actresses.

Roosevelt won an unprecedented third term and the Post reported that the Jews in Germany had 8 p.m. curfews and were required to sew yellow stars onto their clothing so they could be readily identified. I worried about Julius' family, living in the Nazi-occupied Netherlands. Mrs. Sommerfeldt wrote that they were in limbo trying to find a country still willing to accept more Jewish refugees. They'd waited too long deciding to leave and now immigration quotas everywhere, including America, had been reached and the list of possible havens had dwindled down to Argentina and Shanghai, China. It was crazy. I prayed for them every night and also that the war would end soon without the United States' involvement. But Germany and its allies had to be stopped or the entire planet would be nothing but Nazis, racists and victims.

One bright day Julius' ashes arrived and I put them in a gorgeous urn that my mother had gotten at a Sotheby's auction for just that purpose. It looked like something Julius' family's specialty store, Kempner's, would've sold before it was liquidated and sold to the Nazis for the price of a typical beer garden. I placed it on the fireplace mantle at my own new apartment next to the only photograph I had of Julius, Juli and I together.

Daddy was able to get Rutherford Nash's sentence overturned. His extra-long sentence had nagged Julius for years and I made sure to ask my father to file an appeal on his behalf. An appellate judge reduced the sentence to "time served" and ordered "the defendant" to be released "forthwith." He also had some harsh words for the trial judge, calling him a disgrace to the bench and saying he should be removed. Mr. Nash already had his first job – painting my new place. Much to Magdalena's displeasure, I wanted bright yellow and orange walls.

"Orange?" she asked when I showed her the swatches. "Really, Justinia?"

"Alpine rose," I said. "It'll be beautiful."

Daddy also got me a job doing German translation in the State Department. However, I preferred to get something on my own, something that would be more meaningful, less dull. After many months of volunteering, I was hired as a volunteer and special events coordinator at the Red Cross – a Negro first! I helped bring attention to the blood donation program pioneered by the Negro surgeon, Charles Drew. His dehydrated plasma storage initiative became the first Blood Bank. In anticipation of the United States entering the war, blood was collected from civilian donors and would be shipped overseas for transfusions for wounded soldiers. Despite the fact that the military insisted on segregating white and Negro blood – "an idiotic policy!" Dr. Drew railed – promoting the Blood Bank was a fulfilling task. Many lives could be saved. Even Emery donated, and he's terrified of needles.

When I found time, I began writing my memoirs.

A couple years later, Japan, a Nazi ally, bombed our naval base in Hawaii and America became deeply embroiled in the war. Julius' Uncle Sy came by my parents' home one evening to tell us that Gabriel, Gretchen, their parents, Judge and Mrs. Sommerfeldt and *Oma* Zip, along with hundreds of others, had been deported from Amsterdam and shipped to a camp in Auschwitz, Poland. Again I prayed for their safety and survival.

BOOK CLUB GUIDE
Discussion Questions:

1. Was it reasonable for Justinia to be so fickle about her future plans?
2. What do you think about the concept of "passing" for white, Aryan or "other?"
3. Why did Justinia decide to participate in the noose demonstration? Would you have participated? How far would you have been willing to go in the fight for anti-lynching legislation, desegregation and basic civil rights?
4. Why do you think Justinia agreed to marry Xavier?
5. How do you feel about Jasper's questionable past?
6. Was Magdalena a good and loving mother?
7. What do you think about Julius' decision to go back to Germany? What do you think about Julius' family's decision to stay in Germany?
8. What do you think about Justinia's decision to go and to stay in Germany?
9. Do you think Justinia and her family were snobs? Do "blue vein" societies still exist?
10. Do you think Julius or any of his family members had any racial, class or cultural biases? Could the Treadwells and Sommerfeldts have been friends?
11. What did you think of Uncle Sy's opinion about Negroes going to law school?
12. Were there any characters you felt particular sympathy for? Were there any characters you especially disliked? What minor characters should have had a larger role?
13. Did Julius have any flaws, any prejudices?

14. Do you think it was easier being black during the Jim Crow era or Jewish in pre-war Nazi Germany?

15. Should Justinia and Julius have gotten together? Were they really in love?

16. What did you think of the courtroom scenes and do you think contemporary justice is more "just?" Was Julius' father a good judge?

17. Do you understand the Dreschlers' decision to "defriend" the Sommerfeldts? What would you have done? Would you have been a "righteous gentile," someone who risked their life to save Jews from the Nazis and the ensuing Holocaust?

18. Why do you think *Oma* Zip changed and why did it irritate Julius' father?

19. Are the prejudices against blacks and Jews satisfactorily explained or justified? Why were the Germans so welcoming and accepting of Jesse Owens, Justinia and Emery?

20. What was the biggest surprise in the book? What was the most satisfying part? Were there any disappointments?

21. Do you think Justinia "grew" as a result of her experiences? Who had the most influence on her and the decisions she made?

22. What did you think of Justinia's and Julius' experiences and musings regarding religion? What role did religion play in their lives?

23. Do you think having money made living in an era of lynching and segregation easier?

24. Do you think the relationship between blacks and Jews is unique?

25. Do you think a Jim Crow or Nazi society could take root again?

About the Author

Lauren Cecile is a judge in Cleveland, Ohio. She is a graduate of Spelman College and Case Western Reserve University School of Law. She and her husband, Brian, have two children. She is currently working on her second novel.

Contact her at gr8books2015@gmail.com.

Friend her on Facebook: Lauren Cecile

Follow her on Twitter: @AuthorLaurenC

Note: Reviews are gold to authors! If you've enjoyed this book, please consider reviewing it on www.Amazon.com. Thank you!

CPSIA information can be obtained at www.ICGtesting.com
Printed in the USA
LVOW08s1832310316

481608LV00007B/914/P